U0682558

大魚讀品
BIG FISH BOOKS

让日常阅读成为砍向我们内心冰封大海的斧头。

流浪地球

刘慈欣 _ 著
[美] 韩恩立 (Elizabeth Hanlon) 等 _ 译

北京联合出版公司
Beijing United Publishing Co.,Ltd.

图书在版编目（CIP）数据

流浪地球：汉英对照 / 刘慈欣著；（美）韩恩立
（Elizabeth Hanlon）等译. — 北京：北京联合出版公
司，2022.5

ISBN 978-7-5596-6071-8

Ⅰ.①流… Ⅱ.①刘… ②韩… Ⅲ.①幻想小说—小
说集—中国—当代—汉、英 Ⅳ.① I247.7

中国版本图书馆CIP数据核字（2022）第046715号

版权所有©刘慈欣，联合策划方、英文译文版权所有方©中国教育图书
进出口有限公司。由天津磨铁图书有限公司联合策划、发行。

流浪地球：汉英对照

作　　者：刘慈欣
译　　者：［美］韩恩立（Elizabeth Hanlon）等
出 品 人：赵红仕
责任编辑：龚　将

北京联合出版公司出版
（北京市西城区德外大街 83 号楼 9 层　100088）
北京世纪恒宇印刷有限公司印刷　新华书店经销
字数 360 千字　　880 毫米 × 1230 毫米　1/32　　16 印张
2022 年 5 月第 1 版　　2022 年 5 月第 1 次印刷
ISBN 978-7-5596-6071-8
定价：62.00 元

版权所有，侵权必究
未经许可，不得以任何方式复制或抄袭本书部分或全部内容
本书若有质量问题，请与本公司图书销售中心联系调换。电话：010-82069336

编者按

在翻开这本书之前，你或许已经浸淫在科幻故事中多年，或许只是匆匆过客，或许已经读过书中个别篇目，又或许与之素未谋面。前者也好，后者也罢，单纯从阅读的维度来看，这套书无疑会带你进入一场全新的旅途。

你即将读到的 21 篇经典中短篇小说的英译版出自两本科幻作品集：*To Hold Up the Sky* 和 *The Wandering Earth*。这两本沉甸甸的精装书于 2020 年到 2021 年相继面世，是由托尔出版公司对刘慈欣经典科幻中短篇小说进行全新选编而成的。

华语科幻的译介是一场漫漫征途，将英译版作品重新引入国内则是"照镜子"一般的历程。文字的意义是流动的，不同语言、不同译者的文本往往呈现出极具差异化的风貌。编辑过程中，编者在最大限度地保持英译本的独立性和完整性的基础上，对一些规范性的内容进行了统一，与此同时，也在有必要提示之处插入了简短的注释，尽可能减少困惑，消除阅读障碍。

值得注意的修订有：

其一，*To Hold Up the Sky* 和 *The Wandering Earth* 两本书在英文符号的使用上有所不同，为了方便中文读者阅读，在编辑过程中对个别篇目的标点符号进行了修订，做到了统一。

其二，如果你在中英文对照阅读的过程中，发现某些地方英文比中文描述得更详尽，请不必感到困惑，考虑到译者本身的文字风格以及英语表述习惯，对于不影响文意的润色和增减，编者在编辑稿件时尽可能地保留了。

其三，在《带上她的眼睛》一辑中，《吞食者》和《诗云》的故事存在交集，文字和人物也均有"串场"，两位译者对个别人物、段落的表述不同，编辑无意在两个版本中做取舍，于是在文内相应位置添加了脚注，供读者阅读赏析。

其四，对于英译稿存在明显误读的地方，编者进行了修订；除了技术性偏误之外，一些误读是文化传播中出现的认知偏差所致，一些则是顾及文化差异、"入乡随俗"的有心之举——如《梦之海》中改变了主人公的性别。对于上述两类情况，编者分别以直接修订和添加脚注的方式做了处理，尽可能将译介过程中微妙的文意变化呈现出来。

阅读是一场走进心灵的旅途，希望这套作品能够陪伴你探索认知的边界，聆听华语科幻在世界舞台上律动的音符。

公子政

2022.1.18

目录

流浪地球

THE WANDERING EARTH

刹车时代

我没见过黑夜，我没见过星星，我没见过春天、秋天和冬天。

我出生在刹车时代结束的时候，那时地球刚刚停止转动。

地球自转刹车用了四十二年，比联合政府的计划长了三年。妈妈给我讲过我们全家看最后一个日落的情景，太阳落得很慢，仿佛在地平线上停住了，用了三天三夜才落下去。当然，以后没有"天"也没有"夜"了，东半球在相当长的一段时间里（有十几年吧）将处于黄昏中，因为太阳在地平线下并没落深，还在半边天上映出它的光芒。就在那次漫长的日落中，我出生了。

黄昏并不意味着昏暗，地球发动机把整个北半球照得通明。地球发动机安装在亚洲和美洲大陆上，因为只有这两个大陆完整坚实的板块结构才能承受发动机对地球巨大的推力。地球发动机共有 12000 台，分布在亚洲和美洲大陆的各个平原上。从我住的地方可以看到几百台发动机喷出的等离子体光柱。你想象一座巨大的宫殿，有雅典卫城上的神殿那么大，殿中有无数根顶天立地的巨柱，每根柱子像一根巨大的日光灯管那样发出蓝白色的强光。而你，是那巨大宫殿地板上的一个细菌，这样，你就可以想象到我所在的世界是什么样子了。其实这样描述还不是太准确，是地球发动机产生的切线推力分量刹住了地球的自转，因此地球发动机的喷射必须有一定的角度，这样天空中的那些巨型光柱是倾斜的，我们处在一个将要倾倒的巨殿中！南半球的人来到北半球后突然置身于这个环境中，会有许多人精神失常。比这景象更可怕的是发动机带来的酷热，户外气温高达七八十摄氏度，必须穿冷却服才能外出。在这样的气温下常常会有暴雨，而发动机光柱穿过乌云时的景象简直是一场噩梦！光柱蓝白色的强光在云中散射，变成由无数种色彩组成的疯狂涌动的光晕，整个天空仿佛被白热的火山岩浆所覆盖。爷爷老糊涂了，有一次被酷热折磨得实在受不了了，看到下大雨喜出望外，赤膊冲出门去，我们没来得及拦住他。外面的雨点已被地球发动机超高温的等离子光柱烤热，把他身上烫脱了一层皮。

但对于我们这一代在北半球出生的人来说，这一切都很自然，就如同对刹车时代以前的人们来说，太阳、星星和月亮是那样自然。我们把以前人类的历史叫作"前太阳时代"，那真是个让人神往的黄金时代啊！

在我小学入学时，作为一门课程，教师带我们班的三十个孩子进行了一次环球旅行。这时地球已经完全停转，地球发动机除了维持这个行星的这种静止状态外，只进行一些姿态调整。所以在我 3 岁到 6 岁这三年中，光柱的光度大为减弱，这使得我们可以在这次旅行中更好地认识我们的世界。

我们首先近距离见到了地球发动机，是在石家庄附近的太行山出口处看到它的。那是一座金属的高山，它在我们面前赫然耸立，占据了半个天空，同它相比，西边的太行山山脉如同一串小土丘。有的孩子惊叹它如珠峰一样高。我们的班主任小星老师是一位漂亮姑娘，她笑着告诉我们，这座发动机的高度是 11000米，比珠峰还要高 2000 多米，人们管它们叫"上帝的喷灯"。我们站在它巨大的阴影中，感受着它通过大地传来的震动。

地球发动机分为两大类，大一些的叫"山"，小一些的叫"峰"。我们登上了"华北 794 号山"。登"山"比登"峰"花的时间长，因为"峰"是靠巨型电梯上下的，上"山"则要坐汽车沿盘"山"公路走。我们的汽车混在不见首尾的长车队中，沿着光滑的钢铁公路向上爬行。我们的左边是青色的金属峭壁，右边是万丈深渊。车队由 50 吨的巨型自卸卡车组成，车上满载着从太行山上挖下的岩石。汽车很快升到了 5000 米以上，下面的大地已看不清细节，只能看到反射的地球发动机的一片青光。小星老师让我们戴上氧气面罩。随着我们距喷口越来越近，光度和温度都在剧增，面罩的颜色渐渐变深，冷却服中的微型压缩机也大功率地忙碌起来。在 6000 米处，我们见到了进料口，一车车的大石块倒进那闪着幽幽红光的大洞中，一点儿声音都没传出来。我问小星老师地球发动机是如何把岩石做成燃料的。

"重元素聚变是一门很深的学问，现在给你们还讲不明白。你们只需要知道，地球发动机是人类建造的力量最大的机器，比如我们所在的'华北 794 号'，全功率运行时能向大地产生 150 亿吨的推力。"

我们的汽车终于登上了顶峰，喷口就在我们头顶上。由于光柱的直径太大，我们现在抬头看到的是一堵发着蓝光的等离子体巨墙，这堵巨墙向上延伸到无限高。这时，我突然想起不久前的一堂哲学课，那个憔悴的老师给我们出了一个谜语。

"你在平原上走着走着，突然迎面遇到一堵墙，这墙向上无限高，向下无限深，向左无限远，向右无限远，这墙是什么？"

我打了一个寒战，接着把这个谜语告诉了身边的小星老师。她想了好大一会儿，困惑地摇摇头。我把嘴凑到她耳边，把那个可怕的谜底告诉她。

"死亡。"

她默默地看了我几秒钟，突然把我紧紧抱在怀里。我从她的肩上极目望去，迷蒙的大地上，耸立着一片金属的巨峰，从我们周围一直延伸到地平线。巨峰吐出的光柱，如一片倾斜的宇宙森林，刺破我们摇摇欲坠的天空。

我们很快到达了海边，看到城市摩天大楼的尖顶伸出海面，退潮时白花花的海水从大楼无数的窗子中流出，形成一道道瀑布……刹车时代刚刚结束，其对地球的影响已触目惊心：地球发动机加速造成的潮汐吞没了北半球三分之二的大城市，发动机带来的全球高温融化了极地冰川，更使这大洪水雪上加霜，波及南半球。爷爷在三十年前目睹了百米高的巨浪吞没上海的情景，他现在讲这事的时候眼睛还直勾勾的。事实上，我们的星球还没启程就已面目全非了，谁知道在以后漫长的外太空流浪中，还有多少苦难在等着我们呢？

我们乘上一种叫船的古老交通工具在海面上航行。地球发动机的光柱在后面越来越远，一天以后就完全看不见了。这时，大海处在两片霞光之间，一片是西面地球发动机的光柱产生的青蓝色霞光，另一片是东方海平面下的太阳产生的粉红色霞光。它们在海面上的反射使大海也分成了闪耀着两色光芒的两部分，我们的船就行驶在这两部分的分界处，这景色真是奇妙。但随着青蓝色霞光的渐渐减弱和粉红色霞光的渐渐增强，一种不安的气氛在船上弥漫开来。甲板上见不到孩子们了，他们都躲在船舱里不出来，舷窗的帘子也被紧紧拉上。一天后，我们最害怕的那一刻终于到来了，我们集合在那间用作教室的大舱中，小星老师庄严地宣布：

"孩子们，我们要去看日出了。"

没有人动，我们目光呆滞，像突然冻住一样僵在那儿。小星老师又催了几次，还是没人动。她的一位男同事说：

"我早就提过，环球体验课应该放在近代史课前面，学生在心理上就比较容易适应了。"

"没那么简单，在近代史课前，他们早就从社会知道一切了。"小星老师说，她接着对几位班干部说："你们先走，孩子们，不要怕，我小时候第一次看日出也很紧张的，但看过一次就好了。"

孩子们终于一个个站了起来，朝着舱门挪动脚步。这时，我感到一只湿湿的小手抓住了我的手，回头一看，是灵儿。

"我怕……"她嘤嘤地说。

"我们在电视上也看到过太阳，反正都一样的。"我安慰她说。

"怎么会一样呢，你在电视上看蛇和看真蛇一样吗？"

"……反正我们得上去，要不这门课会被扣分的！"

我和灵儿紧紧拉着手，和其他孩子一起战战兢兢地朝甲板走去，去面对我们人生中的第一次日出。

"其实，人类把太阳同恐惧连在一起也只是这三四个世纪的事。在这之前，人类是不怕太阳的。相反，太阳在他们眼中是庄严和壮美的。那时地球还在转动，人们每天都能看到日出和日落。他们对着初升的太阳欢呼，赞颂落日的美丽。"小星老师站在船头对我们说。海风吹动着她的长发，在她身后，海天连线处射出几道光芒，好像海面下的一头大得无法想象的怪兽喷出的鼻息。

终于，我们看到了那令人胆寒的火焰，开始时只是天水连线上的一个亮点，亮点很快增大，渐渐显示出了圆弧的形状。这时，我感到自己的喉咙被什么东西掐住了，恐惧使我窒息，脚下的甲板仿佛突然消失，我在向海的深渊坠下去，坠下去……和我一起下坠的还有灵儿，她那蛛丝般柔弱的小身躯紧贴着我颤抖着；还有其他孩子，其他的所有人；整个世界，都在下坠。这时我又想起了那个谜语，我曾问过哲学老师那堵墙是什么颜色的，他说应该是黑色的。我觉得不对，我想象中的死亡之墙应该是雪亮的，这就是为什么那道等离子体墙让我想起了它。这个时代，死亡不再是黑色的，它是闪电的颜色，当那最后的闪电到来时，世界将在瞬间变成蒸气。

三个多世纪前，天体物理学家们就发现太阳内部氢转化为氦的速度突然加快，于是他们发射了上万个探测器穿过太阳，最终建立了这个恒星完整精确的数学模型。巨型计算机对这个模型计算的结果表明，太阳的演化已向主星序外偏移，氦元素的聚变将在很短的时间内传遍整个太阳内部，由此产生一次叫氦闪的剧烈爆炸。之后，太阳将变为一颗巨大但暗淡的红巨星，它膨胀到如此之大，乃至地球将在太阳内部运行！事实上，在这之前的氦闪爆发中，我们的星球已被气化了。

这一切将在四百年内发生，现在已过了三百八十年。

太阳的灾变将炸毁和吞没太阳系所有适合居住的类地行星，并使所有类木行星完全改变形态和轨道。自第一次氦闪后，随着重元素在太阳中心的反复聚集，太阳氦闪将在一段时间反复发生，这"一段时间"是相对于恒星演化来说的，其长度可能相当于上千个人类历史。所以，人类在以后的太阳系中已无法生存下去，唯一的生路是向外太空恒星际移民。而照人类目前的技术力量，全人类移民唯一可行的目标是半人马座比邻星，这是距我们最近的恒星，有 4.3 光年的路程。以上看法人们已达成共识，争论的焦点在移民方式上。

为了加强教学效果，我们的船在太平洋上折返了两次，又给我们制造了两次日出。现在我们已完全适应了，也相信了南半球那些每天面对太阳的孩子确实能活下去。

之后我们就在太阳下航行了，太阳在空中越升越高，这几天凉爽下来的天气又热了起来。我正在自己的舱里昏昏欲睡，听到外面有骚乱的人声。灵儿推开门探进头来。

"嘻，飞船派和地球派又打起来了！"

我对这事儿不感兴趣，他们已经打了四个世纪了，但我还是到外面看了看。在打成一团的几个男孩儿中，我一眼就看出了挑事儿的是阿东，他爸爸是个顽固的飞船派，因参加一次反联合政府的暴动，现在还被关在监狱里，有其父必有其子。

小星老师和几名粗壮的船员好不容易才拉开架，阿东鼻子血糊糊的，振臂高呼："把地球派扔到海里去！"

"我也是地球派，也要扔到海里去？"小星老师问。

"地球派都扔到海里去！"阿东毫不示弱，现在全世界飞船派情绪又呈上升趋势，所以他们又狂起来了。

"为什么这么恨我们？"小星老师问。

其他几个飞船派小子接着喊了起来：

"我们不和地球派傻瓜在地球上等死！"

"我们要坐飞船走！飞船万岁！"

……

小星老师按了一下手腕上的全息显示器，我们面前的空中立刻显示出一幅全息图像，孩子们的注意力立刻被它吸引过去，暂时安静下来。那是一个晶莹透明的密封玻璃球，直径大约有10厘米，球里有三分之二充满了水，水中有一只小虾、一小枝珊瑚和一些绿色的藻类植物，小虾在水中悠闲地游动着。小星老师说："这是阿东自然课设计的一件作业，小球中除了这几样东西外，还有一些看不见的细菌。它们在密封的玻璃球中相互依赖、相互作用。小虾以海藻为食，从水中摄取氧气，然后排出含有机物质的粪便和二氧化碳废气；细菌将这些东西分解成无机物质和二氧化碳；然后海藻利用这些无机物质与人造阳光进行光合作用，制造营养物质，进行生长和繁殖，同时放出氧气供小虾呼吸。这样的生态循环应该能使玻璃球中的生物在只有阳光的情况下生生不息。这是我见过的最好的课程设计，我知道，这里面凝聚了阿东和所有飞船派孩子的梦想，这就是你们梦中飞船的缩影啊！阿东告诉我，他按照计算机中严格的数学模型，对球中每一样生物进行了基因设计，使它们的新陈代谢正好达到平衡。他坚信，球中的生命世界会长期活下去，直到小虾寿命的终点。老师们都很钟爱这件作业，我们把它放到所要求强度的人造阳光下，也坚信阿东的预测，默默地祝福他创造的这个小小的世界。但现在，时间只过去了十几天……"

小星老师从随身带来的一个小箱子中小心翼翼地拿出了那个玻璃球，死去的小虾漂浮在水面上，水已混浊不堪，腐烂的藻类植物已失去了绿色，变成一团没有生命的毛状物覆盖在珊瑚上。

"这个小世界死了。孩子们，谁能说出为什么？"小星老师把那个死亡的世界举到孩子们面前。

"它太小了！"

"说得对，太小了，小的生态系统，不管多么精确，也是经不起时间的风浪的。飞船派想象中的飞船也一样。"

"我们的飞船可以造得像上海或纽约那么大。"阿东说，声音比刚才低了许多。

"是的，按人类目前的技术也只能造这么大，同地球相比，这样的生态系统还是太小了，太小了。"

"我们会找到新的行星。"

"这连你们自己也不相信。半人马座没有行星，最近的有行星的恒星在 850 光年以外，目前人类能建造的最快的飞船也只能达到光速的百分之零点五，这样就需要 17 万年时间才能到那儿，飞船规模的生态系统连这十分之一的时间都维持不了。孩子们，只有像地球这样规模的生态系统、这样气势磅礴的生态循环，才能使生命万代不息！人类在宇宙间离开了地球，就像婴儿在沙漠里离开了母亲！"

"可……老师，我们来不及的，地球来不及的，它还来不及加速到足够快、航行到足够远，太阳就爆炸了！"

"时间是够的，要相信联合政府！这话我说了多少遍，如果你们还不相信，我们就退一万步说，人类将自豪地去死，因为我们尽了最大的努力！"

人类的逃亡分为五步：第一步，用地球发动机使地球停止转动，使发动机喷口固定在地球运行的反方向；第二步，全功率地开动地球发动机，使地球加速到逃逸速度，飞出太阳系；第三步，在外太空继续加速，飞向比邻星；第四步，在中途使地球重新自转，掉转发动机方向，开始减速；第五步，地球泊入比邻星轨道，成为这颗恒星的卫星。人们把这五步分别称为刹车时代、逃逸时代、流浪时代Ⅰ（加速）、流浪时代Ⅱ（减速）和新太阳时代。

整个移民过程将延续两千五百年时间，一百代人。

我们的船继续航行，到了地球黑夜的部分，在这里，阳光和地球发动机的光柱都照不到，在大西洋清凉的海风中，我们这些孩子第一次看到了星空。天啊，那是怎样的景象啊，美得让我们心醉！小星老师用一只手搂着我们，另一只手指着星空："看，孩子们，那就是半人马座，那就是比邻星，那就是我们的新家！"说完她哭了起来，我们也都跟着哭了，周围的水手和船长，这些铁打的汉子也流下了眼泪。所有的人都用泪眼望着老师指的方向，星空在泪水中扭曲抖动，唯有那个星星是不动的，那是黑夜大海狂浪中远方陆地的灯塔，那是冰雪荒原中快要冻死的孤独旅人前方隐现的火光，那是我们心中的星星，是人类在未来一百代人的苦海中唯一的希望和支撑……

在回家的航程中，我们看到了起航的第一个信号：夜空中出现了一颗巨大的彗星，那是月球。人类带不走月球，就在月球上也安装了行星发动机，把它推离地球轨道，以免在地球加速时相撞。月球上的行星发动机产生的巨大彗尾使大海笼罩在一片蓝光之中，群星看不见了。月球移动产生的引力潮汐使大海巨浪冲天，我们改乘飞机向北半球的家飞去。

起航的日子终于到了！

我们一下飞机，就被地球发动机的光柱照得睁不开眼，这些光柱比以前亮了几倍，而且所有光柱都由倾斜变成笔直。地球发动机开到了最大功率，加速产生的百米巨浪轰鸣着滚上每个大陆，灼热的飓风夹着滚烫的水沫，在林立的顶天立地的等离子光柱间疯狂呼啸，拔起了陆地上所有的大树……这时从宇宙空间看，我们的星球也成了一个巨大的彗星，蓝色的彗尾刺破了黑暗的太空。

地球上路了，人类上路了。

就在起航时，爷爷去世了，他身上的烫伤已经感染。弥留之际，他反复念叨着一句话：

"啊，地球，我的流浪地球啊……"

逃逸时代

学校要搬入地下城了，我们是第一批入城的居民。校车钻进了一个高大的隧洞，隧洞呈不大的坡度向地下延伸。走了有半个钟头，我们被告知已入城了。可车窗外哪有城市的样子？只看到不断掠过的错综复杂的支洞和洞壁上无数的密封门，在高高洞顶的一排泛光灯下，一切都呈单调的金属蓝色。想到后半生的大部分时光都要在这个世界中度过，我们不禁黯然神伤。

"原始人就住在洞里，我们又住进洞里了。"灵儿低声说，但这话还是让小星老师听见了。

"没有办法，孩子们，地面的环境很快就要变得很可怕。那时，冷的时候，吐一口唾沫，还没掉到地上呢，就冻成小冰块儿了；热的时候，再吐一口唾沫，还没掉到地上，就变成蒸气了！"

"冷我知道，因为地球离太阳越来越远了，可为什么还会热呢？"同车的一个低年级的小娃娃问。

"笨，没学过变轨加速吗？"我没好气地说。

"没。"

灵儿耐心地解释起来，好像是为了分散刚才的悲伤："是这样的，跟你想的不同，地球发动机没那么大劲儿，它只能给地球很小的加速度，不能把地球一下子推出太阳轨道。在地球离开太阳前，还要绕着它转十五个圈呢！在这十五个圈中地球慢慢加速。现在，地球绕太阳转着一个挺圆的圈儿，可它的速度越快呢，这圈就越扁，越快越扁，太阳越来越移到这个扁圈的一边，所以后来地球有时离太阳会很远，当然冷了……"

"可……还是不对！地球到最远的地方是很冷，可在扁圈的另一头，它离太阳……嗯，我想想，按轨道动力学，还是现在这么近啊，怎么会更热呢？"

真是个小天才，记忆遗传技术使这样的小娃娃成了平常人，这是人类的幸运，否则，像地球发动机这样连神都不敢想的奇迹，是不会在四个世纪内变成现实的。

我说："可还有地球发动机呢，小傻瓜，现在，1 万多台那样的大喷灯全功率开动，地球就成了火箭喷口的护圈了……你们安静点吧，我心里烦！"

我们就这样开始了地下的生活，像这样在地下 500 米处、人口超过百万的城市遍布各个大陆。在这样的地下城中，我读完小学并升入中学。学校教育都集中在理工科上，艺术和哲学之类的教育已压缩到最少，人类没有这份闲心了。这是人类最忙的时代，每个人都有做不完的工作。很有意思的是，地球上所有的宗教在一夜之间消失得无影无踪，人们现在终于明白，就算真有上帝，他也是个王八蛋。历史课还是有的，只是课本中前太阳时代的人类历史对我们来说就像伊甸园中的神话一样。

父亲是空军的一名近地轨道宇航员，在家的时间很少。记得在变轨加速的第五年，在地球处于远日点时，我们全家到海边去过一次。运行到远日点顶端那一天，是一个如同新年或圣诞节一样的节日，因为这时地球距太阳最远，人们都有一种虚幻的安全感。像以前到地面上去一样，我们必须穿上带有核电池的全密封加热服。外面，地球发动机林立的刺目光柱是主要能看见的东西，地面世界的其他部分都湮没于光柱的强光中，也看不出变化。我们乘飞行汽车飞了很长时间，到了光柱照不到的地方，到了能看见太阳的海边。这时的太阳已成了一个棒球大小，一动不动地悬在天边，它的光芒只在自己的周围映出了一圈晨曦似的亮影，天空呈暗暗的深蓝色，星星仍清晰可见。举目望去，哪有海啊，眼前是一片白茫茫的冰原。在这封冻的大海上，有大群狂欢的人。焰火在暗蓝色的空中开放，冰冻海面上的人们以一种不正常的忘情在狂欢着，到处都是喝醉了在冰上打滚的人，更多的人在声嘶力竭地唱着不同的歌，都想用自己的声音压住别人的声音。

"每个人都在不顾一切地过自己想过的生活，这也没有什么不好。"爸爸突然想起了一件事，"呵，忘了告诉你们，我爱上了任小星，我要离开你们和她在一起。"

"她是谁？"妈妈平静地问。

"我的小学老师。"我替爸爸回答。我升入中学已两年，不知道爸爸和小星老师是怎么认识的，也许是在两年前的毕业仪式上。

"那你去吧。"妈妈说。

"过一阵儿我肯定会厌倦的，那时我就回来，你看呢？"

"你要愿意当然行。"妈妈的声音像冰冻的海面一样平稳，但很快激动起来，"啊，这一颗真漂亮，里面一定有全息散射体！"她指着刚在空中开放的一朵焰火，真诚地赞美着。

在这个时代，人们在看四个世纪以前的电影和小说时都莫名其妙，他们不明白，前太阳时代的人怎么会在无关生死的事情上倾注那么多的感情。当看到男女主人公为爱情而痛苦或哭泣时，他们的惊奇是难以言表的。在这个时代，死亡的威胁和逃生的欲望压倒了一切，除了当前太阳的状态和地球的位置，没有什么能真正引起他们的注意并能打动他们了。这种注意力高度集中的关注，渐渐从本质上改变了人类的心理状态和精神生活，对于爱情这类东西，他们只是用余光瞥一下而已，就像赌徒在盯着轮盘的间隙抓住几秒钟喝口水一样。

过了两个月，爸爸真从小星老师那儿回来了，妈妈没有高兴，也没有不高兴。

爸爸对我说："任小星对你印象很好，她说你是一个有创造力的学生。"

妈妈一脸茫然："她是谁？"

"小星老师嘛，我的小学老师，爸爸这两个月就是跟她在一起的！"

"哦，想起来了！"妈妈摇头笑了，"我还不到40岁，记忆力就成了这个样子。"她抬头看看天花板上的全息星空，又看看四壁的全息森林，"你回来挺好，把这些图像换换吧，我和孩子都看腻了，但我们都不会调整这玩意儿。"

当地球再次向太阳跌去的时候，我们全家都把这事忘了。

有一天，新闻报道海在融化，于是我们全家又到海边去了。这是地球通过火星轨道的时候，按照这时太阳的光照量，地球的气温应该仍然是很低的，但由于地球发动机的影响，地面的气温正适宜。能不穿加热服或冷却服去地面，那感觉真令人愉快。地球发动机所在的这个半球天空还是那个样子，但到达另一个半球时，真正感到了太阳的临近：天空是明朗的纯蓝色，太阳在空中已同起航前一样明亮了。可我们从空中看到海并没融化，还是一片白色的冰原。当我们失望地走出飞行汽车时，听到惊天动地的隆隆声，那声音仿佛来自这颗星球的最深处，真像地球要爆炸一样。

"这是大海的声音！"爸爸说，"因为气温骤升，厚厚的海冰层受热不均匀，这很像陆地上的地震。"

突然，一声雷霆般尖厉的巨响插进这低沉的隆隆声中，在我们后面看海的人们欢呼起来。我看到海面上裂开一道长缝，其开裂速度之快，如同广阔的冰原上突然出现的一道黑色闪电。接着在不断的巨响中，这样的裂缝一条接一条地在海冰上出现，海水从所有的裂缝中喷出，在冰原上形成一条条迅速扩散的急流……

回家的路上，我们看到荒芜已久的大地上，野草在大片大片地钻出地面，各种花朵在怒放，嫩叶给枯死的森林披上绿装……所有的生命都在抓紧时间释放着活力。

随着地球与太阳的距离越来越近，人们的心也一天天揪紧了。到地面上来欣赏春色的人越来越少，大部分人都躲进了地下城中，这不是为了躲避即将到来的酷热、暴雨和飓风，而是为了躲避那随着太阳越来越近的恐惧。有一天在我睡下后，听到妈妈低声对爸爸说："可能真的来不及了。"

爸爸说："前四个近日点时也有这种谣言。"

"可这次是真的，我是从钱德勒博士夫人口中听说的，她丈夫是航行委员会的天文学家，你们都知道他的。他亲口告诉她已观测到氦的聚集在加速。"

"你听着，亲爱的，我们必须抱有希望，这并不是因为希望真的存在，而是因为我们要做高贵的人。在前太阳时代，做一个高贵的人必须拥有金钱、权力或才能，而在今天只要拥有希望，希望是这个时代的黄金和宝石，不管活多长时间，我们都要拥有它！明天把这话告诉孩子。"

和所有的人一样，我也随着近日点的到来而心神不宁。有一天放学后，我不知不觉走到了城市中心广场，在广场中央有喷泉的圆形水池边呆立着，时而低头看着蓝莹莹的池水，时而抬头望着广场圆形穹顶上梦幻般的光波纹，那是池水反射上去的。这时我看到了灵儿，她拿着一个小瓶子和一根小管子，在吹肥皂泡。

每吹出一串，她都呆呆地盯着空中飘浮的泡泡，看着它们一个个消失，然后再吹出一串……

"都这么大了还干这个，这好玩吗？"我走过去问她。

灵儿见了我以后喜出望外："我们俩去旅行吧！"

"旅行？去哪儿？"

"当然是地面啦！"她挥手在空中画了一下，手腕上的计算机甩出一幅全息景象，显示出一个落日下的海滩，微风吹拂着棕榈树，道道白浪，金黄的沙滩上有一对对的情侣，他们在铺满碎金的海面前呈一对对黑色的剪影。"这是梦娜和大刚发回来的，他们俩现在还满世界转呢，他们说外面现在还不太热，外面可好呢，我们去吧！"

"他们因为旷课刚被学校开除了。"

"哼，你根本不是怕这个，你是怕太阳！"

"你不怕吗？别忘了你因为怕太阳还看过精神科医生呢。"

"可我现在不一样了，我受到了启示！你看！"灵儿用小管子吹出了一串肥皂泡。"盯着它看！"她用手指着一个肥皂泡说。

我盯着那个泡泡，看到它表面上光和色的狂澜，那狂澜以人的感觉无法把握的复杂和精细在涌动，好像那个泡泡知道自己生命的长度，疯狂地把自己浩如烟海的记忆中无数的梦幻和传奇向世界演绎。很快，光和色的狂澜在一次无声的爆炸中消失了，我看到了一小片似有似无的水汽，这水汽也只存在了半秒钟，然后什么都没有了，好像什么都没有存在过。

"看到了吗？地球就是宇宙中的一个小水泡，啪的一下，什么都没了，有什么好怕的呢？"

"不是这样的，据计算，在氦闪发生时，地球被完全蒸发掉至少需要一百个小时。"

"这就是最可怕之处了！"灵儿大叫起来，"我们在这地下500米，就像馅饼里的肉馅一样，先被慢慢烤熟了，再蒸发掉！"

一阵冷战传遍我的全身。

"但在地面就不一样了，那里的一切瞬间被蒸发，地面上的人就像那泡泡一样，啪的一下……所以，氦闪时还是在地面上为好。"

不知为什么，我没同她去，她就同阿东去了，我以后再也没见过他们。

氦闪并没有发生，地球高速掠过了近日点，第六次向远日点升去，人们绷紧的神经松弛下来。由于地球自转已停止，在太阳轨道的这一面，亚洲大陆上的地球发动机正对它的运行方向，所以在通过近日点前都停了下来，只是偶尔做一些调整姿态的运行，我们这儿处于宁静而漫长的黑夜之中。美洲大陆上的发动机则全功率运行，那里成了火箭喷口的护圈。由于太阳这时也处于西半球，那儿的高温更是可怕，草木生烟。

地球的变轨加速就这样年复一年地进行着。每当地球向远日点升去时，人们的心也随着地球与太阳距离的日益拉长而放松；而当它在新的一年向太阳跌去时，人们的心也一天天紧缩起来。每次到达近日点，社会上就谣言四起，说太阳氦闪就要在这时发生了；直到地球再次升向远日点，人们的恐惧才随着天空中渐渐变小的太阳平息下来，但又在准备着下一次的恐惧……人类的精神像在荡着一个宇宙秋千，更恰当地说，在经历着一场宇宙俄罗斯轮盘赌：升上远日点和跌向太阳的过程是在转动弹仓，掠过近日点时则是扣动扳机！每扣一次时的神经比上一次更紧张，我就是在这种交替的恐惧中度过了自己的少年时代。其实仔细想想，即使在远日点，地球也未脱离太阳氦闪的威力圈，如果那时太阳爆发，地球不是被气化而是被慢慢液化，那种结果还真不如在近日点。

在逃逸时代，大灾难接踵而至。

由于地球发动机产生的加速度及运行轨道的改变，地核中铁镍核心的平衡被扰动，其影响穿过古腾堡不连续面，波及地幔，各个大陆地热逸出，火山横行，这对人类的地下城市是致命的威胁。从第六次变轨周期后，在各大陆的地下城中，岩浆渗入灾难频繁发生。

那天当警报响起来的时候，我正走在放学回家的路上，听到市政厅的广播："F112市全体市民注意，城市北部屏障已被地应力破坏，岩浆渗入！岩浆渗入！现在岩浆流已到达第四街区！公路出口被封死，全体市民到中心广场集合，通过升降梯向地面撤离。注意，撤离时按《危急法》第五条行事，强调一遍，撤离时按《危急法》第五条行事！"

我环视了一下四周迷宫般的通道，地下城现在看上去并没有什么异常。但我知道现在的危险：只有两条通向外部的地下公路，其中一条去年因加固屏障的需要已被堵死，如果剩下的这条也堵死了，就只有通过经竖井直通地面的升降梯逃命了。升降梯的载运量很小，要把这座城市的36万人运出去需要很长时间。但也没有必要去争夺生存的机会，联合政府的《危急法》把一切都安排好了。

古代曾有过一个伦理学问题：当洪水到来时，一个只能救走一个人的男人，是去救他的父亲呢，还是去救他的儿子？在这个时代的人看来，提出这个问题很不可理解。

当我到达中心广场时，看到人们已按年龄排起了长长的队。最靠近电梯口的是由机器人保育员抱着的婴儿，然后是幼儿园的孩子，再往后是小学生……我排在队伍中间靠前的部分。爸爸现在在近地轨道值班，城里只有我和妈妈，我现在看不到妈妈，就顺着几公里长的队伍向后跑，没跑多远就被士兵拦住了。我知道她在最后一段，因为这座城市主要是学校集中地，家庭很少，她已经算年纪大的那批人了。

长队以让人心里着火的慢速度向前移动，三个小时后轮到我跨进升降梯时，我心里一点儿都不轻松，因为这时在妈妈和生存之间，还隔着 2 万多名大学生呢！而我已闻到了浓烈的硫黄味……

我到达地面两个半小时后，岩浆就在 500 米深的地下吞没了整座城市。我心如刀绞地想象着妈妈最后的时刻：她同没能撤出的一万八千人一起，看着岩浆涌进市中心广场。那时已经停电，整个地下城只有岩浆那可怖的暗红色光芒。广场那高大的白色穹顶在高温中渐渐变黑，所有的遇难者可能还没接触到岩浆，就被这上千摄氏度的高温夺去了生命。

但生活还在继续，在这严酷恐惧的现实中，爱情仍不时闪现出迷人的火花。为了缓解人们的紧张情绪，在第十二次到达远日点时，联合政府居然恢复了中断达两世纪之久的奥运会。我作为一名机动雪橇拉力赛的选手参加了奥运会，比赛项目是驾驶机动雪橇，从上海出发，从冰面上横穿封冻的太平洋，到达终点纽约。

发令枪响过之后，上百只雪橇在冰冻的海洋上以每小时二百公里左右的速度出发了。开始还有几只雪橇相伴，但两天后，他们或前或后，都消失在地平线之外。这时背后地球发动机的光芒已经看不到了，我正处于地球最黑暗的部分。在我眼中，世界就是由广阔的星空和向四面无限延伸的冰原组成的，这冰原似乎一直延伸到宇宙的尽头，或者它本身就是宇宙的尽头。而在由无限的星空和无限的冰原组成的宇宙中，只有我一个人！雪崩般的孤独感压倒了我，我想哭。我拼命地赶路，名次已无关紧要，只是为了在这可怕的孤独感杀死我之前尽早地摆脱它，而那想象中的彼岸似乎根本就不存在。

就在这时，我看到天边出现了一个人影。近了些后，我发现那是一个姑娘，正站在她的雪橇旁，她的长发在冰原上的寒风中飘动着。你知道这时遇见一个姑娘意味着什么，我们的后半生由此决定了。她是日本人，叫山彬加代子。女子组比我们先出发十二个小时，她的雪橇卡在冰缝中，把一根滑竿卡断了。我一边帮她修雪橇，一边把自己刚才的感觉告诉她。

"您说得太对了，我也是那样的感觉！是的，好像整个宇宙中就只有你一个人！知道吗，我看到您从远方出现时，就像看到太阳升起一样！"

"那你为什么不叫救援飞机？"

"这是一场体现人类精神的比赛，要知道，流浪地球在宇宙中是叫不到救援的！"她挥动着小拳头，以日本人特有的执着说。

"不过现在总得叫了，我们都没有备用滑竿，你的雪橇修不好了。"

"那我坐您的雪橇一起走好吗？如果您不在意名次的话。"

我当然不在意，于是我和加代子一起在冰冻的太平洋上走完了剩下的漫长路程。经过夏威夷后，我们看到了天边的曙光。在这被那个小小的太阳照亮的无际冰原上，我们向联合政府的民政部发去了结婚申请。

当我们到达纽约时，这个项目的裁判们早等得不耐烦，收摊走了。但有一个民政局的官员在等着我们，他向我们致以新婚的祝贺，然后开始履行他的职责：他挥手在空中划出一个全息图像，上面整齐地排列着几万个圆点，这是这几天全世界向联合政府登记结婚的数目。由于环境的严酷，法律规定每三对新婚配偶中只有一对有生育权，抽签决定。加代子对着半空中那几万个点犹豫了半天，点了中间的一个。当那个点变为绿色时，她高兴得跳了起来。但我的心中却不知是什么滋味，我的孩子出生在这个苦难的时代，是幸运还是不幸呢？那个官员倒是兴高采烈，他说每当一对"点绿"的时候他都十分高兴，他拿出了一瓶伏特加，我们三个轮着一人一口地喝着，都为人类的延续干杯。我们身后，遥远的太阳用它微弱的光芒给自由女神像镀上了一层金辉，对面是已无人居住的曼哈顿的摩天大楼群，微弱的阳光把它们的影子长长地投在纽约港寂静的冰面上，醉意阑珊的我，眼泪涌了出来。

地球，我的流浪地球啊！

分手前，官员递给我们一串钥匙，醉醺醺地说："这是你们在亚洲分到的房子，回家吧，哦，家多好啊！"

"有什么好的？"我漠然地说，"亚洲的地下城充满危险，你们在西半球当然体会不到。"

"我们马上也有你们体会不到的危险了，地球又要穿过小行星带，这次是西半球对着运行方向。"

"上几个变轨周期也经过小行星带，不是没什么大事吗？"

"那只是擦着小行星带的边缘走，太空舰队当然能应付，他们可以用激光和核弹把地球航线上的那些小石块都清除掉。但这次……你们没看新闻？这次地球要从小行星带正中穿过去！舰队得去对付那些大石块，唉……"

在回亚洲的飞机上，加代子问我："那些石块很大吗？"

我父亲现在就在太空舰队干那份工作，所以尽管政府为了避免惊慌照例封锁消息，我还是知道一些情况。我告诉加代子，那些石块大得像一座大山，五千万吨级的热核炸弹只能在上面打出一个小坑。"他们就要使用人类手中威力最大的武器了！"我神秘地告诉加代子。

"你是说反物质炸弹？！"

"还能是什么？"

"太空舰队的巡航范围是多远？"

"现在他们力量有限，我爸说只有150万千米左右。"

"啊，那我们能看到了！"

"最好别看。"

加代子还是看了，而且是没戴护目镜看的。反物质炸弹的第一次闪光是在我们起飞不久后从太空传来的，那时加代子正在欣赏飞机舷窗外空中的星星，这使她的双眼失明了一个多小时，以后的一个多月眼睛都红肿流泪。那真是让人心惊肉跳的时刻，反物质炮弹不断击中小行星，湮灭的强光此起彼伏地在漆黑的太空中闪现，仿佛宇宙中有一群巨人在围着地球用闪光灯疯狂地拍照似的。

半个小时后，我们看到了火流星，它们拖着长长的火尾划破长空，给人一种恐怖的美感。火流星越来越多，每一个在空中划过的距离越来越长。突然，机身在一声巨响中震颤了一下，紧接着又是连续的巨响和震颤。加代子惊叫着扑到我怀中，她显然以为飞机被流星击中了，这时机舱里响起了机长的声音。

"请各位乘客不要惊慌，这是流星冲破音障产生的超声速爆音，请大家戴上耳机，否则您的听觉会受到永久损害。由于飞行安全已无法保证，我们将在夏威夷紧急降落。"

这时我盯住了一个火流星，那个火球的体积比别的大出许多，我不相信它能在大气中烧完。果然，那火球疾驰过大半个天空，越来越小，但还是坠入了冰海。我们从万米高空看到，海面被击中的位置出现了一个小白点，那白点立刻扩散成一个白色的圆圈，圆圈迅速在海面扩大。

"那是浪吗？"加代子颤着声儿问我。

"是浪，上百米的浪。不过海封冻了，冰面会很快使它衰减的。"我自我安慰地说，不再看下面。

我们很快在檀香山降落，由当地政府安排去地下城。我们的汽车沿着海岸走，天空中布满了火流星，那些红发恶魔好像是从太空中的某一个点同时迸发出来的。一颗流星在距海岸不远处击中了海面，没有看到水柱，但水蒸气形成的白色蘑菇云高高地升起。波浪从冰层下传到岸边，厚厚的冰层轰隆隆地破碎了，冰面显出了浪的形状，好像有一群柔软的巨兽在下面排着队游过。

"这块有多大？"我问那位来接应我们的官员。

"不超过五公斤，不会比你的脑袋大吧。不过刚接到通知，在北方 800 千米的海面上，刚落下一颗 20 吨左右的。"

这时他手腕上的通信机响了，他看了一眼后对司机说："来不及到 204 号门了，就近找个入口吧！"

汽车拐了个弯，在一个地下城入口前停了下来。我们下车后，看到入口外有几个士兵，他们都一动不动地盯着远方的一个方向，眼里充满了恐惧。我们都顺着他们的目光看去，在海天连线处，我们看到一层黑色的屏障，乍一看好像是天边低低的云层，但那"云层"的高度太齐了，像一堵横在天边的长墙，再仔细看，墙头还镶着一线白边。

"那是什么呀？"加代子怯生生地问一个军官，得到的回答让我们汗毛直立。

"浪。"

地下城高大的铁门隆隆地关上了，约莫过了十分钟，我们感到从地面传来了低沉的声音，咕噜噜的，像一个巨人在地面打滚。我们面面相觑，大家都知道，百米高的巨浪正在滚过夏威夷，也将滚过各个大陆。但另一种震动更吓人，仿佛有一只巨拳从太空中不断地击打地球，在地下这震动并不大，只能隐约感到，但每一个震动都直达我们灵魂深处。这是流星在不断地击中地面。

我们的星球所遭到的残酷轰炸断断续续持续了一个星期。

当我们走出地下城时，加代子惊叫："天啊，天怎么是这样的！"

天空是灰色的，这是因为高层大气弥漫着小行星撞击陆地时产生的灰尘，星星和太阳都消失在这无际的灰色中，仿佛整个宇宙在下着一场大雾。地面上，滔天巨浪留下的海水还没来得及退去就封冻了，城市幸存的高楼形单影只地立在冰面上，挂着长长的冰凌柱。冰面上落了一层撞击尘，于是这个世界只剩下一种颜色：灰色。

我和加代子继续回亚洲的旅途。在飞机越过早已无意义的国际日期变更线时，我们见到了人类所见过的最黑的黑夜，飞机仿佛潜行在墨汁的海洋中。看着机舱外那没有一丝光线的世界，我们的心情也暗到了极点。

"什么时候能到头呢？"加代子喃喃地说。我不知道她指的是这次旅程还是这充满苦难和灾难的生活，我现在觉得两者都没有尽头。是啊，即使地球航出了氦闪的威力圈，我们得以逃生，那又怎么样呢？我们只是那漫长阶梯的最下级，当我们的一百代重孙爬上阶梯的顶端，见到新生活的光明时，我们的骨头都变成灰了。我不敢想象未来的苦难和艰辛，更不敢想象要带着爱人和孩子走过这条看不到头的泥泞路，我累了，实在走不动了……就在我被悲伤和绝望逼得快要窒息的时候，机舱里响起了一声女人的惊叫：

"啊！不！不能！亲爱的！"

我循声看去，见那个女人正从旁边的一个男人手中夺下一支手枪，他刚才显然想把枪口凑到自己的太阳穴上。这人很瘦弱，目光呆滞地看着前方无限远处。女人把头埋在他膝上，嘤嘤地哭了起来。

"安静。"男人冷冷地说。

哭声消失了，只有飞机发动机的嗡嗡声在轻响，像不变的哀乐。在我的感觉中，飞机已被粘在这巨大的黑暗中，一动不动；而整个宇宙，除了黑暗和飞机，什么都没有了。加代子钻进我怀里，浑身冰凉。

突然，机舱前部一阵骚动，有人在兴奋地低语。我向窗外看去，发现飞机前方出现了一片朦胧的光亮，那光亮是蓝色的，没有形状，十分均匀地出现在前方弥漫着撞击尘的夜空中。

那是地球发动机的光芒。

西半球的地球发动机已被陨石击毁了三分之一，但损失比起航前的预测要少；东半球的地球发动机由于背向撞击面，完好无缺。从功率上来说，它们是能使地球完成逃逸航行的。

在我眼中，前方朦胧的蓝光，如同从深海漫长的上浮后看到的海面的亮光，我的呼吸又顺畅起来。

我又听到那个女人的声音："亲爱的，痛苦呀、恐惧呀这些东西，也只有在活着时才能感觉到，死了，死了什么也没有了，那边只有黑暗。还是活着好，你说呢？"

那瘦弱的男人没有回答，他盯着前方的蓝光看，眼泪流了下来。我知道他能活下去了，只要那希望的蓝光还亮着，我们就都能活下去，我又想起了父亲关于希望的那些话。

一下飞机，我和加代子没有去我们在地下城中的新家，而是到设在地面的太空舰队基地去找父亲，但在基地，我只见到了追授他的一枚冰冷的勋章。这勋章是一名空军少将给我的，他告诉我，在清除地球航线上的小行星的行动中，一块被反物质炸弹炸出的小行星碎片击中了父亲的单座微型飞船。

"当时那个石块和飞船的相对速度有每秒一百公里，撞击使飞船座舱瞬间气化了，他没有一点儿痛苦，我向你保证，没有一点儿痛苦。"将军说。

当地球又向太阳跌回去的时候，我和加代子又到地面上来看春天，但没有看到。世界仍是一片灰色，阴暗的天空下，大地上分布着由残留海水形成的一个个冰冻湖泊，见不到一点儿绿色。大气中的撞击尘挡住了阳光，使气温难以回升。甚至在近日点，海洋和大地都没有解冻，太阳呈一个朦胧的光晕，仿佛是撞击尘后面的一个幽灵。

三年以后，空中的撞击尘才有所消散，人类终于最后一次通过近日点，向远日点升去。在这个近日点，东半球的人有幸目睹了地球历史上最快的一次日出和日落。太阳从海平面上一跃而起，迅速划过长空，大地上万物的影子在很快变换着角度，仿佛是无数根钟表的秒针。这也是地球上最短的一个白天，只有不到一个小时。当一个小时后太阳跌入地平线，黑暗降临大地时，我感到一阵伤感。这转瞬即逝的一天，仿佛是对地球在太阳系四十五亿年进化史的一个短暂的总结。直到宇宙的末日，它不会再回来了。

"天黑了。"加代子忧伤地说。

"最长的一夜。"我说。东半球的这一夜将延续两千五百年，一百代人后，半人马座的曙光才能再次照亮这个大陆。西半球也将面临最长的白天，但比这里的黑夜要短得多。在那里，太阳将很快升到天顶，然后一直静止在那个位置上渐渐变小，在半个世纪内，它就会融入星群难以分辨了。

按照预定的航线，地球升向与木星的会合点。航行委员会的计划是：地球第十五圈的公转轨道是如此之扁，以至于它的远日点到达木星轨道，地球将与木星在几乎相撞的距离上擦肩而过，在木星巨大引力的拉动下，地球将最终达到逃逸速度。

离开近日点两个月后，就能用肉眼看到木星了，它开始只是一个模糊的光点，但很快显出圆盘的形状。又过了一个月，木星在地球上空已有满月大小了，呈暗红色，能隐约看到上面的条纹。这时，十五年来一直垂直的地球发动机光柱中有一些开始摆动，地球在做会合前最后的姿态调整，木星渐渐沉到了地平线下。以后的三个多月，木星一直处在地球的另一面，我们看不到它，但知道两颗行星正在交会之中。

有一天，我们突然被告知东半球也能看到木星了。于是人们纷纷从地下城中来到地面。当我走出城市的密封门来到地面时，发现开了十五年的地球发动机已经全部关闭了，我再次看到了星空，这表明同木星最后的交会正在进行。人们都在紧张地盯着西方的地平线，地平线上出现了一片暗红色的光，那光区渐渐扩大，延伸到整个地平线的宽度。我现在发现那暗红色的区域上方同漆黑的星空有一道整齐的边界，那边界呈弧形，那巨大的弧形从地平线的一端跨到了另一端，在缓缓升起，巨弧下的天空都变成了暗红色，仿佛一块同星空一样大小的暗红色幕布在把地球同整个宇宙隔开。当我回过神来时，不由得倒吸一口冷气，那暗红色的幕布就是木星！我早就知道木星的体积是地球的 1300 倍，现在才真正感觉到它的巨大。这个宇宙巨怪在整个地平线上升起时，让人产生的那种恐惧和压抑感是难以用语言描述的，一名记者后来写道："不知是我身处噩梦中，还是整个宇宙都是一个造物主巨大而变态的头脑中的噩梦！"木星恐怖地上升着，渐渐占据了半个天空。这时，我们可以清楚地看到它云层中的风暴，那风暴把云层搅动成让人迷茫的混乱线条，我知道那厚厚的云层下是沸腾的液氢和液氦的大洋。著名的大红斑出现了，这个在木星表面维持了几十万年的大旋涡大得可以吞下整个地球。这时木星已占满了整个天空，地球仿佛是浮在木星沸腾的暗红色云海上的一只气球！而木星的大红斑就处在天空正中，如一只红色的巨眼盯着我们的世界，大地笼罩在它那阴森的红光中……这时，谁都无法相信小小的地球能逃出这巨大怪物的引力场。从地面上看，地球甚至连成为木星的卫星都不可能，我们就要掉进那无边云海覆盖着的地狱中了！但领航工程师们的计算是精确的，暗红色的、迷乱的天空在缓缓移动着，不知过了多长时间，西方的天边露出了黑色的一角，那黑色迅速扩大，其中有星星在闪烁，地球正在冲出木星的引力魔掌。这时警报尖叫起来，木星产生的引力潮汐正在向内陆推进，后来得知，这次大潮中百多米高的巨浪再次横扫了整个大陆。在跑进地下城的密封门时，我最后看了一眼仍占据半个天空的木星，发现木星的云海中有一道明显的划痕。后来知道，那是地球引力作用在木星表面的痕迹，我们的星球也在木星表面拉起了如山的液氢和液氦的巨浪。这时，木星巨大的引力正在把地球加速甩向外太空。

离开木星时，地球已达到了逃逸速度，它不再需要返回潜藏着死亡的太阳，而向广袤的外太空飞去，漫长的流浪时代开始了。

就在木星暗红色的阴影下，我的儿子在地层深处出生了。

叛乱

离开木星后，亚洲大陆上一万多台地球发动机再次全功率开动，这一次它们要不停地运行五百年，不停地加速地球。这五百年中，发动机将把亚洲大陆上一半的山脉用作燃料消耗掉。

从四个多世纪死亡的恐惧中解脱出来，人们长出了一口气。但预料中的狂欢并没有出现，接下来发生的事情超出所有人的想象。

在地下城的庆祝集会后，我一个人穿上密封服来到地面。童年时熟悉的群山已被超级挖掘机夷为平地，大地上只有裸露的岩石和坚硬的冻土，冻土上到处有白色的斑块，那是大海潮留下的盐渍。面前那座爷爷和爸爸度过了一生的曾有千万人口的大城市现在已是一片废墟，高楼钢筋外露的残骸在地球发动机光柱的蓝光中拖着长长的影子，好像是史前巨兽的化石……一次次的洪水和小行星的撞击已摧毁了地面上的一切，各大陆上的城市和植被都荡然无存，地球表面已变成与火星一样的荒漠。

这一段时间，加代子心神不定。她常常扔下孩子不管，一个人开着飞行汽车出去旅行，回来后，只是说她去了西半球。最后，她拉我一起去了。

我们的飞行汽车以四倍声速飞行了两个小时，终于能够看到太阳了，它刚刚升出太平洋，这时看上去只有棒球大小，给冰封的洋面投下一片微弱的、冷冷的光芒。加代子把飞行汽车悬停在5000米的空中，然后从后面拿出了一个长长的东西，去掉封套后，我看到那是一架天文望远镜，业余爱好者用的那种。加代子打开车窗，把望远镜对准太阳，让我看。

从有色镜片中我看到了放大几百倍的太阳，我甚至清楚地看到太阳表面缓缓移动的明暗斑点，还有日球边缘隐隐约约的日珥。

加代子把望远镜同车内的计算机联起来，把一个太阳影像采集下来。然后，她又调出了另一个太阳图像，说："这个是四个世纪前的太阳图像。"接着，计算机对两个图像进行比较。

"看到了吗？"加代子指着屏幕说，"它们的光度、像素排列、像素概率、层次统计等参数都完全一样！"

我摇摇头说："这能说明什么？一架玩具望远镜、一个低级图像处理程序，加上你这个无知的外行……别自寻烦恼了，别信那些谣言！"

"你是个白痴。"她说着，收回望远镜，把飞行汽车向回开去。这时，在我们的上方和下方，我又远远地看到了几辆飞行汽车，同我们刚才一样悬在空中，从每辆车的车窗中都伸出一架望远镜对着太阳。

以后的几个月中，一个可怕的说法像野火一样在全世界蔓延。越来越多的人自发地用更大型、更精密的仪器观测太阳。后来，一个民间组织向太阳发射了一组探测器，它们在三个月后穿过日球。探测器发回的数据最后证实了那个事实。

同四个世纪前相比，太阳没有任何变化。

现在，各大陆的地下城已成了一座座骚动的火山，局势一触即发。一天，按照联合政府的法令，我和加代子把儿子送进了养育中心。回家的路上我们俩都感到维系我们关系的唯一纽带已不存在了。走到市中心广场，我们看到有人在演讲，另一些人在演讲者周围向市民分发武器。

"公民们！地球被出卖了！人类被出卖了！文明被出卖了！我们都是一个超级骗局的牺牲品！这个骗局巨大且可怕，上帝都会为之休克！太阳还是原来的太阳，它不会爆发，过去、现在、将来都不会，它是永恒的象征！爆发的是联合政府中那些人阴险的野心！他们编造了这一切，只是为了建立他们的独裁帝国！他们

34

毁了地球！他们毁了人类文明！公民们，有良知的公民们！拿起武器，拯救我们的星球！拯救人类文明！我们要推翻联合政府，控制地球发动机，把我们的星球从这寒冷的外太空开回原来的轨道！开回太阳的温暖怀抱中！"加代子默默地走上前去，从分发武器的人手中接过了一支冲锋枪，加入那些拿到武器的市民队列中，她没有回头，同那支庞大的队列一起消失在地下城的迷雾里。我呆呆地站在那儿，手在衣袋中紧紧攥着父亲用生命和忠诚换来的那枚勋章，它的边角把我的手扎出了血……

三天后，叛乱在各个大陆同时爆发了。

叛军所到之处，人民群起响应，到现在，很少有人怀疑自己受骗了。但我加入了联合政府的军队，这并非出于对政府的坚信，而是我三代前辈都有过军旅生涯，他们在我心中种下了忠诚的种子，不论在什么情况下，背叛联合政府对我来说都是一件不可想象的事。

美洲、非洲、大洋洲和南极洲相继沦陷，联合政府收缩防线死守地球发动机所在的东亚和中亚。叛军很快对这里构成包围态势，他们对政府军占有压倒性优势，之所以在相当长一段时间里攻势没有取得进展，完全是因为地球发动机。叛军不想毁掉地球发动机，因此在这一广阔的战区没有使用重武器，联合政府得以苟延残喘。双方这样对峙了三个月，联合政府的十二个集团军相继临阵倒戈，中亚和东亚防线全线崩溃。两个月后，大势已去的联合政府连同不到十万军队在靠近海岸的地球发动机控制中心陷入重围。

我就是这残存军队中的一名少校。控制中心有一座中等大小的城市，它的中心是地球驾驶室。我拖着一只被激光束烧焦的手臂，躺在控制中心的伤兵收容站里。就是在这儿，我得知加代子已在澳洲战役中阵亡。我和收容站里所有的人一样，整天喝得烂醉，对外面的战事全然不知，也不感兴趣。不知过了多久，听到有人在高声说话。

"知道你们为什么这样吗？你们在自责，在这场战争中，你们站到了反人类的一边，我也一样。"

我转头一看，发现讲话的人肩上有一颗将星，他接着说："没关系的，我们还有最后的机会拯救自己的灵魂。地球驾驶室距我们这儿只有三个街区，我们去占领它，把它交给外面理智的人类！我们为联合政府已尽到了责任，现在该为人类尽责任了！"

我用那只没受伤的手抽出手枪，随着这群突然狂热起来的受伤和没受伤的人，沿着钢铁的通道，向地球驾驶室冲去。出乎意料，一路上我们几乎没遇到抵抗，倒是有越来越多的人从错综复杂的钢铁通道的各个分支中加入我们。最后，我们来到了一扇巨大的门前，那钢铁大门高得望不到顶。它轰隆隆地打开了，我们冲进了地球驾驶室。

尽管以前无数次在电视中看到过，所有的人还是被驾驶室的宏伟震惊了。从视觉上看不出这里的大小，因为驾驶室淹没在一幅巨型全息图中，那是一幅太阳系的模拟图。整个图像实际就是一个向所有方向无限延伸的黑色空间，我们一进来，就悬浮在这空间之中。由于尽量反映真实的比例，太阳和行星都很小很小，小得像远方的萤火虫，但能分辨出来。以那遥远的代表太阳的光点为中心，一条醒目的红色螺旋线扩展开来，像广阔的黑色洋面上迅速扩散的红色波圈，那是地球的航线。在螺旋线最外面的一点上，航线变成明亮的绿色，那是地球还没有完成的路程。那条绿线从我们的头顶掠过，顺着看去，我们看到了灿烂的星海，绿线消失在星海的深处，我们看不到它的尽头。在这广漠的黑色空间中，还飘浮着许多闪亮的灰尘，其中几个尘粒飘近，我发现那是一块块虚拟屏幕，上面翻滚着复杂的数字和曲线。

我看到了令全人类瞩目的地球驾驶台，它好像是飘浮在黑色空间中的一个银白色的小行星，看到它我更难以把握这里的巨大——驾驶台本身就是一个广场，现在上面密密麻麻地站着五千多人，包括联合政府的主要成员，负责实施地球航行计划的星际移民委员会的大部分成员，以及那些最后忠于政府的人。这时我听到最高执政官的声音在整个黑色空间响了起来。

"我们本来是可以战斗到底的，但这可能导致地球发动机失控，这种情况一旦发生，过量聚变的物质将烧穿地球，或蒸发全部海洋，所以我们决定投降。我们理解所有的人，因为已经进行了四十代人，在要延续一百代人的艰难奋斗中，永远保持理智确实是奢求。但也请所有的人记住我们，站在这里的这五千多人，这里有联合政府的最高执政官，也有普通的列兵，是我们把信念坚持到了最后。我们都知道自己看不到真理被证实的那一天，但如果人类得以延续万代，以后所有的人将在我们的墓前洒下自己的眼泪，这颗叫地球的行星，就是我们永恒的纪念碑！"

控制中心巨大的密封门隆隆开启，那五千多名最后的地球派一群群走了出来，在叛军的押送下向海岸走去。一路上两边挤满了人，所有人都冲他们吐唾沫，用冰块和石块砸他们。他们中有的人密封服的面罩被砸裂了，外面零下一百多摄氏度的严寒使那些人的脸麻木了，但他们仍努力地走下去。我看到一个小女孩，举起一大块冰用尽全身力气狠狠地向一个老者砸去，她那双眼睛透过面罩射出疯狂的怒火。

当我听到这五千多人全部被判处死刑时，觉得太宽容了。难道仅仅一死吗？这一死就能偿清他们的罪恶吗？！能偿清他们用一个离奇变态的想象和骗局毁掉地球、毁掉人类文明的罪恶吗？他们应该死一万次！这时，我想起了那些做出太阳爆发预测的天体物理学家，那些设计和建造地球发动机的工程师，他们在一个世纪前就已作古，我现在真想把他们从坟墓中挖出来，让他们也死一万次。

真感谢死刑的执行者们，他们为这些罪犯找了一种好的死法：他们收走了每个被判死刑的人密封服上加热用的核能电池，然后把他们丢在大海的冰面上，让零下百摄氏度的严寒慢慢夺去他们的生命。

这些人类文明史上最险恶、最可耻的罪犯在冰海上站了黑压压的一片，在岸上有十几万人在看着他们，十几万颗牙齿咬得嘣嘣响，十几万双眼睛喷出和那个小女孩一样的怒火。

这时，所有的地球发动机都已关闭，壮丽的群星出现在冰原之上。

我能想象出严寒像无数把尖刀刺进他们的身体，他们的血液在凝固，生命从他们的体内一点点流走，这想象中的感觉变成一种快感，传遍我的全身。看到他们在严寒的折磨中慢慢死去，岸上的人们快活起来，他们唱起了《我的太阳》。我唱着，眼睛看着星空的一个方向，在那个方向上，有一颗稍大些刚刚显出圆盘形状的星星发出黄色的光芒，那就是太阳。

啊，我的太阳，生命之母，万物之父，我的大神，我的上帝！还有什么比您更稳定，还有什么比您更永恒？我们这些渺小的、连灰尘都不如的碳基细菌，拥挤在围着您转的一粒小石头上，竟敢预言您的末日，我们怎么能蠢到这个程度？！

一个小时过去了，海面上那些反人类的罪犯虽然还全都站着，但已没有一个活人，他们的血液已被冻结了。

我的眼睛突然什么都看不见了，几秒钟后，视力渐渐恢复，冰原、海岸和岸上的人群又在眼前慢慢显影，最后完全清晰了，而且比刚才更清晰，这个世界现在笼罩在一片强烈的白光中，刚才我眼睛的失明正是由于这突然出现的强光的刺激造成的。但星空没有重现，所有的星光都被这强光所淹没，仿佛整个宇宙都被强光熔化了，这强光从太空中的一点迸发出来，那一点现在成了宇宙中心，那一点就在我刚才盯着的方向。

太阳氦闪爆发了。

《我的太阳》的合唱戛然而止，岸上的十几万人呆住了，似乎同海面上那些人一样，冻成了一片僵硬的岩石。

太阳最后一次把它的光和热洒向地球。地面上的冰结的二氧化碳干冰首先融化，腾起了一阵白色的蒸气；然后海冰表面也开始融化，受热不均的大海冰层发出惊天动地的巨响。渐渐地，照在地面上的光柔和起来，天空出现了微微的蓝色；后来，强烈的太阳风产生的极光在空中出现，苍穹中飘动着巨大的彩色光幕……

在这突然出现的灿烂阳光下，海面上最后的地球派们仍稳稳地站着，仿佛五千多尊雕像。

太阳爆发只持续了很短的时间，两个小时后强光开始急剧减弱，很快熄灭了。在太阳的位置上出现了一个暗红色球体，它的体积慢慢膨胀，最后从这里看它，已达到了在地球轨道上看到的太阳大小，那么它的实际体积已大到越出火星轨道，而水星、火星和金星这三颗地球的伙伴行星，这时已在上亿摄氏度的辐射中化为一缕轻烟。但它已不是太阳，它不再发出光和热，看上去如同贴在太空中的一张冰冷的红纸，它那暗红色的光芒似乎是周围星光的散射。这就是小质量恒星演化的最后归宿：红巨星。

五十亿年的壮丽生涯已成为飘逝的梦幻，太阳死了。

幸运的是，还有人活着。

流浪时代

当我回忆这一切时，半个世纪已过去了。二十年前，地球航出了冥王星轨道，航出了太阳系，在寒冷广漠的外太空继续着它孤独的航程。

最近一次去地面是十几年前的事了，那是儿子和儿媳陪我去的，儿媳是一个金发碧眼的姑娘，就要做母亲了。

到地面后，我首先注意到，虽然所有的地球发动机仍全功率地运行，巨大的光柱却看不到了，这是因为地球大气已消失，等离子体的光芒没有散射。我看到地面上布满了奇怪的黄绿相间的半透明晶体块，这是固体氧氮，是已冻结的空气。有趣的是，空气并没有均匀地冻结在地球表面，而是形成了小山丘似的不规则的隆起，在原来平滑的大海冰原上，这些半透明的小山形成了奇特的景观。银河系的星河纹丝不动地横过天穹，也像被冻结了，但星光很亮，看久了还刺眼呢。

地球发动机将不间断地开动五百年，到时地球将加速至光速的千分之五，然后地球将以这个速度滑行一千三百年，之后地球就走完了三分之二的航程，它将掉转发动机的方向，开始长达五百年的减速，地球在航行两千四百年后到达比邻星，再过一百年时间，它将泊入这颗恒星的轨道，成为它的一颗卫星。

我知道已被忘却
流浪的航程太长太长
但那一时刻要叫我一声啊
当东方再次出现霞光

我知道已被忘却
起航的时代太远太远
但那一时刻要叫我一声啊
当人类又看到了蓝天

我知道已被忘却
太阳系的往事太久太久
但那一时刻要叫我们一声啊
当鲜花重新挂上枝头
……

每当听到这首歌，一股暖流就涌进我这年迈僵硬的身躯，我干涸的老眼又湿润了。我好像看到半人马座三颗金色的太阳在地平线上依次升起，万物沐浴在它温暖的光芒中。固态的空气熔化了，变成了碧蓝的天。两千多年前的种子从解冻的土层中复苏，大地绿了。我看到我的第一百代孙子孙女们在绿色的草原上欢笑，草原上有清澈的小溪，溪中有银色的小鱼……我看到了加代子，她从绿色的大地上向我跑来，年轻美丽，像个天使……

啊，地球，我的流浪地球……

微纪元

THE
MICRO-
ERA

回归

先行者知道，他现在是全宇宙中唯一的人了。

他是在飞船掠过冥王星时知道的，从这里看去，太阳是一颗暗淡的星星，同三十年前他飞出太阳系时没有两样。但飞船计算机刚刚进行的视行差测量告诉他，冥王星的轨道外移了许多，由此可以计算出太阳比他启程时损失了4.74%的质量，又可推论出另外一个使他的心先是颤抖然后冰冻的结论。

那事已经发生过了。

其实，在他启程时人类已经知道那事要发生了，通过发射上万个穿过太阳的探测器，天体物理学家们确定了太阳将要发生一次短暂的能量闪烁，并损失大约5%的质量。

如果太阳有记忆，它不会对此感到不安，在那几十亿年的漫长生涯中，它曾经历过比这大得多的剧变。当它从星云的旋涡中诞生时，它的生命的剧变是以毫秒为单位的，在那辉煌的一刻，引力的坍缩使核聚变的火焰照亮星云混沌的黑暗……它知道自己的生命是一个过程，尽管现在处于这个过程中最稳定的时期，偶然的、小小的突变总是免不了的，就像平静的水面上不时有一个小气泡浮起并破裂。能量和质量的损失算不了什么，它还是它，一颗中等大小、视星等为 –26.8 的恒星。甚至太阳系的其他部分也不会受到太大的影响，水星可能被熔化，金星稠密的大气将被剥离。再往外围的行星所受的影响就更小了，火星颜色可能由于表面的熔化而由红变黑；地球嘛，只不过表面温度升高至4000 摄氏度，这可能会持续一百个小时左右，海洋肯定会被蒸发，各大陆表面岩石也会熔化一层，但仅此而已。以后，太阳又将很快恢复原状，由于质量的损失，各行星的轨道会稍微后移，这影响就更小了。比如地球，气温可能稍稍下降，平均降到零下一百一十摄氏度左右，这有助于熔化的表面重新凝结，并使水和大气能够被多少保留一些。

那时人们常谈起一个笑话，说的是一个人同上帝的对话。上帝啊，一万年对你是多么短啊！上帝说：就一秒钟。上帝啊，一亿元对你是多么少啊！上帝说：就一分钱。上帝啊，给我一分钱吧！上帝说：请等一秒钟。

现在，太阳让人类等了"一秒钟"：预测能量闪烁的时间是在一万八千年之后。这对太阳来说确实只是一秒钟，却可以使目前活在地球上的人类对"一秒钟"后发生的事采取一种超然的态度，甚至当作一种哲学理念。影响不是没有，人类文化一天天变得玩世不恭起来，但人类至少还有四五百代的时间可以从容地想想逃生的办法。

两个世纪以后，人类采取了第一个行动：发射了一艘恒星际飞船，在周围一百光年以内寻找带有可移民行星的恒星，飞船被命名为"方舟号"，这批宇航员都被称为"先行者"。

"方舟号"掠过了六十颗恒星，也是掠过了六十个炼狱。其中只有一颗恒星有一颗卫星，那是一滴直径8000千米的处于白炽状态的铁水，因其为液态，所以在运行中不断改变着形状……"方舟号"此行唯一的成果，就是进一步证明了人类的孤独。

"方舟号"航行了二十三年的时间，但这是"方舟时间"，由于飞船以接近光速行驶，地球时间已过了两万五千年。

本来"方舟号"是可以按预定时间返回的。

由于在接近光速时无法同地球通信，必须把速度降至光速的一半以下，这需要消耗大量的能量和时间。所以，"方舟号"一般每月减速一次，接收地球发来的信息，而当它下一次减速时，收到的已是地球一百多年后发出的信息了。"方舟号"和地球的时间，就像从高倍瞄准镜中看目标一样，瞄准镜稍微移动一下，镜中的目标就跨越了巨大的距离。"方舟号"收到的最后一条信息是在"方舟时间"自起航十三年，地球时间自起航一万七千年时从地球发出的，"方舟号"一个月后再次减速，发现地球方向已寂静无声了。一万多年前对太阳的计算可能稍有误差，在"方舟号"这一个月，地球这一百多年间，那事发生了。

"方舟号"真成了一艘方舟，但已是一艘只有诺亚一人的方舟。其他的七名先行者，有四名死于一颗距飞船四光年处突然爆发的新星的辐射，两人死于疾病，一人（是男人）在最后一次减速通信时，听着地球方向的寂静开枪自杀了。

以后，这唯一的先行者曾使"方舟号"保持在可通信速度很长时间，后来他把飞船加速到光速，心中那微弱的希望之火又使他很快把速度降下来聆听，由于减速越来越频繁，回归的行程也被拖长了。

寂静仍持续着。

"方舟号"在地球时间启程两万五千年后回到太阳系，比预定的时间晚了九千年。

纪念碑

穿过冥王星轨道后，"方舟号"继续飞向太阳系深处，对于一艘恒星际飞船来说，在太阳系中的航行如同海轮行驶在港湾中。太阳很快大了亮了，先行者曾从望远镜中看了一眼木星，发现这颗大行星的表面已面目全非，大红斑不见了，风暴纹似乎更加混乱。他没再关注别的行星，径直飞向地球。

先行者用颤抖的手按动了一个按钮，高大舷窗的不透明金属窗帘正在缓缓打开。啊，我的蓝色水晶球，宇宙的蓝眼珠，蓝色的天使……先行者闭起双眼默默祈祷着，过了很长时间，才强迫自己睁开双眼。

他看到了一个黑白相间的地球。

黑色的是熔化后又凝结的岩石，那是墓碑的黑色；白色的是蒸发后又冻结的海洋，那是殓布的白色。

"方舟号"进入低轨道，从黑色的大陆和白色的海洋上空缓缓掠过。先行者没有看到任何遗迹，一切都被熔化了，文明已成过眼烟云。但总该留个纪念碑，一座能耐 4000 摄氏度高温的纪念碑。

先行者正这么想着，纪念碑就出现了。飞船收到了从地面发上来的一束视频信号，计算机把这信号显示在屏幕上，先行者首先看到了用耐高温摄像机拍下的两千多年前的大灾难景象。能量闪烁时，太阳并没有像他想象中那样亮度突然增强，太阳迸发出的能量主要以可见光之外的辐射传出。他看到，蓝色的天空突然变成地狱般的红色，接着又变成噩梦般的紫色；他看到，纪元城市中他熟悉的高楼群在几千摄氏度的高温中先是冒出浓烟，然后像火炭一样发出暗红色的光，最后像蜡一样熔化了；灼热的岩浆从高山上流下，形成了一道道巨大的瀑布，无数道这样的瀑布又汇成一条条发着红光的岩浆大河，大地上火流的洪水在泛滥；原来是大海的地方，只有蒸气形成的高大的蘑菇云，这形状狰狞的云山下部映射着岩浆的红色，上部透出天空的紫色，云山在急剧扩大，很快一切都消失在这蒸气中……

当蒸气散去，又能看到景物时，已是几年以后了。这时，大地已从烧熔状态初步冷却，黑色的波纹状岩石覆盖了一切。还能看到岩浆河流，它们在大地上形成了错综复杂的火网。人类的痕迹已完全消失，文明如梦一样无影无踪了。又过了几年，水在高温状态下离解成的氢氧又重新化合成水，大暴雨从天而降，灼热的大地上再次蒸气迷漫，这时的世界就像在一个大蒸锅中一样阴暗闷热和潮湿。暴雨连下几十年，大地被进一步冷却，海洋渐渐恢复了。又过了上百年，因海水蒸发形成的阴云终于散去，天空现出蓝色，太阳再次出现了。再后来，由于地球轨道外移，气温急剧下降，大海完全冻结，天空万里无云，已死去的世界在严寒中变得宁静了。

先行者接着看到了一座城市的图像：先看到如林的细长的高楼群，镜头从高楼群上方降下去，出现了一个广场，广场上一片人海。镜头再下降，先行者看到所有的人都在仰望着天空。镜头最后停在广场正中的一个平台上，平台上站着一个漂亮姑娘，好像只有十几岁，她在屏幕上冲着先行者挥挥手，娇滴滴地喊："喂，我们看到你了，像一颗飞得很快的星星！你是'方舟一号'？！"

在旅途的最后几年，先行者的大部分时间是在虚拟现实游戏中度过的。在那个游戏中，计算机接收玩家的大脑信号，根据玩家思维构筑一幅三维画面，这画面中的人和物还可根据玩家的思想做出有限的活动。先行者曾在寂寞中构筑过从家庭到王国的无数个虚拟世界，所以现在他一眼就看出这是一幅这样的画面。但这幅画面造得很拙劣，由于大脑中思维的飘忽性，这种由想象构筑的画面总有些不对的地方，但眼前这幅画面中的错误太多了：首先，当镜头移过那些摩天大楼时，先行者看到有很多人从楼顶窗子中钻出，径直从几百米高处跳下来，经过让人头晕目眩的下坠，这些人平安无事地落到地上；同时，地上有许多人一跃而起，像会轻功一样一下就跃上几层楼的高度，然后他们的脚踏到了楼壁上伸出的一小块踏板上（这样的踏板每隔几层就有一个，好像专门为此而设），再一跃，又飞上几层，就这样一直跳到楼顶，从某个窗子钻进去。仿佛这些摩天大楼都没有门和电梯，人们就是用这种方式进出的。当镜头移到那个广场平台上时，先行者看到人海中有用线吊着的几个水晶球，那球直径可能有一米多。有人把手伸进水晶球，很轻易地抓出水晶球的一部分，在他们的手移出后晶莹的球体立刻恢复原状，而人们抓到手中的那部分立刻变成了一个小水晶球，那些人就把那个透明的小球扔进嘴里……除了这些明显的谬误外，有一点最能反映这幅计算机画面的思维变态和混乱：在这座城市的所有空间，都飘浮着一些奇形怪状的物体，它们大的有两三米，小的也有半米，有的像一块破碎的海绵，有的像一根弯曲的大树枝。那些东西缓慢地飘浮着，有一根大树枝飘向平台上的那个姑娘，她轻轻推开了它，那大树枝又打着转儿向远处飘去……先行者理解这些，在一个濒临毁灭的世界中，人们是不会有清晰和正常的思维的。

这可能是某种自动装置，在这场大灾难前被人们深埋于地下，躲过了高温和辐射，后来又自动升到这个已经毁灭的地面世界上。这种装置不停地监视着太空，监测到零星回到地球的飞船时就自动发射那个画面，给那些幸存者以这样糟糕透顶又滑稽可笑的安慰。

"这么说后来又发射过方舟飞船？"先行者问。

"当然，又发射了十二艘呢！"那姑娘说。不说这幅荒诞变态的画面的其他部分，这个姑娘造得倒是真不错，她那融合东西方精华的姣好的面容露出一副天真的样子，仿佛她仰望的整个宇宙是一个大玩具。那双大眼睛好像会唱歌，还有她的长发，好像失重似的永远飘在半空不落下，使她看上去像身处海水中的美人鱼。

"那么，现在还有人活着吗？"先行者问，他最后的希望像野火一样燃烧起来。

"您这样的人吗？"姑娘天真地问。

"当然是我这样的真人，不是你这样用计算机造出来的虚拟人。"

"前一艘'方舟号'是在七百三十年前回来的，您是最后一艘回归的'方舟号'了。请问您船上还有女人吗？"

"只有我一个人。"

"您是说没有女人了？！"姑娘吃惊地瞪大了眼。

"我说过只有我一人。在太空中还有没回来的其他飞船吗？"

姑娘把两只白嫩的小手儿在胸前交叉着："没有了！我好难过好难过啊，您是最后一个这样的人了，如果，呜呜……如果不克隆的话……呜呜……"这美人儿捂着脸哭起来，广场上的人群也是一片哭声。

先行者的心沉到了底，人类的毁灭最后被证实了。

"您怎么不问我是谁呢？"姑娘又抬起头来仰望着他说，她又恢复了那副天真的神色，好像转眼忘了刚才的悲伤。

"我没兴趣。"

姑娘娇滴滴地大喊："我是地球领袖啊！"

"对，她是地球联合政府的最高执政官！"下面的人也都一齐闪电般地由悲伤转为兴奋，这真是个拙劣到家的制品。

先行者不想再玩这种无聊的游戏了，他起身要走。

"您怎么这样？！首都的全体公民都在这儿迎接您，前辈，您不要不理我们啊！"姑娘带着哭腔喊。

先行者想起了什么，转过身来问："人类还留下了什么？"

"照我们的指引着陆，您就会知道！"

首都

先行者进入了着陆舱，把"方舟号"留在轨道上，在那束信息波的指引下开始着陆。他戴着一副视频眼镜，可以从其中的一个镜片上看到信息波传来的那幅画面。

"前辈，您马上就要到达地球首都了，这虽然不是这个星球上最大的城市，但肯定是最美丽的城市，您会喜欢的！不过您的降落点要离城市远些，我们不希望受到伤害……"画面上那个自称地球领袖的姑娘还在喋喋不休。

先行者在视频眼镜中换了一个画面，显示出着陆舱正下方的区域，现在高度只有一万多米了，下面是一片黑色的荒原。

后来，画面上的逻辑更加混乱起来，也许是几千年前那个画面的构造者情绪沮丧到了极点，也许是发射画面的计算机内存在这几千年的漫长岁月中老化了。画面上，那姑娘开始唱起歌来：

> 啊，尊敬的使者，你来自宏纪元！
> 辉煌的宏纪元，
> 伟大的宏纪元，
> 美丽的宏纪元，
> 你是烈火中消逝的梦……

唱着唱着，这个漂亮的歌手开始跳起来，她一下从平台跳上几十米的半空，落到平台上后又一跳，居然飞越了大半个广场，落到广场边上的一座高楼顶上，又一跳，飞过整个广场，落到另一边，看上去像一只迷人的小跳蚤。她在空中抓住一根几米长的奇形怪状的飘浮物，那根大树干载着她在人海上空盘旋，她在上面优美地扭动着苗条的身躯。

下面的人海沸腾起来，所有人都大声合唱："宏纪元，宏纪元……"每个人轻轻一跳就能升到半空，以至于整个人群看起来如撒到震动鼓面上的一片沙子。

先行者实在受不了了，他把声音和图像一起关掉。他现在知道，大灾难前的人们忌妒他们这些跨越时空的幸存者，所以做了这些变态的东西来折磨他们。但过了一会儿，当那画面带来的烦恼消失一些后，当感觉到着陆舱接触地面的震动时，他产生了一种幻觉：也许他真的降落在一座高空看不清楚的城市中？当他走出着陆舱，站在那一望无际的黑色荒原上时，幻觉消失，失望使他浑身冰冷。

先行者小心地打开宇宙服的面罩，一股寒气扑面而来，空气很稀薄，但能维持人的呼吸。气温在零下 40 摄氏度左右。天空呈一种大灾难前黎明和黄昏时的深蓝色，但现在太阳在正空照耀着，先行者摘下手套，没有感到它的热力。由于空气稀薄，阳光散射较弱，天空中能看到几颗较亮的星星。脚下是刚凝结了两千年左右的大地，到处可见岩浆流动的波纹形状，地面虽已开始风化，但仍然很硬，土壤很难见到。这带波纹的大地伸向天边，其间有一些小小的丘陵。在另一个方向，可以看到冰封的大海在地平线处闪着白光。

先行者仔细打量四周，看到了信息波的发射源，那儿有一个镶在地面岩石中的透明半球护面，直径大约有一米，半球护面下似乎扣着一片很复杂的结构。他还注意到远处的地面上还有几个这样的透明半球，相互之间相隔二三十米，像地面上的几个大水泡，反射着阳光。

先行者又在他的左镜片中打开了画面，在计算机的虚拟世界中，那个恬不知耻的小骗子仍在那根飘浮在半空中的大树枝上忘情地唱着扭着，并不时向他送飞吻，下面广场上所有的人都在向他欢呼。

……
宏伟的宏纪元！
浪漫的宏纪元！
忧郁的宏纪元！
脆弱的宏纪元！
……

先行者木然地站着，深蓝色的苍穹中，明亮的太阳和晶莹的星星在闪耀，整个宇宙围绕着他——最后一个人类。

孤独像雪崩一样埋住了他，他蹲下来捂住脸抽泣起来。

歌声戛然而止，虚拟画面中的所有人都关切地看着他，那姑娘骑在半空中的大树枝上，突然嫣然一笑。

"您对人类就这么没信心吗？"

这话中有一种东西使先行者浑身一震，他真的感觉到了什么，站起身来。他突然注意到，左镜片画面中的城市暗了下来，仿佛阴云在一秒钟内遮住了天空。他移动脚步，城市立即亮了起来。他走到那个透明半球前，俯身向里面看，他看不清里面那些密密麻麻的细微结构，但看到左镜片中的画面上，城市的天空立刻被一个巨大的东西占据了。

那是他的脸。

"我们看到您了！您能看清我们吗？！去拿个放大镜吧！"姑娘大叫起来，广场上的人海再次沸腾起来。

先行者明白了一切。他想起了那些跳下高楼的人，在微小环境下重力是不会造成伤害的，同样，在那样的尺度下，人也可以轻易地跃上几百米的高楼。那些大水晶球实际上就是水，在微小的尺度下水的表面张力处于统治地位，那是一些小水珠，人们从这些水珠中抓出来喝的水珠就更小了。城市空间中飘浮的那些看上去有几米长的奇怪东西，包括载着姑娘飘浮的大树枝，只不过是空气中细微的灰尘。

那座城市不是虚拟的，它就像两万五千年前人类的所有城市一样真实，它就在这个一米直径的半球形透明玻璃罩中。

人类还在，文明还在。

在微型城市中，飘浮在树枝上的姑娘——地球联合政府最高执政官，向几乎占满整个宇宙的先行者自信地伸出手来。

"前辈，微纪元欢迎您。"

微人类

"在大灾难到来前的一万七千年中，人类想尽了逃生的办法，其中最容易想到的是恒星际移民，但包括您这艘在内的所有方舟飞船都没有找到带有可居住行星的恒星。即使找到了，以大灾难前一个世纪人类的宇航技术，连移民千分之一的人类都做不到。另一个设想是移居到地层深处，躲过太阳能量闪烁后再出来。这不过是拖长死亡的过程而已，大灾难后地球的生态系统将被完全摧毁，是养活不了人类的。

"有一段时期，人们几乎绝望了。但某位基因工程师的脑海中闪现了一个这样的火花：如果把人类的体积缩小到原来十亿分之一会怎么样？这样人类社会的尺度也缩小到了原来的十亿分之一，只要有很微小的生态系统，消耗很微小的资源就可生存下来。很快全人类都意识到这是拯救人类文明唯一可行的办法。这个设想是以两项技术为基础的，其一是基因工程，在修改人类基因后，人类将缩小至 10 微米左右，只相当于一个细胞大小，但其身体的结构完全不变。做到这点是完全可能的，人和细菌的基因本来就没有太大的差别。其二是纳米技术，这是一项在 20 世纪就发展起来的技术，那时人们已经能造出细菌大小的发电机了，后来人们可以在纳米尺度造出从火箭到微波炉等一切设备，只是那些纳米工程师做梦都不会想到他们的产品的最后用途。

"培育第一批微人类类似克隆：从一个人的细胞中抽取全部遗传信息，然后培育出同主体一模一样的微人，但其体积只是主体的十亿分之一。以后他们就同宏人（微人对你们的称呼，他们还把你们的时代叫宏纪元）一样生育后代了。

"第一批微人的亮相极富戏剧性，有一天，大约是您的飞船起航后一万两千年吧，全球的电视上都出现了一个教室，教室中有三十个孩子在上课，画面极其普通，孩子是普通的孩子，教室是普通的教室，看不出任何特别之处。但镜头拉开，人们发现这个教室是在显微镜下拍摄的……"

"我想问……"先行者打断最高执政官的话，"以微人这样微小的大脑，能达到宏人的智力吗？"

"那么您认为我是个傻瓜了？鲸鱼也并不比您聪明！智力不是由大脑的大小决定的，以微人大脑中的原子数目和它们量子状态的数目来说，其信息处理能力像宏人大脑一样绰绰有余……嗯，您能请我们到那艘大飞船上去转转吗？"

"当然，很高兴，可……怎么去呢？"

"请等我们一会儿！"

于是，最高执政官跳上了半空中一个奇怪的飞行器，那飞行器就像一片带螺旋桨的大羽毛。接着，广场上的其他人也都争着向那片"羽毛"上跳。这个社会好像完全没有等级观念，那些从人海中随机跳上来的人肯定是普通平民，他们有老有少，但都像最高执政官姑娘一样一身孩子气，兴奋地吵吵闹闹。这片"羽毛"上很快挤满了人，空中不断出现新的"羽毛"，每片刚出现，就立刻挤满了跳上来的人。最后，城市的天空中飘浮着几百片载满微人的"羽毛"，它们在最高执政官那片"羽毛"的带领下，浩浩荡荡地向一个方向飞去。

先行者再次伏在那个透明半球上方，仔细观察着里面的微城市。这一次，他能分辨出那些摩天大楼了，它们看上去像一片密密麻麻的直立的火柴棍。先行者穷极自己的目力，终于分辨出那些像羽毛的交通工具，它们像一杯清水中漂浮的细小的白色微粒，如果不是几百片连成一群，根本无法分辨出来。凭肉眼看到人是不可能的。

在先行者视频眼镜的左镜片中，那个由微人摄像师用小得无法想象的摄像机实况拍摄的画面仍很清晰，现在那摄像师也在一片"羽毛"上。先行者发现，在微城市的交通中，碰撞是一件随时都在发生的事。那群快速飞行的"羽毛"不时互相撞在一起，撞在空中飘浮的巨大尘粒上，甚至不时迎面撞到高耸的摩天大楼上！但飞行器和它的乘员都安然无恙，似乎没有人去注意这种碰撞。其实这是个初中生都能理解的物理现象：物体的尺度越小，整体强度就越高，两辆自行车碰撞与两艘万吨轮船碰撞的后果是完全不一样的，如果两粒尘埃相撞，它们会毫无损伤。微世界的人们似乎都有金刚之躯，毫不担心自己会受伤。当"羽毛"群飞过时，旁边的摩天大楼上不时有人从窗中跃出，想跳上其中的一片，这并不总是能成功的，于是那人就从几百米处开始了令先行者头晕目眩的下坠，而那些下坠中的微人，还在神情自若地同经过的大楼窗子中的熟人打招呼！

"呀，您的眼睛像黑色的大海，好深好深，带着深深的忧郁呢！您的忧郁罩住了我们的城市，您把它变成一个博物馆了！呜呜呜……"最高执政官又伤心地哭了起来，别的人也都同她一起哭，任他们乘坐的"羽毛"在摩天大楼间撞来撞去。

先行者也从左镜片中看到了城市的天空中自己那双巨大的眼睛，那放大了上亿倍的忧郁深深震撼了他。"为什么是博物馆呢？"先行者问。

"因为只有在博物馆中才有忧郁，微纪元是无忧无虑的纪元！"地球领袖高声欢呼，尽管泪滴还挂在她那娇嫩的脸上，但她已完全没有悲伤的痕迹了。

"我们是无忧无虑的纪元！！"其他人也都忘情地欢呼起来。

先行者发现，微纪元人类的情绪变化比宏纪元快上百倍，这变化主要表现在悲伤和忧郁这类负面情绪上，他们能在一瞬间从这种情绪中跃出。还有一个发现让他更惊奇，由于这类负面情绪在这个时代十分少见，以至于微人们把它当成了稀罕物，一有机会就迫不及待地去体验。

"您不要像孩子那样忧郁，您很快就会发现，微纪元没有什么可忧虑的！"

这话使先行者万分惊奇，他早看到微人的精神状态很像宏时代的孩子，但孩子的精神状态还要夸张许多倍才真正像他们。"你是说，在这个时代，人们越长越……越幼稚？！"

"我们越长越快乐！"领袖女孩说。

"对，微纪元是越长越快乐的纪元！"众人大声应和着。

"但忧郁也是很美的，像月光下的湖水，它代表着宏时代的田园爱情，呜呜……呜……"地球领袖又大放悲声。

"对，那是一个多美的时代啊！"其他微人也眼泪汪汪地附和着。

先行者笑起来："你们根本不知道什么是忧郁，小人儿，真正的忧郁是哭不出来的。"

"您会让我们体验到的！"最高执政官又恢复到兴高采烈的状态。

"但愿不会。"先行者轻轻地叹息说。

"看，这就是宏纪元的纪念碑！"当"羽毛"群飞过另一个城市广场时，最高执政官介绍说。先行者看到那个纪念碑是一根粗大的黑色柱子，有过去的巨型电视塔那么粗，表面覆盖着无数片车轮大小的黑色巨瓦，叠合成鱼鳞状，高耸入云，他看了好长时间才明白，那是一根宏人的头发。

宴会

"羽毛"群从半球形透明罩上的一个看不见的出口飞了出来，这时，最高执政官在视频画面中对先行者说："我们距您那个飞行器有100多千米呢，我们还是落到您的手指上，您把我们带过去快些。"

先行者回头看看身后不远处的着陆舱，心想他们可能把计量单位也都微缩了。他伸出手，"羽毛"群落了上来，看上去像是在手指上飘落了一小片细小的白色粉末。

先行者从视频画面中看到，自己的指纹如一道道半透明的山脉，降落在其上的"羽毛"飞行器显得很小。最高执政官第一个从"羽毛"上跳下来，立刻摔了个四脚朝天。

"太滑了，您是油性皮肤！"她抱怨着，脱下鞋子远远地扔出去，光着脚丫好奇地来回转着，其他人也都下了"羽毛"，手指上的半透明山脉间现在有了一片人海。先行者粗略估计了一下，他的手指上现在有一万多人！

先行者站起来，伸着手指小心翼翼地向着陆舱走去。

刚进入着陆舱，微人群中就有人大喊："哇，看那金属的天空，人造的太阳！"

"别大惊小怪，像个白痴！这只是小渡船，上面那个才大呢！"最高执政官训斥道，但她自己也惊奇地四下张望，然后又同众人一起唱起那支奇怪的歌来：

> 辉煌的宏纪元，
> 伟大的宏纪元，

忧郁的宏纪元，

你是烈火中消逝的梦……

在着陆舱起飞飞向"方舟号"的途中，地球领袖继续讲述微纪元的历史。

"微人社会和宏人社会共存了一个时期，在这段时间里，微人完全掌握了宏人的知识，并继承了他们的文化。同时，微人在纳米技术的基础上，发展起了一种十分先进的技术文明。在宏纪元向微纪元的过渡时期大概有，嗯，二十代人吧。

"后来，大灾难临近，宏人不再进行传统生育了，他们的数量一天天减少；而微人的人口飞快增长，社会规模急剧增大，很快超过了宏人。这时，微人开始要求接管世界政权，这在宏人社会中激起了轩然大波，顽固派们拒绝交出政权，用他们的话说，怎么能让一帮细菌领导人类。于是，在宏人和微人之间爆发了一场世界大战！"

"那对你们可太不幸了！"先行者同情地说。

"不幸的是宏人，他们很快就被击败了。"

"这怎么可能呢？他们一个人用一把大锤就可以捣毁你们一座上百万人的城市。"

"可微人不会在城市里同他们作战的。宏人的那些武器对付不了微人这样看不见的敌人，他们能使用的唯一武器就是消毒剂，而他们在整个文明史上一直用这种东西同细菌作战，最后也并没有取得胜利。他们现在要战胜的是和他们一样智力的微人，取胜就更没可能了。他们看不到微人军队的调动，而微人可以轻而易举地在他们眼皮底下销蚀掉他们的计算机芯片，没有计算机，他们还能干什么呢？大不等于强大。"

"现在想想是这样。"

"那些战犯得到了应有的下场，几千名微人的特种部队带着激光钻头空降到他们的视网膜上……"领袖女孩恶狠狠地说。

"战后，微人取得了世界政权，宏纪元结束了，微纪元开始了！"

"真有意思！"

登陆舱进入了近地轨道上的"方舟号"，微人们乘着"羽毛"四处观光，这艘飞船之巨大令微人们目瞪口呆。先行者本想从他们那里听到赞叹的话，但最高执政官这样告诉他自己的感想：

"现在我们知道，就是没有太阳的能量闪烁，宏纪元也会灭亡的。你们对资源的消耗是我们的几亿倍！"

"但这艘飞船能够以接近光速的速度飞行，可以到达几百光年远的恒星，小人儿，这件事，只能由巨大的宏纪元来做。"

"我们目前确实做不到，我们的飞船目前只能达到光速的十分之一。"

"你们能宇宙航行？！"先行者大惊失色。

"当然不如你们。微纪元的飞船队最远能到达金星，刚收到他们的信息，说那里现在比地球更适合居住。"

"你们的飞船有多大？"

"大的有你们时代的……嗯，足球那么大，可运载十几万人；小的只有高尔夫球那么大，当然是宏人的高尔夫球。"

现在，先行者最后一点儿优越感也荡然无存了。

"前辈，您不请我们吃点什么吗？我们饿了！"当所有"羽毛"飞行器重新聚集到"方舟号"的控制台上时，地球领袖代表所有人提出要求，几万个微人在控制台上眼巴巴地看着先行者。

"我从没想到会请这么多人吃饭。"先行者笑着说。

"我们不会让您太破费的！"女孩怒气冲冲地说。

先行者从贮藏舱拿出一听午餐肉罐头，打开后，他用小刀小心地剜下一小块，放到控制台上那一万多人的旁边。他能看到他们所在的位置，那是控制台上一小块比硬币大些的圆形区域，那区域只是光滑度比周围差些，像在上面呵了口气一样。

"怎么拿出这么多？这太浪费了！"地球领袖指责道，从面前的大屏幕上可以看到，在她身后，人们拥向一座巍峨的肉山，从那粉红色的山体里抓出一块块肉来大吃着。再看看控制台上，那小块肉丝毫不见减少。屏幕上，拥挤的人群很快散开了，有人还把没吃完的肉扔掉，领袖女孩拿着一块肉咬了一口，摇摇头。

"不好吃。"她评价道。

"当然，这是生态循环机中合成的，味道肯定好不了。"先行者充满歉意地说。"我们要喝酒！"地球领袖又提出要求，这又引起了微人们的一片欢呼。先行者吃惊不小，因为他知道酒是能杀死微生物的！

"喝啤酒吗？"先行者小心翼翼地问。

"不，喝苏格兰威士忌或莫斯科伏特加！"地球领袖说。

"茅台酒也行！"有人喊。

先行者还真有一瓶茅台酒，那是他自起航时一直保留在"方舟号"上，准备在找到新殖民行星时喝的。他把酒拿出来，把那白色瓷瓶的盖子打开，小心地把酒倒在盖子中，放到人群的边上。他在屏幕上看到，人们开始攀登瓶盖那道似乎高不可攀的悬崖绝壁，光滑的瓶盖在微尺度下有大块的凸出物，微人用他们上摩天大楼的本领很快攀到了瓶盖的顶端。

"哇,好美的大湖!"微人们齐声赞叹。从屏幕上,先行者看到那个广阔酒湖的湖面由于表面张力而呈巨大的弧形。微人记者的摄像机一直跟着最高执政官,这个女孩先用手去抓酒,但够不着,她接着坐到瓶盖沿上,用一只白嫩的小脚在酒面上划了一下,她的脚立刻包在一个透明的酒珠里,她把脚伸上来,用手从脚上那个大酒珠里抓出了一个小酒珠,放进嘴里。

"哇,宏纪元的酒比微纪元的好多了。"她满意地点点头。

"很高兴我们还有比你们好的东西,不过你这样用脚够酒喝,太不卫生了。"

"我不明白。"她不解地仰望着他。

"你光脚走了那么长的路,脚上会有病菌什么的。"

"啊,我想起来了!"地球领袖大叫一声,从旁边一个随行者的手中接过一个箱子,她把箱子打开,从中取出一个活物,那是一个足球大小的圆家伙,长着无数只乱动的小腿,她抓着其中一条小腿把那东西举起来。"看,这是我们的城市送您的礼物!乳酸鸡!"

先行者努力回忆着他的微生物学知识:"你说的是……乳酸菌吧!"

"那是宏纪元的叫法,这就是使酸奶好吃的动物,它是有益的动物!"

"有益的细菌。"先行者纠正说,"现在我知道细菌确实伤害不了你们,我们的卫生观念不适合微纪元。"

"那不一定,有些动物,呵,细菌,会咬人的,比如大肠杆狼,战胜它们需要体力,但大部分动物,像酵母猪,是很可爱的。"地球领袖说着，又从脚上取下一团酒珠送进嘴里。当她抖掉脚上剩余的酒球站起来时，已喝得摇摇晃晃了，舌头也有些打不过转来。

"真没想到人类连酒都没有失传！"

"我……我们继承了人类所有美好的东西，但那些宏人却认为我们无权代……代表人类文明……"地球领袖可能觉得天旋地转，又一屁股坐在地上。

"我们继承了人类所有的哲学，西方的、东方的，希腊的、中国的！"人群中有一个声音说。

地球领袖坐在那儿向天空伸出双手大声朗诵着："没人能两次进入同一条河流；道生一，一生二，二生三，三生万……万物！"

"我们欣赏凡·高的画，听贝多芬的音乐，演莎士比亚的戏剧！"

"活着还是死了，这是个……是个问题！"领袖女孩又摇摇晃晃地站起来，扮演起哈姆雷特。

"但在我们的纪元，你这样的女孩是做梦也当不了世界领袖的。"先行者说。

"宏纪元是忧郁的纪元，有着忧郁的政治；微纪元是无忧无虑的纪元，需要快乐的领袖。"最高执政官说，她现在看起来清醒了许多。

"历史还没……没讲完，刚才讲到，哦，战争，宏人和微人间的战争，后来微人之间也爆发过一次世界大战……"

"什么？不会是为了领土吧？"

"当然不是，在微纪元，要是有什么取之不尽的东西的话，那就是领土了。是为了一些……一些宏人无法理解的事，在一场最

66

大的战役中，战线长达……哦，按你们的计量单位吧，一百多米，那是多么广阔的战场啊！"

"你们所继承的宏纪元的东西比我想象中多多了。"

"再到后来，微纪元就集中精力为即将到来的大灾难做准备了。微人用了五个世纪的时间，在地层深处建造了几千座超级城市，每座城市在您看来是一个直径两米的不锈钢大球，可居住上千万人。这些城市都建在地下 8 万千米深处……"

"等等，地球半径只有 6000 千米。"

"哦，我又用了我们的单位，那是你们的，嗯，800 米深吧！当太阳能量闪烁的征兆出现时，微世界便全部迁移到地下。然后，然后就是大灾难了。

"在大灾难后的四百年，第一批微人从地下城中沿着宽大的隧道（大约有宏人时代的自来水管那么粗），用激光钻透凝结的岩浆来到地面。又过了五个世纪，微人在地面上建起了人类的新世界，这个世界有上万座城市，一百八十亿人口。

"微人对人类的未来是乐观的，这种乐观之巨大、之毫无保留，是宏纪元的人们无法想象的。这种乐观的基础，就是微纪元社会尺度的微小，这种微小使人类在宇宙中的生存能力增强了上亿倍。比如您刚才打开的那听罐头，够我们这座城市的全体居民吃一到两年，而那个罐头盒，又能满足这座城市一到两年的钢铁消耗。"

"作为一个宏纪元的人，我更能理解微纪元文明这种巨大的优势，这是神话，是史诗！"先行者由衷地说。

"生命进化的趋势是向小的方向，大不等于伟大，微小的生命更能同大自然保持和谐。巨大的恐龙灭绝了，而同时代的蚂蚁却生存了下来。现在，如果有更大的灾难来临，一艘像您的着陆舱那样大小的飞船就能把全人类运走。在太空中一块不大的陨石上，微人也能建立起一种文明，创造一种过得去的生活。"

沉默了许久，先行者对着他面前占据硬币般大小面积的微人人海庄严地说："当我再次看到地球时，当我认为自己是宇宙中最后一个人时，我是全人类最悲哀的人，哀莫大于心死，没有人曾面对过那样让人心死的境地。但现在，我是全人类最幸福的人，至少是宏人中最幸福的人，我看到了人类文明的延续，其实用文明的延续来形容微纪元是不够的，这是人类文明的升华！我们都是一脉相传的人类，现在，我请求微纪元接纳我作为你们社会中一名普通的公民。"

"在我们探测到'方舟号'时我们已经接纳您了，您可以到地球上生活，微纪元供应您一个宏人的生活还是不成问题的。"

"我会生活在地球上，但我需要的一切都能从'方舟号'上得到，飞船的生态循环系统足以维持我的残生了，宏人不能再消耗地球的资源了。"

"但现在情况正在好转，除了金星的气候正变得适于人类生存外，地球的气温也正在转暖，海洋正在融化，可能到明年，地球上很多地方将会下雨，将能生长植物。"

"说到植物，你们见过吗？"

"我们一直在保护罩内种植苔藓，那是一种很高大的植物，每个分支有十几层楼高呢！还有水中的小球藻……"

"你们听说过草和树木吗？"

"您是说那些像高山一样巨大的宏纪元植物吗？唉，那是上古时代的神话了。"

先行者微微一笑："我要办一件事情，回来时，我将给你们看我送给微纪元的礼物，你们会很喜欢那些礼物的！"

新生

先行者独自走进了"方舟号"上的一间冷藏舱，冷藏舱内整齐地摆放着高大的支架，支架上放着几十万个密封管。那是种子库，其中收藏了地球上几十万种植物的种子，这是"方舟号"准备带往遥远的移民星球上去的。还有几排支架，那是胚胎库，冷藏了地球上十几万种动物的胚胎细胞。

明年气候变暖时，先行者将到地球上去种草，这几十万类种子中，有生命力极强的能在冰雪中生长的草，它们肯定能在现在的地球上种活。

只要地球的生态能恢复到宏时代的十分之一，微纪元就拥有了一个天堂中的天堂，事实上地球能恢复的程度可能远不止于此。先行者沉醉在幸福的想象之中，他想象着当微人们第一次看到那棵顶天立地的绿色小草时的狂喜。那么一小片草地呢？一小片草地对微人意味着什么？一个草原！一个草原又意味着什么？那是微人的一个绿色的宇宙了！草原中的小溪呢？当微人们站在草根下看着清澈的小溪时，那在他们眼中是何等壮丽的奇观啊！地球领袖说过会下雨，会下雨就会有草原，就会有小溪！还一定会有树，天啊，树！先行者想象一支微人探险队，从一棵树的根部出发，开始他们漫长而奇妙的旅程，每一片树叶，对他们来说都是一个一望无际的绿色平原……还会有蝴蝶，它的双翅是微人眼中横贯天空的彩云；还会有鸟，它的每一声啼鸣在微人耳中都是一声来自宇宙的洪钟……是的，地球生态资源的千亿分之一就可以哺育微纪元的一千亿人口！现在，先行者终于理解了微人们向他反复强调的一个事实。

微纪元是无忧无虑的纪元。

没有什么能威胁到微纪元，除非……

先行者打了一个寒战，他想起了自己要来干的事，这事一秒钟也不能耽搁了。他走到一排支架前，从中取出了一百支密封管。

这是他同时代人的胚胎细胞，宏人的胚胎细胞。

先行者把这些密封管放进激光废物焚化炉，然后又回到冷藏库仔细看了好几遍，他在确认没有漏掉这类密封管后，回到焚化炉边，丝毫不动感情地摁下了按钮。

在激光束几十万摄氏度的高温下，装有胚胎的密封管瞬间气化了。

全频带阻塞干扰

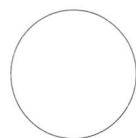

FULL-
SPECTRUM
BARRAGE
JAMMING

写在前面：将这篇小说以深深的敬意献给俄罗斯人民，他们的文学影响了我的一生。

　　在战场电磁干扰形式选择上，本手册主张采用对某一特定频率或信道进行瞄准式干扰，而不主张同时干扰一个较宽频带的阻塞式干扰，因为后者对己方的电磁通信和电子支援措施也会产生影响。

　　　　　　　　　　——摘自 1993 年美国陆军《电子战手册》

1 月 5 日，斯摩棱斯克前线

失陷的城市已经看不见了，战线在一夜之间后退了 40 千米。

在凌晨的天光下，雪原呈现出一种寒冷的暗蓝色。在远方的各个方向，被击中的目标冒出一道道黑色的烟柱，几乎无风，这些烟柱笔直地向高空升去，好像是连接天地的一条条细长的黑纱。顺着这些烟柱向上看，卡琳娜吃了一惊，刚刚显现晨光的天空被一团巨大的白色乱麻充塞着，这纷乱的白色线条仿佛是一个精神错乱的巨人疯狂地画在天上的。那是混杂在一起的歼击机的航迹，是俄罗斯空军和北约空军为争夺制空权所进行的一夜激战留下的。

来自空中和远方的精确打击也持续了一夜，在一位非专业人士看来，打击似乎并不密集，爆炸声每隔几秒钟甚至几分钟才响一次。但卡琳娜知道，每一次爆炸都意味着一个重要目标被击中，几乎不会打空。这一声声爆炸，仿佛是昨夜这篇黑色文章中的一个个闪光的标点符号。当凌晨到来时，卡琳娜不知道防线还剩下多少力量，甚至不知道防线是否还存在，似乎整个世界只有她一人在抵抗。

卡琳娜少校所在的电子对抗排是在半夜被毁灭的，当时这个排所在的位置上落下了6颗激光制导炸弹。卡琳娜侥幸逃生，那辆装载干扰机的BMP-2装甲车还在燃烧，这个排的其他电子战车辆现在都变成散落在周围雪地上的一堆堆黑色金属块。卡琳娜所在的弹坑中的余热正在散去，她感到了寒冷。她用手撑着坐直身子，右手触到了一团黏糊糊的、冰冷绵软的东西，看上去像一个沾满了黑色弹灰的泥团。她突然意识到那是一块残肉，她不知道它属于身体的哪一部分，更不知道属于哪个人。在昨夜的那次致命打击中，1名中尉、2名少尉和8名士兵阵亡。卡琳娜呕吐起来，但除了酸水什么也没吐出来。她的双手拼命地在雪里擦，想把手上的血迹擦掉，但那黑红色的血迹在寒冷中很快在手上凝固，还是那么醒目。

令人窒息的死寂已持续了半个小时，这意味着新一轮的地面进攻就要开始了。卡琳娜拧大了别在左肩上的对讲机的音量，但传出来的只有沙沙的噪声。突然，有几句模糊的话语传了出来，仿佛是大雾中朦胧飞过的几只鸟儿。

"……06 观察站报告，1437 阵地正面，M1A2 有 37 辆，平均间隔 60 米；布莱德雷运兵车 41 辆，距 M1A2 攻击前锋 500 米；M1A2 有 24 辆，勒克莱尔 8 辆，正在向 1633 阵地侧翼迂回，已越过同 1437 的接合部，1437、1633、1752，准备接敌！"

卡琳娜克制住因寒冷和恐惧引起的颤抖，使地平线在望远镜视野中稳定下来，她看到了天边出现的一团团模糊的雪雾，给地平线镶上了一道毛茸茸的边儿。

这时卡琳娜听到了身后传来的发动机的轰鸣声，一排 T90 式坦克越过她的位置冲向敌人，在后面，更多的俄罗斯坦克正在越过高速公路的路基。卡琳娜又听到了另一种轰鸣声，敌人的攻击直升机群在前方的天空中出现，它们队形整齐，在黎明惨白的天空中形成一片黑色的点阵。卡琳娜周围坦克的发烟管启动了，接着是一阵低沉的爆破声，阵地笼罩在一片白色的烟雾中。透过白雾的缝隙，她看到俄罗斯的直升机群正从头顶掠过。

坦克上的 125 毫米炮急风骤雨般地响了起来，白雾变成了疯狂闪烁的粉红色光幕。几乎与此同时，敌人的第一批炮弹落了下来，白雾中粉红色的光芒被爆炸产生的刺眼的蓝白色闪电所代替。卡琳娜伏在弹坑的底部，她感到身下的大地在密集的巨响中像一张震动的鼓皮，身边的泥土和小石块被震得飞起好高，落满了她的后背。在这爆炸声中，还可隐约听到反坦克导弹发射时的嘶鸣声。卡琳娜感到整个宇宙都在这撕人心肺的巨响中化为碎片，并向无限深处坠落……就在她的神经几乎崩溃时，这场坦克战结束了，它只持续了约 30 秒钟。

当白雾和浓烟散去时，卡琳娜看到面前的雪地上散布着被击中的俄罗斯坦克，燃起一堆堆裹着黑烟的熊熊大火。她举目望去，不用望远镜也能看到，远方同样有一大片被击毁的北约坦克，它们看上去像雪原上一个个冒出浓烟的黑点。但更多的敌人坦克正越过那一片残骸冲过来，它们裹在由履带搅起的一团团雪雾中，艾布拉姆斯那凶猛的扁宽前部不时从雪雾中露出来，仿佛是一只只从海浪中冲出的恶龟，滑膛炮炮口的闪光不时亮起，好像恶龟闪亮的眼睛……低空中，直升机的混战仍在继续，卡琳娜看到一架阿帕奇在不远处的半空爆炸，一架米 28 拖着漏出的燃料，摇晃着掠过她的头顶，在几十米之外坠地，炸成了一团火球。近距空空导弹的尾迹，在低空拉出了无数条平行的白线……

卡琳娜听到"咣"的一声响，她转身一看，不远处一辆被击中后冒出浓烟的 T90 后部的底门打开了，没看到有人出来，只见门下方垂下一只手。卡琳娜从弹坑中跃出，冲到那辆坦克后面抓住那只手向外拉，车内响起一声沉闷的爆炸声，一股灼热的气浪把卡琳娜向后冲了几步远。她的手上抓住了一团黏软的、很烫的东西，那是从坦克手的手上拉脱的一团烧熟的皮肤。卡琳娜抬头看到一股火焰从底门中喷出，她通过底门，看到车内已成了一座小型的炼狱，在那暗红色的透明的火焰中，坦克手一动不动的身影清晰可见，像在水中一样波动着。

卡琳娜又听到两声尖啸，这是她左前方的一个导弹班把最后的两枚反坦克导弹发射了出去，其中一枚有线制导的"赛格"导弹成功地击毁了一辆艾布拉姆斯，另一枚无线制导的导弹则被干扰，向斜上方冲去，失去了目标。这时，那个导弹班的 6 个人撤出掩体向卡琳娜所在的弹坑跑来，一架科曼奇直升机向他们俯冲下来，它那棱角分明的机体看上去像一只凶猛的鳄鱼。一长排机枪子弹打在雪地上，激起的雪和土如同一道突然立起又很快倒下的栅栏，这栅栏从那支小小的队伍中穿过，击倒了其中的 4 个人，只有一名中尉和一名士兵到达了弹坑。这时卡琳娜才注意到那名中尉戴着坦克防震帽，可能来自一辆已被击毁的坦克。他们每人手中都拿着一管反坦克火箭筒。跳进弹坑后，中尉首先向距他们最近的一辆敌坦克射击，击中了那辆 M1A2 的正面，诱发了它的反应装甲，火箭弹和反应装甲的爆炸声混在一起，听起来很怪异。坦克冲出了爆炸的烟雾，反应装甲的残片挂在它前面，像一件破烂的衣衫。那名年轻的士兵继续对着它瞄准，他手中的火箭筒随着坦克的起伏而抖动，一直没有把握击中。当距他们只有四五十米的坦克冲进一个低洼地时，那名士兵只能站到弹坑的边缘向斜下方瞄准，他手中的火箭筒与那辆艾布拉姆斯的 120 毫米炮同时响了。坦克的炮手情急之中发射的是一发不会爆炸的贫铀穿甲弹，初速每秒 800 米的炮弹击中了那个士兵，把他上半身打成了一团飞溅的血花！卡琳娜感觉到细碎的血肉有力地打在她钢盔上，噼啪作响。她睁开眼睛，看到就在她眼前的弹坑边缘，那名士兵的两条腿如同两根黑色的树桩，无声地滚落到弹坑底部她的脚下，他身体被粉碎的其他部分，在雪地上溅出了一大片放射状的红色斑点。火箭击中了艾布拉姆斯，聚能爆炸的热流切穿了它的装甲，车体冒出了浓烟。但那个钢铁怪兽仍拖着浓烟向他们冲来，直冲到距他们 20 米左右才在车体内的一声爆炸中停了下来，那声爆炸把它炮塔的顶盖高高地掀了上去。

　　紧接着，北约的坦克阵线从他们周围通过，地皮在履带沉重的撞击下微微颤抖。但这些坦克对他们俩所在的弹坑并没有加以理会。当第一拨坦克冲过去后，中尉一把抓住卡琳娜的手，拉着她跃出弹坑，来到一辆已布满弹痕的吉普车旁。在 200 多米远处，第二次装甲攻击波正快速冲过来。

　　"躺下装死！"中尉说。卡琳娜于是躺到了吉普车的轮子边，闭上双眼。"睁开眼更像！"中尉又说，并在她脸上抹了一把不知是谁的血。他也躺下，与卡琳娜呈直角，头紧挨着卡琳娜的头，他的钢盔滚到了一边，粗硬的头发扎着卡琳娜的太阳穴。卡琳娜大睁着双眼，看着几乎被浓烟吞没的天空。

　　两三分钟后，一辆半履带式布莱德雷运兵车在距他们十几米处停下来，从车上跳下几名身穿蓝白相间雪地迷彩服的美军士兵，他们中大部分平端着枪呈散兵线向前去了，只有一个朝这辆吉普车走来。卡琳娜看到两只沾满雪尘的伞兵靴踏到了紧靠她脸的地方，她能清楚地看到插在伞兵靴上的匕首刀柄上 82 空降师的标志：一匹帕加索斯飞马。那个美国人俯身看她，他们的目光相遇了，卡琳娜尽最大努力使自己的目光呆滞无神，面对着那双透出惊愕的蓝色瞳仁。

　　"Oh! God!"

　　卡琳娜听到了一声惊叹，不知是惊叹这名肩上有一颗校星的姑娘的美丽，还是她那满脸血污的惨相，也许两者都有。他接着伸手解她领口的衣扣，卡琳娜浑身起了鸡皮疙瘩，把手向腰间的手枪移动了几厘米，但这个美国人只是扯下了她脖子上的标志牌。

　　他们等的时间比预想的长，敌人的坦克和装甲车源源不断地从他们两旁轰鸣着通过。卡琳娜感到自己的身体在雪地上都快冻僵了，她这时竟想起了一首军队诗歌中的两句，那首诗是她在一本记述马特洛索夫事迹的旧书上读到的："士兵躺在雪地上，就像躺在天鹅绒上一样。"她得到博士学位的那天，曾把这两句诗写到日记上，那也是一个雪夜，她站在莫斯科大学科学之宫顶层的窗前，那夜的雪也真像天鹅绒，雪雾中，首都的万家灯火时隐时现。第二天她就报名参军了。

　　这时，有一辆吉普车在距他们不远处停了下来，三名北约军官在车上抽着雪茄聊天。这时，卡琳娜和中尉的周围空旷起来，他们跳上吉普车，中尉把车发动，沿着早已看好的路飞快驶去。他们身后响起了冲锋枪的射击声，子弹从头顶飞过，其中一颗打碎了一个后视镜。吉普车急拐进了一个燃烧着的居民点，敌人没有追过来。

　　"少校，你是博士，是吗？"中尉开着车问。

　　"你在哪儿认识的我？"

　　"我见过你和列夫森科元帅的儿子在一起。"

　　沉默了一会儿，中尉又说："现在，他的儿子可是世界上离战争最远的人了。"

　　"你这话什么意思，你要知道……"

　　"没什么意思，说说而已。"中尉淡淡地说，他们的心思都不在这个话题上，他们都在想着还抱有的那一线希望。

　　但愿整个战线只有这一处被突破。

1月5日，近日轨道，"万年风雪号"

米沙感到了一个人独居一座城市的孤独。

"万年风雪号"太空组合体确实有一座小城市那么大，它的体积相当于两艘巨型航空母舰，能使 5000 人同时在太空中生活。当组合体处于旋转重力状态时，里面甚至有一个游泳池和一条小河流，这在当今的太空工作环境中，可以说是绝无仅有的奢侈。但事实是，"万年风雪号"是自"和平号"以来俄罗斯航天界一贯的节俭思维的结果。它的设计思想是，在一个构造中组合太阳系内太空探索的所有功能，这样虽一次性投资巨大，但从长远来看还是十分经济的。"万年风雪号"被西方戏称为太空的瑞士军刀，它可作为空间站在地球各个高度的轨道上运行，它可以方便地移动到绕月球轨道，或做行星际探索飞行。"万年风雪号"已进行过金星和火星飞行，并探测过小行星带。以它那巨大的体积，等于把一个研究院搬到了太空中，就太空科学研究而言，它比西方那些数量众多但小巧玲珑的飞船具有更大的优势。

当"万年风雪号"准备开始前往木星的为期三年的航行时，战争爆发了。当时它上面的 100 多名乘员全都返回了地面，他们大部分是空军军官，只留下了米沙一个人。这时"万年风雪号"暴露出它的一个缺陷：在军事上它目标太大，且没有任何防御能力。没有预见到后来太空军事化的进程，是设计者的一个失误。战争爆发后，"万年风雪号"只能进行躲避飞行。向外太空飞是不行的，在木星轨道之内，有大量的北约无人航行器，它们体积都不大，武装或非武装，每一个对"万年风雪号"都是致命的威胁。于是，它只有航向近日空间，"万年风雪号"引以为傲的主动制冷式热屏蔽系统，使它可以比目前人类的任何太空航行器都更接近太阳。现在"万年风雪号"已到达水星轨道，距太阳5000万千米，距地球1亿千米。

虽然"万年风雪号"上的大部分舱室已经关闭，但留给米沙的空间仍大得惊人。透过广阔的透明穹顶，比地球上看去大三倍的太阳在照耀着，可以清楚地看到太阳表面的斑耀和紫色日冕中奇丽的日珥，有时甚至还可以看到光球表面因对流而产生的米粒组织。这里的宁静是虚假的，外面，太阳抛出的粒子流和射电波的狂风巨浪在呼啸，"万年风雪号"就是这动荡海洋中漂浮的一粒小小的种子。

一束如游丝般的电波把米沙同地球连接起来，也把那遥远世界的忧虑带给了他。他刚刚得知，莫斯科近郊的控制中心已被巡航导弹摧毁，对"万年风雪号"的控制转由设在古比雪夫的第二控制中心执行。他每隔五个小时接收一份从地球传来的战争新闻，每到这时，他就想起了父亲。

1月5日，俄罗斯军队总参谋部

米哈伊尔·谢米扬诺维奇·列夫森科元帅觉得自己面对着一堵墙，实际上他面前是一面平放的莫斯科战区全息战场地图。而以前当他面对挂在墙上的宽大的纸质地图时，却能看到广阔而深邃的空间。不管怎样，他还是喜欢传统的地图。记不清有多少次，要找的位置在地图的最下方，他和参谋们只好趴在地上看，现在想起来让他微微一笑。他又想起在多次演习前，在野战帐篷中用透明胶带把刚发下来的作战地图拼贴起来，他总贴不好，倒是第一次随他看演习的儿子一上手就比他贴得好……发现自己又想起儿子时，他警觉地打住了思绪。

作战室中只有他和西部集群司令两人，后者一根接一根地抽烟，他们凝神地盯着全息地图上方变幻的烟团，仿佛那就是严峻的战局。

西部集群司令说："北约在斯摩棱斯克一线的兵力已达 75 个师，攻击正面有 100 千米宽，已突破多处。"

"东线呢？"列夫森科元帅问。

"第 11 集团军的大部分也倒向右翼，这您是知道的。右翼军队的兵力已达 24 个师，但他们对雅罗斯拉夫尔的攻击仍然是试探性的。"

地面的一次爆炸把微微的震动传了下来，作战室里充满了随着顶板上的挂灯而轻轻摇晃的影子。

"现在，已有人谈论退守莫斯科，凭借城市外围建筑和工事进行巷战了，像 70 多年前一样。"

"胡说八道！我们一旦从西线收缩，北约就可能从北部迂回，在加里宁同右翼军队会合，莫斯科将不战自乱。下一步作战方针，第一是反击，第二是反击，第三还是反击。"

西部集群司令叹了一口气，无言地看着地图。

列夫森科元帅接着说："我知道西线力量不够，准备从东线抽调一个集团军加强西线。"

"什么？现在的雅罗斯拉夫尔防守已经很难了。"

列夫森科元帅笑了笑："现在相当多指挥官的误区，就是只从军事角度考虑问题，严峻的形势让我们钻进去出不来了。从目前的态势看，你认为右翼军队没有力量攻下雅罗斯拉夫尔吗？"

"我认为不是，像第 14 集团军这样的精锐部队，集中了如此密集的装甲和低空攻击力量，在没有遭受太大损失的情况下一天的推进还不到 15 千米，显然是有意放慢的。"

"这就对了，他们在观望，在观望西线战局！如果我们在西线夺回战场主动权，他们就会继续观望下去，甚至有可能在东线单方面停火。"

西部集群司令把刚拿出的一根烟夹在手上，忘了点火。

"东线的几个集团军的叛变确实是在我们背后捅了一刀，但一些指挥官在心理上把这当作借口，使我们的作战方针趋向消极，这种心态必须转变！当然，应当承认，要从根本上扭转战局，莫斯科战区的力量不够，我们的最终希望寄托在增援的高加索集群和乌拉尔集群上。"

"较近的高加索集群要完成集结并进入出击位置，最少也需一个星期，考虑到制空权的因素，时间可能还要长。"

1 月 5 日，莫斯科

卡琳娜和那位中尉的吉普车开进城时已是下午 3 点多，空袭警报刚刚响过，街上空荡荡的。

中尉长叹了一口气说："少校，我真想念我那辆 T90 啊！4 年前从装甲学院毕业的时候，也正是我失恋的时候，可刚到部队的我一看到那辆坦克，心情一下子由阴转晴了。我摸着它的装甲，光溜溜、温乎乎的，像摸着女孩子的手。嗐，那个女孩儿算什么，这才是男人真正的伴侣！可今天早上，它中了一颗西北风，唉，可能现在火还没灭呢……"

这时，城市西北方向传来密集的爆炸声，这是现代空袭中很少见的野蛮的面积型轰炸。

中尉仍沉浸在早上的战斗中："唉，不到30秒钟，整整一个坦克营就完了。"

"敌人的伤亡也很大。"卡琳娜说，"我注意观察了战果，双方被击毁的装甲目标的数量相差并不大。"

"双方坦克的对毁率大约 1∶1.2 吧，直升机差一些，但也不会超过 1∶1.4。"

"要是这样的话，战场的主动权应在我们这边，我们在数量上占很大优势，仗怎么会打成这样呢？"

中尉扭头看了卡琳娜一眼："你是搞电子战的，还不明白为什么？你们的那套玩意儿，什么第五代 C3I、什么三维战场显示，还有动态态势模拟、攻击方案优化之类的，在演习中很像回事，可一到实战中，我面前的液晶屏上显示最多的就两句：COMMUNICATIONERROR 和 COULDNOTLOGIN。就说今天早上吧，我的正面和两翼的情况全不清楚，只接到一个命令：接敌。唉……假如再投入一半的增援兵力，敌人就不会在我们的位置突破。整个战线的情况，大概都这德行。"

卡琳娜知道，在刚刚过去的战斗中，双方在整个战线上投入的坦克总数可能超过一万辆，还有相当于坦克数目一半的武装直升机。

这时他们的车驶入了阿尔巴特街，昔日的步行街现在空空荡荡的，古玩店和艺术品商店的门前堆着做工事的沙袋。

"我的那辆钢铁情人不亏本儿。"中尉仍沉浸在早上的战斗中不能自拔，"我肯定打中了一辆挑战者，但我最想打中的是一辆艾布拉姆斯，知道吗，一辆艾布拉姆斯……"

这时，卡琳娜指着一家古玩店的门口："那儿，我爷爷就死在那儿。"

"可这儿好像没有遭到空袭。"

"我说的是 20 年前的事了，那时我才 4 岁。那个冬天真冷啊。暖气停了，房间里结了冰，我只好抱着电视机取暖，听着总统在我怀中向俄罗斯人许诺一个温暖的冬天。我哭着喊冷、喊饿，爷爷默默地看着我，终于下了决心，拿出了他珍藏的勋章，带着我走了出去，来到这里。那时这儿是自由市场，从伏特加到政治观点，人们什么都卖。一个美国人看上了爷爷的勋章，但只肯出 40 美元。他说红旗勋章和红星勋章都不值钱的，但如果有赫梅利尼茨基勋章，他肯出 100 美元；光荣勋章，150 美元；纳希莫夫勋章，200 美元；乌沙科夫勋章，250 美元；最值钱的胜利勋章当然不可能有，那只授给元帅，但苏沃洛夫勋章也值钱，他可以出450 美元……爷爷默默地走开了。我们沿着寒风中的阿尔巴特街走啊走，后来爷爷走不动了，天也快黑了，他无力地坐到那家古玩店的台阶上，让我先回家。第二天人们发现他冻死在那里，一只手伸进怀中，握着他用鲜血换来的勋章，睁大双眼看着这个他在 70 多年前从古德里安的坦克群下拯救的城市……"

1月5日，俄罗斯军队总参谋部

一个星期以来，列夫森科元帅第一次走出了地下作战室，他踏着厚厚的白雪散步，同时寻找太阳，这时太阳已在挂满雪的松林后面落下了一半。在他的想象中，有一个小黑点正在夕阳那橘红色的表面缓缓移动，那是"万年风雪号"，他的儿子在上面，那是这个星球上离父亲最远的儿子了。

这件事在国内引起了许多流言蜚语，在国际上，敌人更是充分利用它。《纽约时报》用大得吓人的黑体字登出了一个标题：战争史上逃得最远的逃兵！下面是米沙的照片，照片的注脚是：在3亿俄罗斯人用鲜血淹没入侵者时，他们最高军事统帅的儿子却乘着这个国家唯一的一艘巨型飞船，逃到了距战场1亿千米的地方，他是目前这个国家最安全的人了。

但列夫森科元帅的心中很坦然。从中学到博士后，米沙周围几乎没有人知道他父亲是谁。航天控制中心做出这个决定，仅仅是因为米沙的研究专业是恒星的数学模型，"万年风雪号"这次接近太阳，对他的研究是一次难得的机会，而组合体不能完全遥控飞行，上面至少应有一个人。总指挥也是后来从西方的新闻中才得知米沙的身份的。

另外，不管列夫森科元帅是否承认，在他的内心深处，确实希望儿子远离战争。但这并不仅仅是出于血肉之情，列夫森科元帅总觉得自己的儿子不属于战争，是的，他是世界上最不属于战争的人了。但列夫森科元帅又知道自己这想法有问题：谁是属于战争的呢？

况且，米沙就属于恒星吗？他喜欢恒星，把全部生命投入对它的研究上面，但他自己却是恒星的反面。他更像冥王星，像那颗寂静、寒冷的行星，孤独地运行在尘世之光照不到的遥远空间。米沙的性格，加上他那白皙清秀的外表，使人很容易觉得他像个女孩子。但列夫森科元帅心里清楚，儿子从本质上一点儿不像女孩子，女孩儿都怕孤独，但米沙喜欢孤独，孤独是他的营养、他的空气。

米沙是在东德出生的，儿子的生日对元帅来说是一生中最黯淡的一天。那天傍晚，还是少校的他，在西柏林蒂加尔登苏军烈士墓前，同部下一起为烈士们站40多年来的最后一班岗。他的前面，是一群满脸笑容的西方军官，以及几个牵着狼狗来换防的吊儿郎当的德国警察，还有那些高呼"红军滚出去"的光头新纳粹；他的身后，是大尉连长和士兵们含泪的眼睛，他控制不住自己，只好也让泪水模糊了这一切。天黑后回到已搬空的营地，在这回国前的最后一夜，他得知米沙出生了，但妻子因难产而死……回国后日子也很难，同从欧洲撤回的40万军人和12万文职人员一样，他没有住房，同米沙住在一间冬冷夏热的临时铁皮屋里。他昔日的同志为了生活什么都干，有的向黑社会出售武器，有的甚至到夜总会跳脱衣舞。但他一直像军人一样正直地生活着，米沙也在艰辛中默默地长大，和别的孩子不同，他似乎天生就会忍受，因为他有自己的世界。

早在上小学的时候，米沙每天都在自己的小房间里静悄悄地一个人度过整个晚上。元帅开始以为儿子在看书，但有一次他无意中发现，儿子是站在窗前一动不动地看着星星。

"爸爸，我喜欢星星，我要看一辈子星星。"他这样对父亲说。

11 岁生日那天，米沙向父亲提出了迄今为止唯一的一个要求：想要一架天文望远镜，而在这之前，他一直用列夫森科元帅的军用望远镜观察星星。后来，那架天文望远镜就成了米沙唯一的伴侣，他在阳台上看星星可以一直看到东方发白。有不多的几次，他们父子俩一起在阳台上看星星，元帅总是把望远镜对准夜空中看起来最亮的一颗星，但儿子不以为意地摇摇头："那颗没意思，爸爸，那是金星，金星是行星，我只喜欢恒星。"

但其他男孩子喜欢的东西米沙却一点儿兴趣都没有。隔壁空降兵参谋长家的那个小胖子，偷拿父亲的手枪玩，结果枪走火把自己的大腿打穿了；参谋部将军们的那些男孩子，如果能让爸爸领着到部队的靶场上打一次枪，就是得到最高的奖赏了。男孩子对武器的这种天生的依恋，在米沙身上丝毫没有出现，从这点上来说，他确实不像男孩子。元帅对此很不安，他几乎无法容忍自己的儿子对武器无动于衷，以至于后来他做出了一件至今想起来仍让他很不好意思的事：有一次，他把自己的那支马卡诺夫式手枪悄悄放到了儿子的书桌上。米沙放学回来后不久，就拿着枪从他的小房间中出来，他拿枪像女人那样，小心地握着枪管。他把枪轻轻地放到父亲面前，淡淡地说："爸，以后别把这东西乱放。"

在对待米沙的前途问题上，元帅是一个开明的人，他不像自己周围的那些将军，一心让儿子甚至女儿延续自己的军旅生涯。但米沙离父亲的事业确实太远太远了。

列夫森科元帅不是一个脾气暴躁的人，但作为一名全军统帅，他不止一次地在上万名官兵面前斥责一位将军。但对米沙，他却从来没有发过火。这固然因为米沙一直默默地沿着自己的轨道成长，很少让父亲操心。更重要的是，米沙身上似乎生来就有一种非同寻常的超脱的气质，这气质有时甚至让列夫森科元帅感到有些敬畏。就如同他在花盆中随意埋下一颗种子，却长出来绝世珍稀的植物，他敬畏地看着这植物一天天成长，小心地呵护着它，等着它开出花朵。他的期望没有落空，儿子现在已成为世界上最出色的天体物理学家。

这时太阳已在松林后面完全落下去，地上的雪由白色变成浅蓝色。列夫森科元帅收回了思绪，回到了地下作战室。开作战会议的人都到齐了，他们包括西部集群和高加索集群的主要指挥官。

另外还有更多的电子战指挥官，他们从少将到上尉都有，大部分是刚从前线回来的。作战室里正在进行着一场激烈的争论，争论的双方是西部集群的陆战部队和电子战部队的军官们。

"我们正确判明了敌人主攻方向的转变。"塔曼摩步师的费利托夫师长说，"我们的装甲力量和陆航低空攻击力量的机动性也并不差，但通信系统被干扰得一塌糊涂，C3I指挥系统几乎瘫痪！集团军中的电子战单位，级别从营升到了团，从团又升到了师，这两年在这上面的资金投入比常规装备的投入都多，就这么个结果？！"

负责指挥战区电子战的一位中将看了身边的卡琳娜一眼，同其他刚从前线归来的军官一样，她的迷彩服上满是污迹和焦痕，脸上还残留着血迹。中将说："卡琳娜少校在电子战研究方面很有造诣，同时也是总参派往前线的电子战观察员，她的看法可能更有说服力一些。"像卡琳娜这样年轻的博士军官大多心直口快，无所顾忌，往往被人当枪使，这次也不例外。

卡琳娜站起来说："大校，话不能这么说！比起北约，我们这些年对 C3I 的投入微不足道。"

"那电子反制呢？"师长问，"敌人能干扰我们，你们就不能干扰他们？！我们的 C3I 瘫痪了，北约的却运转得很好，像上了润滑油似的，今天早上我对面的陆战一师能那么快速地转变攻击方向就是一个证明！"

卡琳娜苦笑了一下："提起对敌干扰，费利托夫大校，不要忘了，就是在你们师的阵地上，你的人用枪顶着操作员的脑袋，使集团军电子对抗部队的干扰机停下来！"

"怎么回事？"列夫森科元帅问，这时人们才发现他进来，都起身敬礼。

"是这样……"师长对元帅解释说，"对我们的通信指挥系统来说，他们的干扰比北约的更厉害！在北约的干扰中，我们还能维持一定的无线通信，可他们的干扰机一开，就把我们全盖住了！"

卡琳娜说："可同时敌人也全被盖住了！这是我军目前实施电子反制可选择的唯一战略。北约目前在战场通信中，已广泛采用诸如跳频、直接序列扩频、零可控自适应天线、猝发、单频转发和频率捷变这类技术[1]，我们用频率瞄准方式进行干扰根本不起作用，只能采用全频带段阻塞式干扰。"

1　跳频：发射机和接收机以同样的序列变换频率。直接序列扩频：使信号能量分散在很宽的频带上，以给侦听和干扰带来困难。零可控自适应天线：一种覆盖范围似肾形的天线，凹点指向天线无响应的敌方干扰机，以便在其他方向与己方天线通信。猝发：短时间采用宽频带或长时间采用很窄频带发送信息。频率捷变：在遭到干扰时自动改频。（以上为电子战术语简介）

第 5 集团军的一位上校质问:"少校,北约采用的可全是频率瞄准式干扰,频带还相当窄,而我们的 C3I 系统也普遍采用了你提到的那些通信技术,为什么他们对我们的干扰那样有效呢?"

"这原因很简单,我们的 C3I 系统是建立在什么样的软硬件平台上? UNIX,LINUX,甚至 WINDOWS2010,CPU 是 INTEL 和 AMD!这是用人家养的狗给自己看门!在这种情况下,敌人可以很快掌握诸如跳频规律之类的电子战情报,同时用更多更有效的纯软件攻击,加强其干扰效果。总参谋部曾经大力推广过国产操作系统,但到了下面阻力重重,你们集团军就是一个最顽固的堡垒……"

"好了,你们所说的问题和矛盾正是今天会议要解决的,开会!"列夫森科元帅打断了这场争论。

当大家在电子沙盘前坐好后,列夫森科元帅叫过一位少校参谋。这个身材细高的年轻人双眼眯缝着,好像不适应作战室中的光线。"介绍一下,这位是邦达连科少校,他的最大特点就是深度近视,他的眼镜与众不同,别人的眼镜镜片在镜框里边,他的镜片在镜框外面,哈,就像茶杯底那么厚啊!我们现在看不到它了,早上,少校在吉普车遇到空袭时眼镜被砸了,好像隐形眼镜也弄丢了?"

"报告首长,那是五天前在明斯克,我的眼睛是在半年内变成这样的,这变化早些的话我进不了伏龙芝。"少校立正说。

虽然谁也不知道元帅为什么介绍这位少校,人群中还是响起了几声低低的笑声。

"战争爆发以来的事实说明,虽然有白俄罗斯战场的失利,但在空中和陆上常规武器方面,我们并不比敌人差多少,但在电子战方面，我们的差距之大出乎意料。造成这样的局面有很深远的历史原因，这不是我们今天要讨论的。我们要明确的是以下一点：目前，电子战是我军夺回战争主动权的关键！我们首先必须承认敌人在电子战方面的优势，甚至是压倒性优势。然后我们必须以我军现有的电子战软硬件条件为基础，制定出一套行之有效的战略战术，这套战略战术的目的是，要在短时间内，使我军和北约在电子战方面形成某种力量上的平衡。也许大家认为这不可能：我军自 20 世纪末以来的战争理论，主要是基于局部有限战争的，对目前在军事上如此强大的敌人的全面进攻，确实研究得不够。在这样严峻的形势下，我们必须采用一种全新的思维方式，下面我要介绍的统帅部新的电子战战略，就可以看作这种思维的结果。"

灯灭了，电脑屏幕和电子沙盘都关闭了，重重的防辐射门也紧紧关闭，作战室淹没于伸手不见五指的黑暗之中。

"是我让关的灯。"黑暗中传来元帅的声音。

时间在黑暗和沉默中慢慢流逝，这样过了有一分钟。

"大家现在有什么感觉？"列夫森科元帅问。

没有人问答，浓重的黑暗使军官们仿佛沉没在夜之海的海底，他们觉得呼吸都有些困难。

"安德烈将军，你说说看。"

"这几天在战场上的感觉。"第 5 集团军军长说，黑暗中又响起了一阵低低的笑声。

"别的人呢？大概都与他有同感吧。"元帅说。

"当然，您想想，耳机里除了沙沙声什么也没有，屏幕上一片空白，对作战命令和周围的战场态势一无所知，可不就是这种感觉嘛！这黑暗，压得人喘不过气来啊！"

"但并非所有人都是这种感觉，邦达连科少校，你呢？"列夫森科元帅问。

邦达连科少校的声音从作战室的一角传来："我的感觉不像他们这么糟糕，在亮着灯的时候，我看周围也是模模糊糊的。"

"你甚至还有一种优越感吧？"列夫森科元帅问。

"是的元帅，您可能听说过，在那次纽约大停电时，是一些瞎子带领人们走出摩天大楼的。"

"但安德烈将军的感觉也是可以理解的，他有一双鹰眼，还是个神枪手，他喝酒时常用手枪在十几米远处开酒瓶盖。想想他和邦达连科少校在这时用手枪决斗，可是一件很有意思的事。"

黑暗中的作战室又陷入了沉默，指挥官们都在思考。

灯亮了，人们都眯起了双眼，与其说这是不能适应突然出现的亮光，不如说是对元帅刚刚暗示的思想感到震惊。

列夫森科元帅站起来说："我想，刚才我已把我军下一步的电子战新战略表达清楚了：全频段大功率的阻塞干扰，在电磁通信上，制造一个双方'共享'的全黑暗战场！"

"这样将使我军的战场指挥系统全面瘫痪！"有人惊恐地说。

"北约也一样！瞎大家一起瞎，聋大家一起聋，在这样的情况下同敌人达到电子战的力量平衡，这就是新战略的核心思想。"

"那总不至于让我们用通信员骑摩托车去发布作战命令吧？！"

"要是路不好，他们还得骑马。"列夫森科元帅说，"我们粗略估计了一下，这样的全频段阻塞干扰，至少可覆盖北约70%的战场通信系统，这就意味着他们的 C3I 系统全面瘫痪。同时，还可使敌人50%～60%的远程打击武器失去作用，其中最明显的例子就是战斧巡航导弹：现在这种导弹的制导系统同20世纪有了很大的改变，那时的战斧主要使用地形匹配和小型测高雷达来导航，现在这种导航方式只用作末端制导，而其射程的大部分依靠卫星全球定位系统。通用动力公司和麦克唐纳·道格拉斯公司认为他们所做的这种改进是一大进步，美国人太相信来自太空中的导航电波了，但GPS系统的电波传输一旦被干扰，战斧就成了瞎子。这种对GPS的依赖在北约大部分远程打击武器中都存在。在我们所设想的战场电磁条件出现时，就会逼着敌人同我们打常规战，这样就能充分发挥我们的优势。"

"我还是心里没底。"被从东线调往西线的第12集团军军长忧心忡忡地说，"在这样的战场通信条件下，我甚至怀疑我的集团军能不能从东线顺利地调到西线。"

"你肯定能的！"列夫森科元帅说，"这段距离，对库图佐夫来说都很短，我不信今天的俄罗斯军队离了无线电就走不过去了！被现代化装备惯坏的应该是美国人，而不是我们。我知道，当整个战场都处于电磁黑暗中时，你们心中肯定感到恐惧，这时要记住，敌人比你们恐惧10倍！"

当看着卡琳娜的身影混在这群穿迷彩服的军官中，在作战室的出口消失的时候，列夫森科元帅的心悬了起来。她将重返前线，而她所在的电子战部队将是敌人火力最集中的地方。昨天，在同1亿千米远的儿子那来回延时达五分钟的通话中，元帅曾告诉他卡琳娜很好，但在早上的战斗中，她就险些没回来。

米沙和卡琳娜是在一次演习中认识的。那天元帅和儿子一起吃晚饭，同往常一样，他们默默地吃着，米沙早逝的母亲在远处的镜框中默默地看着他们。米沙突然说:"爸爸,我想起明天就是您51岁生日了,我应该送您一件生日礼物。我是看见那架天文望远镜才想起来的,那件礼物真好。"

"送我几天时间吧。"

儿子抬头静静地看着父亲。

"你有你的事业,我很高兴。但做父亲的想让儿子了解自己的事业,这总不算过分吧!明天你和我一起去看军事演习怎么样?"

米沙笑着点点头,他很少笑的。

这是21世纪国内规模最大的一场演习。演习开始的前夜,米沙对公路上那滚滚而过的钢铁洪流没什么兴趣,一下直升机,他就钻进野战帐篷,用透明胶带替父亲粘贴刚发下来的作战地图。在第二天演习的整个过程中,米沙也没表现出丝毫的兴趣,这早在列夫森科元帅的预料之中,但有一件事使他感到莫大的安慰。

上午进行的演习项目是一个装甲师进攻一个高地,米沙同一群地方官员一起坐在观摩台的北侧。这次观摩台的位置虽在安全距离上,但应那些猎奇的地方官员的要求,比过去大大靠前了。图-22轰炸机群掠过高地上空,重磅航空炸弹雨点般落下,使那座山头变成一个喷发的火山口。这时,那群地方官员才明白真实战场同电影里的区别,在那地动山摇的巨响中,他们全都用双臂抱住脑袋伏在桌子上,有几位女士甚至尖叫着往桌子底下钻。但元帅看到,那里只有米沙一个人仍直直地坐着,仍是那副冷漠的表情,静静地、无动于衷地看着那座可怕的火山,任爆炸的火光在他的墨镜中狂闪。这时,一股暖流冲击着列夫森科元帅的心田,儿子,你的身上到底流着军人的血啊!

这天晚上，父子俩在白天的演习现场散步，远处，各种装甲车辆的前灯如繁星洒满山谷和平原，空气中还残留着淡淡的硝烟味。

"这场演习要花多少钱？"米沙问。

"直接费用大约3亿卢布。"

米沙叹了口气："我们的课题组，想搞第三代恒星演化模型，申请了35万经费都批不下来。"

列夫森科元帅把他早就想对儿子说的话说了出来："我们两个的世界相差太远了，你的恒星，最近的也有4光年吧，它同地球上的军队与战争真是毫不相干。我对你的事业知之不多，但很为之感到骄傲。作为军人，我们也是最想让儿子了解自己事业的人，哪一个父亲不把对儿子讲述自己的戎马生涯当作最大的幸福？而你对我的事业却总抱着一种冷漠的态度。事实上，我的事业是你的事业的基础和保障，一个国家，如果没有足够数量和质量的武装力量保证它的和平的话，像你从事的这种纯基础研究根本不可能进行。"

"爸爸，你把事情说反了。如果人们都像我们这样，用全部的生命去探索宇宙的话，他们就能领略到宇宙的美，它的宏大和深远后面的美。而一个对宇宙和自然的内在美有深刻感觉的人，是不会去进行战争的。"

"你这种想法真是幼稚到家了，如果战争是因为人们缺乏美感造成的，那和平可太容易了！"

"您以为让人类感受这种美就那么容易吗？"米沙指指夜空中灿烂的星海，"您看这些恒星，人们都知道它们是美的，但有多少人能够真正体会到这种美的最深层呢？这无数的天体，它们从星云到黑洞的演化是那么壮丽，它们喷发的能量是那么巨大狂暴，但您知道吗，只用数量不多的几个优美的方程式就能精确地描述这一切，用这些方程式建造的数学模型能极其精确地预言恒星的一切行为。甚至我们对自己星球上大气层的数学模型，精确度都要比它低几个数量级。"

列夫森科元帅点点头："这是可能的，据说人类对月球的了解比对地球海底的了解还要多。但对你所说的宇宙和自然深层次美的感受还是制止不了战争，没有人比爱因斯坦更能感受这种美了，原子弹不还是在他的建议下造出来的吗？"

"爱因斯坦在他的后期研究中没什么建树，很大程度上是由于他过多地介入了政治。我是不会走他的老路的。但，爸爸，到了需要的时候，我也会尽自己的责任。"

米沙在演习区域待了五天，元帅不知儿子是什么时候认识卡琳娜的，第一次看到他们在一起的时候，他们已经谈得很融洽了，他们谈恒星，而卡琳娜对此知道得很多。看着还是一个天真烂漫的女孩儿的卡琳娜，因为她的博士学位，早早就扛上了一颗校星，他的心里就多少有些别扭。不过除此之外，他对卡琳娜的印象还是很好的。第二次见到米沙和卡琳娜在一起时，列夫森科元帅看到他们已有了一些亲密感，他们谈话的内容让他很意外：他们在谈电子战。当时他们俩在距元帅的吉普车不远的一辆坦克边，对于谈话内容，他们并没有避开别人的意思。

元帅听到米沙说："你们现在只关注一些纯软件的高层次的东西，比如C3I、病毒攻击、数字战场等，可你想过没有，你们可能握着一把木头做的剑。"看着卡琳娜惊奇的目光，米沙继续说，"你想过这些东西的基础吗，也就是位于网络七层协议最下面的物理层？对于民用网络，可以使用像光纤和定向激光这样一些东西作为通信媒介，但对于用于战场的 C3I 系统，它的各个终端是快速移动和位置不定的，所以只能主要依赖电磁波来进行信息联结。而电磁波这东西，你知道，在干扰下像薄冰一样脆弱……"

元帅真的吃惊不小，他从未与儿子交流过这些，米沙更不可能偷看他的机密文件，但他却把自己在电子战上多年来形成的思想简明准确地表达出来！米沙的这番话对卡琳娜的影响更大，居然使她偏离了自己的研究方向，研制出了一种代号"洪水"的电磁干扰装置。"洪水"的大小可以装入一辆装甲车，它能同时发出 3kHz～30GHz 的强烈的电磁干扰波，覆盖了除毫米波之外的所有电磁通信波段。这种武器在西伯利亚某基地进行的第一次试验就为军队惹来了一屁股官司："洪水"使附近那座城市的电磁波通信全部中断，手机不通了，传呼机不响了，电视机和收音机都收不到信号，对银行和股市的影响更是灾难性的，地方上把造成的损失说成了天文数字。"洪水"的灵感来自一种电磁炸弹，这种武器是通过高爆炸药在一次性线圈中产生强烈的电磁脉冲。所以"洪水"工作起来如同火箭发动机一样，产生的音响震破了附近的玻璃窗，这就决定了它只能遥控操作，而距它两三千米处的操作人员还得穿上防微波辐射的防护服。"洪水"在总装备部和总参的电子战指挥机构引起了很大的争论，很多人认为它没什么实战价值，在有限战场上使用它，就如同在巷战中使用核武器，对敌我的杀伤力都一样大。但在元帅的坚持下，"洪水"还是批量生产了二百多台。现在，在统帅部新的电子战战略中，它将担当主要角色。

儿子爱上了一个军中的姑娘，元帅深感意外，他的结论是米沙对卡琳娜的感情同她的职业无关。后来米沙带卡琳娜到家里来过几次，第一次卡琳娜穿着一件靓丽的连衣裙，走时元帅听到米沙对卡琳娜说："下次穿军装来。"这事使元帅否定了自己先前的结论，他现在知道，米沙爱上卡琳娜，与她是一名少校军官并非一点儿关系也没有。他又有了演习第一天上午的那种感受，卡琳娜肩上的那颗校星他现在也觉得无比美丽了。

1月6日，莫斯科战区

强烈的电磁波在战区上空很快聚集，最后形成了巨大的电磁台风。战后人们回忆，当时在远离前线的山村里，人们也看到动物和鸟儿骚动不安；在灯火管制的城市中，人们能看到电视天线上感应出的微小火花……

从东线调往西线的第12集团军的一个装甲团正在疾速行军，团长站在停在路边的吉普车边，满意地看着漫天雪尘中疾速行进的部队。敌人的空袭远没有预料的强度，所以部队可以在白天赶路了。这时，三枚战斧导弹低低地从他们头顶掠过，冲压发动机低沉的嗡嗡声也清晰可闻。不一会儿，远处响起了三声爆炸。团长身边的通信员拿着只有沙沙声的耳机无事可做，转头看看爆炸的方向，然后惊叫起来，让团长看，团长让通信员不要大惊小怪，但旁边的一位少校营长也让他看，他就看了，然后困惑地摇了摇头。战斧不是每枚都能命中目标，但像这样三枚各自相距上千米落到空无一物的田野上，真是少见。

两架苏 27 孤独地飞行在战区 5000 米上空。他们本来属于一支歼击机中队，但这个中队刚刚在海上同一支北约的 F22 中队发生了一场遭遇战，在空中混战中，他们和中队失散了。在以前，重新会合是轻而易举的事，但现在，无线电联络不通了，原来对于高速歼击机很狭小的空域现在在感觉上变得如宇宙一样广阔，要想会合如同大海捞针。这对长僚机只能紧贴着飞行，距离之近像在飞特技，只有这样，他们才能听到对方的无线电呼叫。

"左上方发现可疑目标，方位 220，仰角 30！"僚机报告，长机飞行员沿那个方位看去，冬日雪后的晴空一碧如洗，能见度极好，两架飞机向斜上方靠近目标观察。那个目标与他们同一方向飞行，但速度慢了许多，所以他们很快追上了它。

当他们看清目标的形状后，真觉得白天见了鬼。那是一架北约的 E-4A 预警飞机，这是歼击机最不可能遇到的敌方飞机，就像一个人不可能看到自己的后脑勺一样。E-4A 预警飞机上的雷达监视面积可达 100 万平方千米，环视一圈只需 5 秒钟，它能发现远离防区 2000 千米处的目标，可以提供 40 分钟以上的预警时间，能发现 1000~2000 千米范围内的 800~1000 个电磁信号，它的每次扫描可询问和识别 2000 个海陆空各类目标。预警机从不需护航，它强有力的千里眼可使自己远远地避开歼击机的威胁，所以长机飞行员理所当然地认为这可能是一个圈套。他和僚机向四周的空域仔细搜索了一遍，明净寒冷的空中看不到任何东西，长机决定冒一次险。

"雷球雷球，我将发起攻击，你向 317 方位警戒，但注意不要超出目视距离！"

看着僚机向着他认为最可能有埋伏的方位飞去后，他打开加力，猛拉操纵杆。苏27拖着加速的黑烟，如一条仰起的眼镜蛇向斜上方的预警机扑去。这时E-4A也发现了向它逼近的威胁，它急忙向东南方向做逃脱的机动飞行，干扰热寻导弹的镁热弹不断地从机尾蹦出，那一串小小的光球仿佛是它那被吓出壳的灵魂。一架预警飞机在歼击机面前就如同一辆自行车在摩托车面前一样，是无法逃脱的。这时长机飞行员才感到他刚才给僚机的命令是多么自私。他在E-4A的后上方远远跟着它，欣赏着到手的猎物。E-4A背上蓝白相间的雷达天线罩线条优美，像一件可人的圣诞玩具；它那粗大的白色机身，如同摆在盘子里的一只肥美的炖鸭，令他垂涎欲滴，又不忍下刀叉。但直觉使他不敢拖延，他首先用20毫米机炮做了一个点射，击碎了雷达天线罩，他看到，西屋公司制造的AN/PY-3型雷达的天线的碎片飞散在空中，如圣诞节银色的纸花。他接着用机炮切断了E-4A的一个机翼。最后，射速达每分钟6000发的双管机炮射出的死亡之鞭，从已经翻滚下坠的E-4A拦腰切过，把它击成两截。苏27沿着一条下降的盘旋线跟着两块坠落的机体，飞行员看到，人员和设备不停地从机舱中掉出来，就像从盒中掉出的糖果一样，有几朵伞花在空中绽开。他想起了在刚过去的空战中，一个战友被击落时的情景：一架F22三次从战友的降落伞上方掠过，伞被冲翻了，他看着战友像一块石头一样渐渐消失在大地的白色背景中。他克制了这样做的冲动，同僚机会合后，双机编队以最快的速度脱离这个空域。

　　他们仍觉得这可能是个圈套。

走散的飞机并不止那两架。在战线的上空，一架隶属于美国陆军骑一师的"科曼奇"在漫无目的地飞着，驾驶员沃克中尉却倍感兴奋。他刚从"阿帕奇"转飞"科曼奇"不久，对这种20世纪末才大量装备陆军的武装攻击直升机不太适应，他不适应"科曼奇"的没有脚踏的操纵系统，并觉得它的双目头盔瞄准镜还不如"阿帕奇"的单目镜让人感到舒服，但让他感到最不适应的还是坐在前面的攻击指挥员哈尼上尉。他们第一次见面时，哈尼说："中尉，你要清楚自己的位置，我是这架直升机的大脑，你只是它电子和机械部件的一部分，你要尽一个部件的责任！"而沃克最讨厌作为一个部件而存在。记得一位年近百岁的参加过"二战"的前海军飞行员参观他们的基地，他看了看"科曼奇"的座舱，摇摇头："唉，孩子们，我当年那架野马式，座舱里的仪表还不如现在的微波炉上多，我最好的仪表是它！"他拍了拍沃克的屁股，"我们两代飞行员的区别，就是空中骑士和电脑操作员的区别。"沃克想当空中骑士，现在机会来了。在俄罗斯人那近乎变态的疯狂干扰下，这架直升机上的什么"作战任务设备一体化"系统、什么"目标探测系统"、什么"辅助目标探察分类系统"、什么"真实视觉场面发生器"，还有"资料突发系统"等，全休克了！只剩下那两台1200马力的T800型引擎还在忠实地转动着。哈尼平时就是全凭那些电子玩意儿活着的，现在他那张喋喋不休的臭嘴也随着这些东西沉默下来。这时，他听到了内部送话系统传来哈尼的话音：

"注意，发现目标，好像在左前方，好像在那个小山包旁边，有一支装甲部队，好像是敌人的，你……看着办吧。"

沃克差点笑出声来，哈，这小子，听他以前是怎么指挥的：

"发现目标，方位 133，90 式坦克 17 辆，89 式运兵车 21 辆，向 391 方位以平均速度 43.5 千米运动，平均间隔 31.4 米，按 AJ041 号优化攻击方案，从 179 方位以 37 度倾角进入……"现在呢，"好像"有装甲部队，"好像"在"山包那边"，这还用你说？我早看见了！还让我看着办。你是废物了，哈尼，现在是我的天下，我要用屁股当仪表做一个骑士了！这架"科曼奇"在我的手中将不辜负它那英勇的印第安部落的名字。

"科曼奇"向着那显而易见的目标冲去，把机上的 62 枚 27.5 英寸的蜂巢火箭全部发射出去，沃克陶醉地看着他那群拖着火尾的小蜜蜂欢快地向目标飞去，把敌人的车队淹没于一片火海之中。但当他迂回飞行观察战果时却发现事情不对，地面上敌人的士兵没有隐蔽，而是全都站在雪地上冲他指点着，像是在破口大骂。沃克飞近了一些，清楚地看到了一辆被击毁的装甲车上的那个标志，那是个三环同心圆，中间是蓝色，然后是一个白圈儿和一个红圈儿。沃克眼前一黑，感到世界变成了地狱，他也破口大骂起来：

"你个狗娘养的白痴，你瞎眼了？！"

但他还是聪明地远远飞开，以防对方还击。"你个狗娘养的，你现在大概在想到军事法庭上怎样把责任推给我，你推不掉的，你是负责目标甄别的，你要明白这一点！"

"也许……我们还有机会补救。"哈尼怯生生地说，"我又发现了一支部队，就在对面……"

"去你妈的吧！"沃克没好气地说。

"这次没错，他们正在同法国人交火！"

这下沃克又来了精神，他驾机向新目标冲去，看到对方主要是步兵，装甲力量不多，这倒证实了哈尼的判断。沃克把仅剩的4枚"地狱火"导弹发射出去，然后把加特林双管机枪的射速调到每分钟1500发并开始射击。他舒服地感觉到机枪通过机体传来的微微震动，看到地面敌人的散兵线被撒上了一层白色的"胡椒面"。但一名老练的武装直升机驾驶员的直觉告诉他有危险，他扭头一看，只见一枚肩射导弹刚刚从左下方一名站在吉普车上的士兵肩上发射出来。沃克手忙脚乱地发射了诱饵镁热弹，又向后方做摆脱飞行，但还是晚了些，那枚导弹拖着蛛丝般的白烟击中了"科曼奇"的机头下方。沃克从爆炸带来的短暂眩晕中醒来时，发现直升机已坠落到雪地上。沃克拼命爬出全是白烟的机舱，在雪地上抱住一棵刚被螺旋桨齐腰砍断的树，回头看见前舱中被炸成肉酱的哈尼上尉。他又看到前方一群端着冲锋枪的士兵正在向他跑来，他们那斯拉夫人的面孔清晰可见。沃克颤抖着掏出手枪放到面前的雪地上，然后掏出俄语会话本读了起来：

"吾已放下武器，吾是战俘，日内瓦……"

他后脑挨了一枪托，肚子上又挨了一脚，当他翻倒在雪地上时却大笑起来，他可能被揍个半死，但不会全死，他看到了那些士兵衣领上波兰军队的鹰形领章标志。

1月7日，明斯克，北约军队作战指挥中心

"把那个该死的军医叫来！"托尼·帕克上将烦躁地喊道。当那名瘦弱的上校军医跑到他面前时，他恼怒地说："怎么搞的？你折腾了两次，我的假牙还在嗡嗡响！"

"将军，这是我见过的最奇怪的事，也许是您的神经系统有问题，要不我给您打一针局部麻醉？"

这时，一位少校参谋走过来说："将军，请把假牙给我，我有办法。"帕克取下假牙，放到了少校递过来的纸巾上。

关于将军掉的两颗门牙，媒体的普遍说法是在波斯湾战争中他所在的坦克被击中时造成的，只有将军自己知道这不是真的。那次是断了下颌，牙则是更早些时候掉的。那是在克拉克空军基地，当时的世界好像除了火山灰外什么都没有，天是灰的、地是灰的、空气也是灰的，就连他和基地最后一批人员将要登上的那架"大力神"，机顶上也落了厚厚的、白白的一层。火山岩浆的暗红色火光在这灰色的深处时隐时现。那个菲律宾女职员还是找来了，说基地没了，她失业了，房子也压在火山灰下，让她和肚子里的孩子怎么活？她拉着他，求他一定带她到美国去，他告诉她这不可能，于是她脱下高跟鞋朝他脸上打，打掉了他的两颗门牙。看着灰色的海水，帕克默念：我的孩子，现在你在哪儿？你是和母亲在马尼拉的贫民窟中度日吗？你的父亲现在在某种程度上是为你而战，战后当俄罗斯的民主政府上台后，北约的前锋将抵达中国边境，苏比克和克拉克将重新成为美国在太平洋上的海空军基地，那里将比 20 世纪更繁荣，你会在那儿找到工作的！如果你是个女孩，说不定像你妈妈（她叫什么来着，哦，阿莲娜）一样能认识个美国军官……

那位修牙的少校回来了，打断了将军的胡思乱想，将军拿过那个纸巾上的假牙，装上感觉了几秒后惊奇地看着少校："嗯？你是怎么做到的？"

"将军，您的假牙响是因为它对电磁波产生了共振。"

将军盯着少校，分明不相信他的话。

"将军，真是这样！也许您以前也暴露在强烈的电磁波下，比如在雷达的照射范围内，但那些电磁波的频率同您的假牙的固有频率不吻合。而现在，空中所有频带的电磁波都很强烈，于是产生了这种情况。我把假牙进行了一些加工，使它的共振频率提高了许多，它现在仍然共振，但您感觉不到了。"

少校离开后，帕克将军的目光落到了电子作战图旁的一台座钟上，钟座是骑着大象的汉尼拔塑像，上面刻着"战必胜"三个字。原来它摆放在白宫的蓝厅，当时总统发现他的目光总落在那玩意儿上，就亲自拿起了那台在那儿放了一百多年的钟赠给了他。

"上帝保佑美国，将军，现在您就是上帝！"

帕克沉思了很久，缓缓地说："命令全线停止进攻，用全部空中力量搜寻并摧毁俄罗斯人的干扰源。"

1月8日，俄罗斯军队总参谋部

"敌人停止进攻了，你好像并不感到高兴。"列夫森科元帅对刚从前线归来的西部集群司令说。

"是高兴不起来，北约的全部空中力量已集中打击我们的干扰部队，这种打击确实是很奏效的。"

"这在我们的预料之中。"列夫森科元帅平静地说，"我们的战术在开始会使敌人手足无措，但他们总会想出对付的办法的。用于阻塞式干扰的干扰机，由于其强烈的全频道发射，很容易被探测和摧毁。好在我们已争取了相当长的时间，现在全部希望都寄托在两个集群的快速集结上了。"

"情况可能比预想的严峻。"西部集群司令说，"在我们失去电子战优势之前，可能没给高加索集群进入出击位置留下足够的时间。"

西部集群司令走后，列夫森科元帅看着电子沙盘上的前线地形，想起了正处于敌人密集火力下的卡琳娜，由此又想起了米沙。那天，米沙回到家里，脸上青一块紫一块的。在这之前他已听到传言，说他儿子是那所大学中唯一的一名反战分子，结果被学生们打了。

"我只是说不要轻言战争，我们真的不能同西方达成一种理智的和平吗？"米沙对父亲解释说。

元帅用他从未有过的严厉对儿子说："你知道自己的位置，你可以不说话，但以后绝不许出现类似的言行。"

米沙点点头。

晚上一进家门，元帅就告诉米沙："俄共上台了。"

米沙看了父亲一眼，淡淡地说："吃饭吧。"

再往后，西方宣布俄罗斯新政府为非法，杜波列夫组织极右联盟并发动内战，列夫森科元帅都不需要告诉米沙了，父子俩每天晚上都像往常一样默默地吃饭。直到有一天，米沙接到航天基地的通知，打起行装走了。两天后，他乘航天飞机登上了在近地轨道运行的"万年风雪号"。

又过了一周，战争全面爆发了，这是一场由空前强大的敌人从预料不到的方向发起的、旨在彻底肢解俄罗斯的世界大战。

1月9日，近日轨道，"万年风雪号"掠过水星

由于"万年风雪号"的速度很快，它不可能成为水星的卫星，只能从这颗行星面对太阳的那一面高速掠过。这是人类第一次用肉眼直接对水星表面进行近距离观察。米沙看到，水星表面高达2千米的峭壁蜿蜒数百千米，穿过布满巨大坑穴的平原。他还看到了被行星地质学家们称作"不可思议的地形"的、名叫"卡托里萨"的盆地，它的直径有1300千米。它的不可思议之处在于，在水星的另一面，有一个面积相仿的盆地正对着它，人们猜测，这是一颗巨大的彗星撞击了水星，强烈的震波穿过了整个星体，在两个半球同时形成了极其相似的两个盆地。米沙还发现了许多新的、令人激动的东西，他发现水星表面有许多明亮的光斑，当他在屏幕上把那些光斑放大后，激动得屏住了呼吸。

那是水星上的水银湖泊，它们的平均面积达上千平方千米。

米沙想象，在水星那漫长的白天，在那1800摄氏度的酷热下，站在水银湖岸边的情形。即使在狂风中，水银湖也会很平静，而水星没有大气，没有风，湖的表面如广阔的镜子平原，太阳和银河毫不失真地投射在上面。

"万年风雪号"掠过水星后，将继续靠近太阳，一直航行到它那由核聚变制冷装置支持的绝热层所能忍受的极限距离。太阳的高温将是它最好的掩护，北约的任何太空航行器都不可能飞进这个酷热的地狱。

看看这广阔的宇宙，再想想那1亿千米之外的母亲星球上的战争，米沙再次哀叹人类目光的狭隘。

1月10日，斯摩棱斯克前线

看着敌人渐渐靠近的散兵线，卡琳娜明白了为什么当周围的干扰点相继被摧毁后，只有她这里幸存下来：敌人想夺取一台完整的"洪水"。

这支由3架"科曼奇"和4架"黑鹰"组成的直升机群轻而易举地发现了这台"洪水"的位置。由于"洪水"巨大的电磁发射，对它的遥控只能通过光缆进行，这又使敌人顺着光缆的走向发现了卡琳娜所在的、距那台"洪水"3000米的遥控站，这是一间被废弃的孤立的小库房。

那4架运载着40多名敌人步兵的"黑鹰"就在距库房不到200米处降落了。当时遥控站中除卡琳娜之外，还有一名上尉和一名上士。上士听到引擎声响，刚拉开库房的门，就被直升机上的狙击手射出的一颗子弹掀开了头盖骨。敌人随后的火力很谨慎也很节制，显然怕伤了库房里的他们想得到的设备，这就使得卡琳娜和那名上尉多坚守了一段时间。

现在，在卡琳娜的左前方，上尉的冲锋枪声沉默了，这枪声是她在这里唯一的安慰。她看到在那个作为掩体的树桩后面，上尉的身体一动不动，一圈殷红的鲜血正在他周围的雪地上扩散。卡琳娜现在在库房前由几个沙袋堆成的简易掩体后面，她的脚下散落着8个冲锋枪弹夹，滚烫的枪管在沙袋上面的积雪中发出咝咝的声音。每当卡琳娜射击时，对面的敌人就卧倒，子弹在他们前面溅起一团团雪花，而半圆形包围圈另一个方向的敌人则跃起快步推进一段距离。现在，卡琳娜只剩下3个弹夹了，她开始打单发，这没有经验的举动等于告诉敌人她子弹不多了，使他们更快、更大胆地推进。当卡琳娜再次换弹夹时，她听到沙袋顶上厚厚的积雪"吱"地响了一声，有什么东西从中飞快地钻了过来，她感到右胁被什么猛推了一下，没有疼痛，只有一阵很快扩散的麻木感，她感到温热的血顺着右侧身体流下去。她坚持着，几乎是漫无目的地打完了这个弹夹。当她伸手拿起沙袋顶上最后一个弹夹时，一颗子弹打断了她的前臂，弹夹掉到雪地上，只剩下一条与皮肤相连的手臂来回摆动。卡琳娜站起身，回头向库房门走去，她身后的雪地上留下了一条细细的血迹。当她拉开门时，又一颗子弹穿透了她的左肩。

这支由瑞特·唐纳森上尉率领的美国海军陆战队"海豹"突击队的小分队，谨慎地靠近库房。当唐纳森和两名陆战队员越过那名俄罗斯上士的尸体，踹开门冲进帐篷时，发现里面只有一名年轻女军官。她坐在他们的目标——"洪水"遥控仪旁边，一只被打断的手臂无力地垂在控制台上，对着显示屏上映出的影子，她用另一只手整理着自己的头发，不断滴下的鲜血在她的脚下积成了小小的血洼。她对着冲进来的美国人和那一排枪口笑了一下，算是打了招呼。唐纳森长出了一口气，但这口出来的气再也没有吸回去：他看到她整理头发的手从控制台上拿起了一个墨绿色长圆形的东西，把它悬在半空中。唐纳森立刻认出了那是一枚气体炸弹，由于是装备武装直升机的，体积很小。那东西由激光近炸引信引爆，在距地面半米处发生两次爆炸，第一次扩散气体炸药，第二次引爆炸药雾，他现在就算是一支箭也飞不出它的威力圈。

他朝她伸出一只手向下压着："镇静，少校，镇静下来，不要激动。"他朝周围示意了一下，陆战队员们的枪口垂了下来，"您听我说，事情没您想的那么严重，您将得到最好的医疗，您将被送到德国最好的医院，然后，会作为第一批交换的战俘……"少校又对他笑了一下，这使他多少受到了一些鼓励，"您完全没必要采用这么野蛮的方式，这是一场文明的战争，它本来是很顺利的，这一点在 20 天前越过波俄边境时我就感觉到了。当时你们的大部分火力都被摧毁，只有零星的机枪声恰到好处地点缀着我们这场光荣而浪漫的远征，您看，一切都会很顺利的，没必要……"

"我还知道另一次更美妙的开始。"少校用纯正的英语说，她轻柔的声音如来自天堂，能让火焰熄灭、钢铁变软，"美丽的沙滩，有棕榈树，树上挂着欢迎的横幅；到处是漂亮的姑娘，留着齐腰的长发，穿着沙沙作响的丝袜，在年轻的士兵群中移动，用红色和粉红色的花环装点着他们，并羞怯地对着目瞪口呆的士兵们微笑……上尉，您知道这次登陆吗？"

唐纳森困惑地摇摇头。

"这就是 1965 年 3 月 8 日上午 9 点，在岘港，美国首批海军陆战队登上越南土地的情景，也是越战的开端。"

唐纳森觉得自己一下子掉进了冰窟窿，刚才的镇静瞬间消失了，他的呼吸急促起来，声音开始颤抖。"不，别这样少校，你这样对待我们是不公平的！我们没有杀过多少人，杀人的是他们！"他指着窗外半空中悬停着的直升机说，"是那些飞行员，还有那些在很远的航空母舰上操作电脑指引巡航导弹的先生，但他们也都是些体面的先生，他们所面对的目标都是屏幕上漂亮的彩色标记，他们按了一下按钮或动一下鼠标，耐心地等一会儿，那些标志就消失了。他们都是文明的先生，他们没有恶意，真的没有恶意……您在听我说吗？"

少校笑着点点头，谁说死神是丑恶的、恐怖的，死神真美。

"我有一个女朋友，她在马里兰大学读博士，她像您一样美丽，真的，她还参加反战游行……"我真该听她的，唐纳森想，"您在听我说吗？您也说点什么吧，求求您说点什么……"

美丽的少校最后对敌人微笑了一次："上尉，我得尽责任。"

赶来增援的俄军104摩步师的一支部队这时距那个"洪水"遥控站还有500米距离，他们首先听到了一声沉闷的爆炸，并远远看到那间孤立在宽阔田野中的小库房隐没于一团白雾之中。紧接着是一声比刚才响百倍的巨响，地动山摇，一团巨大的火球在库房的位置出现。火焰裹在黑色的浓烟中高高升起，化作一团高耸的蘑菇云，如绽放在天地之间的一朵绝美的生命之花。

1月11日，俄罗斯军队总参谋部

"我知道你想要什么东西，别废话，要吧！"列夫森科元帅对高加索集群司令说。

"我想让前两天的战场电磁条件再持续四天。"

"你清楚，我们的战场干扰部队现在70%已被摧毁，我现在连四个小时都无法给你了！"

"那我的集群无法按时到达出击位置，北约的空中打击大大迟滞了部队的集结速度。"

"要是那样的话，您就把一颗子弹打进自己脑袋里去吧。现在敌人已逼近莫斯科，已到了70年前古德里安到过的位置。"

在走出地下作战室的途中，高加索集群司令在心里默念：莫斯科，坚持啊！

1月12日，莫斯科防线

塔曼师师长费利托夫大校清楚，他们的阵地最多只能再承受一次进攻了。

敌人的空中打击和远程打击渐渐猛烈起来，而俄军的空中掩护却越来越少了。这个师的装甲力量和武装直升机都所剩无几，这最后的坚守几乎全靠血肉之躯了。

师长拖着被弹片削断的腿，拄着一支步枪走出掩蔽部。他看到战壕挖得不深，这也难怪，现在阵地上大部分都是伤员了。但他惊奇地发现，在战壕的前面构起了一道整齐的约半米高的胸墙。师长很奇怪这胸墙是用什么材料这么快筑起的，他看到被雪覆盖的胸墙上伸出几条树枝一样的东西，走近一看，那是一只只惨白僵硬的手臂……他勃然大怒，一把抓住一位上校团长的衣领。

"浑蛋！谁让你们用士兵的尸体筑掩体的？！"

"是我命令这样干的。"师参谋长的声音从师长身后平静地响起，"昨天晚上进入新阵地太快，这里又是一片农田，实在没有什么别的材料了。"

他们沉默相视着，从参谋长额头绷带上流出的血在脸上一道道地冻结了。这样过了一会儿，他们两人沿战壕慢慢地走去，沿着这堵用青春和生命筑成的胸墙走去。师长的左手拄着做拐杖的步枪，右手扶正了钢盔，向着胸墙行军礼，他们在最后一次检阅自己的部队……他们路过了一个被炸断双腿的小士兵，从断腿中流出的血把下面的雪和土混成了红黑色的泥，这泥的表面现在又冻住了。他正躺着把一颗反坦克手雷往自己怀里放。他抬起没有血色的脸，朝师长笑了笑："我要把这玩意儿塞进艾布拉姆斯的履带里。"

寒风卷起道道雪雾，发出凄厉的啸声，仿佛在奏着一首上古时代的战歌。

"如果我比你先阵亡，请你也把我砌进这道墙里，这确实是一个好归宿。"师长说。

"我们两个不会相差太长时间的。"参谋长用他那特有的平静语调说。

1月12日，俄罗斯军队总参谋部

一个参谋来告诉列夫森科元帅，航天部部长急着要见他，事情很紧急，是有关米沙和电子战的事。

听到儿子的名字，列夫森科元帅心里一震。他已知道了卡琳娜阵亡的消息，同时他也无法想象1亿千米之外的米沙同电子战有什么关系，他甚至想象不出米沙现在和地球有什么关系。

部长一行人走了进来，他没有多说话，把一片3英寸光盘递给了列夫森科元帅："将军，这是我们一个小时前收到的米沙从'万年风雪号'上发回的信息，后来他又补充说，这不是私人信息，希望您能当着所有有关人员的面播放它。"

作战室中的所有人听着来自 1 亿千米以外的声音："我从收到的战争新闻中得知，如果电磁干扰不能再持续三到四天的话，我们可能输掉这场战争。如果这是真的，爸爸，我能给您这段时间。

"以前，您总认为我所研究的恒星与现实相距太远，我自己也是这么认为的，现在看来我们都错了。我记得对您提起过，恒星产生的能量虽然巨大，但它本身却是一个相对单纯和简单的系统。比如我们的太阳，组成它的只是两种最简单的元素：氢和氦。它的运行也只是由核聚变和引力平衡两种机制构成的。这样，同我们的地球相比，它的运行状态在数学模型上就比较容易把握了。现在，对太阳的研究已经建立了十分精确的太阳数学模型，其中也有我做的工作。通过这个数学模型，我们可以对太阳的行为做出十分精确的预测。这就使我们可以利用一个微小的扰动，在短时间内局部打破太阳运行的某种平衡。方法很简单：用'万年风雪号'精确撞击太阳表面的某点。

"也许您认为，这不过是把一块小石头投入海洋，但事实不是这样的，爸爸，这是一粒沙子掉进了眼睛！

"从数学模型中我们得知，太阳是一个极其精细和敏感的能量平衡系统。如果计算得当，一个微小的扰动就能在太阳表面和相当的深度产生连锁反应，这种反应扩散开来，使其局部平衡被打破。历史上有过这样的先例：最近的记载是在 1972 年 8 月初，在太阳表面一个很小的区域发生了一次剧烈的爆发，这次爆发引起了对地球产生巨大影响的一次电磁暴。飞机和轮船上的罗盘指针胡乱跳动；远距离无线电通信中断；在北极地区，夜空中闪动着炫目的红光；在乡村，电灯时亮时灭，如同处于雷暴的中心。

这种效应在当时持续了一个多星期。现在比较可信的一种解释是：当时一颗比'万年风雪号'还小的天体撞击了太阳表面。这样的太阳表面平衡扰动在历史上一定多次发生，但它大部分发生在人类发明无线电接收装置以前，所以没被察觉。这些对太阳表面的撞击都是随机的、偶然的，因而它们所能产生的平衡扰动在强度和范围上都是有限的。

"但'万年风雪号'对太阳的撞击点是经过精确计算的，它所产生的扰动比上面提到的自然产生的扰动要大几个数量级。这次扰动将使太阳向空间喷发出强烈的电磁辐射，这种辐射包括从极低频到甚高频的所有频带的电磁波。同时，太阳射出的强烈的 X 射线将猛烈撞击对于短波通信十分重要的电离层，从而改变电离层的性质，使通信中断。在扰动发生时，地球表面除毫米波外的绝大部分无线电通信将中断。这种效应在晚上可能相对弱一些，但在白天甚至超过了你们前两天进行的电磁干扰。据计算，这次扰动大约可持续一周。

"爸爸，以前我们两个人一直生活在相距遥远的两个世界中，我们互相交流很少。但现在，我们这两个世界融为一体，我们在为一个共同的目标而战，我为此自豪。爸爸，像您的每一个士兵一样，我在等着您的命令。"

航天部部长说："米哈伊尔博士所说的都是事实。去年，我们向太阳发射过一个探测器，它依据数学模型的计算对太阳表面进行了一次小型的撞击实验，证实了模型所预言的扰动。庄博士和他的研究小组还提出了一个设想：将来也许可以用这种方法适当地改变地球的气候。"

列夫森科元帅走进了一个小隔间，拿起了一个直通总统府的红色电话，过了不一会儿，他就从隔间走了出来。历史对这一时刻的记载是不同的，有人说他马上说出了那句话，也有人说他沉默了一分钟之久，但那句话是肯定的。

"告诉米沙，照他说的去做吧。"

1月12日，近日轨道，"万年风雪号"冲向太阳

"万年风雪号"的10台核聚变发动机全部打开，每台发动机的喷口都喷出了长达上百千米的等离子体射流，它在做最后的轨道和姿态修正。

在"万年风雪号"的正前方，有一道巨大的美丽日珥，那是从太阳表面盘旋而上的灼热的氢气气流。它像一条长长的轻纱，飘浮在太阳火的海洋上空，梦幻般地变幻着形状和姿态，它的两端都连着日球表面，形成了一座巨大的拱门。"万年风雪号"从这高达40万千米的凯旋门正中缓缓地、庄严地通过。前方又出现了几道日珥，它们只有一头同太阳相连，另一头伸进了太空深处。发动机闪着蓝光的"万年风雪号"像穿行在几棵大火树中的一只小小的萤火虫。后来，那蓝光渐渐熄灭，发动机停止了，"万年风雪号"的轨道已精确设定，剩下的一切都将由万有引力定律来完成了。

当飞船进入了太阳的上层大气日冕时，上方太空黑色的背景变成了紫红色，这紫红色的光辉弥漫了这里的所有空间。在下方，可以清楚地看到太阳色球中的景象，在那里，成千上万的针状体在闪闪发光。那些东西在19世纪就被天文学家们观察到了，

它们是从太阳表面射向高空的发光的气体射流，这些射流使得太阳大气看上去像一片燃烧的大草原，每棵草都有上千千米长。在这燃烧的大草原下面就是太阳的光球，那是无边无际的火的海洋。

从"万年风雪号"发回的最后的图像中，人们看到米沙从巨大的监视屏前起身，摁下按钮打开了透明穹顶外面的防护罩，壮丽的火的大洋展现在他面前，他想亲眼看看他童年梦幻中的世界。火之海在抖动变形，那是半米厚的绝热玻璃在熔化，很快那上百米高的玻璃壁化作一片透明的液体滚落下来。像一个初见海洋的人陶醉地面对海风，米沙伸开双臂迎接那向他呼啸而来的6000摄氏度的飓风。在摄像机和发射设备被烧熔之前发回的最后几秒钟图像中，可以看到米沙的身体燃烧起来，最后他的整个身体都变成了一根跳动的火炬，和太阳的火海融为一体……

接下来的景象只能猜想了："万年风雪号"的太阳能电池板和凸出结构将首先熔化，这些熔化的部分由于其表面张力，在飞船的表面形成一个个银色的小球。当"万年风雪号"越过色球和日冕的交界处时，它的主体开始熔化，当它深入色球2000千米后，整个色球完全熔化了。一个个分开的金属液珠合并成一个巨大的银色液球，它精确地沿着那已化为液体的计算机所设定的目标高速飞去。太阳大气的作用开始显示，液球的周围出现了一圈淡蓝色的火焰，这火焰向后拖了几百千米长，颜色也向后由淡蓝渐变为黄色，在尾部变成美丽的橘红色。

最后，这美丽的火凤凰消失在浩渺的火海之中。

1月13日，地球

人类回到了马可尼之前的世界。

入夜，即使在赤道地区，夜空也充满了涌动的极光。

面对着一片雪花的电视屏幕，大多数人只能猜测和想象那块激战中的广阔土地上的情形。

1月13日，莫斯科前线

帕克将军推开了企图把他拉上直升机的82空降师的师长和几名前线指挥官，举起望远镜继续看着远方，那里，俄罗斯人的阵线滚滚而来。

"定标4000米，9号弹药装填，缓发引信，放！"

听着来自后方的射击声，帕克知道，还有不到30门105毫米的榴弹炮可以射击，这是他目前唯一可以用于防守的重武器了。

一个小时前，这个阵地上唯一的一支装甲力量——德军的一个坦克营，以令人钦佩的勇气发起反冲锋，并取得了优秀的战果：在距此8000米处击毁了相当于他们坦克数目一倍半的俄罗斯坦克。但由于数量上的绝对劣势，他们在俄罗斯人的钢铁洪流面前如正午太阳下的露珠一样消失了。

"定标3500米，放！"

炮弹飞行的嘶鸣声过后，在俄罗斯人的坦克阵前面掀起了一道由泥土和火焰构成的高墙。但就如同洪水面前的一道塌方一样，塌下的泥土暂时挡住了洪水，但洪水最终还是漫了过来。爆炸激起的泥土落下后，俄罗斯人的装甲前锋又在浓烟中显现出来。帕克看到他们的编队十分密集，如同在接受检阅。如果在前几天用这种队形进攻是自取灭亡，但是现在，在北约的空中和远程打击火力几乎全部瘫痪的情况下，这却是一种可以采用的队形。它可以最大限度地集中装甲攻击力量，以确保在战线一点上的突破。

防线配置的失误是在帕克将军预料之中的，因为在这样的战场电磁条件下，要想准确快速地判明敌人的主攻方向几乎是不可能的。对下一步的防守他心中一片茫然，在 C3I 系统全面瘫痪的情况下，快速调整防御布局是十分困难的。

"定标 3000 米，放！"

"将军，您在找我？"法军司令若斯凯尔中将走了过来。他身边只跟着一名法军中校和一名直升机驾驶员。他没穿迷彩服，胸前的勋表和肩上的将星擦得亮亮的，却戴着钢盔并提着一支步枪，显得不伦不类。

"听说在我们的左翼，幼鹿师正在撤出阵地。"

"是的，将军。"

"若斯凯尔将军，在我们的身后，70 万北约部队正在撤退，他们的成功突围取决于我们的坚固防守！"

"是取决于你们的坚固防守。"

"我能得到更明白的说明吗？"

"您什么都明白！你们对我们隐瞒了真实战局，你们早就知道右翼联盟的军队要在东线单方面停火！"

"作为北约军队最高指挥官，我有权这样做。将军，我想您也明白，您和您的部队有接受指挥的职责。"

......

"定标 2500 米，放！"

......

"我只遵守法兰西共和国总统的命令。"

"我不相信现在您能收到这样的命令。"

"几个月前就收到了，在爱丽舍宫的国庆招待会上，总统亲自向我说明了在这种情况下法国军队的行为准则。"

"你们这些杂种，这几十年来你们一直没变！[1]"帕克终于失去控制。

"话别说得这么难听，将军，如果您不走，我也一个人留下来，我们一起光荣地战死在这广阔的雪原上。拿破仑在这儿也失败过，我们不丢人。"若斯凯尔向帕克挥动着那支 FAMS 法军制式步枪说。

......

"定标 2000 米，放！"

......

帕克慢慢地转过身来，面对着他面前的一群前线指挥官："请你们向坚守阵地的美军部队传达我下面的话：我们并非生来就是一支只靠电脑才能打仗的军队，我们是一支来自庄稼汉的军队。几十年前，在瓜达卡纳尔岛，我们在热带丛林中一个地洞一个地洞地同日本人争夺；在溪山，我们用圆锹挡开北越士兵的手榴弹；更远一些的时候，在那个寒冷的冬夜，伟大的华盛顿领着那

1　1966 年，戴高乐将军使法国退出北约军事一体化组织，这对当时"冷战"中的北约是一次沉重打击。

些没有鞋穿的士兵渡过冰封的特连顿河，创造了历史……"

"定标 1500 米，放！"

"我命令，销毁文件和非战斗辎重……"

"定标 1200 米，放！"

帕克将军戴上钢盔，穿上防弹衣，并把他那支 9 毫米手枪别在左腋下。这时榴弹炮的射击声沉默了，炮手正把手榴弹填进炮膛中，接着响起了一阵杂乱的爆炸声。

"全体士兵！"帕克将军看着已像死亡屏障一样在他们面前展开的俄罗斯坦克群说，"上刺刀！"

战场的浓烟后面，太阳时隐时现，给血战中的雪野投上变幻的光影。

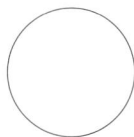

地球大炮
CANNONBALL

随着各大陆资源的枯竭和环境的恶化，世界把目光投向南极洲。南美突然崛起的两大强国在世界政治格局中取得了举足轻重的地位，使得《南极条约》成为一纸空文。但人类的理智在另一方面取得了胜利，全球彻底销毁核武器的最后进程开始了，随着全球无核化的实现，人类对南极大陆的争夺变得安全了一些。

一、新固态

走在这个巨洞中，沈华北如同置身于没有星光的夜空下的黑暗平原上。脚下，在核爆的高温中熔化的岩石已经冷却凝固，但仍有强劲的热力透过隔热靴底使脚板出汗。远处洞壁上还没有冷却的部分发着在黑暗中才能看到的红光，如同这黑暗平原尽头的朦胧晨曦。沈华北的左边走着他的妻子赵文佳，前面是他们8岁的儿子沈渊，这孩子穿着笨重的防辐射服仍蹦蹦跳跳的。在他们周围，是联合国核查组的人员，他们密封服头盔上的头灯在黑暗中射出许多道长长的光柱。

全球核武器的最后销毁采用两种方式：拆卸和地下核爆炸。这是位于中国的地下爆炸销毁点之一。

核查组组长凯文斯基从后面赶上来，他的头灯在洞底投向前面三人晃动的长影子："沈博士，您怎么把一家子都带来了？这里可不是郊游的好去处。"

沈华北停下脚步，等着这位俄罗斯物理学家赶上来："我妻子是销毁行动指挥中心的地质工程师，至于儿子，我想他喜欢这种地方。"

"我们的儿子总是对怪异和极端的东西着迷。"赵文佳对丈夫说，透过防辐射面罩，沈华北看到了她脸上忧虑的表情。

小男孩在前面手舞足蹈地说："这个洞开始时才只有菜窖那么大点儿呢，两次就给炸成这么大了！想想原子弹的火球像个被埋在地下的娃娃，哭啊叫啊蹬啊踹啊，真的很有趣呢！"

沈华北和赵文佳交换了一下眼神，前者面露微笑，后者脸上的忧虑又加深了一些。

"孩子，这次是八个娃娃！"凯文斯基笑着对沈渊说，然后转向沈华北："沈博士，这正是我现在想要同您谈的。这次销毁的是八颗巨浪型潜射导弹的弹头，每颗当量10万吨级，这八颗核弹放在一个架子上呈正立方体布置……"

"有什么问题吗？"

"起爆前我从监视器中清楚地看到，在这个由核弹头构成的立方体正中，还有一个白色的球体。"

沈华北再次停住脚步，看着凯文斯基说："博士，《销毁条约》规定了向地下放的东西不能少于多少，好像不禁止多放进去些什么。既然爆炸的当量用五种观测方式都核实无误，其他的事情应该是无所谓的。"

凯文斯基点点头："这正是我在爆炸后才提这个问题的原因，只是出于好奇心。"

"我想您听说过'糖衣'吧。"

沈华北的话如同一句咒语，使这巨洞中的一切都僵滞不动了，所有的人都停下了脚步，指向各个方向的头灯光柱也都不再晃动了。由于谈话是通过防辐射服里的无线电对讲系统进行的，远处的人也都能清楚地听到沈华北的话。短暂的静默后，核查组的成员们从各个方向会聚过来，这些不同国籍的人大部分是核武器研究领域的精英。

"那东西真的存在？"一个美国人盯着沈华北问，后者点点头。

裂变核弹的关键技术是向心压缩，核弹引爆时，裂变物质被包裹着它的常规炸药的爆炸力压缩成一个致密的球体，达到临界密度而引发剧烈的链式反应，产生核爆炸。这一切要在百万分之一秒内发生，对裂变物质的向心压缩必须极其精确，向心压力极微小的不平衡都可能在裂变物质还没有达到临界密度前将其炸散，那样的话，所发生的就只是一次普通的化学爆炸。自核武器诞生以来，研究者们用复杂的数学模型设计出各种形状的压缩炸药，近年来，又尝试用最新技术通过各种手段得到精确的向心压缩，"糖衣"就是这类技术设想中的一种。

"糖衣"是一种纳米材料，它用来在裂变弹中包裹核炸药，外面再包裹一层常规炸药。"糖衣"具有自动平衡分配周围压应力的功能，即使外层炸药爆炸时产生的压应力不均匀，经过"糖衣"的应力平衡分配，它包裹的核炸药仍能得到精确的向心压缩。

沈华北说："你们看到的由八颗核弹头围绕的那个白色球体，是用'糖衣'包裹的一种合金材料，它将在核爆中受到巨大的向心压力。这是我们计划在整个销毁过程中进行的一项研究，这毕竟是一个难得的机会，当核弹全部消失后，短时期内地球上很难再产生这么大的瞬间压应力了。在如此巨大的向心压力下，实验材料会变成什么、会发生些什么，将是很有意思的事。我们希望通过这项研究，为'糖衣'技术在民用领域找到一个光明的前景。"

一位联合国官员说："你们应该把石墨包在'糖衣'中放进去，那样我们每次爆炸都能得到一大块钻石，耗资巨大的核销毁工程说不定变得有利可图呢。"

耳机里传来几声笑，没有技术背景的官员在这种场合总是受到轻视的。"80万吨级核爆炸产生的压力，不知比将石墨转化为金刚石的压力大多少个数量级。"有人说。

沈渊清亮的童音突然在大家的耳机中响起："这大爆炸产生的当然不是金刚石，我告诉你们是什么吧，是黑洞！一个小小的黑洞！它将把我们都吸进去，把整个地球吸进去！通过它，我们将钻到一个更漂亮的宇宙中！"

"呵呵，孩子，那这次核爆炸的压力又太小了……沈博士，您儿子的小脑袋真的不同寻常！"凯文斯基说，"那么实验结果呢？那块合金变成了什么？我想你们多半找不到它了吧？"

"我也还不知道呢，我们去看看吧。"沈华北向前指了指说。核爆炸使这个巨洞呈规则的球形，因而洞的底面是一个小盆地，在远方盆地的正中央，晃动着几盏头灯。"那是'糖衣'实验项目组的人。"

大家向盆地中央走去，感觉像在走下一道长长的山坡。这时，凯文斯基突然站住了，接着蹲下来用双手贴着地面："地下有震动！"

其他人也感觉到了："不会是核爆炸诱发的地震吧？"

赵文佳摇摇头："销毁点所在地区的地质结构是经过反复勘测的，绝对不会诱发地震。这震动不是地震，它在爆炸后就出现了，持续不断直到现在，邓伊文博士说它与'糖衣'实验有关，具体的我也不清楚。"

随着他们接近盆地中心，由地层深处传来的震动渐渐增强，直到使脚底发麻，仿佛大地深处有一个粗糙的巨轮在疯狂旋转。当他们来到盆地中心时，这一小群人中有一个站起身来，他就是赵文佳刚才提到的邓伊文——材料核爆压缩实验项目的负责人。

"你手里拿的什么？"沈华北指着邓伊文手中一大团白色的东西问。

"钓鱼线。"邓博士说。分开围成一圈蹲在地上的那群人，他们正盯着地上的一个小洞看，那个洞出现在熔化后又凝结的岩石表面，直径约 10 厘米，呈很规则的圆形，边缘十分光滑，像钻机打的孔，邓伊文手中的钓鱼线正源源不断地向洞中放下去。"瞧，已经放了 1 万多米了，还远没到底呢。经雷达探测，这洞已有 3 万多米深，并且还在不断延长。"

"它是怎么来的？"有人问。

"是那块被压缩后的实验合金钻出来的，它沉到地层中去了，就像石块在海面上沉下去一样，这震动就是它穿过致密的地层时传上来的。"

"天啊，这可真是奇迹！"凯文斯基惊叹道，"我还以为那块合金会被核爆的高温蒸发掉了呢。"

邓伊文说："如果没有包裹'糖衣'的话会是那样的结果，但这次它还没来得及被蒸发，就被'糖衣'焦聚的向心压力压缩成一种新的物质形态，叫超固态比较合适，可物理学中已经有了这个名称，我们就叫它新固态吧。"

"您是说，这东西的比重与地层的比重相比，就如同石块与水的比重相比？"

"比那要大得多，石块在水中下沉主要是因为水是液体，水结冰后比重变化不大，但放在上面的石块就沉不下去。现在新固态物质竟然在固态的岩石中下沉，可见它的密度是多么惊人！"

"您是说它成了中子星物质？"

邓伊文摇摇头："我们现在还没有精确测定，但可以肯定它的密度比中子星的简并态物质小得多，这从它的下沉速度就可以看出来。如果真是一块中子星物质，那么它在地层中的下沉将如同陨石坠入大气层一样快，那会引起火山爆发和大地震。它是介于普通固态和简并态之间的一种物质形态。"

"它会一直沉到地心吗？"沈渊问。

"也许会吧，孩子。因为在下沉到一定深度后，地层物质将变成液态的，那将更有利于它的下沉！"

"真好玩！真好玩！"

在人们都把注意力集中到那个洞上的时候，沈华北一家三口悄悄地离开了人群，远远地走到黑暗之中。除了脚下地面的震动外，这里很静，他们头灯的光柱照不了多远就消失于黑暗中，仿佛他们只是无际虚空中三个抽象的存在。他们把对讲系统调到私人频道，在这里，小沈渊将做出一个决定一生的选择：是跟爸爸还是跟妈妈。

沈渊的父母面临着一个比离婚更糟的处境：沈华北现在已是血癌晚期。沈华北不知道他的病是否与他所从事的核科学研究有关，但可以肯定自己已活不过半年了。幸运的是人体冬眠技术已经成熟，他将在冬眠中等待治愈血癌的技术出现。沈渊可以和父亲一起冬眠，然后再一同醒来，也可以同妈妈一起继续生活。从各方面考虑，显然后者是一个明智的选择，但孩子倾向于同爸爸一起到未来去，现在沈华北和赵文佳试图再次说服他。

"妈妈，我和你留下来，不同爸爸去睡觉了！"沈渊说。

"你改变主意了？！"赵文佳惊喜地问。

"是的，我觉得不一定非要去未来，现在就很好玩，比如刚才那个沉到地心去的东西，多好玩！"

"你决定了？"沈华北问，赵文佳瞪了他一眼，显然怕孩子又改变主意。

"当然！我去看那个洞了……"说着，小沈渊向远处头灯晃动的盆地中心跑去。

赵文佳看着孩子的背影，忧虑地说："我不知道能不能带好他，这孩子太像你了，整日生活在自己的梦中，也许未来真的更适合他。"

沈华北扶着妻子的双肩说："谁也不知道未来是什么样，再说像我有什么不好，总要有爱做梦的人。"

"生活在梦中没什么可怕，我就是因为这个爱上你的，但你难道没有发现这孩子的另一面？他在学校竟然同时当上了两个班的班长！"

"这我也是刚知道，真不明白他是怎么做到的。"

"他的权力欲像刀子一样锋利，而且不乏实现它的能力和手段，这与你是完全不同的。"

"是啊，这两种性格怎么可能融为一体呢？"

"我更担心的是这种融合将来会发生什么。"

这时孩子的身影已完全融入远方那一群头灯中，他们将目光收回，关掉头灯，将自己完全融入黑暗中。

沈华北说："不管怎样，生活还得继续。我所等待的技术，也许在明年就能出现，也许要等上一个世纪，也许……永远也不会出现。你再活 40 年没有问题，一定要答应我一个请求：如果 40 年后那项技术还没出现，也一定要让我苏醒一次，我想再看看你和孩子，千万不要让这一别成为永别。"

黑暗中赵文佳凄凉地笑笑："到未来去见一个老太婆妻子和一个比你大 10 岁的儿子？不过，像你说的，生活还得继续。"

他们就在这核爆炸形成的巨洞中默默地度过了在一起的最后时光。明天，沈华北将进入无梦的长眠，赵文佳将和他们那个生活在梦中的孩子一起，继续沿着莫测的人生之路，走向不可知的未来。

二、苏醒

他用了一整天时间才真正醒来。意识初萌时，世界在他的眼中只是一团白雾；十个小时后这白雾中出现了一些模糊的影子，也是白色的；又过了十个小时，他才辨认出那些影子是医生和护士。冬眠中的人是完全没有时间感的，所以沈华北这时绝对肯定自己的冬眠时间仅是这模糊的一天，他认定冬眠维持系统在自己刚失去知觉后就出了故障。视力进一步恢复后，他打量了一下这间病房，很普通的白色墙壁，安在侧壁上的灯发出柔和的光芒，形状看上去也很熟悉，这些似乎证实了他的感觉。但接下来他知道自己错了：病房白色的天花板突然发出明亮的蓝光，并浮现出醒目的白字——

您好！承担您冬眠服务的大地生命冷藏公司已于 2089 年破产，您的冬眠服务已全部移交绿云公司，您现在的冬眠编号是 WS368200402-118，并享有与大地公司所签订合同中的全部权利。您已经完成全部治疗程序，您的全部病症已在苏醒前被治愈，请接受绿云公司对您获得新生的祝贺。

您的冬眠时间为 74 年 5 个月 7 天零 13 个小时，预付费用没有超支。

现在是 2125 年 4 月 16 日，欢迎您来到我们的时代。

又过了 3 个小时他才渐渐恢复听力，并能够开口说话，在 74 年的沉睡后，他的第一句话是："我妻子和儿子呢？"

站在床边的那位瘦高的女医生递给他一张折叠的白纸："沈先生，这是你妻子给你的信。"

我们那时已经很少有人用纸写信了……沈华北没把这话说出来，只是用奇怪的目光看了医生一眼，但当他用还有些麻木的双手展开那张纸后，得到了自己跨越时间的第二个证据：纸面一片空白，接着发出了蓝莹莹的光，字迹自上而下显示出来，很快铺满了纸面。他在进入冬眠前曾无数次想象过醒来后妻子对他说的第一句话，但这封信的内容超出了他最怪异的想象：

亲爱的，你正处于危险中！

当你看到这封信时，我已不在人世。给你这封信的是郭医生，她是一个你可以信赖的人，也许是这个世界上你唯一可以信赖的人，一切听从她的安排。

请原谅我违背了诺言，没有在40年后唤醒你。我们的渊儿已成为一个你无法想象的人，干了你无法想象的事。作为他的母亲我不知该如何面对你，我伤透了心，已过去的一生对于我毫无意义，你保重吧。

"我儿子呢？沈渊呢？！"沈华北吃力地支起上身问。

"他五年前就死了。"医生的回答极其冷酷，丝毫不顾及这消息带给这位父亲的刺痛。接着她似乎多少觉察到这一点，安慰说："你儿子也活了78岁。"

郭医生掏出一张卡片递给沈华北："这是你的新身份卡，里面存储的信息都在刚才那封信上。"

沈华北翻来覆去地看那张纸，上面除了赵文佳那封简短的信外什么都没有，当他翻动纸张时，褶皱的部分发出水样的波纹，很像用手指按压他以前所在时代的液晶显示器时发生的现象。郭医生伸手拿过那张纸，在右下角按了一下，纸上显示被翻过一页，出现了一个表格。

"对不起，真正意义上的纸张已经不存在了。"

沈华北不解地抬头看着她。

"因为森林已经不存在了。"她耸耸肩说，然后逐项指着表格上的内容，"你现在的名字叫王若，出生于2097年，父母双亡，也没有任何亲属。你的出生地在呼和浩特，但现在的居住地在这里——这是宁夏一个很偏僻的山村，是我能找到的最理想的地方，不会引人注意……不过你去那里之前需要整容……千万不要与人谈起你儿子，更不要表现出对他的兴趣。"

"可我出生在北京，是沈渊的父亲！"

郭医生直起身来，冷冷地说："如果你到外面去这样宣布，那你的冬眠和刚刚完成的治疗就全无意义了，你活不过一个小时。"

"到底发生了什么？！"

郭医生笑笑："这个世界上大概只有你不知道……好了，我们要抓紧时间，你先下床练习行走吧，我们要尽快离开这里。"

沈华北还想问什么，突然响起了震耳的撞门声，门被撞开后，有六七个人冲了进来，围在他的床边。这些人年龄各异，衣着也不相同，他们的共同点是都有一顶奇怪的帽子，或戴在头上或拿在手中，这种帽子有齐肩宽的圆檐，很像过去农民戴的草帽；他们的另一个共同之处就是都戴着一个透明的口罩，其中有些人进屋后已经把它从脸上扯了下来。这些人齐盯着沈华北，脸色阴沉。

"这就是沈渊的父亲吗？"问话的人看上去是这些人中最老的一位，留着长长的白胡须，像是有80多岁了，不等医生回答，他朝周围的人点点头："很像他儿子。医生，您已经尽到了对这个病人的责任，现在他属于我们了。"

"你们是怎么知道他在这儿的？"郭医生冷静地问。

不等老者回答，病房一角的一位护士说："我，是我告诉他们的。"

"你出卖病人？！"郭医生转身愤怒地盯着她。

"我很高兴这样做。"护士说，她那秀丽的脸庞被狞笑扭曲了。

一个年轻人揪住沈华北的衣服把他从床上拖了下来，冬眠带来的虚弱使他瘫在地上。一个姑娘一脚踹在他的小腹上，那尖尖的鞋头几乎扎进他的肚子里，剧痛使他在地板上像虾似的弓起身体。那个老者用有力的手抓住他的衣领，把他拎了起来，像竖一根竹竿似的想让他站住，看到不行后一松手，他又仰面摔倒在地，后脑撞到地板上，眼前直冒金星，他听到有人说：

"真好，那个杂种欠这个社会的，总算能够部分偿还了。"

"你们是谁？"沈华北无力地问，他在那些人的脚中间仰视着他们，好像在看着一群凶恶的巨人。

"你至少应该知道我。"老者冷笑着说。从下面向上看去，他的脸十分怪异，让沈华北胆寒。"我是邓伊文的儿子，邓洋。"

"邓伊文"这个熟悉的名字使沈华北心里一动，他翻身抓住老者的裤脚，激动地喊道："我和你父亲是同事和最好的朋友，你和我儿子还是同班同学，你不记得了？天啊，你就是洋洋？！真不敢相信，你那时……"

"放开你的脏爪子！"邓洋吼道。

那个拖他下床的人蹲下来，把凶悍的脸凑近沈华北说："听着小子，冬眠的年头是不算岁数的，他现在是你的长辈，你要表现出对长辈的尊敬。"

"要是沈渊活到现在，他就是你爸爸了！"邓洋大声说，引起了一阵哄笑，接着他挨个儿指着周围的人向他介绍，"在这个小伙子4岁时，他的父母同时死于中部断裂灾难；这姑娘的父母也在螺栓失落灾难中遇难，当时她还不到2岁；这几位，在得知用毕生的财富进行的投资化为乌有时，有的自杀未遂，有的患了精神分裂症……至于我，被那个杂种诱骗，把自己的青春和才华都扔到那项该死的工程中，现在得到的只是世人的唾骂！"

躺在地板上的沈华北迷惑地摇着头，表示他听不懂。

"你面对的是一个法庭，一个由南极庭院工程的受害者组成的法庭！尽管这个国家的每个公民都是受害者，但我们要独享这种惩罚的快感。真正的法庭当然没有这么简单，事实上比你们那时还要复杂得多，所以我们才不会把你送到那里去，让他们和那些律师扯一年之后宣布你无罪，就像他们对你儿子那样。我们会让你得到真正的审判，当一个小时后这个审判执行时，你会发现如果七十多年前就死于白血病是一件多么幸运的事。"

周围的人又齐声狞笑起来。接着有两个人架起沈华北的双臂把他向门外拖去，他的双腿无力地拖在地板上，连挣扎的力气都没有。

"沈先生，我已经尽力了。"在他被拖出门前，郭医生在后面说。他想回头再看看她，看看这个被妻子称为他在这个冷酷时代唯一可以信任的人，但这种被拖着的姿势使他无力回头，只听到她又说："其实，你不必太沮丧，在这个时代，活着也不是一件容易的事。"当他被拖出门后，听到郭医生在喊："快把门关上，把空净器开大，你要把我们呛死吗？！"听她的口气，显然不再关心他的命运。

出门后，他才明白医生最后那句话的意思：空气中有一股刺鼻的味道，让人难以呼吸。他被拖着走过医院的走廊，出了大门后，那两个人不再拖他，把他的胳膊搭到肩上架着走。来到外面后他如释重负，深深地吸了一口气，但吸入的不是他想象的新鲜空气，而是比医院大楼内更污浊、更呛人的气体，他的肺里火辣辣的，让他爆发出持续不断的剧烈咳嗽，就在他咳到要窒息时，听到旁边有人说："给他戴上呼吸膜吧，要不在执行前他就会完蛋。"接着有人给他的口鼻罩上了一个东西，虽然只是一种怪味代替了另一种，但他至少可以顺畅地呼吸了。他又听到有人说："防护帽就不用给他了，反正在他能活的这段时间里，紫外线什么的不会导致第二次白血病的。"这话又引起了其他人的一阵怪笑。当他喘息稍定，因窒息而流泪的双眼视野清晰后，便抬起头来第一次打量未来世界。

他首先看到街道上的行人，他们都戴着被称为呼吸膜的透明口罩和叫作防护帽的大草帽；他还注意到，虽然天气很热，但人们穿得都很严实，没有人露出皮肤。接着他看到了周围的世界，这里仿佛处于一个深深的峡谷中，这峡谷是由高耸入云的摩天大楼构成的——说高耸入云一点儿都不夸张，这些高楼全都伸进半空中的灰云里。在狭窄的天空上，他看到太阳呈一团模糊的光晕在灰云后出现，那光晕移动着黑色的烟纹，他这才知道遮盖天空的不是云而是烟尘。

"一个伟大的时代，不是吗？"邓洋说，他的那些同伙又哈哈大笑起来，好像很久没有这么开心了。

他被架着向不远处的一辆汽车走去，车的形状有些变化，但他肯定那是汽车，大小同过去的小客车一样，能坐下这几个人。接着有两个人超过了他们，向另一个方向走去，他们戴着头盔，身上的装束与过去有很大不同，但沈华北还是一眼就认出了他们的身份，并冲他们大喊起来：

"救命！我被绑架了！救命！"

那两个警察猛地回头，跑过来打量着沈华北，看了看他的病号服，又看了看他光着的双脚，其中一个问："您是刚苏醒的冬眠人吧？"

沈华北无力地点点头："他们绑架我……"

另一名警察对他点点头说："先生，这种事情是经常发生的，这一时期苏醒的冬眠人数量很多，为安置你们占用了大量的社会保障资源，因而你们经常受到仇视和攻击。"

"好像不是这么回事……"沈华北说，但那警察挥手打断了他。

"先生，您现在安全了。"然后那名警察转向邓洋一伙人："这位先生显然还需要继续治疗，你们中的两个人送他回医院，这位警官将一同去了解情况，我同时通知你们，你们七个人已经因绑架罪而被逮捕。"说着他抬起手腕对着上面的对讲机呼叫支援。

邓洋冲过去制止他："等一下警官，我们不是那些迫害冬眠人的暴徒，你们看看这个人，不面熟吗？"

两个警察仔细地盯着沈华北看，还短暂地摘下他的呼吸膜以更好地辨认："他……好像是米西西！"

"不是米西西，他是沈渊的父亲！"

两个警察瞪大双眼在邓洋和沈华北之间来回看着，像是见了鬼。中部断裂灾难留下的孤儿把他们拉到一边低声说着，这过程中两个警察不时抬头朝沈华北这边看看，每次的目光都有变化，在最后一次朝这边投来的目光中，沈华北绝望地读出这些人已是邓洋一伙的同谋了。

两个警察走过来，没有朝沈华北看一眼，其中一位警惕地环视四周做放哨状，另一名径直走到邓洋面前，压低了声音说："我们就当没看见吧，千万不要让公众注意到他，否则会引起骚乱的。"

让沈华北恐惧的不仅仅是警察话中的内容，还有他说这话时的样子，他显然不在乎让沈华北听到这些，好像他只是一件放在旁边的没有生命的物件。

那些人把沈华北塞进汽车，他们也都上了车。在车开的同时，车窗的玻璃就变得不透明了，车是自动驾驶的，没有司机，前面也看不到可以手动的操纵杆件。一路上车里没有人说话，仅仅是为了打破这令人窒息的沉默，沈华北随口问："谁是米西西？"

"一个电影明星。"坐在他旁边的螺栓失落灾难留下的孤女说，"因扮演你儿子而出名，沈渊和外星撒旦是目前影视媒体上出现最多的两个大反派角色。"

沈华北不安地挪挪身体，与她拉开一条缝，这时他的手臂无意间触碰到了车窗下的一个按钮，窗玻璃立刻变得透明了。他向外看去，发现这辆车正行驶在一座巨大而复杂的环状立交桥上，桥上挤满了汽车，车与车的间距只有不到两米的样子。这景象令人恐惧的是，这时并不是处于塞车状态，就在这塞车时才有的间距下，所有的车辆都在高速行驶，可能超过了每小时 100 千米！

这使得整个立交桥像一个由汽车构成的疯狂大转盘。他们所在的这辆车正在以令人目眩的速度冲向一个岔路口，在这辆车就要撞入另一条车流时，车流中正好有一个空当在迎接它，这种空当以令人难以觉察的速度在岔路口不断出现，使两条湍急的车流无缝地合为一体。沈华北早就注意到车是自动驾驶的，人工智能已把公路的利用率发挥到极限。

后面有人伸手又把玻璃调暗了。

"你们真想在我对这一切都一无所知的情况下杀死我吗？"沈华北问。

坐在前排的邓洋回头看了他一眼，懒洋洋地说："那我就简单地给你讲讲吧。"

三、南极庭院

"想象力丰富的人在现实中往往手无缚鸡之力。相反，那些把握历史走向的现实中的强者，大多只有一个想象力贫乏的大脑。你儿子，是历史上少有的把这二者合为一体的人。在大多数时间，现实只是他幻想海洋中的一座小小的孤岛，但如果他愿意，可以随时把自己的世界翻转过来，使幻想成为小岛而现实成为海洋，在这两个海洋中他都是最出色的水手……"

"我了解自己的儿子，你不必在这上面浪费时间。"沈华北打断邓洋说。

"但你无论如何也不会想到沈渊在现实中爬到了多高的位置，拥有了多大的权力，这使他有能力把自己最变态的狂想变成现实。可惜，社会没有及早发现这个危险。也许历史上曾有过他这样的人，但都像擦过地球的小行星一样，没能在这个世界上释放自己的能量就消失在茫茫太空中了。不幸的是，历史给了你儿子用变态狂想制造灾难的机会。

"在你进入冬眠后的第五年，世界对南极大陆的争夺有了一个初步结果：这个大陆被确定为全球共同开发的区域，但各个大国都为自己争得了大面积的专属经济区。尽早使自己在南极大陆的经济区繁荣起来，并尽快开发那里的资源，是各大国摆脱因环境问题和资源枯竭而带来的经济衰退的唯一希望，'未来在地球顶上'成为当时尽人皆知的口号。

"就在这时，你儿子提出了那个疯狂设想，声称这个设想的实现将使南极大陆变为这个国家的庭院，到时从北京去南极将比从北京去天津还方便。这不是比喻，是真的，旅行的时间要比去天津的短，消耗的能源和造成的污染都比去天津的少。那次著名的电视演讲开始时，全国观众都笑成一团，像在看滑稽剧，但他们很快安静下来，因为他们发现这个设想真的能行！这就是南极庭院设想，后来根据它开始了灾难性的南极庭院工程。"

说到这里，邓洋陷入了沉默。

"接着说呀，南极庭院的设想是什么？"沈华北催促道。

"你会知道的。"邓洋冷冷地说。

"那你至少可以告诉我，我与这一切有什么关系？"

"因为你是沈渊的父亲，这不是很简单吗？"

"现在又盛行血统论了？"

"当然没有，但你儿子的无数次表白使血统论适合你们。当他变得举世闻名时，就真诚地宣称他思想和人格的绝大部分是在 8 岁前从父亲那里形成的，以后的岁月不过是进行一些知识细节方面的补充而已。他还声明，南极庭院设想的最初创造者也是父亲。"

"什么？！我？南极……庭院？！这简直是……"

"再听我说完最后一点，你还为南极庭院工程提供了技术基础。"

"你指的什么？！"

"当然是新固态材料，没有它，南极庭院设想只是一个梦，而有了它，这个变态的狂想立刻变得现实了。"

沈华北困惑地摇摇头，他实在想象不出，那超高密度的新固态材料如何能把南极大陆变成一个国家的庭院。

这时车停了。

四、地狱之门

下车后，沈华北迎面看到一座奇怪的小山，山体呈单一铁锈色，光秃秃的，看不到一棵草。邓洋向小山一偏头说："这是一座铁山。"看到沈华北惊奇的目光，他又加上一句，"就是一大块铁。"沈华北举目四望，发现这样的铁山在附近还有几座，它们以怪异的色彩突兀地出现在这广阔的平原上，使这里有一种异域的景色。

沈华北这时已恢复到可以行走，他脚步蹒跚地随着这伙人走向远处一座高大的建筑物。那个建筑物呈完美的圆柱形，有上百米高，表面光滑一体，没有任何开口。他们走近后，一扇沉重的铁门轰隆隆地向一边滑开，露出一个入口。一行人走了进去，门在他们身后密实地关上了。

在暗弱的灯光下，沈华北看到他们身处一个像是密封舱的地方，光滑的白色墙壁上挂着一长排像太空服一样的密封装。人们各自从墙上取下一套密封装穿了起来，在两个人的帮助下他也开始穿上其中的一件。在这过程中他四下打量，看到对面还有一扇紧闭的密封门，门上亮着一盏红灯，红灯旁边有一个发光的数码显示器，他看出显示的是大气压值。当他那沉重的头盔被旋紧后，在面罩的右上角出现一块透明的液晶显示区，显示出飞快变化的数字和图形，他只看出那是这套密封服内部各个系统的自检情况。接着，他听到外面响起低沉的嗡嗡声，像是什么设备启动了，然后注意到对面那扇门上方显示的大气压值在迅速减小，在大约三分钟后减到零，旁边的红灯转换为绿灯。门开了，露出这个密封建筑物黑洞洞的内部。沈华北证实了自己的猜测：这是一个由大气区域进入真空区域的过渡舱。如此说来，这个巨大圆柱体的内部是真空的。

一行人走进了那个入口，门又在后面关上了，他们身处浓浓的黑暗之中，有几个人密封服头盔上的灯亮了，黑暗中出现几道光柱，但照不了多远。一种熟悉的感觉出现了，沈华北不由得打了个寒战，心里有一种莫名的恐惧。

"向前走。"他的耳机中响起了邓洋的声音。头灯的光晕在前方照出了一座小桥，不到一米宽，另一头伸进黑暗中，所以看不清有多长，桥下漆黑一片。沈华北迈着颤抖的双腿走上了小桥，密封服沉重的靴子踏在薄铁板桥面上发出空洞的声响。他走出几米，回过头来想看看后面的人是否跟上来了，这时所有人的头灯同时灭了，黑暗吞没了一切。但这只持续了几秒钟，小桥的下面突然出现了蓝色的亮光。沈华北回头看，只有他上了桥，其他人都挤在桥边看着他，在从下向上照的蓝光中，他们像一群幽灵。他扶着桥边的栏杆向下看去，几乎使血液凝固的恐惧攫住了他。

他站在一口深井上。

这口井的直径约 10 米，井壁上每隔一段距离就有一个环绕光圈，在黑暗中标示出深井的存在。他此时正站在横过井口的小桥的正中央，从这里看去，井深不见底，井壁上无数的光圈渐渐缩小，直至成为一点，他仿佛在俯视着一个发着蓝光的大靶标。

"现在开始执行审判，去偿还你儿子欠下的一切吧！"邓洋大声说着，然后用手转动安装在桥头的一个转轮，嘴里念念有词，"为了我被滥用的青春和才华……"小桥倾斜了一个角度，沈华北抓住另一面的栏杆努力使自己站稳。

接着邓洋把转轮让给了中部断裂灾难留下的孤儿，后者也用力转了一下："为了我被熔化的爸爸妈妈……"小桥倾斜的角度又增加了一些。

转轮又传到螺栓失落灾难留下的孤女手中，姑娘怒视着沈华北用力转动转轮："为了我被蒸发的爸爸妈妈……"

因失去所有财富而自杀未遂者从螺栓失落灾难留下的孤女手中抢过转轮："为了我的钱、我的劳斯莱斯和林肯车、我的海滨别墅和游泳池，为了我那被毁的生活，还有我那在寒冷的街头排队领救济的妻儿……"小桥已经转动了 90 度，沈华北此时只能用手抓着上面的栏杆坐在下面的栏杆上。

因失去所有财富而患精神分裂症的人也扑过来，同因失去所有财富而自杀未遂者一起转动转轮，他的病显然还没完全好，没说什么，只是对着下面的深井笑。小桥完全倾覆了，沈华北双手抓着栏杆倒吊在深井上方。

这时的他并没有多少恐惧，望着脚下深不见底的地狱之门，自己不算长的一生闪电般地掠过脑海：他的童年和少年时代是灰色的，在那些时光中记不起多少快乐和幸福；走入社会后，他在学术上取得了成功，发明了"糖衣"技术，但这并没有使生活接纳他；他在人际关系的蛛网中挣扎，却被越缠越紧；他从未真正体验过爱情，婚姻只是不得已而为之；当他打定主意永远不要孩子时，孩子来到了人世……他是一个生活在自己的思想和梦想中的人，一个令大多数人讨厌的另类，从来不可能真正地融入人群；他的生活是永远的离群索居，永远的逆水行舟，他曾寄希望于未来，但这就是未来了：已去世的妻子、已成为人类公敌的儿子、被污染的城市、这些充满变态仇恨的人……这一切已使他对这个时代和自己的生活心灰意懒。本来他还打定主意，要在死前知道事情的真相，现在这也无关紧要了，他是一个累极了的行者，唯一渴望的就是解脱。

在井边那群人的欢呼声中，沈华北松开了双手，向那发着蓝光的命运的靶标坠下去。

他闭着眼睛沉浸在坠落的失重中，身体仿佛变得透明，一切生命不能承受之重已离他而去。在这生命的最后几秒钟，他的脑海中突然响起了一首歌，这是父亲教他的一首古老的苏联歌曲，在他冬眠前的时代已没有人会唱了。后来他作为访问学者到莫斯科去，希望在那里找到知音，但这首歌在俄罗斯也失传了，所以这成了他自己的歌。在到达井底之前他也只能在心里吟唱一两个音符，但他相信，当自己的灵魂最后离开躯体时，这首歌会在另一个世界继续传唱……不知不觉中，这首旋律缓慢的歌已在他的心中唱出了一半，过了好长时间，他的意识猛然警醒，他睁开双眼，看到自己正在飞快地穿过一个又一个蓝色光环。

坠落仍在继续。

"哈哈哈哈……"他的耳机中响起了邓洋的狂笑声，"快死的人，感觉很不错吧？！"

他向下看去，看到一串扑面而来的发着蓝光的同心圆，他不停地穿过最大的一个圆，在圆心处不断有新的小圆环出现并很快扩大；向上看，也是一个同心圆，但其运动是前一个画面的反演。

"这井有多深？"他问。

"放心，你总会到底的，井底是一块坚硬平滑的钢板，啪的一下，你摔成的那张肉饼会比纸还薄的！哈哈哈哈……"

这时，他注意到面罩右上角的那块液晶显示区又出现了，有一行发着红光的字：

您现在已到达 100 千米深度，速度 1.4 千米 / 秒，您已经穿过莫霍不连续面，由地壳进入地幔。

沈华北再次闭上双眼，这次他的脑海中不再有歌声，而是像一台冷静的计算机般飞快地思索着。当半分钟后他再次睁开眼睛时，已经明白了一切：这就是南极庭院工程，那块坚硬平滑的井底钢板并不存在，这口井没有底。

这是一条贯穿地球的隧道。

五、大隧道

"它是走切线，还是穿过地心？"沈华北问，只是思维以语言的形式冒了一下头。

"聪明的头脑，这么快就想到了！"邓洋惊叹道。

"很像他儿子。"有人跟着说，听上去可能是中部断裂灾难留下的孤儿。

"是穿过地心，由中国的漠河穿过地球到达南极大陆的最东端南极半岛。"邓洋回答沈华北说。

"刚才那座城市是漠河？！"

"是的，它因作为地球隧道起点而繁荣起来。"

"据我所知，从那里贯穿地球应该到达阿根廷南部。"

"不错，但隧道有轻微的弯曲。"

"既然隧道是弯曲的，我会不会撞上井壁呢？"

"如果隧道笔直地直达阿根廷，你倒是肯定会撞上，那种笔直的地球隧道只有在贯穿两极之间的地轴上才能实现，这种与地轴成一定角度的隧道必须考虑地球的自转因素，它的弯曲正好能让你平滑地通过。"

"呵，伟大的工程！"沈华北由衷地赞叹道。

您现在已到达 300 千米深度，速度 2.4 千米/秒，已进入地幔黏性物质区。

他看到自己穿过光圈的频率正在加快，下面和上面那两个同心圆的密度增加了许多。

邓洋说："关于建造穿过地球的隧道，不是什么新想法，18世纪就有两个人提出了这个设想，一位是叫莫泊都的数学家，另一位则是举世闻名的伏尔泰。到后来，法国天文学家弗拉马里翁又把这个计划重新提了出来，并且首先考虑了地球的自转因素……"

沈华北打断他问："那你怎么说这想法是从我这里来的呢？"

"因为前面那些人不过是在做思想实验，而你的设想影响了一个人，这人后来用自己魔鬼般的才能促成了这个狂想的实现。"

"可……我不记得向沈渊提起过这些。"

"真是个健忘的人，你做了一个后来改变人类历史进程的设想，却忘了。"

"我真的想不起来。"

"那你总能想起那个叫贝加多的阿根廷人，还有他送给你儿子的生日礼物吧？"

您现在已到达 1500 千米深度，速度 5.1 千米／秒，已进入地幔刚性物质区。

沈华北终于想起来了。那是沈渊 6 岁生日时，沈华北请在北京的阿根廷物理学家贝加多博士到家里做客。当时南美两强已经崛起，阿根廷对南极大陆的大片陆地提出领土要求，并向南极大量移民。在后来的全球无核化进程中，阿根廷加入联合国销毁委员会，沈华北和贝加多都是这个委员会中一个技术小组的专家。

那次贝加多给沈渊带来的礼物是一个地球仪，它是用一种最新的玻璃材料制成的。那种玻璃是阿根廷飞速发展的技术水平的一个体现，它的折射率与空气相同，因而看不出玻璃球的存在，地球仪上的大陆仿佛是悬浮在两极之间，沈渊很喜欢这个礼物。

在晚饭后的聊天中，贝加多拿出了一张国内的大报，让沈华北看上面的一幅政治漫画，画上一位阿根廷球星正在踢地球。

"我不喜欢这个。"贝加多说,"中国人对我的国家的了解好像只限于足球,并把这种了解引申到国际政治上。"

"您要知道,阿根廷毕竟是在地球上与中国相距最远的一个国家,你们正在地球的对面。"赵文佳微笑着说,从沈渊的手中拿过那个全透明的地球仪,在上面,中国和阿根廷隔着那个超透明的球体重叠在一起。

"其实我有个办法能够使两国更好地交流。"沈华北拿过地球仪说,"只需从中国挖一条通过地心贯穿地球的隧道就行了。"

贝加多说:"那条隧道也有 12000 多千米长,并不比飞机航线短多少。"

"但旅行时间会短许多的,想想您带着旅行包从隧道的这一端跳进去……"

沈华北的本意是想把话题从政治上引开,他成功了,贝加多来了兴趣:"沈,你的思维方式总是与众不同……让我们看看,我跳进去后会一直加速,虽然我的加速度会随坠落深度的增加而减小,但确实会一直加速到地心,通过地心时我的速度达到最大值,加速度为零;然后开始减速上升,这种减速度的值会随着上升而不断增加,当到达地球的另一端——阿根廷的地面时,我的速度正好为零。如果我想回中国,只需从那端再跳下去就行了,如果我愿意,可以在南北半球之间做永恒的简谐振动。嗯,妙极了,可是旅行时间……"

"让我们计算一下吧。"沈华北打开电脑。

计算结果很快出来了,以地球理想的平均密度,从中国跳进地球隧道,穿过直径 12000 多千米的地球,坠落到阿根廷,需 42 分钟 12 秒。

"快捷的旅行！"贝加多高兴地说。

……

您现在已到达 2800 千米深度，速度 6.5 千米 / 秒，您正在穿过古腾堡不连续面，进入地核。

坠落中的沈华北又听到邓洋说："在那个晚上，你一定没有注意到，你的儿子瞪圆了那双充满灵气的大眼睛，出神地听着你的话，你更不可能知道，他盯着床头的那个透明地球仪一夜没睡。当然，你对儿子的这种影响可能有过无数次，你在沈渊的心灵中播下了许多狂想的种子，这只是其中开出花朵的一颗。"

沈华北凝视着周围距自己四五米远处的那一圈飞速上升的井壁，高频掠过的环绕光圈使井壁的表面有些模糊。

"这是新固态材料吗？"他问。

"还能是其他什么？有什么别的材料具有建造这样的隧道的强度吗？"

"这样巨量的新固态物质是如何生产出来的？这种比重大得能沉入地层的材料又是怎样搬运和加工的呢？"

"只能最简略地说说。新固态物质是通过连续不断的小型核爆炸生产出来的，核心技术当然是你的'糖衣'，其生产线是庞大而复杂的。新固态材料有多种密度级别，较低密度的材料不会沉入地层，用它造出一个面积较大的基础，将高密度材料放置于其上，其压强被基础分散，就能够浮在地面上了，用类似的原理，也可以进行这种材料的运输。至于新固态材料的加工，技术更加复杂，以你的知识水平可能无法理解。总之，新固态材料已经是一个庞大的产业，其经济规模超过了钢铁，它并不只是用于南极庭院工程。"

"那么这条隧道是如何建成的呢？"

"首先告诉你一点，建构隧道的基本构件是井圈，每个井圈长约100米，整条隧道是由大约24万个井圈连接而成的。至于具体的施工过程，你是个聪明人，也许自己能想出来。"

您现在已到达4100千米深度，速度7.5千米/秒，正处于液态地核中部。

"沉井？"

"是的，是用沉井工艺，第一步是从中国和南极将井圈沉入地层，并拼接成贯穿地球的一条线；第二步是将连接后的井圈中的地层物质掏出，隧道就形成了。你在隧道入口的外面看到的那些铁山，就是由从隧道的地核部分中掏出的铁镍合金堆成的。具体的施工要由地下船来进行，这种能在地层中行驶的机器也是由新固态材料制造的，有的型号能在地核深度行驶，它们能在地层中使下沉的井圈定位。"

"这样算下来，只需12万个井圈。"

"超固态物质承受地球深处的压力和高温是没有问题的，但地下还有许多流动体，较浅处是流动的岩浆，更危险的是地核中的液态铁镍流，它们会对隧道产生巨大的剪切冲击。新固态材料的强度能够承受这种冲击，但井圈之间的连接处就不行了，所以隧道由内外两层井圈构成。内层的井圈紧贴外层井圈，两层井圈间相互交错，这样就使隧道形成了足够的抗剪切强度。"

您现在已到达5400千米深度，速度7.7千米/秒，正在接近固态地核。

"下面，我想你要告诉我南极庭院工程带来的灾难了。"

六、灾难

"南极庭院工程的第一次灾难发生于二十五年前，那时工程进入最后的勘探设计阶段，需要进行大量的地下航行。在一次勘探航行中，一艘名叫'落日六号'的地下船在地幔中失事，并下沉到地核中。船上三名乘员中有两人遇难，只有一名年轻的女领航员幸存，但她现在仍被封闭在地心中，将在狭窄的地下船中度过余生。那艘船上的中微子通信设备已失去发射功能，但可能仍能接收。顺便说一句，她的名字叫沈静，是您的孙女。"

沈华北的心抽搐了一下。

在这疯狂的速度下，井壁上的光圈在沈华北眼中已连为一体，使这巨井的井壁发出刺目的蓝光，正在其中飞速坠落的沈华北，仿佛在穿过时光隧道，进入那并不遥远但他不曾经历过的过去。

您现在已到达 5800 千米深度，速度 7.8 千米 / 秒，您已进入固态地核，正在接近地心！

"南极庭院工程进行到第六年，发生了惨烈的中部断裂灾难。前面说过，隧道是由内外两层相互交错的井圈构成的，在装入内层井圈时，必须首先将已连接好的外层井圈中的地下物质掏空，以免两层井圈间混入杂质，影响它们之间贴合的紧密度。在施工中采用掏空一段外井圈放入一个内井圈的工艺，这就意味着在地核段的施工中，在一段外井圈被掏空而内井圈还未到位的这段时间里，包括接合部在内的两个外井圈将单独承受地核铁镍流的冲击。本来，两段井圈间的接合部采用十分坚固的铆接技术，在设计中，应该能够在相当长的时间里承受铁镍流的冲击。但在进入地核 490 多千米处，两段刚刚掏空的井圈处有一股异常强大的铁镍流，其流速是以前的大量勘探中观测到的最高值的 5 倍。强大的冲击力使两个井圈错位，高温高压的地核物质瞬间涌入隧道，并沿着已建成的隧道飞速上升。在得知断裂发生后，作为工程总指挥的沈渊立刻下令关闭了位于古腾堡不连续面处的安全闸门，它被称为古腾堡闸。这时在闸门下近 500 千米的隧道中，有 2500 多名工程人员在施工，在得知断裂发生后，他们同时乘坐隧道中的高速升降机撤离。共有 130 多部升降机，最后一部升降机与沿隧道上升的铁镍流保持着 30 千米左右的距离。结果只有 61 部升降机来得及通过古腾堡闸，其余都在闸门关闭后被 4000 多摄氏度高温的地核激流吞没，1527 人殒命地心。

　"中部断裂灾难举世震惊，沈渊同时受到了来自两方面的强烈谴责：一方认为他完全可以等所有升降机都通过古腾堡闸后再关闭闸门，这时铁镍流距闸门还有 30 千米，虽然时间很短，但还是来得及的。即使这道闸门没来得及关闭，在上面的莫霍不连续面（地表和地幔的交界面）还有一道安全闸——莫霍闸。那些极端愤怒的遇难者家属控告沈渊犯故意杀人罪。对此，沈渊在媒体面前只有一句话：'我怕出娄子啊！'这娄子确实出不得，有不止一部以南极庭院工程为题材的灾难片，其中最著名的是《铁泉》，在影片中有地核物质冲出地表的噩梦般的景象：一股铁镍液柱高高冲上同温层，在那个高度上散成一朵巨大的死亡之花，它发出的刺目白光使北半球的黑夜变成白昼，大地上下起了灼热的铁水暴雨，亚洲大陆成了一口炼钢炉，人类最终面临恐龙的命运……这描述并不夸张，正因如此，沈渊又面临着另一项与上面完全相反的指控：他应该更早些关闭古腾堡门，根本没有必要等那 61 部升降机通过。有更多的人支持这项指控，舆论给他安上了一项临时杜撰的罪名：因渎职而反人类罪。虽然在法律上两项指控最终都没有成立，但沈渊因此辞职，离开了南极庭院工程的指挥层，他拒绝了另外的任命，以后一直作为一名普通工程师在隧道中工作。"

这时，井壁发出的蓝光突然变成红色。

您现在已到达 6300 千米深度，速度 8 千米／秒，正在穿过地心！

耳机里响起了邓洋的声音："你现在已达到可以飞出地球的速度，却正处在这个星球的中心，地球正在围着你旋转，所有的海洋和大陆，所有的城市和所有的人，都在围着你旋转。"

沐浴在这庄严的红光中，沈华北的脑海中又响起了音乐，这次是一首宏伟的交响曲，他以第一宇宙速度穿过发着红光的地心隧道，仿佛漂行在地球的血管中，这使他热血沸腾。

邓洋又说："虽然新固态材料有良好的绝热性能，但是现在你周围的温度仍超过了 1500 摄氏度，你的密封服中的冷却系统正在全功率运行。"

井壁的红光只延续了十多秒钟，又变回宁静的蓝光。

您已通过地心，现在正在上升，并开始减速。您已经上升了500 千米，速度 7.8 千米／秒，仍在固态地核中。

蓝光使沈华北冷静下来，他已适应了失重，现在缓缓地转动身体，使头部向着前进的方向，以找到上升的感觉。他问邓洋："好像还有第三次灾难？"

"螺栓失落灾难发生在五年前，那时南极庭院工程已经完工，地球隧道已投入了正式运营，每时每刻都有地心列车穿行于其中。地心列车的车厢是直径 8 米、长 50 米的圆柱体，每列地心列车最多可由二百节车厢组成，可运载两万吨货物或近万名乘客，穿过地球的单程需 42 分钟。运输过程只是自由坠落，不消耗任何能源。

"当时，在漠河起点站，一名维修工人不小心将一颗直径不到 10 厘米的螺栓掉进隧道，这枚螺栓是用一种能够吸收电磁波的新材料制造的，因而没有被安全监测系统的雷达检测到。螺栓在隧道中一直坠落，穿过地球到达南极站，又从那里向回坠落，在到达地心时击中了一列正在向南极上升的地心列车。螺栓与列车的相对速度高达每秒 16 千米，这样的动能使它像一颗炸弹。它穿透了头两节车厢，把沿路的一切都汽化了，这两节车厢的爆炸，使整列列车以每秒 8 千米的速度擦到井壁上，在一瞬间就被撕得粉碎。大量的碎片在隧道中来回运行，有的一次次穿过整个地球，大部分则因撞击失去了部分速度，只是在地核附近摆动。用了一个月时间才把隧道中的碎片完全清理干净，列车上 3000 名乘客的遗体没有找到，地核的高温已把他们彻底火化了。"

您现在已从地心上升了 2200 千米，速度 7.5 米／秒，已重新进入地核的液态部分。

"但最大的灾难还是这个超级工程本身，南极庭院工程在技术上是人类史无前例的壮举，而在经济上的愚蠢也是空前绝后的。直到现在，人们对这样一个在经济规划上近乎白痴的工程竟得以实施仍百思不得其解。沈渊那魔鬼般的才能固然起了作用，根本原因可能还在于人们对开发新大陆的狂热和对技术的盲目崇拜。在经济学上，南极庭院工程的完工之日，也就是它的死亡之时。虽然通过地球隧道的运输极其快捷，且几乎不消耗能量，用当时人们的话说，'扔下去就到了'或'跳下去就到了'。但由于工程巨大的投资，使得地心列车的运输费用极其昂贵，这抵消了它快捷的长处，使得地心列车在与传统运输方式的竞争中没什么明显优势。"

您现在已从地心上升了 3500 千米，速度 6.5 千米／秒，正在穿过古腾堡不连续面，重新进入地幔。

"人类的南极梦很快破灭了，蜂拥而来的工业和过度的开发很快毁掉了这个地球上仅存的洁净世界，使南极大陆与其他大陆一样，成了一个弥漫着烟尘的垃圾场。南极上空的臭氧层被完全破坏，其影响波及全球，即使在北半球，强烈的紫外线已使人们必须加以防护才能出门，南极冰盖的加速融化也使全球的海平面急剧升高。在经历了一个痛苦的过程后，人类的理智再次占了上风，联合国所有的成员国签署了新的《南极公约》，使人类全面撤出南极大陆，再次把南极变成人迹罕至的地方，期望那里的环境能够慢慢恢复。随着向南极运输需求的骤减，在螺栓失落灾难后，地心列车完全停止了运营，地球隧道被封闭，到现在已有八年了。但南极庭院工程带来的经济灾难一直在持续，无数购买了南极庭院公司股票的人血本无归，引发了严重的社会动乱，投资的黑洞使国家经济到了崩溃的边缘，现在，我们还在这场灾难的低谷中痛苦地徘徊着……好了，这就是南极庭院工程的故事。"

随着速度的降低，井壁上本来稳定平滑的蓝光开始闪烁。渐渐地，周围的井壁能够分辨出单个的环绕光圈在掠过，向两个方向看，那密密的同心圆靶标又开始呈现出来。

您现在已从地心上升了 4800 千米，速度 5.1 千米／秒，正在穿过地幔的刚性物质区。

七、沈渊之死

"我儿子后来怎么样了？"沈华北问。

"隧道封闭后，沈渊作为留守人员待在漠河起点站。有一天我给他打了个电话，他只说了一句'我同女儿在一起'。后来我知道，他在这几年中一直过着一种不可思议的生活：每天都穿着密封服在地球隧道中来回坠落，睡觉都在里面，只有在吃饭和为密封服补充能量时才回到起点站。他每天要穿过地球三十次左右，就这样日复一日，年复一年，在漠河和南极半岛间，做着周期为84分钟、振幅为12600千米的简谐振动。"

您现在已从地心上升了6000千米，速度2.4千米/秒，正在穿过地幔的黏性物质区。

"谁也不知道沈渊在这永恒的坠落中都干些什么，但据他的同事说，每次通过地心时，他都会通过中微子通信设备与女儿打招呼，他更是常常在坠落中与女儿长谈。当然只是他一个人在说话，但生活在随着铁镍流在地核中运行的'落日六号'中的沈静应该能够听到的。

"他的身体长时间处于失重状态中，但由于必须在起点站吃饭和给密封服充电，每天还要在地面经受两到三次的正常地球重力，这样的折腾使他年老的心脏变得很脆弱。他在一次坠落中死于心脏病，当时没人注意到，于是他的遗体又在地球隧道中运行了两天。密封服的能量耗尽，停止制冷，地球隧道成了他的火葬炉，遗体在最后一次通过地心时被烧成了灰。我相信，你儿子对于这个归宿是很满意的。"

您现在已从地心上升了6200千米，速度1.4千米/秒，已经

穿过莫霍不连续面，进入地壳。注意，您正在接近地球隧道的南极顶点！

"这也是我的归宿，对吗？"沈华北平静地问。

"你也应该感到满足，临死前，你已经看到了自己想看的东西。本来我们是想在不穿密封服的情况下把你扔进地球隧道的，但现在让你穿上了，让你完整地看到了你儿子创造的东西。"

"是的，我很满足，此生足矣，我真诚地谢谢各位了！"

没有回答，耳机中的嗡嗡声骤然消失，地球另一端的那几个复仇者中断了通信。

沈华北看到上方的同心圆已经很稀疏了，他两三秒才能穿过一个光圈，而且这间隔还在急剧地拉长，这时耳机中响起了一声蜂鸣，面罩上显示：

您已经到达地球隧道的南极顶点！

他看到同心圆的圆心变空了，不再有新的光圈浮现，中间那个光圈越来越大，终于，他穿过了最后一个蓝色光圈，以不太快的速度升向一座与隧道另一端一模一样的横过井口的小桥。小桥上站着几个穿密封服的人，在他升出井口时，这些人一起伸手抓住了他，把他拉上桥。

南极站的内部也处于黑暗之中，只有井壁上光圈的蓝光照上来。他抬起头，迎面看到上方悬着一个巨大的圆柱体，其直径比井口稍小。他走到小桥尽头的井边，再向上看，隐约看到上方有一排这样的圆柱体，他数出了四个，再后面的就隐没到高处的黑暗中了。他知道，这就是停运的地心列车。

八、南极

半个小时后，沈华北同那几名救他命的警察一起，走出地球隧道的南极站，站在已没有积雪的南极平原上，远处可以看到被废弃的城市。低垂在地平线上的太阳把软弱无力的光芒投在这广阔而没有生气的大陆上，这里的空气比地球的另一端要好些，不用戴呼吸膜。

一名警官告诉沈华北，他们是在南极空城中留守的少数警务人员，接到郭医生的报警后，立刻赶到了南极站。当时井口是被封闭的，他们紧急联系地球隧道管理部门打开井盖，正好看见沈华北在蓝光中升向井口，仿佛从深海中浮出来一般。如果晚几秒钟，沈华北必死无疑，密封的井盖将挡住他，使他开始向北半球再次坠落，而在他再次通过地心之前，密封服的能量就会耗尽，他将像他的儿子一样在地心熔炉中化为灰烬。

"以邓洋为首的那几个家伙已经被逮捕，他们将被以杀人罪起诉，不过……"警官冷冷地盯着沈华北说，"我理解他们的想法。"

沈华北仍然沉浸在失重带来的眩晕中，他看着天边的太阳，长出了一口气，又说了一句："我此生足矣——"

"要是这样，您对自己今后的命运就比较容易接受了。"另一名警官说。

"命运？"沈华北清醒过来，扭头看着那名警官。

"您不能在这个时代生活，否则这样的事还会发生。好在政府有一个时间移民计划，为了减轻人口对环境的压力，强制一部分人口进入冬眠，让他们到未来去生活。现在政府已经决定，您将作为时间移民的一员，重新进入冬眠，这一次要多长时间才能被唤醒，我可说不准。"

沈华北好一会儿才理解了这话的意思，对警官深深地鞠躬："谢谢，我怎么总是这样幸运？"

"幸运？"警官不解地看着他说，"即使是这个时代的冬眠移民，也不可能适应未来社会的生活，别说您这样来自过去的人了！"

沈华北的脸上浮现出微笑："无所谓，关键是，我将看到地球隧道再次成为人类的骄傲！"

警官们发出了几声笑："怎么可能呢？这个完全失败的超级工程，只能永远作为你们父子俩的耻辱。"

"哈哈哈哈……"沈华北大笑起来，失重的虚弱使他站立不稳，但在精神上他已亢奋到极点，"长城和金字塔都是完全失败的超级工程，前者没能挡住北方游牧民族的南下，后者也没能使其中的法老木乃伊复活，但时间使这些都无关紧要，只有凝结于其上的人类精神永远光彩照人！"他指指身后高高耸立的地球隧道南极站，"与这条伟大的地心长城相比，你们这些哭哭啼啼的孟姜女是多么可怜！哈哈哈哈……"

沈华北张开双臂，让南极的寒风吹透自己的身体。"渊儿，我们此生足矣——"他幸福地说。

尾声

沈华北再次苏醒是半个世纪以后，他醒来后，几乎经历了与五十年前那次苏醒时一样的事：被一群陌生人带上车，进入地球隧道的漠河站，穿上密封服（令他不可理解的是，这密封服竟然比五十年前的那身笨重了许多），再次被扔进地球隧道开始漫长的坠落。五十年之后，地球隧道看上去没什么变化，仍是一条由无数蓝色光圈标示出的不见底的深井。

不过这次，有一个人陪着他下坠，是一个美丽的姑娘，她自我介绍说是他的导游。

"导游？对了，我的预感对了，地球隧道真的成为长城和金字塔了！"坠落中的沈华北兴奋地说。

"不，地球隧道没有成为长城和金字塔，它成了——"导游姑娘在失重中拉着沈华北的手，小心地与他在坠落中保持着同步。

"成了什么？"

"地球大炮！"

"什么？！"沈华北吃惊地打量着周围飞速掠过的井壁。

导游开始回忆："在您冬眠后，全球的环境进一步恶化，污染和臭氧层破坏使各大陆最后的植被迅速消失，可呼吸的空气已成了商品……这时，要想拯救地球生态，只有关闭人类所有的重工业和能源工业。"

"那样也许能让地球生态恢复，却会使人类文明毁灭。"沈华北插嘴说。

"面对当时的惨状，真有许多人愿意做出这种选择。不过更多的人在寻找另外的出路，最可行的办法，是把地球上的所有工业转移到太空和月球上。"

"那么，你们建立了太空电梯？"

"没有，试了试才知道那比挖地球隧道还难。"

"那么，发明了反重力飞船？"

"更没有，倒是从理论上证明了它根本不可能。"

"核动力火箭？"

"这倒是有，但其运输成本与传统火箭不相上下。如果用这些手段向太空转移工业，就又会发生地球隧道式的经济灾难了。"

"这么说，你们什么也转移不了了。"沈华北咧嘴苦笑，"上面是后人类时代了？"

导游没有回答，两人在沉默中向那无底深渊继续坠下去，周围飞掠而过的光环越来越密，最后井壁成为发出蓝光的平滑的一体。又过了十分钟，蓝光变成红光，他们默默地以每秒 8 千米的速度通过地心，井壁很快又发出蓝光，导游姑娘灵巧地使身体旋转 180 度，变为头向上的上升姿态，沈华北也笨拙地跟着这样做了。

"哦——"沈华北突然发出一声惊叫，从面罩右上角的显示中，他看到现在他们的速度是每秒 8.5 千米。

通过地心后，他们仍在加速！

让沈华北惊恐的另一件事是：他感到了重力，在这穿过地球的坠落过程中，本应自始至终是失重的，可他真的感到了重力！科学家的直觉很快告诉他，这不是重力，是推力，正是这推力使他们克服了不断增长的地球引力，保持加速。

"你一定还记得凡尔纳的登月大炮吧？"导游突然问。

"小时候看过的最愚蠢的一本书。"沈华北心不在焉地回答着，四下张望，想搞清这突然出现的怪事。

"一点儿都不愚蠢，用大炮进行发射，是人类大规模进入太空最理想、最快捷的方式。"

"除非你想在炮弹中被压成肉浆。"

"被压成肉浆是因为加速度太大，加速度太大是因为炮管太短，如果有足够长的炮管，炮弹就能以温柔的加速度射出去，就像你现在感觉到的一样。"

"这么说，我们是在凡尔纳大炮里？"

"我说过，它叫地球大炮。"

沈华北仰望着发出蓝光的隧道，努力把它想象成一根炮管。由于速度太快，井壁看上去浑然一体，已没有任何运动感了，他们仿佛一动不动地悬浮在这发着蓝光的巨管中。

"在你冬眠后的第四年，我们又研制出一种新型的新固态材料，除了具有以前这类材料的性质外，它还是优良的导体。现在，在这一半的地球隧道外表面，就缠绕着一圈用这种材料制成的粗导线，使这一半地球隧道变为一根长达 6300 千米的电磁线圈。"

"线圈中的电流从哪里来？"

"地核中有强大丰富的电流，正是这些电流产生了地球的磁场。我们用地核船拖着那种新固态导线，在地核中拉了上百个大回路，每个回路都有几千千米长，用这些回路来采集地核中的电流，并将它汇聚到隧道线圈上，使隧道中充满了强磁场。我们的密封服的肩部和腰部有两个超导线圈，线圈中的电流产生方向相反的磁场，推力就是这样产生的。"

由于继续加速，上升段很快要走完了，井壁再次发出红光。

"注意，现在我们的速度已达到每秒 15 千米，超过了第二宇宙速度，我们就要飞出炮口了！"

这时，在地球隧道的南极出口，停放地心列车的高大建筑早已拆除，地球隧道的圆形出口直接面对着天空，上面有一个密封盖板。扩音器中传出这样的声音："游客们请注意，地球大炮将进行今天的第 43 次发射，请您戴上护目镜和耳塞，否则对您的视力和听觉将造成永久的损害。"

　　十秒钟后，隧道口的密封盖板哗地滑向一边，露出了直径 10 米的圆形井口，空气涌入真空的井内，发出尖厉的呼啸声。一声巨响，井口喷出了一道长长的火舌，其亮度使南极天边低垂的太阳也黯然失色，密封盖板又迅速滑回原位盖住井口。井内的抽气机发出低沉的轰鸣声，抽空刚才盖板打开的三秒钟进入井内的空气，以准备下一次发射。人们抬头仰望，只见两颗拖着火尾的流星正在疾速上升，很快消失在南极深蓝色的苍穹中。

　　沈华北并没有像想象中那样看到隧道出口迎面扑来，速度太快，他不可能看清。他只看到，身处其中的那条发着红光似乎通向无限高处的隧道在瞬间消失，代之以南极的蓝天，二者之间没有任何过渡，快得像屏幕上两幅图像的切换。他猛地回头，看到脚下的大地正在疾速退去，他认出了那座南极城市，那座城市很快变成了一块篮球场大小的长方形。他抬起头，看到天空的颜色正在迅速地由蓝变黑，速度之快，像一块正在被调暗的屏幕。再低头，他看到了南极半岛狭长弯曲的形状，看到了围绕着半岛的大海。他的身后拖着一条长长的火尾，看看身上才发现密封服的表面在燃烧，他被裹在一层薄薄的火焰中。看看在距他十几米处与他一起上升的导游，也被裹在火焰中，像一个拖着长长火尾的小怪物。巨大的空气阻力像一个巨掌狠狠地压在他的头上和肩上，但随着天空的变黑，这巨掌像被另一个更加强大的力量征服了，它的压力渐渐放松。低头看，南极大陆已显示出了完整的形状，沈华北惊喜地发现这块大陆又恢复了它的白色。向远处看，地球已显示出了弧形，太阳正从地球边缘移上来，在薄薄的大气层中散射出绚丽的暮曙光。再向上看，群星已在太空中出现，沈华北第一次见到如此晶莹灿烂的星星。身上的火光熄灭了，他们已冲出大气层，飘浮在寂静的太空中。沈华北有种身轻如燕的感觉，他发现自己身上的密封服——太空服变薄了许多，表面的那层散热物质已在与大气的剧烈摩擦中蒸发了。这时，高速通过大气层时的通信盲区已过，他的耳机中响起了导游的声音：

"穿过大气层时的阻力消耗了一部分速度，但我们现在的速度仍超过了逃逸值，我们正在飞离地球。你看那儿——"

导游指着下面已经变得很小的南极半岛，沈华北在地球隧道出口所在的位置看到了闪光，接着一颗拖着火尾的流星从半岛缓慢地飞升而上，在飞出大气层后火光熄灭了。

"那是地球大炮刚刚发射的一艘太空船，它将接我们回去。地球大炮的炮管中每时每刻都同时运行着五六颗'炮弹'，这样它每过八到十分钟就射出一艘太空船，所以现在进入太空就如同乘地铁一样便捷。在二十年前工业大迁移开始时，是发射最频繁的时期，炮管中往往同时有二十多颗'炮弹'在加速，地球大炮以两三分钟一发的频率向太空急促地射击。一批批太空船组成了上升的流星雨，那是人类向命运的庄严挑战，真是壮观！"

这时，沈华北在群星中发现了许多快速移动的星星，它们的运动在静止的星空背景上很容易看出来，那些东西一定就在地球轨道上。再细看，它们中相当一部分可以看出形状，有环形的、圆柱形的，还有多个形状组合而成的不规则体，像漆黑太空上精美的小饰件。

"那是宝山钢铁公司。"导游指着一个发光的圆环说，然后又依次指点着其他几个亮点，"那几个是中国石化，当然它们现在不处理石油了；那几个圆柱形的是欧洲冶金联合体；那些是用微波向地球供电的太阳能电站，发光的只是它们的控制中心，太阳能电池组和传输电能的天线阵列是看不到的……"

沈华北被这情景陶醉了，再看看下面蔚蓝色的地球，他的眼泪涌了出来。他现在最大的愿望，就是让参加过南极庭院工程的每一个人，故去的和健在的，都看看这些，他特别想到了其中的一个人，一个在所有人心目中永远年轻的女性。

"找到我的孙女了吗？"他问。

"没有，我们缺少在地核中进行远距离探测的技术，那是一个广阔的区域，谁也不知道铁镍流把她带到哪里了。"

"能不能把我们看到的这些用中微子发向地心？"

"一直在这么做呢，相信她会看到的。"

乡村教师

THE VILLAGE TEACHER

作者附言：

　　这篇小说同我以前的作品相比有一些变化，主要是不那么"硬"了，重点放在营造意境上。不要被开头所迷惑，它不是你想象的那种东西。我不敢说它的水准高到哪里去，但从中你将看到中国科幻史上最离奇、最不可思议的意境。

　　他知道，这最后一课要提前讲了。

　　又一阵剧痛从肝部袭来，几乎使他晕厥过去。他已没有气力下床了，便艰难地移近床边的窗口。月光映在窗纸上，银亮亮的，使小小的窗户看上去像是通向另一个世界的门，那个世界的一切一定都是银亮亮的，像用银子和不冻人的雪做成的盆景。他颤抖着抬起头，从窗纸的破洞中望出去，幻觉立刻消失了，他看到了远处自己度过了一生的村庄。

村庄静静地卧在月光下，像是百年前就没人似的。那些黄土高原上特有的平顶小屋，形状上同村子周围的黄土包没啥区别，在月夜中颜色也一样，整个村子仿佛已融入这黄土坡之中。只有村前那棵老槐树很清晰，树上干枯枝杈间的几个老鸦窝更是黑黑的，像是滴在这暗银色画面上的几滴醒目的墨点……其实村子也有美丽温暖的时候，比如秋收时，外面打工的男人女人们大都回来了，村里有了人声和笑声，家家屋顶上是金灿灿的玉米，打谷场上的娃们在秸秆堆里打滚。再比如过年的时候，打谷场被汽灯照得通亮，在那里连着几天闹红火、摇旱船、舞狮子。那几个狮子只剩下咔嗒作响的木头脑壳，上面油漆都脱了，村里没钱置新狮子皮，就用几张床单代替，玩得也挺高兴……但正月十五一过，村里的青壮年都外出打工挣生活去了，村子一下没了生气。只有每天黄昏，当稀拉拉几缕炊烟升起时，村头可能出现一两个老人，扬起山核桃一样的脸，眼巴巴地望着那条通向山外的路，直到被老槐树挂住的最后一抹夕阳消失。天黑后，村里早早就没了灯光，娃娃和老人们睡得都早，电费贵，现在到了一块八一度了。

这时村里隐约传出了一声狗叫，声音很轻，好像那狗在说梦话。他看着村子周围月光下的黄土地，突然觉得那好像是纹丝不动的水面。要真是水就好了，今年是连着第五个旱年了，要想有收成，又要挑水浇地了。想起田地，他的目光向更远方移去，那些小块的山田，在月光下像一个巨人登山时留下的一个个脚印。在这只长荆条和毛蒿的石头山上，田也只能是这么东一小块西一小块的，别说农机，连牲口都转不开身，只能凭人力种了。去年

172

一家什么农机厂到这儿来，推销一种微型手扶拖拉机，可以在这些巴掌大的地里干活儿。那东西真是不错，可村里人说他们这是闹笑话哩！他们想过那些巴掌地能产出多少东西来吗？就是绣花似的种，能种出一年的口粮就不错了，遇上这样的旱年，可能种子钱都收不回来呢！为这样的田买那三五千一台的拖拉机，再搭上两块多一升的柴油？！唉！这山里人的难处，外人哪能知晓呢？

这时，窗前走过了几个小小的黑影，这几个黑影在不远的田垄上围成一圈蹲下来，不知要干什么。他知道这都是自己的学生，其实只要他们在近旁，不用眼睛他也能感觉到他们的存在，这直觉是他一生积累出来的，只是在这生命的最后时间里更敏锐了。

他甚至能认出月光下的那几个孩子，其中肯定有刘宝柱和郭翠花。这两个孩子都是本村人，本来不必住校的，但他还是收他们住了。刘宝柱的爹十年前买了个川妹子成亲，生了宝柱，五年后娃大了，对那女人看得也松了，结果有一天她跑回四川了，还卷走了家里所有的钱。这以后，宝柱爹也变得不成样儿了，开始是赌，同村子里那几个老光棍一样，把家折腾得只剩四堵墙、一张床。然后是喝，每天晚上都用八毛钱一斤的地瓜烧把自己灌得烂醉，拿孩子出气，每天一小揍，三天一大揍，直到上个月的一天半夜，抢了根烧火棍差点把宝柱的命要了。郭翠花更惨了，要说她妈还是正经娶来的，这在这儿可是个稀罕事，男人也很荣光了。可好景不长，喜事刚办完大家就发现她是个疯子，之所以迎亲时没看出来，大概是吃了什么药。本来嘛，好端端的女人哪会到这穷得鸟都不拉屎的地方来？但不管怎么说，翠花还是生下来了，并艰难地长大。但她那疯妈妈的病也越来越重，犯起病来，白天拿菜刀砍人，晚上放火烧房，更多的时间还是在阴森森地笑，那声音让人汗毛直竖……

剩下的都是外村的孩子了，他们的村子距这里最近的也有十里山路，只能住校了。在这所简陋的乡村小学里，他们一住就是一个学期。娃们来时，除了带自己的铺盖，每人还背了一袋米或面，十多个孩子在学校的那个大灶做饭吃。当冬夜降临时，娃们围在灶边，看着菜面糊糊在大铁锅中翻腾，灶膛里秸秆橘红色的火光映在他们脸上……这是他一生中看到过的最温暖的画面，他会把这画面带到另一个世界的。

窗外的田垄上，在那圈娃中间，亮起了几点红色的小火星星，在这一片银灰色的月夜的背景上，火星星的红色格外醒目。这些娃在烧香，接着他们又烧起纸来，火光使娃们的形象以橘红色在冬夜银灰色的背景上显现出来，这使他又想起了那灶边的画面。他脑海中还出现了另外一个类似的画面：当学校停电时（可能是因为线路坏了，但大多数时间是因为交不起电费），他给娃们上晚课。他手里举着一根蜡烛照着黑板，问："看见不？""看不显！"娃们总是这样回答。那么一点点亮光，确实难看清，但娃们缺课多，晚课是必须上的。于是他再点上一根蜡，手里举着两根蜡。"还是不显！"娃们喊。他于是再点上一根，虽然还是看不清，但娃们不喊了，他们知道再喊老师也不会加蜡了，蜡太多了也是点不起的。烛光中，他看到下面那群娃的面容时隐时现，像一群用自己的全部生命挣脱黑暗的小虫虫。

娃们和火光，娃们和火光，总是娃们和火光，总是夜中的娃们和火光，这是这个世界深深刻在他脑子中的画面，但他始终不明其含义。

　　他知道娃们是在为他烧香和烧纸，他们以前多次这么干过，只是这次，他已没有力气像以前那样斥责他们迷信了。他用尽了一生在娃们的心中燃起科学和文明的火苗，但他明白，同笼罩着这偏远山村的愚昧和迷信相比，那火苗是多么弱小，像这深山冬夜中教室里的那根蜡烛。半年前，村里的一些人来到学校，要从本来就已经很破旧的校舍取下椽子木，说是修村头的老君庙用。问他们校舍没顶了，娃们以后住哪儿，他们说可以睡教室里嘛。他说那教室四面漏风，大冬天能住？他们说反正都是外村人。他拿起一根扁担和他们拼命，结果被人家打断了两根肋骨。好心人抬着他走了三十多里山路，送到了镇医院。

　　就是在那次检查伤势时，意外发现他患了食道癌。这并不稀奇，这一带是食道癌高发区。镇医院的医生恭喜他因祸得福，因为他的食道癌现处于早期，还未扩散，动手术就能治愈，食道癌是手术治愈率最高的癌症之一，他算捡了条命。

　　于是他去了省城，去了肿瘤医院，在那里，他问医生动一次这样的手术要多少钱，医生说像你这样的情况可以住我们的扶贫病房，其他费用也可适当减免，最后算下来不会太多的，也就两万多元吧。想到他来自偏远山区，医生接着很详细地给他介绍住院手续怎么办，他默默地听着，突然问："要是不手术，我还有多长时间？"

　　医生呆呆地看了他好一阵儿，才说："半年吧。"并不解地看到他长出了一口气，好像得到了很大安慰。

　　至少能送走这届毕业班了。

　　他真的拿不出这两万多元。虽然民办教师工资很低，但干了这么多年，孤身一人无牵无挂，按说也能攒下一些钱了。只是他把钱都花在娃们身上了，他已记不清给多少学生代交了学杂费，最近的就有刘宝柱和郭翠花。更多的时候，他看到娃们的饭锅里没有多少油星星，就用自己的工资买些肉和猪油回来……反正到现在，他全部的钱也只有手术所需用的十分之一。

沿着省城那条宽敞的大街，他向火车站走去。这时天已黑了，城市的霓虹灯开始发出迷人的光芒，那光芒之多彩之斑斓，让他迷惑；还有那些高楼，一入夜就变成了一盏盏高耸入云的巨大彩灯；音乐声在夜空中飘荡，疯狂的、轻柔的，走一段一个样。

就在这个不属于他的世界里，他慢慢地回忆起自己不算长的一生。他很坦然，各人有各人的命，早在二十年前初中毕业回到山村小学时，他就选定了自己的命。再说，他这条命很大一部分是另一位乡村教师给的。他就是在自己现在任教的这所小学度过童年的，他爹妈死得早，那所简陋的乡村小学就是他的家，他的小学老师把他当亲儿子待，日子虽然穷，但他的童年并不缺少爱。那年，放寒假了，老师要把他带回自己的家里过冬。老师的家很远，他们走了很长的积雪的山路，当看到老师家所在的村子的一点灯光时，已是半夜了。这时他们看到身后不远处有四点绿莹莹的亮光，那是两双狼眼。那时山里狼很多，学校周围就能看到一堆堆狼屎。有一次他淘气，把那灰白色的东西点着扔进教室里，使浓浓的狼烟充满了教室，把娃们都呛得跑了出来，让老师很生气。现在，那两只狼向他们慢慢逼近，老师折下一根粗树枝，挥动着它拦住狼的来路，同时大声喊着让他向村里跑。他当时吓糊涂了，只顾跑，只想着那狼会不会绕过老师来追他，只想着会不会遇到其他的狼。当他上气不接下气地跑进村子，然后同几个拿猎枪的汉子去接老师时，发现他躺在一片已冻成糊状的血泊中，半条腿和整只胳膊都被狼咬掉了。老师在被送往镇医院的路上就咽了气，当时在火把的光芒中，他看到了老师的眼睛，老师的腮帮被深深地咬下一大块，已说不出话，但用目光把一种心急如焚的牵挂传给了他。他读懂了那牵挂，记住了那牵挂。

初中毕业后，他放弃了在镇政府里一个不错的工作机会，直接回到了这个举目无亲的山村，回到了老师牵挂的这所乡村小学。这时，学校因为没有教师已荒废好几年了。

前不久，教委出台新政策，取消了民办教师，其中的一部分经考试考核转为公办。当他拿到教师资格证时，知道自己已成为一名国家承认的小学教师了，很高兴，但也只是高兴而已，不像别的同事那么激动。他不在乎什么民办公办，他只在乎那一批又一批的娃，从他的学校读完了小学，走向生活。不管他们是走出山去还是留在山里，他们的生活同那些没上过一天学的娃总是有些不一样的。

他所在的山区，是这个国家最贫困的地区之一。但穷不是最可怕的，最可怕的是那里的人们对现状的麻木。记得那是好多年前了，搞包产到户，村里开始分田，然后又分其他的东西。对于村里唯一的一台拖拉机，大伙对于油钱怎么出、机时怎么分配总也谈不拢，最后唯一大家都能接受的办法是把拖拉机分了，真的分了，你家拿一个轮子，他家拿一根轴……再就是两个月前，有一家工厂来扶贫，给村里安了一台潜水泵，考虑到用电贵，人家还给带了一台小柴油机和足够的柴油。挺好的事儿，但人家前脚走，村里后脚就把机器都卖了，连泵带柴油机，只卖了1500块钱，全村好吃了两顿，算是过了个好年……一家皮革厂来买地建厂，什么也不清楚就把地卖了，那厂子建起后，硝皮子的毒水流进了河里，渗进了井里，人一喝了那些水浑身起红疙瘩，就这也没人在乎，还沾沾自喜那地卖了个好价钱……看村里那些娶不上老婆的光棍汉，每天除了赌就是喝，但不去种地，他们能算清：穷到了头，县里每年总会有些救济，那钱算下来也比在那巴掌大的山地里刨一年土坷垃挣得多……没有文化，人们都变得下作了，那里的穷山恶水固然让人灰心，但真正让人感到没指望的，是山里人那呆滞的目光。

　　他走累了，就在人行道边坐下来。他面前，是一家豪华的大餐馆，那餐馆靠街的一整堵墙全是透明玻璃，华丽的枝形吊灯把光芒投射到外面。整个餐馆像一个巨大的鱼缸，里面穿着华贵的客人们则像一群多彩的观赏鱼。他看到在靠街的一张桌子旁坐着一个胖男人，这人头发和脸似乎都在冒油，使他看上去像用一大团表面涂了油的蜡做的。他两旁各坐着一个身材高挑、穿着暴露的女郎，那男人转头对一个女郎说了句什么，把她逗得大笑起来，那男人跟着笑起来，而另一个女郎则娇嗔地用两个小拳头捶那个男的……真没想到还有个子这么高的女孩子，秀秀的个儿，大概只到她们一半……他叹了口气，唉，又想起秀秀了。

　　秀秀是本村唯一一个没有嫁到山外的姑娘，也许是因为她从未出过山，怕外面的世界，也许是别的什么原因。他和秀秀好过两年多，最后那阵好像就成了，秀秀家里也通情达理，只要1500块的肚疼钱[1]。后来，村子里一些出去打工的人赚了些钱回来，和他同岁的二蛋虽不识字但脑子活，去城里干起了挨家挨户清洗抽

1　西北一些农村地区彩礼的一个名目，意思是对娘生女儿肚子疼的补偿。

油烟机的活儿，一年下来竟能赚个万把块，前年回来待了一个月，秀秀不知怎的就跟这个二蛋好上了。秀秀一家全是睁眼瞎，家里粗糙的干打垒墙壁上，除了贴着一团一团用泥巴和起来的瓜种子，还画着长长短短的道道儿，那是她爹多年来记的账……秀秀没上过学，但自小对识文断字的人有好感，这是她同他好的主要原因。但二蛋的一瓶廉价香水和一串镀金项链就把这种好感全打消了。"识文断字又不能当饭吃。"秀秀对他说。虽然他知道识文断字是能当饭吃的，但具体到他身上，吃的确实比二蛋差好远，所以他也说不出什么。秀秀看他那样儿，转身走了，只留下一股让他皱鼻子的香水味。

和二蛋成亲一年后，秀秀生娃儿死了。他还记得那个接生婆，把那些锈不拉儿的刀刀铲铲放到火上烧一烧就向里捅，秀秀可倒霉了，血流了一铜盆，在送去镇医院的路上就咽气了。成亲办喜事儿的时候，二蛋花了三万块，那排场在村里真是风光死了，可他怎的就舍不得花点儿钱让秀秀到镇医院去生娃呢？后来他一打听，这花费一般也就二三百，就二三百呀。但村里历来都是这样儿，生娃是从不去医院的。所以没人怪二蛋，秀秀就这命。后来他听说，比起二蛋妈来，她还算幸运。生二蛋时难产，二蛋爹从产婆那儿得知是个男娃，就决定只要娃了。于是二蛋妈被放到驴子背上，让那驴子一圈圈走，硬是把二蛋挤出来，听当时看见的人说，在院子里血流了一圈……

想到这里他长出了一口气，笼罩着家乡的愚昧和绝望使他窒息。

但娃们还是有指望的，对于那些在冬夜寒冷的教室中盯着烛光照着的黑板的娃来说，他就是那蜡烛，不管能点多长时间，发出的光有多亮，他总算是从头点到尾了。

　　他站起身来继续走，没走多远就拐进了一家书店，城里就是好，还有夜里开门的书店。除了回程的路费，他把身上所有的钱都买了书，以充实他的乡村小学里那小小的图书室。半夜，提着那两捆沉重的书，他踏上了回家的火车。

　　在距地球五万光年的远方，在银河系的中心，一场延续了两万年的星际战争已接近尾声。

　　那里的太空中渐渐现出一个方形区域，仿佛灿烂的群星的背景被剪出一个方口，这个区域的边长约为 10 万千米，区域的内部是一种比周围太空更黑的黑暗，让人感到一种虚空中的虚空。从这黑色的正方形中，开始浮现出一些实体，它们形状各异，都有月球大小，呈耀眼的银色。这些物体越来越多，并组成一个整齐的立方体方阵。这银色的方阵庄严地驶出黑色正方形，两者构成了一幅挂在宇宙永恒墙壁上的镶嵌画，这幅画以绝对黑体的正方形天鹅绒为衬底，由纯净的银光耀眼的白银小构件整齐地镶嵌而成。这又仿佛是一首宇宙交响乐的固化。渐渐地，黑色的正方形消融在星空中，群星填补了它的位置，银色的方阵庄严地悬浮在群星之间。

　　银河系碳基联邦的星际舰队，完成了本次巡航的第一次时空跃迁。

　　在舰队的旗舰上，碳基联邦的最高执政官看着眼前银色的金属大地，大地上布满了错综复杂的纹路，像一块无限广阔的银色蚀刻电路板。不时有几个闪光的水滴状的小艇出现在大地上，沿着纹路以令人目眩的速度行驶几秒钟，然后无声地消失在一口突然出现的深井中。时空跃迁带过来的太空尘埃被电离，成为一团团发着暗红色光的云，笼罩在银色大地的上空。

最高执政官以冷静著称，他周围那似乎永远波澜不惊的淡蓝色智能场就是他人格的象征，但现在，像周围的人一样，他的智能场也微微泛出黄光。

"终于结束了。"最高执政官的智能场振动了一下，把这个信息传送给站在他两旁的参议员和舰队统帅。

"是啊，结束了。战争的历程太长太长，以至于我们都忘记了它的开始。"参议员回答。

这时，舰队开始了亚光速巡航，它们的亚光速发动机同时启动，旗舰周围突然出现了几千个蓝色的太阳，银色的金属大地像一面无限广阔的镜子，把蓝太阳的数量又复制了一倍。

远古的记忆似乎被点燃了，其实，谁能忘记战争的开始呢？这记忆虽然遗传了几百代，但在碳基联邦的万亿公民的脑海中，它仍那么鲜活，那么让人刻骨铭心。

两万年前的那一时刻，硅基帝国从银河系外围对碳基联邦发动全面进攻。在长达一万光年的战线上，硅基帝国的 500 多万艘星际战舰同时开始恒星蛙跳。每艘战舰首先借助一颗恒星的能量打开一个时空蛙洞，然后从这个蛙洞时空跃迁至另一个恒星，再用这颗恒星的能量打开第二个蛙洞继续跃迁……由于打开蛙洞消耗了恒星大量的能量，使得恒星的光谱暂时向红端移动，当飞船从这颗恒星完成跃迁后，它的光谱渐渐恢复原状。当几百万艘战舰同时进行恒星蛙跳时，所产生的这种效应是十分恐怖的：银河系的边缘出现一条长达一万光年的红色光带，这条光带向银河系的中心移过来。这个景象在光速视界是看不到的，但会在超空间监视器上显示出来。那条由变色恒星组成的红带，如同一道一万光年长的血潮，向碳基联邦的疆域涌来。

碳基联邦最先接触硅基帝国攻击前锋的是绿洋星，这颗美丽的行星围绕着一对双星恒星运行，它的表面全部被海洋覆盖。那生机盎然的海洋中漂浮着由柔软的长藤植物构成的森林，温和美丽、身体晶莹透明的绿洋星人在这海中的绿色森林间轻盈地游动，创造了绿洋星伊甸园般的文明。突然，几万道刺目的光束从天而降，硅基帝国舰队开始用激光蒸发绿洋星的海洋。在很短的时间内，绿洋星变成了一口沸腾的大锅，这颗行星上包括50亿绿洋星人在内的所有生物在沸水中极度痛苦地死去，他们被煮熟的有机质使整个海洋变成了绿色的浓汤。最后海洋全部蒸发了，昔日美丽的绿洋星变成了一个由厚厚蒸汽包裹着的地狱般的灰色行星。

这是一场几乎波及整个银河系的星际大战，是银河系中碳基和硅基文明之间惨烈的生存竞争，但双方谁都没有料到战争会持续两万银河年！

现在，除了历史学家，谁也记不清有百万艘以上战舰参加的大战役有多少次了。规模最大的一次超级战役是第二旋臂战役，战役在银河系第二旋臂中部进行，双方投入了上千万艘星际战舰。据历史记载，在那广漠的战场上，被引爆的超新星就达两千多颗，那些超新星像第二旋臂中部黑暗太空中怒放的焰火，使那里变成超强辐射的海洋，只有一群群幽灵似的黑洞漂行于其间。战役的最后，双方的星际舰队几乎同归于尽。15000年过去了，第二旋臂战役现在听起来就像上古时代缥缈的神话，只有那仍然存在的古战场证明它确实发生过。但很少有飞船真正进入过古战场，那里是银河系最恐怖的区域，这并不仅仅是因为辐射和黑洞。当时，双方数量多得难以想象的战舰群为了进行战术机动，进行了大量的超短距离时空跃迁，据说当时的一些星际歼击机在空间格斗时，时空跃迁的距离竟短到令人难以置信的几千米！这样就把古战场的时空结构搞得千疮百孔，像一块内部被老鼠钻了无数长洞的大乳酪。飞船一旦误入这个区域，可能在一瞬间就被畸变的空间扭成一根细长的金属绳，或压成一张面积有几亿平方千米但厚度只有几个原子的薄膜，立刻被辐射狂风撕得粉碎。但更为常见的是飞船变为建造它们时的一块块钢板，或者立刻老得只剩下一个破旧的外壳，内部的一切都变成古老灰尘；人在这里也可能瞬间回到胚胎状态或变成一堆白骨……

但最后的决战不是神话，它就发生在一年前。在银河系第一和第二旋臂之间的荒凉太空中，硅基帝国集结了最后的力量，这支由150万艘星际战舰组成的舰队在自己周围构筑了半径1000光年的反物质云屏障。碳基联邦投入攻击的第一个战舰群刚完成时空跃迁就陷入了反物质云中。反物质云十分稀薄，但对战舰具有极大的杀伤力，碳基联邦的战舰立刻变成一个个刺目的火球，但它们仍奋勇冲向目标。每艘战舰都拖着长长的火尾，在后面留一条发着荧光的航迹，这由30多万个火流星组成的阵列形成了碳硅战争中最为壮观、最为惨烈的画面。在反物质云中，这些火流星渐渐缩小，最后在距硅基帝国战舰阵列很近的地方消失了，但它们用自己的牺牲为后续的攻击舰队在反物质云中打开了一条通道。在这场战役中，硅基帝国的最后舰队被赶到银河系最荒凉的区域：第一旋臂的顶端。

现在，这支碳基联邦舰队将完成碳硅战争中的最后一项使命：

他们将在第一旋臂的中部建立一条 500 光年宽的隔离带，隔离带中的大部分恒星将被摧毁，以制止硅基帝国的恒星蛙跳。恒星蛙跳是银河系中大吨位战舰进行远距离快速攻击的唯一途径，而一次蛙跳的最大距离是 200 光年。隔离带一旦产生，硅基帝国的重型战舰要想进入银河系中心区域，只能以亚光速跨越这 500 光年的距离。这样，硅基帝国实际上被禁锢在第一旋臂顶端，再也无法对银河系中心区域的碳基文明构成任何严重威胁。

"我带来了联邦议会的意愿，"参议员用振动的智能场对最高执政官说，"他们仍然强烈建议：在摧毁隔离带中的恒星前，对它们进行生命级别的保护甄别。"

"我理解议会。"最高执政官说，"在这场漫长的战争中，各种生命流出的血足够形成上千颗行星的海洋了，战后，银河系中最迫切需要重建的是对生命的尊重。这种尊重不仅是对碳基生命的，也是对硅基生命的，正是基于这种尊重，碳基联邦才没有彻底消灭硅基文明。但硅基帝国并没有这种对生命的感情，如果说碳硅战争之前，战争和征服对于它们还仅仅是一种本能和乐趣的话，现在这种东西已根植于它们的每个基因和每行代码之中，成为它们生存的终极目的。由于硅基生物对信息的存储和处理能力大大高于我们，可以预测硅基帝国在第一旋臂顶端的恢复和发展将是神速的，所以我们必须在碳基联邦和硅基帝国之间建成足够宽的隔离带。在这种情况下，对隔离带中数以亿计的恒星进行生命级别的保护甄别是不现实的。第一旋臂虽属银河系中最荒凉的区域，但其带有生命行星的恒星数量仍可能达到蛙跳密度，这种密度足以使中型战舰进行蛙跳。而即使只有一艘硅基帝国的中型战舰闯入碳基联邦的疆域，可能造成的破坏也是巨大的，所以在隔离带中只能进行文明级别的甄别。我们不得不牺牲隔离带中某些恒星周围的低级生命，这是为了拯救银河系中更多的高级和低级生命。这一点我已向议会说明。"

参议员说："议会也理解您和联邦防御委员会，所以我带来的只是建议而不是立法。但隔离带中周围已形成 3C 级以上文明的恒星必须被保护。"

"这一点无须质疑，"最高执政官的智能场闪现出坚定的红色，"对隔离带中带有行星的恒星的文明检测将是十分严格的！"

舰队统帅的智能场第一次发出信息："其实我觉得你们多虑了，第一旋臂是银河系中最荒凉的荒漠，那里不会有 3C 级以上文明的。"

"但愿如此。"最高执政官和参议员同时发出了这个信息，他们智能场的共振使一道弧形的等离子体波纹向银色金属大地的上空扩散开去。

舰队开始了第二次时空跃迁，以近乎无限的速度奔向银河系的第一旋臂。

夜深了，烛光中，全班的娃们围在老师的病床前。

"老师歇着吧，明儿个讲也行的。"一个男娃说。

他艰难地苦笑了一下："明儿个有明儿个的课。"

他想，如果真能拖到明天当然好，那就再讲一堂课，但直觉告诉他怕是不行了。

他做了个手势，一个娃把一块小黑板放到他胸前的被单上，这最后一个月，他就是这样把课讲下来的。他用软弱无力的手接过娃递过来的半截粉笔，吃力地把粉笔头放到黑板上，这时又一阵剧痛袭来，手颤抖了几下，粉笔嗒嗒地在黑板上敲出了几个白点儿。从省城回来后，他再也没去过医院。两个月后，他的肝部疼了起来，他知道癌细胞已转移到那儿了，这种疼痛越来越厉害，最后变成了压倒一切的痛苦。他一只手在枕头下摸索着，找出了一些止痛片，是最常见的用塑料长条包装的那种。对于癌症晚期的剧疼，这药已经没有任何作用，可能是由于精神暗示，他吃了后总觉得好一些。杜冷丁倒也不算贵，但医院不让带出来用，就是带回来也没人给他注射。他像往常一样从塑料条上取下两片药来，但想了想，便把所有剩下的十二片全剥出来，一把吞了下去，他知道以后再也用不着了。他又挣扎着想在黑板上写字，但头突然偏向一边，一个娃赶紧把盆接到他嘴边，他吐出了一口黑红的血，然后虚弱地靠在枕头上喘息着。

娃们中传出了低低的抽泣声。

他放弃了在黑板上写字的努力，无力地挥了一下手，让一个娃把黑板拿走。他开始说话，声音如游丝一般。

"今天的课同前两天一样，也是初中的课。这本来不是教学大纲上要求的，我是想到，你们中的大部分人，这一辈子永远也听不到初中的课了，所以我最后讲一讲，也让你们知道稍深一些的学问是什么样子。昨天讲了鲁迅的《狂人日记》，你们肯定不大懂，不管懂不懂都要多看几遍，最好能背下来，等长大了，总会懂的。鲁迅是个很了不起的人，他的书每一个中国人都应该读读的，你们将来也一定要找来读读。"

他累了，停下来喘息着歇歇，看着跳动的烛光，鲁迅写下的几段文字在他的脑海中浮现出来。那不是《狂人日记》中的，课本上没有，他是从自己那套本数不全已经翻烂的《鲁迅全集》

上读到的，许多年前读第一遍时，那些文字就深深地刻在他脑子里。

"假如一间铁屋子，是绝无窗户而万难破毁的，里面有许多熟睡的人，不久都要闷死了，然而是从昏睡入死灭，并不感到就死的悲哀。现在你大嚷起来，惊起了较为清醒的几个人，使这不幸的少数者来受无可挽救的临终的苦楚，你倒以为对得起他们吗？"

"然而几个人既然起来，你不能说绝没有毁坏这铁屋的希望。"

他用尽最后的力气，接着讲下去。

"今天我们讲初中物理。物理你们以前可能没有听说过，它讲的是物质世界的道理，是一门很深很深的学问。

"这节课讲牛顿三大定律。牛顿是从前的一个英国大科学家，他说了三句话，这三句话很神的，把人间、天上所有的东西的规律都包括进去了，上到太阳、月亮，下到流水、刮风，都跑不出这三句话划定的圈圈。用这三句话，可以算出什么时候日食，就是村里老人说的天狗吃太阳，一分一秒都不差的。人飞上月球，也要靠这三句话。这就是牛顿三大定律。

"下面讲第一定律：当一个物体没有受到外力作用时，它将保持静止或匀速直线运动不变。"

娃们在烛光中默默地看着他，没有反应。

"就是说，你猛推一下谷场上那个石碾子，它就一直滚下去，滚到天边也不停下来。宝柱，你笑什么？是啊，它当然不会那样，这是因为有摩擦力，摩擦力让它停下来，这世界上，没有摩擦力的环境可是没有的……"

是啊，他人生的摩擦力就太大了。在村里他是外姓人，本来就没什么分量，加上他这个倔脾气，这些年来把全村人都得罪下了。他挨家挨户拉人家的娃入学，跑到县里，把跟着爹做买卖的娃拉回来上学，拍着胸脯保证垫学费……这一切并没有赢得多少感激。关键在于，他对过日子的看法同周围人太不一样，成天想的说的，都是些不着边际的事，这是最让人讨厌的。在他查出病来之前，他曾跑到县里，居然从教育局跑回一笔维修学校的款子，村子里只拿出了一小部分，想过节请个戏班子唱两天戏，结果让他搅了。他愣从县里拉过个副县长来，让村里把钱拿回来，可当时戏台子都搭好了。学校倒是修了，但他扫了全村人的兴，以后的日子更难过。先是村里的电工——村长的侄子把学校的电掐了，接着做饭取暖用的秸秆村里也不给了，害得他扔下自个的地，一人上山打柴，更别提后来拆校舍的房椽子那事了……这些摩擦力无所不在，让他心力交瘁，让他无法做匀速直线运动，他不得不停下来了。

也许，他就要去的那个世界是没有摩擦力的，那里的一切都是光滑可爱的，但那有什么意义？在那边，他的心仍留在这个充满灰尘和摩擦力的世界上，留在这所他倾注了全部生命的乡村小学里。他不在了以后，剩下的两个教师也会离去，这所他用力推了一辈子的小学校就会像谷场上那个石碾子一样停下来。他陷入了深深的悲哀，但不论在这个世界还是那个世界，他都无力回天。

"牛顿第二定律比较难懂，我们最后讲，下面先讲牛顿第三定律：当一个物体对第二个物体施加一个力，这第二个物体也会对第一个物体施加一个力，这两个力大小相等，方向相反。"

娃们又陷入了长时间的沉默。

"听懂了没？谁说说？"

班上学习最好的赵拉宝说："我知道是啥意思，可总觉得说不通：晌午我和李权贵打架，他把我的脸打得那么痛，肿起来了，所以作用力不相等的，我受的肯定比他大嘛！"

喘息了好一会儿，他才解释说："你痛是因为你的腮帮子比权贵的拳头软，它们相互的作用力还是相等的……"

他想用手比画一下，但手已抬不起来了，他感到四肢像铁块一样沉，这沉重感很快扩展到全身，他感到自己的躯体像要压塌床板，陷入地下似的。

时间不多了。

"目标编号：1033715；绝对目视星等：3.5；演化阶段：主星序偏上，发现两颗行星，平均轨道半径分别为 1.3 和 4.7 个距离单位，在一号行星上发现生命。这是红 69012 舰报告。"

碳基联邦星际舰队的 10 万艘战舰目前已散布在一条长 1 万光年的带状区域中，这就是正在建立的隔离带。工程刚刚开始，只是试验性地摧毁了 5000 颗恒星，其中带有行星的只有 137 颗，而行星上有生命的这是第一颗。

"第一旋臂真是个荒凉的地方啊。"最高执政官感叹道。他的智能场振动了一下，用全息图隐去了脚下的旗舰和上方的星空，使他、舰队统帅和参议员悬浮于无际的黑色虚空中。接着，他调出了探测器发回的图像：虚空出现了一个发着蓝光的火球。最高执政官的智能场产生了一个白色的方框，那方框调整大小，圈住了这颗恒星并把它的图像隐去了，于是他们又陷入无边的黑暗之中。但这黑暗中有一个小小的黄色光点，图像的焦距开始大幅度调整，行星的图像以令人目眩的速度推向前来，很快占满了半个虚空，三个人都沉浸在它反射的橙黄色光芒中。

这是一颗被浓密大气包裹着的行星，在它那橙黄色的气体海洋上，汹涌的大气运动描绘出了极端复杂的不断变幻的线条。行星图像继续移向前来，直到占据了整个宇宙，三个人被橙黄色的气体海洋吞没了。探测器带着他们在这浓雾中穿行，很快雾气稀薄了一些，他们看到了这颗行星上的生命。

那是一群在浓密大气上层飘浮的气球状生物，表面有着美丽的花纹，那花纹不停地在变幻着色彩和形状，时而呈条纹状，时而呈斑点状，不知这是不是一种可视语言。每个气球都有一条长尾，那长尾的尾端不时炫目地闪烁一下，光沿着长尾传到气球上，化为一片弥漫的荧光。

"开始四维扫描！"红69012舰上的一名上尉值勤军官说。

一束极细的波开始从上至下飞快地扫描那群气球。这束波只有几个原子粗细，但它的波管内的空间维度比外部宇宙多一维。扫描数据传回舰上，在主计算机的内存中，那群气球被切成了几亿亿个薄片，每个薄片的厚度只有一个原子那么大，在这个薄片上，每个夸克的状态都被精确地记录下来。

"开始数据镜像组合！"

主计算机的内存中，那几亿亿个薄片按原有顺序叠加起来，很快，组合成一群虚拟气球。在计算机内部广漠的数字宇宙中，这个行星上的那群生物体有了精确的复制品。

"开始 3C 级文明测试！"

在数字宇宙中，计算机敏锐地定位了气球的思维器官，它是悬在气球内部错综复杂的神经丛中间的一个椭圆体。计算机在瞬间分析了这个大脑的结构，并越过所有低级感官，直接同它建立了高速信息接口。

文明测试是从一个庞大的数据库中任意地选取试题，测试对象如果能答对其中三道，则测试通过；如果头三道题没有答对，测试者有两种选择：可以认为测试没有通过，或者继续测试——题数不限，直到被测试者答对的题数达到三道，这时可认为其通过测试。

"3C 文明测试试题 1 号：请叙述你们已探知的组成物质的最小单元。"

"嘀嘀，嘟嘟嘟，嘀嘀嘀嘀。"气球回答。

"1 号试题测试未通过。3C 文明测试试题 2 号：你们观察到物体中热能的流向有什么特点？这种流向是否可逆？"

"嘟嘟嘟，嘀嘀，嘀嘀嘟嘟。"气球回答。

"2 号试题测试未通过。3C 文明测试试题 3 号：圆的周长和它的直径之比是多少？"

"嘀嘀嘀嘀嘟嘟嘟嘟嘟。"气球回答。

"3 号试题测试未通过。3C 文明测试试题 4 号……"

"到此为止吧，"当测试题数达到十道时，最高执政官说，"我们时间不多。"他转身对旁边的舰队统帅示意了一下。

"发射奇点炸弹！"舰队统帅命令。

奇点炸弹实际上是没有大小的，它是一个严格意义上的几何点，一个原子同它相比都是无穷大。虽然最大的奇点炸弹质量有上百亿吨，最小的也有几千万吨，但当一颗奇点炸弹沿着长长的导轨从红 69012 舰的武器舱中滑出时，却可以看到一个直径达几百米的发着幽幽荧光的球体，这荧光是周围的太空尘埃被吸入这个微型黑洞时产生的辐射。同那些恒星引力坍缩形成的黑洞不同，这些小黑洞在宇宙创世之初就形成了，它们是大爆炸前的奇点宇宙的微缩模型。碳基联邦和硅基帝国都有庞大的船队，它们游弋在银河系银道面外的黑暗荒漠搜集这些微型黑洞，一些海洋行星上的种群把它们戏称为"远洋捕鱼船队"。而这些船队带回的东西，是银河系中最具威慑力的武器之一，是迄今为止唯一能够摧毁恒星的武器。

奇点炸弹脱离导轨后，沿一条由母舰发出的力场束加速，直奔目标恒星。过了不长的一段时间，这个灰尘似的黑洞高速射入了恒星表面火的海洋。想象在太平洋的中部突然出现一个半径 100 千米的深井，就可以大概把握这时的情形。巨量的恒星物质开始被吸入黑洞，那汹涌的物质洪流从所有方向汇聚到一点并消失在那里，物质被吸入时产生的辐射在恒星表面产生一个刺目的光团，仿佛恒星戴上了一个光彩夺目的钻石戒指。随着黑洞向恒星内部沉下去，光团暗淡下来，可以看到它处于一个直径达几百万千米的大旋涡正中，那巨大的旋涡散射着光团的强光，缓缓转动着，呈现出飞速变幻的色彩，使恒星从这个方向看去仿佛是一张狰狞的巨脸。很快，光团消失了，旋涡渐渐消失，恒星表面似乎又恢复了它原来的色彩和光度。但这只是毁灭前最后的平静，随着黑洞向恒星中心下沉，这个贪婪的饕餮者更疯狂地吞食着周围密度急剧增高的物质，它在一秒钟内吸入的恒星物质总量可能相当于上百个中等行星。黑洞巨量吸入时产生的超强辐射向恒星表面蔓延，由于恒星物质的阻滞，只有一小部分到达了表面，但其余的辐射把它们的能量留在了恒星内部。这能量快速破坏着恒星的每一个细胞，从整体上把它飞快地拉离平衡态。从外部来看，恒星的色彩在缓缓变化，由浅红色变为明黄色，从明黄色变为鲜艳的绿色，从绿色变为如洗的碧蓝，从碧蓝变为恐怖的紫色。这时，在恒星中心的黑洞产生的辐射能量已远远大于恒星本身辐射的能量，随着更多的能量以非可见光形式溢出恒星，这紫色在不断加深，这颗恒星看上去像太空中一个在忍受着超级痛苦的灵魂，这痛苦在急剧增大，紫色已深到了极限，这颗恒星用了不到一个小时的时间走完了它未来几十亿年的旅程。

一团似乎吞没整个宇宙的强光闪起，然后慢慢消失，在原来恒星所在的位置上，可以看到一个急剧膨胀的薄球层，像一个被吹大的气球，这是被炸飞的恒星表面。随着薄球层体积的增大，它变得透明了，可以看到它内部的第二个膨胀的薄球层，然后又可以看到更深处的第三个薄球层……这个爆炸中的恒星，就像宇宙中突然显现的一个套一个的一组玲珑剔透的镂花玻璃球，其中最深处的一个薄球层的体积也是恒星原来体积的几十万倍。当爆炸的恒星的第一层膨胀外壳穿过那个橙黄色行星时，它立刻被汽化了。其实在这整个爆炸的壮丽场景中根本就看不到它，同那膨胀的恒星外壳相比，它只是一粒微不足道的灰尘，其大小甚至不能成为那几层镂花玻璃球上的一个小点。

"你们感到消沉？"舰队统帅问，他看到最高执政官和参议员的智能场暗下来了。

"又一个生命世界毁灭了，像烈日下的露珠。"

"那您就想想伟大的第二旋臂战役，当两千多颗超新星被引爆时，有 12 万个这样的世界同碳硅双方的舰队一起化为蒸汽。阁下，时至今日，我们应该超越这种无谓的多愁善感了。"

参议员没有理会舰队统帅的话，他对最高执政官说："这种对行星表面取随机点的检测方式是不可靠的，可能漏掉行星表面的文明特征，我们应该进行面积检测。"

最高执政官说："这一点我也同议会讨论过，在隔离带中我们要摧毁的恒星有上亿颗，这其中估计有 1000 万个行星系，行星数量可能达 5000 万颗，我们时间紧迫，对每颗行星都进行面积检测是不现实的。我们只能尽量加宽检测波束，以增大随机点覆盖的面积，除此之外，只能祈祷隔离带中那些可能存在的文明在其星球表面的分布尽量均匀了。"

"下面我们讲牛顿第二定律……"

他心急如焚，极力想在有限的时间里给娃们多讲一些。

"一个物体的加速度，与它所受的力成正比，与它的质量成反比。首先，加速度，这是速度随时间的变化率，它与速度是不同的。速度大，加速度不一定大；加速度大，速度也不一定大。比如，一个物体现在的速度是 110 米每秒，两秒后的速度是 120 米每秒，那么它的加速度就是 120 减 110 除以 2，即 5 米每秒。呵，不对，5 米每秒的平方。另一个物体现在的速度是 10 米每秒，两秒后的速度是 30 米每秒，那么它的加速度就是 30 减 10 除以 2，即 10 米每秒的平方。看，后面这个物体虽然速度小，但加速度大！呵，刚才说到平方，平方就是一个数自个儿乘自个儿……"

他惊奇自己的头脑如此清晰，思维如此敏捷。他知道，自己生命的蜡烛已燃到根上，棉芯倒下了，把最后的一小块蜡全部引燃了，一团比以前的烛苗亮 10 倍的火焰熊熊燃烧起来。剧痛消失了，身体也不再沉重，其实他已感觉不到身体的存在，他的全部生命似乎只剩下那个在疯狂运行的大脑，那个悬在空中的大脑竭尽全力，尽量多尽量快地把自己存储的信息输出给周围的娃们。但说话是个该死的"瓶颈"，他知道来不及了。他产生了一个幻象：一把水晶样的斧子把自己的大脑无声地劈开，他一生中积累的那些知识，虽不是很多但他很看重，像一把发光的小珠子毫无保留地落在地上，发出一阵悦耳的叮当声。娃们像见到过年的糖果一样抢那些小珠子，抢了摆成一堆……这幻象让他有一种幸福的感觉。

"你们听懂了没？"他焦急地问，他的眼睛已经看不到周围的娃们，但还能听到他们的声音。

"我们懂了！老师快歇着吧！"

他感觉到那团最后的火焰在弱下去："我知道你们不懂，但你们把它背下来，以后慢慢会懂的。一个物体的加速度，与它所受的力成正比，与它的质量成反比。"

"老师，我们真懂了，求求你快歇着吧！"

他用尽最后的力气喊道："背呀！"

娃们抽泣着背了起来："一个物体的加速度，与它所受的力成正比，与它的质量成反比。一个物体的加速度，与它所受的力成正比，与它的质量成反比……"

这几百年前就在欧洲化为尘土的卓越头脑产生的思想，以浓重西北方言的童音在 20 世纪中国最偏僻的山村中回荡，就在这声音中，那烛苗灭了。

娃们围着老师已没有生命的躯体大哭起来。

"目标编号：500921473；绝对目视星等：4.71；演化阶段：主星序正中，带有九颗行星。这是蓝84210号舰报告。"

"一个精致完美的行星系。"舰队统帅赞叹。

最高执政官很有同感："是的，它的固态小体积行星和气液态大体积行星的配置很有韵律感，小行星带的位置恰到好处，像一条美妙的装饰链。还有最外侧那颗小小的甲烷冰行星，似乎是这首音乐最后一个余音未尽的音符，暗示着某种新周期的开始。"

"这是蓝84210号舰，将对最内侧1号行星进行生命检测，检测波束发射。该行星没有大气，自转缓慢，温差悬殊。1号随机点检测，白色结果；2号随机点检测，白色结果……10号随机点检测，白色结果。蓝84210号舰报告，该行星没有生命。"

舰队统帅不以为意地说："这颗行星的表面温度可以当冶炼炉了，没必要浪费时间。"

"开始2号行星生命检测，波束发射。该行星有稠密大气，表面温度较高且均匀，大部为酸性云层覆盖。1号随机点检测，白色结果；2号随机点检测，白色结果……10号随机点检测，白色结果。蓝84210号舰报告，该行星没有生命。"

通过四维通信，最高执政官对1000光年之外蓝84210号舰上的值勤军官说："直觉告诉我，3号行星有生命的可能性很大，在它上面检测30个随机点。"

"阁下，我们时间很紧了。"舰队统帅说。

"照我说的做。"最高执政官坚定地说。

"是，阁下。开始3号行星生命检测，波束发射。该行星有中等密度的大气，表面大部为海洋覆盖……"

来自太空的生命检测波束落到了亚洲大陆靠南一些的一点上，波束在地面上形成了一个直径约 5 千米的圆形。如果是在白天，用肉眼有可能觉察到波束的存在，因为当波束到达时，在它的覆盖范围内，一切无生命的物体都将变成透明状态。现在它覆盖的中国西北的这片山区，那些黄土山在观察者的眼里将如同水晶的山脉，阳光在这些山脉中折射，将是一幅十分奇异壮观的景象。观察者还会看到脚下的大地也变成深不可测的深渊，而被波束判断为有生命的物体则保持原状态不变，人、树木和草在这水晶世界中显得格外清晰醒目。但这效应只持续半秒钟，这期间检测波束完成初始化，之后一切恢复原状。观察者肯定会认为自己产生了一瞬间的幻觉。而现在，这里正是深夜，自然难以觉察到什么了。

　　这所山村小学，正好位于检测波束圆形覆盖区的圆心上。

　　"1 号随机点检测，结果……绿色结果，绿色结果！蓝 84210 号舰报告，目标编号：500921473，第 3 号行星发现生命！"

　　检测波束对覆盖范围内的众多种类生命体进行分类，在以生命结构的复杂度和初步估计的智能等级进行排序的数据库中，在一个方形掩蔽物下的那一簇生命体排在首位。于是波束迅速收缩，汇聚到那个掩蔽物上。

　　最高执政官的智能场接收到从蓝 84210 号舰上发回的图像，并把它放大到整个太空背景上，那所山村小学的影像在瞬间占据了整个宇宙。图像处理系统已经隐去了掩蔽物，但那簇生命体的图像仍不清晰，这些生命体的外形太不醒目了，几乎同周围行星表面的以硅元素为主的黄色土壤融为一体。计算机只好把图像中所有的无生命部分，包括这些生命体中间的那具体形状较大的已没有生命的躯体，全部隐去，这样那一簇生命体就仿佛悬浮在虚空之中。即使如此，他们看上去仍是那么平淡和缺乏色彩，像一簇黄色的植物，一看就知是那种在他们身上不会发生任何奇迹的生物。

一束纤细的四维波束从蓝84210号舰发射而出，这艘有一个月球大小的星际战舰正停泊在木星轨道之外，使太阳系暂时多了一颗行星。那束四维波束在三维太空中以接近无限的速度到达84210那所乡村小学校舍的屋顶，以基本粒子的精度对这18个孩子进行扫描。数据的洪流以人类难以想象的速率传回太空，很快，在蓝84210号舰主计算机那比宇宙更广阔的内存中，孩子们的数字复制体形成了。

18个孩子悬浮在一个无际的空间里，那空间呈一种无法形容的色彩，实际上那不是色彩，虚无是没有色彩的，虚无是透明中的透明。孩子们都不由得想拉住旁边的伙伴，他们看上去很正常，但手从他们身体里毫无阻力地穿过去了。孩子们感到了难以形容的恐惧。计算机觉察到了这一点，它认为这些生命体需要一些熟悉的东西，于是在自己的内存宇宙的这一部分模拟这个行星天空的颜色。孩子们立刻看到了蓝天，没有太阳没有云更没有浮尘，只有蓝色，那么纯净，那么深邃。孩子们的脚下没有大地，也是与头顶一样的蓝天，他们似乎置身于一个无限的蓝色宇宙中，而他们是这宇宙中唯一的实体。计算机感觉到，这些数字生命体仍然处于惊恐中，它用了亿分之一秒想了想，终于明白了：银河系中大多数生命体并不惧怕悬浮于虚空之中，但这些生命体不同，他们是大地上的生物。于是它给了孩子们一个大地，并给了他们重力感。孩子们惊奇地看着脚下突然出现的大地，它是纯白色的，上面有黑线画出的整齐方格，他们仿佛站在一个无限广阔的语文作业本上。他们中有人蹲下来摸摸地面，这是他们见过的最光滑的东西，他们迈开双脚走，但原地不动，这地面是绝对光滑的，摩擦力为零，他们很惊奇自己为什么不会滑倒。这时有个孩子脱下自己的一只鞋子，沿着地面扔出去，那鞋子以匀速直线向前运行滑去，孩子们呆呆地看着它以恒定的速度渐渐远去。

他们看到了牛顿第一定律。

有一个声音空灵而悠扬，在这数字宇宙中回荡。

"开始3C级文明测试，3C文明测试试题1号：请叙述你所在星球生物进化的基本原理，是自然淘汰型还是基因突变型？"

孩子们茫然地沉默着。

"3C文明测试试题2号：请简要说明恒星能量的来源。"

孩子们茫然地沉默着。

……

"3C文明测试试题10号：请说明构成你们星球上海洋的液体的分子构成。"

孩子们仍然茫然地沉默着。

那只鞋在遥远的地平线处变成一个小黑点消失了。

"到此为止吧！"在1000光年之外，舰队统帅对最高执政官说，"不能再耽误时间了，否则我们肯定不能按时完成第一阶段的任务。"

最高执政官的智能场发出了微弱的表示同意的震动。

"发射奇点炸弹！"

载有命令信息的波束越过四维空间，瞬间到达了停泊在太阳系中的蓝84210号舰。那个发着幽幽荧光的雾球滑出了战舰前方长长的导轨，沿着看不见的力场束急剧加速，向太阳扑去。

最高执政官、参议员和舰队统帅把注意力转向了隔离带的其他区域，那里又发现了几个有生命的行星系，但其中最高级的生命是一种生活在泥浆中的无脑蠕虫。接连爆炸的恒星像宇宙中怒放的焰火，使他们想起了史诗般的第二旋臂战役。

不知过了多长时间，最高执政官智能场的一小部分下意识地游移到太阳系，他听到了蓝84210号舰舰长的声音：

"准备脱离爆炸威力圈，时空跃迁准备，30秒倒数！"

"等一下，奇点炸弹到达目标还需多长时间？"最高执政官问。舰队统帅和参议员的注意力也被吸引过来。

"它正越过内侧1号行星的轨道，大约还有10分钟。"

"用5分钟时间，再进行一些测试吧。"

"是，阁下。"

接着听到了蓝84210号舰值勤军官的声音："3C文明测试试题11号：一个三维平面上的直角三角形，它的三条边的关系是什么？"

沉默。

"3C文明测试试题12号：你们的星球是你们行星系的第几颗行星？"

沉默。

"这没有意义，阁下。"舰队统帅说。

"3C文明测试试题13号：当一个物体没有受到外力作用时，它的运行状态如何？"

数字宇宙广漠的蓝色空间中突然响起了孩子们清脆的声音：

"当一个物体没有受到外力作用时，它将保持静止或匀速直线运动不变。"

"3C 文明测试试题 13 号通过！3C 文明测试试题 14 号……"

"等等！"参议员打断了值勤军官，"下一道试题也出关于甚低速力学基本近似定律的。"他又问最高执政官，"这不违反测试准则吧？"

"当然不，只要是测试数据库中的试题都可以。"舰队统帅代为回答，这些令他大感意外的生命体把他的注意力全部吸引过来了。

"3C 文明测试试题 14 号：请叙述相互作用的两个物体间力的关系。"

孩子们说："当一个物体对第二个物体施加一个力，这第二个物体也会对第一个物体施加一个力，这两个力大小相等，方向相反！"

"3C 文明测试试题 14 号通过！3C 文明测试试题 15 号：对于一个物体，请说明它的质量、所受外力和加速度之间的关系。"

孩子们齐声说："一个物体的加速度，与它所受的力成正比，与它的质量成反比！"

"3C 文明测试试题 15 号通过，文明测试通过！确定目标恒星500921473 的 3 号行星上存在 3C 级文明。"

"奇点炸弹转向！脱离目标！！！"最高执政官的智能场急剧闪动着，用最大的能量把命令通过超空间传送到蓝 84210 号舰上。

在太阳系，推送奇点炸弹的力场束弯曲了，这根长几亿千米的力场束此时像一根弓起的长杆，努力把奇点炸弹挑离射向太阳的轨道。蓝84210号舰上的力场发动机以最大功率工作，巨大的散热片由暗红变为耀眼的白炽色。力场束向外的推力分量开始显示出效果，奇点炸弹的轨道开始弯曲，但它已越过水星轨道，距太阳太近了，谁也不知道这努力是否能成功。通过超空间直播，全银河系都在盯着那个模糊的雾团的轨迹，并看到它的亮度急剧增大。这是一个可怕的迹象，说明炸弹已能感受到太阳外围空间粒子密度的增大。舰长的手已放到了那个红色的时空跃迁启动按钮上，以在奇点炸弹击中太阳前的一刹那脱离这个空间。但奇点炸弹最终像一颗子弹一样擦过太阳的边缘，当它以仅几万米的高度掠过太阳表面上空时，由于黑洞吸入太阳大气中大量的物质，亮度增到最大，使得太阳边缘出现了一个刺眼的蓝白色光球，在这一刻看上去像一个紧密的双星系统，这奇观对人类将一直是个难解的谜。蓝白色光球飞速掠过时，下面太阳浩瀚的火海黯然失色。像一艘快艇掠过平静的水面，黑洞的引力在太阳表面划出了一道V形的划痕，这划痕扩展到太阳的整个半球才消失。奇点炸弹撞断了一条日珥，这条从太阳表面升起的百万千米长的美丽轻纱在高速冲击下，碎成一群欢快舞蹈着的小小的等离子体旋涡……奇点炸弹掠过太阳后，亮度很快暗下来，最后消失在茫茫太空的永恒之夜中。

"我们险些毁灭了一个碳基文明。"参议员长出一口气说。

"真是不可思议，在这么荒凉的地方竟会存在3C级文明！"舰队统帅感叹说。

"是啊，无论是碳基联邦，还是硅基帝国，其文明扩展和培植计划都不包括这一区域，如果这是一个自己进化的文明，那可是一件很不寻常的事。"最高执政官说。

"蓝84210号舰，你们继续留在那个行星系，对3号行星进行全表面文明检测，你舰之前的任务将由其他舰只接替。"舰队司令命令道。

同他们在木星轨道之外的数字复制品不一样，山村小学中的那些娃丝毫没有觉察到什么，在那间校舍里的烛光下，他们只是围着老师的遗体哭啊哭。不知哭了多长时间，娃们最后安静下来。

"咱们去村里告诉大人吧。"郭翠花抽泣着说。

"那又咋的？"刘宝柱低着头说，"老师活着时村里的人都腻歪他，这会儿肯定连棺材钱都没人给他出呢！"

最后，娃们决定自己掩埋老师。他们拿了锄头、铁锹，在学校旁边的山地上开始挖墓坑，灿烂的群星在整个宇宙中静静地看着他们。

"天啊！这颗行星上的文明不是3C级，是5B级！！！"看着蓝84210号舰从1000光年之外发回的检测报告，参议员惊呼起来。

人类城市的摩天大楼群的影像在旗舰上方的太空中显现。

"他们已经开始使用核能，并用化学推进方式进入太空，甚至已登上了他们所在行星的卫星。"

"他们基本特征是什么？"舰队统帅问。

"您想知道哪些方面？"蓝84210号上的值勤军官问。

"比如，这个行星上生命体记忆遗传的等级是多少？"

"他们没有记忆遗传，所有记忆都是后天取得的。"

"那么，他们的个体相互之间的信息交流方式是什么？"

"极其原始，也十分罕见。他们身体内有一种很薄的器官，这种器官在这个行星以氧氮为主的大气中振动时可产生声波，同时把要传输的信息调制到声波之中，接收方也用一种薄膜器官从声波中接收信息。"

"这种方式下信息传输的速率是多大？"

"大约每秒 1 比特至 10 比特。"

"什么？！"旗舰上听到这话的所有人都大笑起来。

"真的是每秒 1 比特至 10 比特，我们开始也不相信，但反复核实过。"

"上尉，你是个白痴吗？！"舰队统帅大怒，"你是想告诉我们，一种没有记忆遗传，相互间用声波进行信息交流，并且是以令人难以置信的每秒 1 比特至 10 比特的速率进行交流的物种，能创造出 5B 级文明？！而且这种文明是在没有任何外部高级文明培植的情况下自行进化的？！"

"但，阁下，确实如此。"

"但在这种状态下，这个物种根本不可能在每代之间积累和传递知识，而这是文明进化所必需的！"

"他们有一种个体，有一定数量，分布于这个种群的各个角落，这类个体充当两代生命体之间知识传递的媒介。"

"听起来像神话。"

"不，"参议员说，"在银河文明的太古时代，确实有过这个概念，但即使在那时也极其罕见，除了我们这些星系文明进化史的专业研究者，很少有人知道。"

"你是说那种在两代生命体之间传递知识的个体？"

"他们叫教师。"

"教——师？"

"一个早已消失的太古文明词汇，很生僻，在一般的古词汇数据库中都查不到。"

这时，从太阳系发回的全息影像焦距拉长，显示出蔚蓝色的地球在太空中缓缓转动的画面。

最高执政官说："在银河系联邦时代，独立进化的文明十分罕见，能进化到5B级的更是绝无仅有。我们应该让这个文明继续不受干扰地进化下去，对它的观察和研究，不仅有助于我们对太古文明的研究，对今天的银河文明也有启示。"

"那就让蓝84210号舰立刻离开那个行星系吧，并把这颗行星周围100光年的范围列为禁航区。"舰队统帅说道。

北半球失眠的人，会看到星空突然微微抖动，那抖动从空中的一点发出，呈圆形向整个星空扩展，仿佛星空是一汪静水，有人用手指在水中央点了一下似的。

蓝84210号舰跃迁时产生的时空激波到达地球时已大大衰减，只使地球上所有的时钟都快了3秒，但在三维空间中的人类是不可能觉察到这一效应的。

"很遗憾，"最高执政官说，"如果没有高级文明的培植，他们还要在亚光速和三维时空中被禁锢2000年，至少还需1000年的时间才能掌握和使用湮灭能量，2000年后才能通过多维时空进行通信；至于通过超空间跃迁进行宇宙航行，可能是5000年后的事了；至少要10000年，他们才具备加入银河系碳基文明大家庭的起码条件。"

参议员说："文明的这种孤独进化，是银河系太古时代才有的事。如果那古老的记载正确，我那太古的祖先生活在一个海洋行星的深海中。在那黑暗世界中的无数个王朝后，一个庞大的探险计划开始了，他们发射了第一个外空飞船，那是一个透明的浮力小球，经过漫长的路程浮上海面。当时正是深夜，小球中的先祖第一次看到了星空……你们能够想象，那对他们来说是怎样的壮丽和神秘啊！"

最高执政官说："那是一个让人向往的时代，一粒灰尘样的行星对先祖都是一个无限广阔的世界，在那绿色的海洋和紫色的草原上，先祖敬畏地面对群星……这感觉我们已丢失千万年了。"

"可我现在又找回了它！"参议员指着地球的影像说，它那蓝色的晶莹球体上浮动着雪白的云纹，他觉得它真像一颗来自他祖先星球海洋中的一种美丽的珍珠，"看这个小小的世界，它上面的生命体在过着自己的生活，做着自己的梦，对我们的存在、对银河系中的战争和毁灭全然不知。宇宙对他们来说，是希望和梦想的无限源泉，这真像一首来自太古时代的歌谣。"

他真的吟唱了起来，他们三人的智能场合为一体，荡漾着玫瑰色的波纹。那从遥远得无法想象的太古时代传下来的歌谣听起来悠远、神秘、苍凉，通过超空间，传遍了整个银河系。在这团由上千亿颗恒星组成的星云中，数不清的生命感到了一种消失已久的温馨和宁静。

"宇宙的最不可理解之处在于它是可以理解的。"最高执政官说。

"宇宙的最可理解之处在于它是不可理解的。"参议员说。

当娃们造好那座新坟时，东方已经发亮了。老师是放在从教室拆下来的一块门板上下葬的，陪他入土的是两盒粉笔和一套已翻破的小学课本。娃们在那个小小的坟头上立了一块石板，上面用粉笔写着"李老师之墓"。

　　只要一场雨，石板上那稚拙的字迹就会消失；用不了多长时间，这座坟和长眠在里面的人就会被外面的世界忘得干干净净。

　　太阳从山后露出一角，把一抹金辉投进仍沉睡着的山村；在仍处于阴影中的山谷草地上，露珠在闪着晶莹的光，可听到一两声怯生生的鸟鸣。

　　娃们沿着小路向村里走去，那一群小小的身影很快消失在山谷中淡蓝色的晨雾中。

　　他们将活下去，在这块古老贫瘠的土地上，收获虽然微薄但确实存在的希望。

中国太阳 SUN
OF
CHINA

水娃从娘颤巍巍的手中接过那个小小的包裹，包裹中有娘做的一双厚底布鞋、三个馍、两件打了大块补丁的衣裳、二十块钱。爹蹲在路边，闷闷地抽着旱烟锅。

　　"娃要出门了，你就不能给个好脸？"娘对爹说，爹仍蹲在那儿，还是闷闷地一声不吭，娘又说，"不让娃出去，你能出钱给他盖房娶媳妇啊？！"

　　"走！东一个西一个都走球了，养他们还不如养窝狗！"爹干号着说，头也不抬。

　　水娃抬头看看自己出生和长大的村庄，这个处于永恒干旱中的村庄，只靠着水窖中积下的一点儿雨水过活。水娃家没钱修水泥窖，还是用的土水窖，那水一到大热天就臭了。往年，这臭水烧开了还能喝，就是苦点儿、涩点儿，但今年夏天，那水烧开了喝都拉肚子。听附近部队上的医生说，是地里什么有毒的石头溶进水里了。

水娃又低头看了爹一眼，转身走去，没有再回头。他不指望爹抬头看他一眼，爹心里难受时就那么蹲着抽闷烟，一蹲能蹲几个小时，仿佛变成了黄土地上的一大块土坷垃。但他分明又看到了爹的脸，或者说，他就走在爹的脸上，看周围这广阔的西北土地，干干的黄褐色，布满了水土流失刻出的裂纹，不就是一张老农的脸吗？这里的什么都是这样，树、地、房子、人，黑黄黑黄，皱巴巴的。他看不到这张伸向天边的巨脸的眼睛，但能感觉到它的存在，那双巨眼在望着天空，年轻时那目光充满着对雨的企盼，年老时就只剩呆滞了。其实这张巨脸一直是呆滞的，他不相信这块土地还有过年轻的时候。

一阵干风吹过，前面这条出村的小路湮没于黄尘中，水娃沿着这条路走去，迈出了他新生活的第一步。

这条路，将通向一个他做梦都想不到的地方。

人生第一个目标：喝点不苦的水，挣点钱

"哟，这么些个灯！"

水娃到矿区时天已黑了，这个矿区是由许多私开的小窑煤矿组成的。

"这算啥？城里的灯那才叫多哩！"来接他的国强说，国强也是水娃村里的，出来好多年了。

水娃随国强来到工棚住下，吃饭时喝的水居然是甜丝丝的！国强告诉他，矿上打的是深井，水当然不苦了，但他又加了一句："城里的水才叫好喝呢！"

睡觉时国强递给水娃一包硬邦邦的东西当枕头，打开看，是黑塑料皮包着的一根根圆棒棒，再打开塑料皮，看到那棒棒黄黄的，像肥皂。

"炸药。"国强说，翻身呼呼睡着了。水娃看到他也枕着这东西，床底下还放着一大堆，头顶上吊着一大把雷管。后来水娃知道，这些东西足够把他的村子一窝端了！国强是矿上的放炮工。

矿上的活儿很苦很累，水娃前后干过挖煤、推车、打支柱等活计，每样活计一天下来都把人累得要死。但水娃就是吃苦长大的，他倒不怕活儿重，他怕的是井下那环境，人像钻进了黑黑的蚂蚁窝，开始真像做噩梦，但后来也习惯了。工钱是计件，每月能挣一百五十块，好的时候能挣到二百块出头，水娃觉得很满足了。

但最让水娃满足的还是这里的水。第一天下工后，浑身黑得像块炭，他跟着工友们去洗澡。到了那里后，看到人们用脸盆从一个大池子中舀出水来，从头到脚浇下来，地下流淌着一条条黑色的小溪。当时他就看呆了，妈妈呀，哪有这么用水的，这可都是甜水啊！因为有了甜水，这个黑乎乎的世界在水娃眼中变得美丽无比。

但国强一直鼓动水娃进城，国强以前就在城里打过工，因为偷建筑工地的东西被当作盲流遣送回原籍。他向水娃保证，城里肯定比这里挣得多，也不像这样累死累活的。

就在水娃犹豫不决时，国强在井下出了事。那天他排哑炮时炮炸了，从井下被抬上来时他浑身嵌满了碎石，死前他对水娃说了一句话：

"进城去，那里灯更多……"

人生第二个目标：到灯更多水更甜的城里，挣更多的钱

"这里的夜像白天一样呀！"

水娃惊叹道，国强说得没错，城里的灯真是多多了。现在，他正同二宝一起，一人背着一个擦鞋箱，沿着省会城市的主要大街向火车站走去。二宝是水娃邻村人，以前曾和国强一起在省城里干过。按照国强以前给的地址，水娃费了好大的劲才找到他，他现在已不在建筑工地干，而是干起擦皮鞋来。水娃找到他时，与他同住的一个同行正好有事回家了，他就简单地教了水娃几下子，然后让水娃背上那套家伙什同他一起去擦皮鞋。

水娃对这活计没有什么信心，他一路上寻思，要是修鞋还差不多，擦鞋？谁花一块钱擦一次鞋（要是鞋油好些得三块），这人准有毛病。但到了火车站前，他们摊还没摆好，生意就来了。这一晚上到 11 点，水娃竟挣了十四块！但在回去的路上二宝一脸晦气，说今天生意不好，言下之意显然是水娃抢了他的买卖。

"窗户下那些大铁箱子是啥？"水娃指着前面的一座楼问。

"空调，那屋里现在跟开春儿似的。"

"城里真好！"水娃抹了一把脸上的汗说。

"在这儿只要吃得了苦，赚碗饭吃是很容易的，但要想成家立业可就没门儿啰。"二宝说着用下巴颏儿指了指那幢楼，"买套房，两三千一平方米呢！"

水娃傻傻地问："平方米是啥？"

二宝轻蔑地晃晃头，不屑理他。

水娃和十几个人住在一间合租的简易房中，这些人大都是进

城打工和做小买卖的农民，但在大通铺上位置紧挨着水娃的却是个城里人，不过不是这座城市的。在这里他和大家都差不多，吃的和他们一样，晚上也是光膀子在外面乘凉。但每天早晨，他都西装革履，走出门去像换了一个人，真给人一种鸡窝里飞出金凤凰的感觉。这人姓庄名宇，大伙倒是都不讨厌他，这主要是因为他带来的一样东西。那东西在水娃看来就是一把大伞，但那伞是用镜子做的，里面光亮亮的，把伞倒放在太阳下，在伞把头上的一个托架上放一锅水，那锅底被照得晃眼，锅里的水很快就开了，水娃后来知道这叫太阳灶。大伙用这东西做饭烧水，省了不少钱，可没太阳时不能用。

这把叫太阳灶的大伞没有伞骨，就那么薄薄的一片。水娃最迷惑的时候就是看庄宇收伞：这伞上伸出一根细细的电线一直通到屋里，收伞时庄宇进屋拔下电线的插头，那伞就扑的一下摊到地上，变成了一块银色的布。水娃拿起布仔细看，它柔软光滑，轻得几乎感觉不到分量，表面映着自己变形的怪相，还变幻着肥皂泡表面的那种彩纹，一松手，银布从指缝间无声地滑落到地上，仿佛是一掬轻盈的水银。当庄宇再插上电源的插头时，银布如同一朵开放的荷花般懒洋洋地伸展开来，很快又变成一个圆圆的伞面倒立在地上。再去摸摸那伞面，薄薄的、硬硬的，轻敲时发出悦耳的金属声响，它强度很高，在地面固定后能撑住一个装满水的锅或壶。

庄宇告诉水娃："这是一种纳米材料，表面光洁，具有很好的反光性，强度很高。最重要的是，它在正常条件下呈柔软状态，但在通入微弱电流后会变得坚硬。"

水娃后来知道，这种叫纳米镜膜的材料是庄宇的一项研究成果。申请专利后，他倾其所有投入资金，想为这项成果打开市场，但包括便携式太阳灶在内的几项产品都无人问津，结果他血本无归，现在竟穷到向水娃借钱交房租。虽落到这地步，但这人一点儿都没有消沉，每天仍东奔西跑，努力为这种新材料的应用找出路。他告诉水娃，这是自己跑过的第十三座城市了。

除了那个太阳灶外，庄宇还有一小片纳米镜膜。平时它就像一块银色的小手帕摊放在床边的桌子上，每天早晨出门前，庄宇总要打开一个小小的电源开关，那块银手帕立刻变成硬硬的一块薄片，成了一面光洁的小镜子，庄宇对着它梳理打扮一番。有一天早晨，他对着小镜子梳头时斜视了刚从床上爬起来的水娃一眼，说："你应该注意仪表，常洗脸，头发别总是乱乱的，还有你这身衣服，不能买件便宜点的新衣服吗？"

水娃拿过镜子来照了照，笑着摇摇头，意思是对一个擦鞋的来说，那么麻烦没有用。

庄宇凑近水娃说："现代社会充满着机遇，满天都飞着金鸟儿，说不定哪天你一伸手就抓住一只，前提是你得拿自己当回事儿。"

水娃四下看了看，没什么金鸟儿，他摇摇头说："我没读过多少书呀。"

"这当然很遗憾，但谁知道呢，有时这说不定是一个优势，这个时代的伟大之处就在于其捉摸不定，谁也不知道奇迹会在谁身上发生。"

"你……上过大学吧？"

"我有固体物理学博士学位，辞职前是大学教授。"

庄宇走后，水娃目瞪口呆了好半天，然后又摇摇头，心想庄宇这样的人跑了十三座城市都抓不到那鸟儿，自己怎么行呢？他感到这家伙是在取笑自己，不过这人本身也够可怜、够可笑的了。

这天夜里，屋里的其他人有的睡了，有的聚在一堆打扑克，水娃和庄宇则到门外几步远的一个小饭馆里看人家的电视。这时已是夜里 12 点，电视中正在播出新闻，屏幕上只有播音员，没有其他画面。

"在今天下午召开的新闻发布会上，新闻发言人透露，举世瞩目的中国太阳工程已正式启动，这是一项改造国土生态的超大型工程……"

水娃以前听说过这项工程，知道它将在我们的天空中再建造一个太阳，这个太阳能给干旱的大西北带来更多的降雨。这事对水娃来说太玄乎，像每次遇到这类事一样，他想问庄宇，但扭头一看，见庄宇睁圆双眼瞪着电视，半张着嘴，好像被它摄去了魂儿。水娃用手在他面前晃了晃，他毫无反应，直到那则新闻过去很久才恢复常态，自语道："真是，我怎么就没想到中国太阳呢？！"

水娃茫然地看着他，他不可能不知道这件连自己都知道的事，这事儿哪个中国人不知道呢？他当然知道，只是没想到，那他现在想到了什么呢？这事与他庄宇，一个住在闷热的简易房中的潦倒流浪者，能有什么关系？

庄宇说："记得我早上说的话吗？现在一只金鸟飞到我面前了，好大的一只金鸟儿，其实它以前一直在我的头顶盘旋，我居然没感觉到！"

水娃仍然迷惑不解地看着他。

庄宇站起身来："我要去北京了，赶2点半的火车，小兄弟，你跟我去吧！"

"去北京？干什么？"

"北京那么大，干什么不行？就是擦皮鞋，也比这儿挣得多好多！"

于是，就在这天夜里，水娃和庄宇踏上了一列连座位都没有的拥挤列车，列车穿过夜色中广阔的西部原野，向太阳升起的方向驰去。

人生第三个目标：到更大的城市，见更大的世面，
挣更多的钱

第一眼看到首都时，水娃明白了一件事：有些东西你只能在看见后才知道是什么样儿，凭想象是绝对想不出来的。比如北京之夜，就在他的想象中出现过无数次，最早不过是把镇子或矿上的灯火扩大许多倍，然后是把省城的灯火扩大许多倍，当他和庄宇乘坐的公共汽车从西站拐入长安街时，他知道，过去那些灯火就是扩大一千倍，也不是北京之夜的样子。当然，北京的灯绝对不会有一千个省城的灯那么多、那么亮，但这夜中北京的某种东西，是那座西部的城市怎样叠加也产生不出来的。

水娃和庄宇在一个便宜的地下室旅馆住了一夜后，第二天早上就分了手。临别时庄宇祝水娃好运，并说如果以后有难处可以找他，但当水娃让他留下电话或地址时，他却说自己现在什么都没有。

"那我怎么找你呢？"水娃问。

"过一阵子，看电视或报纸，你就会知道我在哪儿。"

看着庄宇远去的背影，水娃迷惑地摇摇头，他这话可真是费解：这人现在已一文不名，今天连旅馆都住不起了，早餐还是水娃出的钱，甚至连他那个太阳灶，也在起程前留给房东顶了房费，现在，他已是一个除了梦之外什么都没有的乞丐。

与庄宇分别后，水娃立刻去找活儿干，但大都市给他的震撼使他很快忘记了自己的目的。整个白天，他都在城市中漫无目的地闲逛，仿佛行走在仙境中，一点儿都不觉得累。

傍晚，他站在首都的新象征之一——去年落成的五百米高的统一大厦前，仰望着那直插云端的玻璃墙壁。在上面，渐渐暗下去的晚霞和很快亮起来的城市灯海在进行着摄人心魄的光与影的表演，水娃看得脖子酸疼。当他正要走开时，大厦本身的灯也亮了起来。这奇景以一种更大的力量攫住了水娃的全部身心，他继续在那里仰头呆望着。

"你看了很长时间，对这工作感兴趣？"

水娃回头，看到说话的是一个年轻人，典型的城里人打扮，但手里拿着一顶黄色的安全帽。"什么工作？"水娃迷惑地问。

"那你刚才在看什么？"那人问，同时用拿安全帽的手向上一指。

水娃抬头向他指的方向看，看到高高的玻璃墙壁上居然有几个人，从这里看去只是几个小黑点儿。"他们在那么高的地方干什么呀？"水娃问，又仔细地看了看，"擦玻璃？"

那人点点头："我是蓝天建筑清洁公司的人事主管，我们公司主要承揽高层建筑的清洁工程，你愿意干这个工作吗？"

水娃再次抬头看，高空中那几个蚂蚁似的小黑点让人头晕目眩。"这……太吓人了。"

"如果是担心安全那你尽管放心，这工作看起来危险，正是这点使它招工很难，我们现在很缺人手。但我向你保证，安全措施是很完备的，只要严格按规程操作，绝对不会有危险，且工资在同类行业中是最高的，你嘛，每月工资一千五百元，工作日管午餐，公司代买人身保险。"

这钱数让水娃吃了一惊，他呆呆地望着经理，后者误解了水娃的意思："好吧，取消试用期，再加三百元，每月一千八百元，不能再多了。以前这个工种基本工资只有四五百，每天有活儿干再额外计件儿，现在是固定月薪，相当不错了。"

于是，水娃成了一名高空清洁工，英文名字叫蜘蛛人。

人生第四个目标：成为一个北京人

水娃与四位工友从航天大厦的顶层谨慎地下降，用了四十分钟才到达它的第八十三层，这是他们昨天擦到的位置。蜘蛛人最头疼的活儿就是擦倒角墙，即与地面的角度小于 90 度的墙。而航天大厦的设计者为了表现他那变态的创意，把整座大厦设计成倾斜的，在顶部由一根细长的立柱与地面支撑，据这位著名建筑师说，倾斜更能表现出上升感。这话似乎有道理，这座航天大厦也名扬世界，成为北京的又一标志性建筑。但这位建筑大师的祖宗八代都被北京的蜘蛛人骂遍了，清洁航天大厦的活儿对他们来说几乎是一场噩梦，因为这座倾斜的大厦整整一面全是倒角墙，高达四百米，与地面的角度小到 65 度。

到达工作位置后，水娃仰头看看，头顶上这面巨大的玻璃悬崖仿佛正在倾倒下来。他用一只手打开清洁剂容器的盖子，另一只手紧紧抓着吸盘的把手。这种吸盘是为清洁倒角墙特制的，但并不好使，常常脱吸，这时蜘蛛人就会荡离墙面，被安全带吊着在空中打秋千。这种事在清洁航天大厦时多次发生，每次都让人魂飞天外。就在昨天，水娃的一位工友脱吸后远远地荡出去，又荡回来，在强风的推送下直撞到墙上，撞碎了一大块玻璃，在他的额头和手臂上各划了一道大口子，而那块昂贵的镀膜高级建筑玻璃让他这一年的活儿白干了。

到现在为止，水娃干蜘蛛人的工作已经两年多了，这活儿可真不容易。在地面上有二级风力时，百米空中的风力就有五级，而在四五百米的超高层建筑上，风就更大了。危险自不必说，从 21 世纪初开始，蜘蛛人的坠落事故就时有发生。在冬天，那强风就像刀子一样锋利，清洗玻璃时最常用的氢氟酸洗剂腐蚀性很大，使手指甲先变黑再脱落；而到了夏天，为防洗涤药水的腐蚀，还得穿着不透气的雨衣雨裤雨鞋，如果是擦镀膜玻璃，背上太阳暴晒，面前玻璃反射的阳光也让人睁不开眼，这时水娃的感觉真像是被放在庄宇的太阳灶上。

但水娃热爱这个工作，这两年多是他有生以来最快乐的时光。这固然因为在外地来京的低文化层次的打工者中，蜘蛛人的收入相对较高，更重要的是，他从工作中获得了一种奇妙的满足感。他最喜欢干那些别的工友不愿意干的活儿：清洁新近落成的超高建筑。这些建筑的高度都在 200 米以上，最高的达 500 米。悬在这些摩天大楼顶端的外墙上，北京城在下面一览无余地延伸开来，那些 20 世纪建成的所谓高层建筑从这里看下去是那么矮小，再远一些，它们就像一簇簇插在地上的细木条，而城市中心的紫禁城则像是用金色的积木搭起来的。在这座高度听不到城市喧闹的楼上，整个北京成了一个可以一眼望全的整体，成了一个以蛛网般的公路为血脉的巨大的生命，在下面静静地呼吸着。有时，摩天大楼高耸在云层之上，腰部以下笼罩在阴暗的暴雨之中，以上却阳光灿烂，干活儿时脚下是一望无际的滚滚云海。每到这时，水娃总觉得他的身体都被云海之上的强风吹得透明了……

水娃从这经历中学到了一个哲理：事情得从高处才能看清楚。如果你淹没于这座大都市之中，周围的一切是那么纷繁复杂，城市仿佛是一个无边无际的迷宫。但从这高处一看，整座城市不过是一个有一千多万人的大蚂蚁窝罢了，而它周围的世界又是那么广阔。

在第一次领到工资后，水娃到一个大商场转了转，乘电梯上到第三层时，他发现这是一个让自己迷惑的地方。与繁华的下两层不同，这一层的大厅比较空旷，只摆放着几张大得惊人的低桌子，在每张桌子宽阔的桌面上，都有一片小小的楼群，每幢楼有一本书那么高。楼间有翠绿的草地，草地上有白色的凉亭和回廊……这些小建筑好像是用象牙和奶酪做成的，看上去那么可爱，它们与绿草地一起，构成了精致的小世界，在水娃眼中，真像是一个个小天堂的模型。最初他猜测这是某种玩具，但这里见不到孩子，桌边的人们也一脸认真和严肃。他站在一个小天堂边上对着它出神地望了很久，一位漂亮小姐过来招呼他，他这才知道这里是出售商品房的地方。他随便指着一幢小楼，问最顶上那套房多少钱，小姐告诉他那是三室一厅，每平方米三千五百元，总价值三十八万元。听到这数目水娃倒吸一口冷气，但小姐接下来的话让这冷酷的数字温柔了许多："分期付款，每月一千五百到两千元。"

他小心地问："我……我不是北京人，能买吗？"

小姐给了他一个动人的微笑："您可真逗，户口已经取消两年了，还什么北京人不北京人的？您住下不就是北京人了吗？"

水娃走出商场后，漫无目的地在街上走了很长时间。夜幕中的北京在他的周围五光十色地闪耀着，他的手中拿着售房小姐给他的几张花花绿绿的广告页，不时停下来看看。仅在一个多月前，在那座遥远的西部城市的简易房中，在省城拥有一套住房对他来说都还是一个神话，现在，他离买起那套北京的住房还有相当的距离，但这已不是神话了，它由神话变成了梦想，而这个梦想，就像那些精致的小模型一样，实实在在地摆在眼前，可以触摸到了。

这时，有人在里面敲水娃正在擦的这面玻璃，这往往是麻烦事。在办公室窗上出现的高楼清洁工总让超级大厦中的白领们有一种莫名的烦恼，好像这些人真如其名那样是一个个异类大蜘蛛，而他们之间的隔阂远不止那面玻璃。在蜘蛛人干活儿时，里面的人不是嫌有噪声就是抱怨阳光被挡住了，变着法儿和他们过不去。航天大厦的玻璃是半反射型的，水娃很费劲地向里面看，终于看清了里面的人，居然是庄宇！

分手后，水娃一直惦记着庄宇。在他的记忆中，庄宇一直是一个西装革履的流浪汉，在这座大城市中深一脚浅一脚地过着艰难的生活。在一个深秋之夜，正当水娃在宿舍中默默地为庄宇过冬的衣服发愁时，却真的在电视上看到了他！这时，中国太阳工程正在选择构建反射镜的材料，这是工程最关键的技术核心，在十几种材料中，庄宇研制的纳米镜膜最后被选中了。他由一名科技流浪汉变成了中国太阳工程的首席科学家之一，一夜之间举世闻名。从这以后，虽然庄宇频频在各种媒体出现，水娃反而把他忘记了，他觉得他们之间已没有什么关系。

在那间宽大的办公室里，水娃看到庄宇与两年前相比，从里到外都没有变，还穿着那身西装，现在水娃知道，这身当时在他眼中高级华贵的衣服实际上次透了。水娃向他讲述了自己在北京的生活，最后他笑着说："看来咱们俩在北京干得都不错。"

"是的是的，都不错！"庄宇激动地连连点头，"其实，那天早晨对你说那些关于时代和机遇的话时，我几乎对一切都失去了信心，我是说给自己听的，但这个时代真的充满了机遇。"

水娃点点头："到处都是金色的鸟儿。"

接着，水娃打量起这间充满现代感的大办公室来，这里最引人注目的是那一套不同寻常的装饰物：办公室的天花板整个是一幅星空的全息图像，所以在办公室中的人如同置身于一个灿烂星空下的院子。在这星空的背景前悬浮着一个银色的圆形曲面，那是一个镜面，很像庄宇的那个太阳灶，但水娃知道，这个太阳灶面积可能有几十个北京那么大。在天花板的一角，有一盏球形的灯，与这镜面一样，这灯球没有任何支撑地悬浮在空中，发出耀眼的黄光。镜面把它的一束光投射到办公桌旁的一个大地球仪上，在其表面打出一个圆圆的亮点。那个灯球在天花板下缓缓飘移着，镜面转动着追踪它，始终保持着那束投向地球仪的光束。星空、镜面、灯球、光束、地球仪和其表面的亮点，形成了一幅抽象而神秘的构图。

"这就是中国太阳吗？"水娃指着镜面敬畏地问。

庄宇点点头："这是一个面积达 3 万平方千米的反射镜，它在36000 千米高的同步轨道上向地球反射阳光，在地面看上去，天空中像多了个太阳。"

"我一直搞不明白，天上多个太阳，地上怎么会多了雨水呢？"

"这个人造太阳可以以多种方式影响天气，比如通过改变大气的热平衡来影响大气环流、增加海洋蒸发量、移动锋面等，这一两句话说不清楚。其实，轨道反射镜只是中国太阳工程的一部分，另一部分是一个复杂的大气运动模型。它运行在许多台超级计算机上，精确地模拟出某一区域大气的运动状态，然后找准一个关键点，用人造太阳的热量施加影响，就会产生出巨大的效应，足以在一段时间内完全改变目标区域的气候……这个过程极其复杂，不是我的专业，我也不太明白。"

水娃又问了一个庄宇肯定明白的问题，他知道自己的问题太傻，但还是鼓足勇气问了出来："那么大个东西悬在天上，不会掉下来吗？"

庄宇默默地看了水娃几秒钟，又看了看表，一拍水娃的肩膀说："走，我请你吃饭，同时让你明白中国太阳为什么不会掉下来。"

但事情远没有庄宇想的那么简单，他不得不把要讲授的知识线移到底层。水娃知道自己生活在一个圆的地球上，但他意识深处的世界还是一个天圆地方的结构，庄宇费了很大劲才使水娃真正明白了我们的世界只是一颗飘浮在无际虚空中的小石球。这个晚上水娃并没有搞明白中国太阳为什么不会掉下来，但这个宇宙在他的脑海中已完全变了样，他进入了自己的托勒密时代。第二个晚上，庄宇同水娃到大排档去吃饭，并成功地使水娃进入了哥白尼时代。又用了两个晚上，水娃艰难地进入了牛顿时代，知道了（当然仅仅是知道了）万有引力。接下来的一个晚上，借助于办公室中的那个大地球仪，庄宇使水娃迈进了航天时代。在接下来的一个公休日，也是在那个大地球仪前，水娃终于明白了同步轨道是什么意思，同时也明白了中国太阳为什么不会掉下来。

在这一天，庄宇带水娃参观了中国太阳工程的指挥中心，在一个高大的屏幕上映出了同步轨道上中国太阳建设工地的全景：漆黑的空间中飘浮着几块银色的薄片，航天飞机在那些薄片前像几只小小的蚊子。最让水娃感到震撼的是另一个大屏幕上从36000千米高度拍摄的地球。他看到，大陆像漂浮在海洋上的一张张大牛皮纸，山脉像牛皮纸的皱褶，而云层如同牛皮纸上残留的一片片白糖末……庄宇指给水娃看哪里是他的家乡，哪里是北京，水娃呆呆地看了好半天，冒出一句话：

"站在这种高处，人想的事情肯定不一样……"

三个月后，中国太阳的主体工程完工，在国庆节之夜，反射镜首次向地球的黑夜部分投射阳光，并把巨大的光斑固定在京津地区。这天夜里，水娃在天安门广场上同几十万人一起目睹了这壮丽的日出：西边的夜空中，一颗星星的亮度急剧增强，在这颗星的周围有一圈蓝天在扩散，当中国太阳的亮度达到最大时，这圈蓝天已占据了半个天空的面积，在它的边缘，色彩由纯蓝渐渐过渡到黄色、橘红和深紫，这圈渐变的色彩如一圈彩虹把蓝天围在中央，形成了人们所称的"环形朝霞"。

水娃在凌晨4点才回到宿舍，他躺在狭窄的上铺，中国太阳的光芒从窗户照进来，照在墙上那几张商品住宅广告页上，水娃把那几张彩纸从墙上撕了下来。

在中国太阳的天国之光下，他曾为之激动不已的理想显得那么平淡渺小。

两个月后，清洁公司的经理找到水娃，说中国太阳工程指挥中心的庄总让他去一下。自清洁航天大厦的活儿干完后，水娃就再也没见过庄宇。

"你们的太阳真是伟大！"在航天大厦的办公室中见到庄宇后，水娃由衷地赞叹道。

"是我们的太阳，特别是你也有份儿。现在在这里看不到中国太阳了，它正在给你的家乡造雪呢！"

"我爸妈来信说，我们那里今冬的雪真的多了起来！"

"但中国太阳也遇到了大问题。"庄宇指指身后的一块大屏幕，上面显示着两个圆形的光斑，"这是在同一位置拍摄的中国太阳的图像，时隔两个月，你能看出它们有什么差别吗？"

"左边那个亮一些。"

"看，仅两个月，反射率的降低用肉眼都能看出来了。"

"怎么，是大镜子上落灰了吗？"

"太空中没有灰，但有太阳风，也就是太阳喷出的粒子流，时间一长，它使中国太阳的镜面表层发生了质变，镜面就蒙上了一层极薄的雾膜，反射率就降低了。一年以后，镜面将变得像蒙上一层水雾一样，那时中国太阳就变成了中国月亮，可什么事都干不了了。"

"你们开始没想到这些吗？"

"当然想到了……我们还是谈你的事吧，想不想换个工作？"

"换工作？我还能干什么呢？"

"还是干高空清洁工，但是在我们这里干。"

水娃迷惑地四下看看："你们的大楼不是刚清洁过吗？还用专门雇高空清洁工？"

"不，不是让你擦大楼，是擦中国太阳。"

人生第五个目标：飞向太空擦太阳

这是一次由中国太阳工程运行部的高层领导人参加的会议，讨论成立镜面清洁机构的事。庄宇把水娃介绍给大家，并介绍了他的工作。当有人问到学历时，水娃诚实地说他只读过三年小学。

"但我认字的，看书没问题。"水娃对与会者说。

一阵笑声响起。"庄总，你这是在开玩笑吗？！"有人气愤地喊道。

庄宇平静地说："我没开玩笑。如果组成三十个人的镜面清洁队，把中国太阳全部清洁一遍需半年时间，按照清洁周期清洁队需要不停地工作，这需要有六十到九十人进行轮换，如果正在制定中的空间劳动保护法出台，这种轮换可能需要更多的人，也就是说需要一百二十人甚至一百五十人。我们难道要让一百五十名有博士学位的、在高性能歼击机上飞过三千小时的宇航员干这项工作吗？"

"那也得差不多点儿吧？在城市高等教育已经普及的今天，让一个文盲飞向太空？"

"我不是文盲！"水娃对那人说。对方没理他，接着对庄宇说："这是对这个伟大工程的亵渎！"

与会者们纷纷点头赞同。

庄宇也点点头："我早就料到各位会有这种反应。在座的除了这位清洁工之外都具有博士学位，那么好，就让我们看看各位在清洁工作中的素质吧！请跟我来。"

十几名与会者迷惑不解地跟着庄宇走出会议室，走进电梯。这种摩天大楼中的电梯分快、中、慢三种，他们乘坐的是最快的电梯，电梯飞快加速，直上大厦的顶层。

有人说："我是第一次乘这个电梯，真有乘火箭升空的感觉！"

"我们进入同步轨道后，大家还将体验清洁中国太阳的感觉。"庄宇说。周围的人都向他投来奇怪的目光。

走出电梯后，大家又跟着庄宇爬了一段窄扶梯，最后从一扇小铁门走出去，来到了大厦的露天楼顶。他们立刻置身于阳光和强风之中，上面的蓝天似乎比平时看到的清澈了许多，向四周望去，北京城尽收眼底。他们发现楼顶上已经有一小群人在等着，水娃吃惊地发现那竟是清洁公司的经理和他的蜘蛛人工友们！

庄宇大声说："现在，我们就请大家体验一下水娃的工作。"

于是那些蜘蛛人走过来给每一位与会者扎上安全带，然后领他们走到楼顶边缘，让他们小心地站到十几位蜘蛛人作为工作平台的小小的吊板上，然后吊板开始慢慢下降，悬在距楼顶边缘五六米处不动了，被挂在大厦玻璃墙上的与会者们发出了一阵绝不掺假的惊叫声。

"各位，我们继续开会吧！"庄宇蹲着从楼顶边缘探出身去对下面的人喊。

"你个浑蛋！快拉我们上去！"

"你们每人必须擦完一块玻璃才能上来！"

擦玻璃是不可能的，下面的人能做的只是死抓着安全带或吊板的绳索一动不敢动，根本不可能松开一只手去拿起放在吊板上的刷子或打开清洁剂桶的盖子。在他们的日常工作中，这些航天官员每天都在图纸或文件上与几万千米的高度打交道，但在这亲身体验中，四百米的高度已经令他们魂飞天外了。

庄宇站起身，走到一位空军大校的上面，他是被吊下去的十几个人中唯一的镇定自若者。他开始擦玻璃，动作沉稳，最让水娃吃惊的是，他的两只手都在干活儿，并没有抓着什么稳定自己，而他的吊板在强风中贴着墙面一动不动，这对蜘蛛人来说也只有老手才能做到。当水娃认出他就是十多年前"神舟八号"飞船上的一名宇航员时，对眼前所见也就不奇怪了。

庄宇问："张大校，你坦率地说，眼前的工作真的比你们在轨道上的太空行走作业容易吗？"

"如果仅从体力和技巧上来说，相差不是太多。"前宇航员回答说。

"说得好！宇航训练中心的一项研究表明，在人体工程学上，高层建筑清洁工的工作与太空中的镜面清洁工作有许多相似之处：都是在危险的、需要时时保持平衡的位置上，从事重复单调且消耗体力的劳动；都要时时保持着警觉，稍一疏忽就会有意外事故发生。这事故对宇航员来说，可能是错误飘移、工具或材料丢失或生命维持系统失灵等；对蜘蛛人来说，则可能是撞碎玻璃、工具或清洁剂跌落或安全带断裂滑脱等。在体能技巧方面，特别是在心理素质方面，蜘蛛人完全有能力胜任镜面清洁工作。"

前宇航员仰视着庄宇点了点头："这使我想起了那个古老的寓言：卖油人把油通过一个铜钱的方孔倒进油壶中，所需的技巧与将军把箭射中靶心同样高超，差异只在于他们的身份。"

庄宇接着说："哥伦布发现了美洲，库克发现了澳洲，但这些新世界都是由普通人开发的，这些开拓者在当时的欧洲处于社会的最下层。太空开发也一样，国家在下一个五年计划中把近地空间作为第二个西部，这就意味着航天事业的探险时代已经结束，它不再只是由少数精英从事的工作，让普通人进入太空，是太空开发产业化的第一步！"

"好了，好了，你说的都对！快把我们弄上去啊！"下面的其他人声嘶力竭地喊着。

在回去的电梯上，清洁公司的经理凑到庄宇耳边低声说："庄总，您慷慨激昂了半天，讲的道理有点太大了吧？当然，当着水娃和我这些小弟兄的面，您不好把关键之处挑明。"

"嗯？"庄宇询问地看着他。

"谁都知道，中国太阳工程是以准商业方式运行的，中途差点因资金缺口而停工，现在，留给你们的运行费用没有多少了。在商业宇航中，正规宇航员的年薪都在百万元以上，我这些小伙子每年就可以给你们省几千万元。"

庄宇神秘地一笑说："您以为，为这区区几千万我值得冒这个险吗？我这次故意把镜面清洁工的文化程度标准压到最低，这个先例一开，中国太阳运行中在空间轨道的其他工作岗位，我就可以用普通大学毕业生来做，这一下，省的可不止几千万元，如您所说，这也是没办法的办法，我们真的没剩多少钱了。"

经理说："在我的童年和少年时代，进入太空是一种何等浪漫的事业，我清楚地记得，邓小平在访问肯尼迪航天中心时，把一位美国宇航员称作神仙。现在……"他拍着庄宇的后背苦笑着摇摇头，"我们彼此彼此了。"

庄宇扭头看了看那几名蜘蛛人小伙子，放大了声音说："但，先生，我给他们的工资怎么说也是你的八到十倍！"

第二天，包括水娃在内的六十名蜘蛛人进入了坐落在石景山的中国宇航训练中心，他们都是从外地来京打工的农村后生，来自中国广阔田野的各个偏僻角落。

镜面农夫

西昌基地，"地平线号"航天飞机从它的发动机喷出的大团白雾中探出头来，轰鸣着升上蓝天。机舱里坐着水娃和其他十四名镜面清洁工，经过三个月的地面培训，他们从这六十个人中被挑选出来，首批进入太空进行实际操作。

在水娃这时的感觉中，失重远不像传说中那么可怕，他甚至有一种熟悉的舒适感，这是孩子被母亲紧紧抱在怀中的感觉。在他右上方的舷窗外，天空的蓝色在渐渐变深。舱外隐约传来爆破螺栓的啪啪声，助推器分离，发动机声由震耳的轰鸣变为蚊子似的嗡嗡声。天空变成深紫色，最后完全变黑，星星出现了，都不眨眼，十分明亮。嗡嗡声戛然而止，舱内变得很安静，座椅的震动消失了，接着后背对椅面的压力也消失了，失重出现。水娃他们是在一个巨大的水池中进行的失重训练，这时的感觉还真像是浮在水中。

但安全带还不能解开，发动机又嗡嗡地叫了起来，重力又把每个人按回椅子上，漫长的变轨飞行开始了。小小的舷窗中，星空和海洋交替出现，舱内不时充满了地球反射的蓝光和太阳白色的光芒。窗口能看到的地平线的弧度一次比一次大，能看到的海洋和陆地的景色范围也一次比一次大。向同步轨道的变轨飞行整整进行了六个小时，舷窗中星空和地球的景色交替也渐渐有了催眠作用，水娃居然睡着了。但他很快被扩音器中指令长的声音惊醒，那声音说变轨飞行结束了。

舱内的伙伴们纷纷飘离座椅，紧贴着舷窗向外瞅。水娃也解开安全带，用游泳的动作笨拙地飘到离他最近的舷窗前，他第一次亲眼看到了完整的地球。但大多数人挤在另一侧的舷窗边，他也一蹬舱壁蹿了过去，因速度太快在对面的舱壁上碰了脑袋。从舷窗望出去，他才发现"地平线号"已经来到中国太阳的正下方，反射镜已占据了星空的大部分面积，航天飞机如同飞行在一个巨大银色穹顶下的一只小蚊子。"地平线号"继续靠近，水娃渐渐体会到镜面的巨大：它已占据了窗外的所有空间，一点儿都感觉不到它的弧度，他们仿佛飞行在一望无际的银色平原上。距离在继续缩短，镜面上出现了"地平线号"的倒影。可以看到银色大地上有一条条长长的接缝，这些接缝像地图上的经纬线一样织成了方格，成了能使人感觉到相对速度的唯一参照物。渐渐地，银色大地上的经线不再平行，而是向一点汇聚，这趋势急剧加快，好像"地平线号"正在驶向这巨大地图上的一个极点。极点很快出现了，所有经线方向的接缝都汇聚在一个小黑点上，航天飞机向着这个小黑点下降。水娃震惊地发现，这个黑点竟是这银色大地上的一座大楼，这座大楼是一个全密封的圆柱体，水娃知道，这就是中国太阳的控制站，是他们以后三个月在这冷寂太空中唯一的家。

太空蜘蛛人的生活就这样开始了。每天（中国太阳绕地球一周的时间也是二十四小时），镜面清洁工们驾驶着一台台有手扶拖拉机大小的机器擦光镜面。他们开着这些机器在广阔的镜面上来回行驶，很像在银色的大地上耕种着什么，于是西方新闻媒体给他们起了一个更有诗意的名字："镜面农夫"。这些"农夫"的世界是奇特的，他们脚下是银色的平原，由于镜面的弧度，这平原在远方的各个方向缓缓升起，但由于面积巨大，周围看上去如水面般平坦。上方，地球和太阳总是同时出现，后者比地球小得多，倒像是它的一颗光芒四射的卫星。在占据太空大部分的地球上，总能看到一个缓缓移动的圆形光斑，在地球黑夜的一面这光斑尤其醒目，这就是中国太阳在地球上照亮的区域。镜面可以调整形状以改变光斑的大小，当银色大地在远方上升的坡度较陡时，光斑就小而亮，当上升坡度较缓时，光斑就大而暗。

但镜面清洁工的工作是十分艰辛的，他们很快发现，清洁镜面的枯燥和劳累，比在地球上擦高楼有过之而无不及。每天收工回到控制站后，往往累得连太空服都脱不下来。随着后续人员的到来，控制站里拥挤起来，人们像生活在一个潜水艇中。但能够回到站里还算幸运，镜面上距站最远处近 100 千米，清洁到外缘时他们往往下班后回不来，只能在"野外"过"夜"。他们从太空服中吸些流质食物，然后悬在半空中睡觉。工作的危险更不用说，镜面清洁工是人类航天史上进行太空行走最多的人，在"野外"，太空服的一个小故障就足以置人于死地，还有微陨石、太空垃圾和太阳磁暴等。这样的生活和工作条件使控制站中的工程师们怨气冲天，但天生就能吃苦的"镜面农夫"们却默默地适应了这一切。

在进入太空后的第五天，水娃与家里通了话，这时水娃正在距控制站 50 多千米处干活，他的家乡正处于中国太阳的光斑之中。

水娃爹问："娃啊，你是在那个日头上吗？它在俺们头上照着呢，这夜跟白天一样啊！"

水娃答："是，爹，俺是在上面！"

水娃娘问："娃啊，那上面热吧？"

水娃说："说热也热，说冷也冷，俺在地上投了个影儿，影儿的外面有咱那儿十个夏天热，影儿的里面有咱那儿十个冬天冷。"

水娃娘对水娃爹说："我看到咱娃了，那日头上有个小黑点点！"

水娃知道那是不可能的，他的眼泪涌了出来，说："爹、娘，俺也看到你们了，亚洲大陆的那个地方也有两个小黑点点！明天多穿点衣服，我看到一大股寒流从大陆北面向你们那里移过去了！"

……

三个月后换班的第二分队到来，水娃他们返回地球去休为期三个月的假。他们着陆后的第一件事就是每人买了一架单筒高倍望远镜。三个月后他们回到中国太阳上，在工作的间隙大家都用望远镜遥望地球，望得最多的当然还是家乡，但在4万千米的距离上是不可能看到他们的村庄的。他们中有人用粗笔在镜面上写下了一首稚拙的诗：

在银色的大地上我遥望家乡，

村边的妈妈仰望着中国太阳，

这轮太阳就是儿子的眼睛，

黄土地将在这目光中披上绿装。

"镜面农夫"们的工作是出色的，他们逐渐承担了更多的任务，范围都超出了他们的清洁工作。首先是修复被陨石破坏的镜面，后来又承担了一项更高层次的工作：监视和加固应力超限点。

中国太阳在运行中，其姿态总是在不停变化，这些变化是由分布在其背面的三千台发动机完成的。反射镜的镜面很薄，它由背面的大量细梁连成一个整体，在进行姿态或形状改变时，有些位置可能发生应力超限，如果不及时对各发动机的出力给予纠正，或在那个位置进行加固，任其发展，超限应力就可能撕裂镜面。这项工作的技术要求很高，发现和加固应力超限点都需要熟练的技术和丰富的经验。

除了进行姿态和形状调整外，最有可能发生应力超限的时间是在轨道理发时，这项操作的正式名称是：光压和太阳风所致轨道误差修正。太阳风和光压对面积巨大的镜面产生作用力，这种力量在每平方千米的镜面上达两公斤左右，使镜面轨道变扁上移，在地面控制中心的大屏幕上，变形的轨道与正常的轨道同时显示，很像是正常的轨道上长出了头发，这个离奇的操作名称由此而来。轨道理发时镜面产生的加速度比姿态和形状调整时大得多，这时"镜面农夫"们的工作十分重要，他们飞行在银色大地上空，仔细地观察着地面上的每一处异常变化，随时进行紧急加固，每次都出色地完成了任务。他们的收入因此增加很多，但这中间得利最多的，还是已成为中国太阳工程第一负责人的庄宇，他连普通大学毕业生也不必雇了。

但"镜面农夫"们都明白，他们这批人是第一批也是最后一批只有小学文化程度的太空工人了，以后的太空工人最低也得是大学毕业生。但他们完成了庄宇所设想的使命：证明了太空开发中的底层工作最需要的是技巧和经验，是对艰苦环境的适应能力，而不是知识和创造力，普通人完全可以胜任。

但太空也在改变着"镜面农夫"们的思维方式，没有人能像他们这样，每天从36000千米的高空居高临下地看地球。世界在他们面前只是一个一眼便可望过来的小沙盘，地球村对他们来说不是一个比喻，而是眼前实实在在的现实。

"镜面农夫"作为第一批太空工人，曾在全世界引起了轰动。但随着近地空间开发产业化的飞速发展，许多超级工程在太空中出现，包括用微波向地面传送电能的超大型太阳能电站，微重力产品加工厂等，容纳十万人的太空城也开始建设。大批产业工人涌向太空，他们都是普通人，世界渐渐把"镜面农夫"们忘记了。

几年后，水娃在北京买了房子，建立了家庭，又有了孩子。每年他有一半时间在家里，一半时间在太空。他热爱这项工作，在 3 万多千米高空的银色大地上长时间巡行，使他的心中产生了一种超脱的宁静，他觉得自己已找到了理想的生活，未来就如同脚下的银色平原一样平滑地向前伸展。但后来的一件事打破了这种宁静，彻底改变了水娃的心路历程，这就是他与史蒂芬·霍金的交往。

没有人想到霍金能活过 100 岁，这既是医学界的奇迹，也是他个人精神力量的表现。当近地轨道的第一所太空低重力疗养院建立后，他成为第一位疗养者。但上太空的失重差一点儿要了他的命，返回地面也要经受失重，所以在太空电梯或反重力舱之类的运载工具发明之前，他可能回不了地球了。事实上，医生建议他长住太空，因为失重环境对他的身体是最合适不过的。

霍金开始对中国太阳没什么兴趣，他从低轨道再次忍受加速重力（当然比从地面进入太空时小得多）来到位于同步轨道的中国太阳，是想看看在这里进行的一项关于背景辐射强度各向微小异性的宇宙学观测，观测站之所以设在中国太阳背面，是因为巨大的反射镜可以挡住来自太阳和地球的干扰。但在观测完成，观测站和工作小组都撤走后，霍金仍不想走，说他喜欢这里，想多待一阵儿。到底中国太阳的什么东西吸引了他，新闻界做出了各种猜测，但只有水娃知道实情。

在中国太阳生活的日子里，霍金最喜欢做的事就是在镜面上散步，让人不理解的是，他只在反射镜的背面散步，每天散步的时间长达几个小时。空间行走经验最丰富的水娃被站里指定陪博士散步。这时的霍金已与爱因斯坦齐名，水娃当然听说过他，但在控制站内第一次见到他时还是很吃惊。水娃想象不出一位瘫痪到如此程度的人如何做出那么大的成就，尽管他对这位大科学家做了什么还一无所知。但在散步时，丝毫看不出霍金的瘫痪，也许是有了操纵电动轮椅的经验，他操纵太空服上的微型发动机与正常人一样灵活。

霍金与水娃的交流很困难，他虽然植入了由脑电波控制的电子发声系统，说话不像20世纪那么困难了，但他的话要通过实时翻译器译成中文水娃才能听得懂。按领导的交代，为了不影响博士思考问题，水娃从不主动搭话，但博士却很愿意与他交谈。

博士最先是问水娃的身世，然后回忆起自己的早年，他向水娃讲述童年时在圣阿尔班斯住的那幢阴冷的大房子，冬天结了冰的高大客厅中响着维格纳的音乐；还有那辆放在奥斯明顿磨坊牧场的马戏车，他常和妹妹玛丽一起乘着它到海滩去；还有他常与父亲去的齐尔顿领地的爱文豪灯塔……水娃惊叹于这位百岁老人的记忆力，更让他吃惊的是，他们之间居然有共同语言，水娃讲述家乡的一切，博士也很爱听，当走到镜面边缘时还让水娃指给他看水娃家乡的位置。

时间长了，谈话不可避免地转到科学方面，水娃本以为这会结束他们之间难得的交流。但并非如此，向普通人用最通俗的语言讲述艰深的物理学和宇宙学，对博士来说似乎是一种休息，他向水娃讲述了大爆炸、黑洞、量子引力。水娃回去后就啃博士在20世纪写的那本薄薄的小书，再向站里的工程师和科学家请教，居然明白了不少。

"知道我为什么喜欢这里吗？"一次散步到镜面边缘时，博士对着从边缘露出一角的地球对水娃说，"这个大镜面隔开了下面的地球，使我忘记了尘世的存在，能全身心地面对宇宙。"

水娃说："下面的世界好复杂的，可从这里远远地看，宇宙又是那么简单，只是空间中撒着一些星星。"

"是的，孩子，真是这样。"博士点点头说。

反射镜的背面与正面一样，也是镜面，只是多了如一座座小黑塔似的姿态和形状调整发动机。每天散步时，博士和水娃两人就紧贴着镜面缓缓地飘行，常常从中心一直飘到镜面的边缘。没有月亮时，反射镜的背面很黑，表面是星空的倒影。与正面相比，这里的地平线很近，且能看出弧形。星光下，由支撑梁组成的黑色经纬线在他们脚下移动，他们仿佛飘行在一个宁静的小星球的表面。遇上姿态或形状调整，反射镜背面的发动机启动，这小星球的表面被一簇簇小火苗照亮，更使这里显出一种美丽的神秘。在这小小的世界之上，银河在灿烂地照耀着。就在这样的境界中，水娃第一次接触到宇宙最深层的奥秘。他明白了自己所看到的所有星空，在大得无法想象的宇宙中也只是一粒灰尘，而这整个宇宙，不过是百亿年前一次壮丽焰火的余烬。

许多年前，作为蜘蛛人踏上第一座高楼的楼顶时，水娃看到了整个北京；来到中国太阳时，他看到了整个地球；现在，水娃面对着他人生第三个壮丽的时刻，他站到了宇宙的楼顶上，看到了他以前做梦都不会想到的东西，虽然这知识还很粗浅，但足以使那更遥远的世界对他产生一种难以抗拒的吸引力。

有一次水娃向站里的一位工程师说出了自己的一个困惑："人类在 20 世纪 60 年代就登上了月球，为什么后来反而缩了回来，到现在还没登上火星，甚至连月球也不去了？"

工程师说："人类是现实的动物，20世纪中叶那些由理想主义和信仰驱动的东西是没有长久生命力的。"

　　"理想和信仰不好吗？"

　　"不是说不好，但经济利益更好，如果从那时开始人类就不惜代价，做飞向外太空的赔本买卖，地球现在可能还在贫困之中，你我这样的普通人反而不可能进入太空，虽然只是在近地空间。朋友，别中了霍金的毒，他那套东西一般人玩不了的！"

　　水娃从此变了，他仍然像以前一样努力工作，表面平静地生活，但心里却显然在想着更多的事。

　　时光飞逝，二十年过去了。这二十年中，水娃和他的伙伴们从36000千米的高空清楚地看到了祖国和世界的变化。他们看到，三北防护林形成了一条横贯中国东西的绿带，黄色的沙漠渐渐被绿色覆盖，家乡也不再缺少雨水和白雪，村前干枯的河床又盈满了清流……这一切也有中国太阳的一份功劳，它在改变大西北气候的宏大工程中起了很大的作用。除此之外，这些年中国太阳还干了许多不寻常的事，比如融化乞力马扎罗山的积雪以缓解非洲干旱，使举行奥运会的城市成为真正的不夜城……

　　但对于最新的技术来说，用这种方式影响天气显得过于笨拙，且有太多的副作用，中国太阳已完成了它的使命。

　　太空产业部举行了一个隆重的仪式，为人类第一批太空产业工人授勋。这不仅仅是表彰他们二十年来辛勤而出色的工作，更重要的是，这60位只有小学和初中文化程度的青年进入太空工作，标志着太空开发已对所有人敞开了大门。经济学家们一致认为，这是太空开发产业化的真正开端。

这个仪式引起了新闻媒体的极大注意，除了以上的原因，在普通大众心中，"镜面农夫"们的经历具有传奇色彩。同时，在这个追逐与忘却的时代，有一个怀旧的机会也是很不错的。

当年那些憨厚朴实的小伙子现在都已人到中年，但他们看上去变化并不是太大，人们从全息电视中还能认出他们。他们中的大部分人已通过各种方式接受了高等教育，其中有一些人还获得了"太空工程师"的职称，但无论在自己还是公众的眼里，他们仍是那群来自乡村的打工者。

水娃代表伙伴们讲话，他说："随着电磁输送系统的建成，现在进入近地空间的费用，只及乘飞机飞越太平洋费用的一半，太空旅行已变成了一件平常而平淡的事。但新一代人很难想象，在二十年前进入太空对一个普通人来说意味着什么，很难想象那会是怎样令他激动和热血沸腾，我们就是那样一群幸运者。

"我们这些人很普通，没什么可说的，我们能有这样不寻常的经历是因为中国太阳。这二十年来，它已成为我们的第二家园，在我们的心目中它很像一个微缩的地球。最初，我们把镜面上的接缝当作北半球的经纬线，说明自己的位置时总是说在北纬多少度、东经西经多少度；到后来，随着我们对镜面的熟悉，渐渐在上面划分出了大陆和海洋，我们会说自己是在北京或莫斯科，我们每个人的家乡在镜面上也都有对应的位置，对那一块我们擦得最勤……在这个银色的小地球上我们努力地工作，尽了自己的责任。先后有五位镜面清洁工为中国太阳献出了生命，他们有的是在太阳磁暴爆发时没来得及隐蔽，有的则是被陨石或太空垃圾击中。

"现在，这块我们生活和工作了二十年的银色土地就要消失了，我们很难用语言表达自己的感受。"

水娃沉默了，已是太空产业部部长的庄宇接过了话头说："我完全理解你们的感受，但在这里可以欣慰地告诉大家：中国太阳不会消失！这点我想你们也都知道了，对于这样一个巨大的物体，不可能采用 20 世纪的方式，让它坠入大气层烧掉，它将用另一种方式找到自己的归宿：其实很简单，只要停止进行轨道理发，并进行适当的姿态调整，太阳风和光压将最终使它超过第二宇宙速度，离开地球成为太阳的卫星。许多年后，行星际飞船会在遥远的地方找到它，那时我们也许会把它变成一个博物馆，我们这些人会再次回到那银色的平原上，一起回忆我们这段难忘的岁月。"

水娃突然显得激动起来，他大声地问庄宇："部长先生，你真的认为会有这一天，你真的认为会有行星际飞船吗？"

庄宇呆呆地看着水娃，一时说不出话来。

水娃接着说："20 世纪中叶，当阿姆斯特朗在月球上印下第一个脚印时，几乎所有的人都相信人类将在十到二十年之内登上火星。现在，八十六年过去了，别说火星了，月球也再没人去过，理由很简单：那是赔本买卖。

"20 世纪'冷战'结束后，经济准则一天天统治世界，人类在这个准则下也取得了巨大的成就：现在，我们消灭了战争和贫困，恢复了生态，地球正在变成一个乐园。这就使我们更加坚信经济准则的正确性，它已变得至高无上，渗透到我们的每个细胞中，人类社会已变成了百分之百的经济社会，投入大于产出的事再也不会做了。对月球的开发没有经济意义，对行星的大规模载人探测是经济犯罪，至于进行星际航行，那是地地道道的精神变态。现在，人类只知道投入、产出，并享受这些产出了！"

庄宇点点头说："21世纪人类的太空开发仍局限于近地空间，这是事实，它有许多更深刻的原因，已超出了我们今天的话题。"

"没有超出，现在，我们有了一个机会，只需要花很少的钱就能飞出近地空间进行远程宇宙航行。太阳光压可以把中国太阳推出地球轨道，同样能把它推到更远的地方。"

庄宇笑着摇摇头："呵，你是说把中国太阳作为一个太阳帆船？从理论上说是没问题的，反射镜的主体薄而轻，面积巨大，经过长期的光压加速，理论上它会成为人类迄今为止发射过的速度最快的航天器。但这也只是从理论上而言，实际情况是，一艘船只有帆并不能远航，它上面还要有人，一艘无人的帆船只能在海上来回打转，连港口都驶不出去，记得史蒂文森的《金银岛》里对此有生动的描述：要想借助于光压远航并返回，反射镜需要精确而复杂的姿态控制，而中国太阳是为在地球轨道上运行而设计的，离开了人的操作，它自己只能沿着无规则的航线瞎飘一气，而且飘不了太远。"

"不错，但它上面会有人的，我来驾驶它。"水娃平静地说。

这时，通过收视统计系统显示，对这个频道的收视率急剧上升，全世界的目光正在被吸引过来。

"可你一个人同样控制不了中国太阳，它的姿态控制至少需要……"

"至少需要十二个人，考虑到星际航行的其他因素，至少需要十五个到二十个人，我相信会有这么多志愿者的。"

庄宇不知所措地笑笑："真没想到，我们今天的谈话会转移到这个方向。"

"陆部长，二十年前，你不止一次地改变了我的人生方向。"

"可我万万没有想到你沿着那个方向走了这么远，已远远超过我了。"庄宇感慨地说，"好吧，很有意思，让我们继续讨论下去吧！嗯……很遗憾，这个想法是不可行的。中国太阳最合理的航行目标是火星，可你想过没有，中国太阳不可能在火星上登陆，如果要登陆，将又是一笔巨大的开支，会使这个计划失去经济上的可行性；如果不登陆，那和无人探测器没有区别，有什么意思呢？"

"中国太阳不去火星。"

庄宇迷惑地看着水娃："那去哪里？木星？"

"也不是木星，去更远的地方。"

"更远？去海王星？去冥王……"庄宇突然顿住，呆呆地盯着水娃看了好一会儿，"天啊，你不会是说……"

水娃坚定地点点头："是的，中国太阳将飞出太阳系，成为恒星际飞船！"

与庄宇一样，全世界的观众顿时目瞪口呆。

庄宇两眼平视前方，机械地点点头："好吧，我们就当你不是在开玩笑，你让我大概估算一下……"说着他半闭起双眼开始心算。

"我已经算好了。借助太阳的光压，中国太阳最终将加速到光速的十分之一，考虑到加速所用的时间，大约需要四十五年时间到达比邻星。"

"然后再借助比邻星的光压减速，完成对半人马座三星系统的探测后，再向相反的方向加速，再用几十年时间返回太阳系。这听起来是个美妙的计划，但实际上只是一个根本不可能实现的梦想。"

"你又想错了，到达比邻星后中国太阳不减速，以每秒3万多千米的速度掠过它，并借助它的光压再次加速，飞向天狼星。如果有可能，我们还会继续蛙跳，飞向第三颗恒星，第四颗……"

"你到底要干什么？"庄宇失态地大叫起来。

"我们向地球索要的，只是一套高可靠性但规模较小的生态循环系统和……"

"用这套系统维持二十个人上百年的生命？"

"听我说完，和一套生命低温冬眠系统。在航行的大部分时间我们处于冬眠状态，只在接近恒星时才启动生态循环系统，按目前的技术，这足以维持我们在宇宙中航行上千年。当然，这两套系统的价格也不低，但比起人类从头开始一次恒星际载人探测来，它所需资金只有其千分之一。"

"就是一分钱不要，世界也不会允许二十个人去自杀。"

"这不是自杀，这是探险，也许我们连近在眼前的小行星带都过不去，也许我们最远会到达天狼星甚至更远，不试试怎么知道？"

"但有一点与探险不同：你们肯定是回不来了。"

水娃点点头："是的，回不来了。有人满足于老婆孩子热炕头，从不向与自己无关的尘世之外扫一眼；有的人则用尽全部生命，只为看一眼人类从未见过的事物。这两种人我都做过，我们有权选择各种生活，包括在十几光年之遥的太空中飘荡的一面镜子上的生活。"

"最后一个问题，在上千年的时间里，以每秒几万甚至十几万千米的速度掠过一颗又一颗恒星，发回人类要经过几十年甚至几个世纪才能收到的微弱电波，这有太大意义吗？"

水娃微笑着向全世界说："飞出太阳系的中国太阳，将会使享乐中的人类重新仰望星空，唤回他们的宇宙远航之梦，重新燃起他们进行恒星际探险的愿望。"

人生的第六个目标：飞向星海，把人类的目光重新引向宇宙深处

庄宇站在航天大厦的楼顶，凝视着天空中快速移动的中国太阳，在它的光芒下，首都的高楼投下了无数快速移动的影子，使得北京仿佛是一张随着中国太阳转动的大面孔。

这是中国太阳最后一次环绕地球运行，它已达到了第二宇宙速度，将飞出地球的引力场，进入绕太阳运行的轨道。这艘人类第一艘载人恒星际飞船上有二十个人，除水娃外，其他人是从上百万名志愿者中挑选出来的，其中包括三名与水娃共事多年的"镜面农夫"。中国太阳还未启程就达到了它的目标：人类社会对太阳系外宇宙探险的热情再次出现了。

庄宇的思绪回到了二十三年前那个闷热的夏夜，在那个西北城市，他和一个来自干旱土地的农村男孩登上了开往北京的夜行列车。

作为告别，中国太阳把它的光斑依次投向各大城市，让人们最后一次看到它的光芒。然后，中国太阳的光斑投向大西北，水娃出生的那个小村庄就在光斑之中。

村边的小路旁，水娃的爹娘同乡亲们一起注视着向东方飞行的中国太阳。

水娃爹喊道："娃啊，你要到老远的地方去吗？"

水娃从太空中回答："是啊，爹，怕是回不了家了。"

水娃娘问："那地方很远？"

水娃回答："很远，娘。"

水娃爹问："比月亮还远吗？"

水娃沉默了几秒钟，用比刚才低许多的声音说："是的，爹，比月亮远些。"

水娃的爹娘并不觉得特别难受，娃是在那比月亮还远的地方干大事呢！再说，这可是个了不起的年头，即使是远在天涯海角的人，随时都可以和他说话，还可以在小电视上看见他，这跟面对面没啥子区别。但他们不会想到，随着时间的流逝，那小屏幕上的儿子将变得越来越迟钝，对爹娘关切的问话，他要想好长时间才能回答。他想的时间开始只有几秒钟，以后越来越长，一年后，爹娘每问一句话，儿子将呆呆地想一个多小时才能回答。最后儿子将消失，他们将被告之水娃睡觉了，这一觉要睡四十多年。在这以后，水娃的爹娘将用尽余生，继续照顾那块曾经贫瘠现已肥沃起来的土地，过完他们那充满艰辛但已很满足的一生。他们最后的愿望将是：在遥远未来的一天，终于回家的儿子能看到一个更美好的家园。

中国太阳正在飞离地球轨道，它在东方的天空中渐渐暗下去，它周围的蓝天也慢慢缩为一点，最后，它将变为一颗星星融入群星之中，但早在这之前，恒星太阳的曙光就会把它完全淹没。

曙光也照亮了村前的这条小路，现在它的两旁已种上了两排白杨，不远处还有一条与它平行的小河。二十四年前的那天，也是在这清晨时分，在同样的曙光下，一个西北农家的孩子怀着朦胧的希望在这条小路上渐渐远去。

这时北京的天已经大亮，庄宇仍站在航天大厦的楼顶，望着中国太阳最后消失的位置，它已踏上了漫长的不归路。中国太阳将首先进入金星轨道之内，尽可能地接近太阳，以获得更大的加速光压和更长的加速距离，这将通过一系列复杂的变轨飞行来实现，其行驶方式很像大航海时代驶逆向风的帆船。七十天后，它将通过火星轨道；一百六十天后，它将掠过木星；两年后，它将飞出冥王星轨道成为一艘恒星际飞船，飞船上的所有人将进入冬眠；四十五年后它将掠过半人马座，宇航员们将短暂苏醒，自中国太阳启程一个世纪后，地球才能收到他们发回的关于半人马座的探测信息；这时，中国太阳正在飞向天狼星的路上，由于半人马座三星的加速，它的速度将达到光速的15%，将于六十年后，也就是自地球启程一个世纪后到达天狼星，当中国太阳掠过这个由天狼星 A、B 构成的双星系统后，它的速度将增加到光速的十分之二，向星空的更深处飞去。按照飞船上生命冬眠系统能维持的时间极限，中国太阳有可能到达波江座 - ε 星，甚至可能（虽然这种可能性很小很小）最后到达鲸鱼座 79 星，这些恒星被认为可能有行星存在。

谁也不知道中国太阳将飞多远，水娃他们将看到什么样的神奇世界，也许有一天他们对地球发出一声呼唤，要上千年才能得到回音。但水娃始终会牢记母亲行星上的一个叫中国的国度，牢记那个国度西部一片干旱土地上的一个小村庄，牢记村前的那条小路，他就是从那里启程的。

THE WANDERING EARTH
CIXIN LIU

TRANSLATED BY ELIZABETH HANLON ET AL.

北京联合出版公司
Beijing United Publishing Co.,Ltd.

CONTENTS

流浪地球

THE WANDERING EARTH

TRANSLATED BY ELIZABETH HANLON

韩恩立－译

Chapter 1

The Braking Era

I have never seen the night. I have never seen the stars. I have never seen spring, fall or winter. I was born as the Braking Era ended, just as the Earth stopped turning.

It had taken forty-two years to halt Earth's rotation, three years longer than the Coalition had planned. My mother told me about the time our family watched the last sunset. The sun sank very slowly, as if stuck on the horizon. It took three days and three nights to finally set. Of course, afterward there was no more 'day' or 'night'. The Eastern hemisphere was shrouded in perpetual dusk for a long time, maybe a decade or so. The sun lay just below the horizon, its glow filling half the sky. During that endless sunset, I was born.

Dusk did not mean darkness. The Earth Engines brightly illuminated the whole Northern hemisphere. They had been installed all across Asia and America – only the solid tectonic plate structure of these two continents could withstand the enormous thrust they exerted. In total, there were 12,000 engines scattered across the Asian and American plains.

From where I lived, I could see the bright plasma beams of hundreds of engines. Imagine an enormous palace, as big as the Parthenon on the Acropolis. Inside the palace, countless massive columns rise up to the vaulted ceiling, each one blazing with the blue-white light of a fluorescent tube. And you, you are just a microbe on the palace's floor. That was the world I lived in. Actually, that description was not totally accurate. It was the tangential thrust component generated by the engines that halted the Earth's rotation.

Because of this, the engine jets needed to be set at a very precise angle, causing the massive beams to slant across the sky. It was like the grand palace that we lived in was teetering on the verge of collapse! When visitors from the Southern hemisphere were exposed to the spectacle, many of them suffered panic attacks.

But even more terrifying than the sight of the engines was the scorching heat they produced. Temperatures reached as high as seventy or eighty degrees Celsius, forcing us to don cooling suits before we stepped outside. The heat often raised torrential storms. When a plasma beam pierced the dark clouds, it was a nightmarish scene. The clouds would scatter the beam's blue-white light, throwing off frenetic, surging rainbow halos. The entire sky glowed as if covered in white-hot lava. My grandfather had grown senile in his old age. One time, tormented by the implacable heat, he was so overjoyed to see a downpour arrive that he stripped to the waist and ran out the door. We were too late to stop him. The raindrops outside had been heated to boiling point by the superheated plasma beams, and his skin was scalded so badly that it sloughed off in large sheets.

To my generation, born in the Northern hemisphere, all of this was perfectly natural, just as the sun, stars, and moon had been natural to the people who lived before the Braking Era. We called that period of human history the Ante-solar Era – and what a captivating golden age it had truly been!

When I started primary school, as part of the curriculum, our teachers led our class of thirty children on a trip around the world. By then, Earth had completely stopped turning. Except for maintaining this stationary state, the Earth Engines were only being used to make small adjustments to the planet's orientation. Because of this, during the three years from when I was three until I turned six, the plasma beams were less intensely luminous than when the engines were operating at full capacity. It was this period of relative inactivity that allowed us to take a trip to gain a better understanding of our world.

First, we visited an Earth Engine up close. The engine was located near

Shijiazhuang, by the entrance to the railway tunnel that ran through the Taihang mountains. The great metallic mountain loomed over us, filling half the sky. To the west, the Taihang mountain range seemed like a series of gentle hills. Some children exclaimed that it must be as tall as Mount Everest. Our head teacher was a pretty young woman named Ms. Stella. She laughed and told us that the engine was eleven thousand meters tall, two thousand meters taller than Mount Everest.

'People call it "God's Blowtorch",' she said. We stood in its massive shadow, feeling its tremors shake the earth.

There were two main types of Earth Engines. Larger engines were dubbed 'Mountains', while smaller ones were called 'Peaks'. We ascended North China Mountain 794. It took a lot longer to scale Mountains than Peaks. It was possible to ride a giant elevator straight to the top of a Peak, but the top of a Mountain could only be reached via a long drive along a serpentine road. Our bus joined an endless procession of vehicles creeping up the smooth steel road. To our left, there was only a blank face of azure metal; to our right, a bottomless chasm.

The traffic mostly consisted of massive, fifty-ton dump trucks, laden with rubble from the Taihang mountains. Our bus quickly reached five thousand meters. From that height, the ground below appeared blank and featureless, washed out by the bluish glare of the Earth Engine. Ms. Stella instructed us to put on our oxygen masks. As we drew closer to the mouth of the plasma beam, the light and heat increased rapidly. Our masks grew shaded, and the micro-compressors in our cooling suits whirred to life. At six thousand meters, we saw the fuel intake port. Truckload after truckload of rocks tumbled into the dull red glow of the gaping pit, consumed without a sound. I asked Ms. Stella how the Earth Engines turned stones into fuel.

'Heavy element fusion is a difficult field of study, too complex for me to explain it to you at this age,' she replied. 'All you need to know is that the Earth Engines are the most powerful machines ever built by humankind. For instance, North China Mountain 794 – where we are now – exerts fifteen billion tons of thrust upon the earth when operating at full capacity.'

Finally, our bus reached the summit. The mouth of the plasma beam was directly above us. The diameter of the beam was so immense that, when we raised our heads, all we could see was a glowing wall of blue plasma that stretched infinitely into the sky. At that moment, I suddenly recalled a riddle posed to us by our philosophy teacher.

'You are walking across a plain when you suddenly encounter a wall,' our haggard teacher had said. 'The wall is infinitely tall and extends infinitely deep underground. It stretches infinitely to the left and infinitely to the right. What is it?'

A cold shiver washed over me. I recited the riddle to Ms. Stella, who sat next to me. She teased it over for a while, but finally shook her head in confusion. I leaned in close and whispered the riddle's dreadful answer in her ear.

Death.

She stared at me in silence for a few seconds, and then hugged me tightly against her. Resting my head on her shoulder, I gazed into the far distance. Gargantuan metal Peaks studded the hazy earth below, stretching all the way to the horizon. Each Peak spat forth a brilliant jet of plasma, like a tilted cosmic forest, piercing our teetering sky.

Soon after, we arrived at the seashore. We could see the spires of submerged skyscrapers protruding above the waves. As the tide ebbed, frothing seawater gushed from their countless windows, forming cascades of waterfalls... Even the Braking Era just ended, its effects upon the Earth had become horrifyingly apparent. The tides caused by the acceleration of the Earth Engines engulfed two-thirds of the Northern hemisphere's major cities. Then, the rise in global temperatures melted the polar ice caps, which turned the flooding into a catastrophe that spread to the Southern hemisphere. Thirty years ago, my grandfather witnessed giant hundred-meter waves inundate Shanghai. Even now, when he described the sight, his eyes would stare off into space. In fact, our planet had already changed beyond recognition before it even set out on its voyage. Who knew what trials and tribulations awaited us on our endless travels through outer space?

We boarded something called an 'ocean liner' – an ancient mode of transportation – and departed the shore. Behind us, the plasma beams of the Earth Engines grew ever more distant. After a day's travel, they disappeared from view altogether. The sea was bathed in light from two different sources. To the west, the plasma beams still suffused the sky with an eerie bluish glow; to the east, rosy sunlight was creeping over the horizon. The competing rays split the sea in two, and our ship sailed right along the glittering seam where they met on the surface. It was a fantastic sight. But as the blue glow retreated, and the rosy glow strengthened, unease settled over the ship. My classmates and I were no longer to be seen above deck. We stayed hidden away in our cabins, blinds pulled tight across the portholes. A day later, the moment we most dreaded finally arrived. We all gathered in the large cabin that we used as a classroom to listen to Ms. Stella's announcement.

'Children,' she said solemnly, 'we will now go to watch the sun rise.'

No one moved. Every pair of eyes was fixed in a glassy stare, as if abruptly frozen to the spot. Ms. Stella tried to urge us from the cabin, but everyone sat perfectly still. One of the other teachers remarked, 'I've mentioned it before, but we really ought to schedule the Global Experience trip before we teach them modern history. The students would adapt more readily.'

'It's not that simple.' Ms. Stella replied. 'They pick it up from their surroundings long before we teach them modern history.' She turned to the class monitors. 'You children go first. Don't be afraid. When I was young, I was nervous about seeing my first sunrise, too. But once I saw it, I was just fine.'

Finally, we stood up and, one by one, trudged out of the cabin door. I suddenly felt a small clammy hand clasp my own, and looked back to see Ling'er.

'I'm scared . . .' she whimpered.

'We've seen the sun on TV before. It's the same thing,' I assured her.

'How can it be? Is seeing a snake on TV the same as seeing a real live one?'

'. . . Well, we have to go look anyway. Otherwise we'll be marked down!'

Ling'er and I gripped hands tightly as we gingerly made our way to the deck with the other children. Stepping outside, we prepared to face our first sunrise.

'In fact, we only began to fear the Sun three or four centuries ago. Before that, humans were not afraid of the Sun. It was just the opposite. In their eyes, the Sun was noble and majestic. Earth still turned on its axis back then, and people saw the Sun rise and set every single day. They would rejoice at sunrise and praise the beauty of sunset.' Ms. Stella stood at the bow of the ship, the sea breeze playing with her long hair. Behind her, the first few rays of sunlight shot over the horizon, like breath expelled from the blowhole of some unimaginably colossal sea creature.

Finally, we glimpsed the soul-chilling flame. At first, it was just a point of light on the horizon, but it quickly grew into a blazing arc. I felt my throat close up in terror. It seemed as if the deck beneath my feet had suddenly vanished. I was falling into the blackness of the sea, falling...Ling'er fell with me, her spindly frame quivering against mine. Our classmates, everyone else – the entire world even – all fell into the abyss. Then I remembered the riddle. I had asked our philosophy teacher what color the wall was. He told me that it was black. I thought he was wrong. I always imagined the wall of death would be bright as fresh snow. That was why I had remembered it when I saw the wall of plasma. In this era, death was no longer black. It was the glare of a lightning flash, and when that final bolt struck, the world would be vaporized in an instant.

Over three centuries ago, astrophysicists discovered the conversion rate of hydrogen to helium in the interior of the Sun was accelerating. They launched thousands of probes straight into the Sun to investigate, and eventually developed a precise mathematical model of the star.

Using this model, supercomputers calculated that the Sun had already evolved away from the main sequence on the Hertzsprung-Russell diagram. Helium would soon permeate the Sun's core, triggering a violent explosion called a helium flash. Afterward, the Sun would become a massive, cool-burning red giant, swelling until its diameter encompassed Earth's orbit.

But our planet would have been vaporized in the preceding helium flash long before then.

All of this was projected to occur in the next four hundred years. Since then, three hundred and eighty years had passed.

This solar catastrophe would not only raze and consume every inhabitable terrestrial planet in the solar system – it would also completely transform the composition and orbits of the Jovian planets. After the first helium flash, as heavy elements re-accumulated in the Sun's core, further runaway nuclear explosions would occur repeatedly for a period of time. While this period represented only a brief phase of stellar evolution, it might last thousands of times longer than all of human history. As long as we remained in the solar system, humanity stood no chance of surviving such a catastrophe. Interstellar immigration was our only way out. Given the level of technology available to humanity at the time, the only viable target for this migration was Proxima Centauri. It was the star closest to our own, a mere 4.3 light-years away. It was easy to reach a consensus on a destination. The real controversy lay in how to get there.

In order to reinforce the lesson, our ship doubled back twice on the Pacific, giving us two sunrises. By then we were accustomed to the sight, and no longer needed to be convinced that children born in the Southern hemisphere could actually survive daily exposure to the Sun. We sailed on into the dawn. As the sun rose higher in the sky, the cool ocean air of the past few days retreated, and temperatures began to rise. I was drifting off to sleep in my cabin when I heard a commotion outside. My door opened and Ling'er stuck her head in.

'Hey, the Leavers and Takers are at it again!'

I could not have cared less. They had been fighting for the last four centuries. Even so, I got up to take a quick look. Outside, a group of several boys were fighting. One glance told me Tung was up to his usual tricks again. His father was a stubborn Leaver, and he was still serving a prison sentence for his part in an uprising against the Coalition. Tung was a chip off the old block.

With the help of several brawny crewmen, Ms. Stella managed to pull the boys apart. Through a bloody nose, Tung still raised a fist and shouted, 'Throw the Takers overboard!'

'I'm a Taker. Do you want to throw me overboard, too?' asked Ms. Stella.

'I'll throw every single Taker overboard!' Tung refused to yield. Global support for the Takers had been rising of late, and they had grown unruly again.

'Why do you hate us so much?' asked Ms. Stella. Several Leaver children immediately shouted in protest.

'We won't wait to die on Earth with you Taker fools!'

'We will build spaceships and depart! All hail spaceships!'

Ms. Stella pressed the holographic projector on her wrist. An image immediately materialized in the air before us, arresting our attention. We quieted down for a moment. The hologram showed a crystal clear glass sphere with a closed ecosystem. The sphere was about ten centimeters in diameter and two-thirds full of water. It held a small shrimp, a branch of coral, and a bit of green algae. The shrimp swam languidly around the coral.

'This is a project Tung designed for his natural science class,' said Ms. Stella. 'In addition to the things you can all see, the sphere also contains microscopic bacteria. Everything inside the sphere is mutually interdependent. The shrimp eats the algae and draws oxygen from the water, and then discharges organic matter in its faeces and exhales carbon dioxide. The bacteria break down the shrimp's waste into inorganic matter and carbon dioxide. The algae then use the inorganic matter and carbon dioxide to carry out photosynthesis under an artificial light source. They create nutrients, grow and reproduce, and release oxygen for the shrimp to breathe. As long as there is a constant supply of sunlight, the ecological cycle in the glass sphere should be able to sustain itself in perpetuity. This is the best design by a student I have ever seen. I know that this sphere embodies Tung's dream and the dreams of all Leaver children. It is the spaceship you long after, in miniature! Tung told me he designed it according to the output of rigorous mathematical models. He modified the genes of every organism to ensure their metabolisms would be perfectly balanced. He firmly believed that the little world inside the sphere would survive until the shrimp reached the end of its natural life span. The teachers all adored this project. We placed it under an artificial light source at the required intensity. We were persuaded by Tung's predictions, and we silently wished the tiny world he had created would succeed. But now, less than two weeks later . . .'

Ms. Stella carefully withdrew the real glass sphere from a small box. The shrimp floated lifelessly at the surface of the murky water. The decaying algae had lost any hint of green, and had turned into a dead, woolly film that coated the coral.

'The little world is dead. Children, who can tell me why?' Ms Stella raised the lifeless sphere so that everyone could see it.

'It was too small!'

'Indeed, it was too small. Small ecosystems like this, no matter how precisely designed, cannot endure the passage of time. The spaceships of the Leavers are no exception.'

'We will build spaceships as large as Shanghai or New York City,' Tung objected, his voice much lower than before.

'Yes, but anything larger is beyond the limits of human technology, and compared to Earth, those ecosystems would still be much too small.'

'Then we will find a new planet!'

'Even you Leavers don't really believe that,' replied Ms. Stella. 'There are no suitable planets in orbit around Proxima Centauri. The nearest fixed star with inhabitable planets is eight hundred and fifty light-years away. At present, the fastest spaceship we can build can only travel at zero-point-five percent of the speed of light, which means it would take us one hundred and seventy thousand years to get there. A spaceship-sized ecosystem would not last for even one-tenth of the voyage. Children, only an ecosystem the size of Earth, with its unstoppable ecological cycle, could sustain us indefinitely! If humanity leaves Earth behind,' she proclaimed, 'then we would be as vulnerable as an infant separated from its mother in the middle of a desert!'

'But . . .' Tung paused. 'Ms. Stella, it's too late for us and too late for

Earth. The Sun will explode before we accelerate and get far enough away!'

'There is enough time,' she replied firmly. 'You must believe in the Coalition! How many times have I told you? Even if you don't believe, at the very least we can say, 'Humanity dies with pride, for we have done everything that we could!''

Humanity's escape was a five-step process. First, the Earth Engines would generate thrust in the opposite direction of Earth's movement, halting its rotation. Second, operating at full capacity, the engines would accelerate Earth until it reached escape velocity, flinging it from the solar system. Third, Earth would continue to accelerate as it flew through outer space toward Proxima Centauri. Fourth, the engines would reverse direction, restarting Earth's rotation and decelerating gradually. Fifth, Earth would enter into orbit around Proxima Centauri, becoming its satellite. People called these five steps the 'Braking Era', the 'Deserting Era', the 'First Wandering Era' (during acceleration), the 'Second Wandering Era' (during deceleration), and the 'Neosolar Era'.

The entire migration process was projected to last 2,500 years, over one hundred generations.

The ocean liner continued its passage toward the part of the earth shrouded in night. Neither sunlight nor the glow of the plasma beams could be seen here. As the chilly Atlantic breeze nipped at our faces, for the first time in our young lives, we saw the stars in the night sky. God, it was a heartbreakingly beautiful sight! Ms. Stella stood with one arm around Ling'er and I. 'Look, children,' she said, pointing to the stars with her other hand. 'There is Centaurus, and that is Proxima Centauri, our new home!' She began to cry, and we cried along with her. All around us, even the captain and the crew – hardened sailors all – began to tear up. With tearful eyes, everyone gazed in the direction in which Ms. Stella pointed, and the stars shimmered and danced. Only one star held steady; the beam of a distant lighthouse over dark and stormy seas, a flicker of fire beckoning to a lonely traveler freezing on the tundra. That star had taken the place of the Sun in our hearts. It was the only pillar of hope for one hundred future generations as they navigated a sea of troubles.

*

On our voyage home, I saw the first signal for departure. A giant comet appeared in the night sky – the Moon. Because we could not take the Moon with us, engines had been installed on the lunar surface to push it out of Earth's orbit, ensuring that there would be no collision during the acceleration period. The sweeping tail of the Lunar Engines bathed the sea in blue light, obscuring the stars. As it moved past, the Moon's gravitational pull raised towering breakers. We had to transfer to a plane to fly home to the Northern hemisphere.

The day of departure had finally arrived!

As soon as we disembarked, we were blinded by the glare of the Earth Engines. They blazed many times brighter than before, no longer slanted but speared straight toward the sky. The engines were running at maximum power. The planet's acceleration created thunderous, hundred-meter waves that battered every continent. Blistering hurricanes howled through the towering columns of plasma, whipping up boiling froth and uprooting whole forests . . . Our planet had become a gigantic comet, its blue tail piercing the darkness of space.

Earth was on its way; humanity was on its way.

My grandfather passed away just before departure, his burnt body ravaged by infection. In his final moments, he repeated one phrase over and over: 'Ah, Earth, my wandering Earth . . .'

Chapter 2

The Deserting Era

Our school was scheduled to relocate to an underground city, and we were among its first inhabitants. Our school bus entered a massive tunnel, which sloped gently downward into the earth. After driving for half an hour, we were told that we had entered the city, but nothing outside the bus windows resembled any city I had seen before. We whipped past a labyrinth of smaller side tunnels and countless sealed doors set back into cavities in the walls. Under the row of floodlights mounted to the tunnel ceiling, everything assumed a leaden blue cast. We could not help but feel dejected at the realization that, for most of the remainder of our lives, this would be our world.

'Primitive humans lived in caves, and now so will we,' Ling'er said quietly, but Ms. Stella still caught her words.

'It can't be helped, children,' she sighed. 'The surface will soon become a terrible, terrible place. When it is cold, your spit will freeze before it hits the ground. When it is hot, it will evaporate even as it leaves your lips!'

'I know it'll be cold because Earth is travelling away from the Sun, but why will it get hot?' asked a little girl from one of the lower grades.

'Idiot, haven't you studied transfer orbits?' I snapped.

'No.'

Ling'er launched into a patient explanation, as if to dispel her sorrowful thoughts. 'It's like this: the Earth Engines aren't as powerful as you think. They can accelerate Earth a little bit, but they can't just push it out of its solar orbit straight away. Before Earth escapes the Sun, we still need to orbit it fifteen times! Through these fifteen orbits, Earth will gradually accelerate. Right now, Earth's orbit around the Sun is pretty much circular, but as it speeds up, it will become increasingly elliptical. The faster we move, the flatter the ellipse grows, and the more the Sun will be shifted toward one end of the orbit. So when Earth is furthest from the Sun, naturally it will be very cold . . .'

'But . . . that's still not right! It will be cold when Earth is far away from the Sun, but on the other end of the ellipse, its distance from the Sun will be . . . Hmm, let me think.' The girl chewed on her lip. 'Orbital dynamics says Earth won't be any closer to the Sun than it is now, so why would it get hotter?'

She truly was a little genius. Genetic engineering had made this type of exceptional memory the new norm. Humanity was quite fortunate in this respect. Otherwise, unimaginable miracles like the Earth Engines could not have been realized in the span of four centuries.

'Don't forget about the Earth Engines, dummy,' I chimed in. 'Over ten thousand of those giant blowtorches are on full blast. Earth is basically just a ring to hold the rocket nozzles. Now be quiet. I'm getting annoyed.'

*

We began our new lives underground. Located five hundred meters below the surface, our city had space for over one million residents. Many others just like it were scattered across every continent. Here, I finished primary school and entered secondary school. My schooling concentrated on science and engineering. Art, philosophy, and other subjects deemed inessential had been minimized or removed from the curriculum. Humanity had no time for distractions. It was the busiest era in human history. Everyone had work to do, and the work was never finished. Interestingly, every world religion had vanished without a trace overnight. People finally realized that if God truly existed, he was a real bastard. We still studied history, but to us, the Ante-solar Era of human history seemed as mythical as the Garden of Eden.

My father served in the Air Force as an astronaut. He frequently flew low-Earth orbit missions and was rarely at home. I remember in the fifth year of orbital acceleration, when Earth was at aphelion, we took a family trip to the seashore. Aphelion Day was a holiday like New Year's Eve or Christmas. As Earth entered the part of its orbit furthest from the Sun, everyone basked in a false sense of security. We still needed to wear special thermal suits to go to surface. Instead of cooling suits, we donned sealed heating suits powered by nuclear batteries. Outside, we were nearly blinded by the Earth Engines' towering plasma beams. The harsh light eclipsed our view of the surface world, and it was difficult to tell if the landscape had changed at all. We had to fly for a long time in our car before we escaped the glare and we could actually see the shore. The Sun had shrunk to the size of a baseball. It hung motionless in the sky, surrounded by a faint, dawn-like halo. The sky was the deepest blue we had ever seen, and the stars were clearly visible. Looking around, I fleetingly wondered where the ocean had gone. Now, there was only a vast, white icy plain stretching to the horizon. A large crowd of revelers had gathered atop the frozen sea. Fireworks whistled through the darkness. Everyone was carousing with unusual abandon. Drunken party-goers rolled across the ice, while others belted out the words to a dozen different songs, each trying to drown out the competing voices around them.

'Despite it all, everyone is living their own lives. No harm in that,' my father said approvingly. He paused, suddenly remembering something. 'Oh, I forgot to tell you – I've fallen in love with Stella Ren I want to move out to be with her.'

'Who is she?' my mother asked calmly.

'My primary school teacher,' I answered for him. I had started secondary school two years ago, and had no idea how my father knew Ms. Stella. Maybe they had met at my graduation ceremony?

'Then go,' said my mother.

'I'm sure I'll grow tired of her soon enough. I'll come back then. Is that okay by you?'

'If you want to, certainly.' Her voice was as calm and even as the frozen sea. But a moment later, she bubbled with excitement. 'Oh, that one is beautiful! It must have a holographic diffractor inside!' She pointed to a firework blossoming in the night sky, genuinely moved by its beauty.

Movies and novels produced four centuries ago were baffling to modern audiences. It was incomprehensible to us why people in the Ante-solar Era invested so much emotion into matters that had nothing to do with survival. Watching the hero or heroine suffer or weep for love was bizarre beyond words. In this day and age, the threat of death and the desire to escape overrode everything else. Nothing but the most current updates on the solar state and position of Earth could hope to move us or even hold our attention. This hyper-focus gradually changed the essence of human psychology and spirituality. Humans paid scant attention to affairs of the heart, like a gambler taking a swig of water, unable to tear his eyes from the roulette wheel.

Two months later, my father returned from his jaunt with Ms. Stella. My mother was neither happy nor unhappy to see him.

'Stella has a good impression of you,' my father told me. 'She said you were a very creative student.'

'Who said that?' My mother asked with a puzzled expression.

'My primary school teacher, Ms. Stella,' I replied impatiently. 'Dad was living with her for the last two months!'

'Oh, I remember!' She shook her head and laughed. 'Not even forty yet, and my memory is already shot.'

She looked up at the holographic stars on the ceiling and the forest on the walls. 'It's good to have you home. Now you can switch up these images. Your son and I are sick of looking at them, but we don't know how to work the darn thing.'

By the time Earth began its fall back toward the Sun, we had all entirely forgotten the episode.

*

One day, the news reported that the ocean had begun to thaw, so we took another family trip to the seashore. Earth was just passing through Mars' orbit. The available sunlight should not have significantly raised temperatures, but the Earth Engines ensured the surface was warm enough to thaw the sea ice. It felt delightful to step outside without the encumbrance of a thermal suit. The Earth Engines still lit up the sky in our hemisphere, but on the other side of the planet, people could really feel the Sun's approach. Their sky was clear and pure blue, and the Sun was as bright as it had been before departure. But from the air, we spotted no signs of a thaw. We saw only a white expanse of ice. Disappointed, we got out of our car. Just as we closed the doors, we heard an earthshaking rumble that seemed to rise from the very depths of the planet. It sounded like the Earth was about to explode.

'That's the sound of the ocean!' my father shouted over the noise. 'The sharp rise in temperatures is heating the thick ice unevenly – it's like an earthquake on land!'

Suddenly, a sharp noise like a thunderclap pierced the low rumble, eliciting cheers from the people watching the sea behind us. I saw a long crack open up, shooting across the frozen ocean like a black fork of lightning. The rumbling continued as more fissures appeared in the ice. Water gushed from the cracks, forming torrents that rushed across the icy plain.

On the way home, we looked out over the long-desolate land below and saw broad tracts of wild grass sprouting from the earth. All kinds of flowers had burst into full bloom, and withered forests were mantled in tender green leaves. Life was throwing itself into the business of rejuvenation as if there was no time to lose.

Every day the Earth drew closer to the Sun, dread knotted itself tighter in our stomachs. Fewer people made the trip to the surface to admire the spring scenery. Most of us retreated into the depths of the underground city, not to avoid the approaching heat, torrential rains, and hurricane-force winds, but to escape the creeping terror of the Sun. One night, after I had already gone to bed, I overheard my mother tell my father in hushed tones, 'Maybe it really is too late.'

'The same rumour was going around during the last four perihelions,' he replied.

'But this time it's true,' she insisted. 'I heard it from Dr. Chandler. Her husband is an astronomer on the Navigation Commission. You all know him. He told her that they have observed accelerated rates of helium concentration.'

'Listen, my dear, we mustn't give up hope. Not because hope is real, but because we have to conduct ourselves nobly. In the Ante-solar Era, nobility required wealth, power, or talent, but now one just needs hope. It is the gold and jewels of this age. No matter how long we live, we must hold on to it! Tomorrow, we'll tell our son the same thing.'

Like everyone else, I felt restless and uneasy as the perihelion approached.

One day after school, I found myself in the city's central plaza. I stood by the round fountain in the middle of the plaza, looking down at the glittering water in the pool and then up at the ethereal ripples of light reflected on the domed ceiling. Just then I noticed Ling'er. She was holding a little bottle in one hand and a short length of tube in the other. She was blowing soap bubbles, her eyes blankly following each string of bubbles as they drifted away. She watched them vanish one by one, only to blow another stream.

'You still like blowing bubbles at your age?' I asked, walking over.

Ling'er looked pleased to see me. 'Let's take a trip!'

'Take a trip? Where?'

'To the surface, of course!' She swept her hand through the air, using the computer on her wrist to project a hologram of a beach at sunset. A gentle breeze stirred the palm trees, and white surf lapped at the shore. Pairs of lovers dotted the yellow sand, black silhouettes against the gold-flecked sea. 'Mona and Dagang sent me this. They've been traveling all over the world. They said it's not too hot on the surface. It's so nice out. Let's go!'

'They were just expelled for cutting class,' I objected.

Ling'er sniffed. 'That's not what you're really afraid of. You're afraid of the Sun!'

'And you're not? You had to see a psychiatrist because of your heliophobia.'

'I'm a different person now. I've been inspired! Look,' said Ling'er, using the tube to blow another stream of soap bubbles. 'Watch closely.' She pointed to the bubbles.

I singled out a bubble, examining the waves of light and color surging across its surface, the iridescent patterns too complex and intricate for humans to process. It was as if the bubble knew it would lead a short life, and was frantically broadcasting the myriad dreams and legends of its prodigious memory to the world. A moment later, the waves of light and color vanished in a silent explosion. For a half-second, a tiny wisp of vapor remained, but then that, too, was gone, as if the bubble had never existed at all.

'See? The Earth is a Cosmic soap bubble. One pop, and it's gone. So what is there to be afraid of?'

'But it won't happen like that. It's been calculated that after the helium flash it will take one hundred hours before the Earth is completely vaporized.'

'That's exactly the scariest part!' Ling'er cried. 'Five hundred meters underground, we're like meat stuffing in a pasty. First we'll be slowly cooked through, and then we'll be vaporized!'

A cold shiver ran down my entire body.

'But it won't be like that on the surface. Everything will be vaporized in the blink of an eye. Anyone up there will be like soap bubbles, one pop and…' She trailed off. 'So I think it would be better to be on the surface when the flash hits.'

I couldn't say why, but I did not go with her. She went with Tung instead, and I never saw either of them again.

But the helium flash never happened. Earth swept past perihelion and climbed toward aphelion for the sixth time. Humanity breathed a collective sigh of relief. Because Earth no longer rotated, at this point in its orbit around the Sun, the Earth Engines installed in Asia faced into the planet's direction of flight. As a result, the engines were completely powered down, save for occasional adjustments to Earth's orientation. We sailed into a quiet, endless night. In America, however, the engines were operating at full capacity, the continent securing the rocket nozzles to the planet. Because the Western hemisphere also faced the Sun, the heat there was devastating. Grass and trees alike went up in smoke.

Earth's gravity-assisted acceleration progressed like this year after year. When the planet began its ascent toward aphelion, we unwound proportionally to Earth's distance from the Sun; at the new year, when the planet began its long fall toward the Sun, we grew edgier with each passing day. Each time Earth reached perihelion, rumors swirled that the helium flash was imminent. The rumors would persist until Earth climbed again toward aphelion. But even as people's fears subsided as the Sun shrank in the sky, the next wave of panic was already brewing. It was like humanity's morale was dangling from a cosmic trapeze. Or perhaps it was more accurate to say that we were playing Russian Roulette on a planetary scale: every journey from perihelion to aphelion and back was like turning the chamber, and passing the perihelion was like pulling the trigger! Each pull of the trigger was more nerve-wracking than the last. My boyhood was spent alternating between terror and relaxation. Come to think of it, even at aphelion, Earth never left the danger zone of the helium flash. When the Sun exploded, Earth would be slowly liquefied, which was a fate considerably worse than being vaporized at perihelion.

In the Deserting Era, disaster followed disaster in quick succession.

The changes in velocity and trajectory generated by the Earth Engines disturbed the equilibrium of Earth's iron-nickel core. The turbulence passed through the Gutenberg discontinuity and spread to the mantle. As geothermal energy escaped to the surface, volcanic eruptions ravaged every continent, which posed a lethal threat to humanity's underground cities. Beginning in the sixth orbital period onward, catastrophic magma seepage events occurred all too frequently in cities around the world.

On the day it happened, I was on my way home from school when the sirens sounded. It was quickly followed by an emergency broadcast from city hall.

'Attention citizens of City F112! The city's northern barrier has been breached by crustal stress. Magma has entered the city! Magma has entered the city! Magma flows have already reached Block Four! Highway exits have been sealed off. All citizens should report to the central plaza and evacuate by lift. Please note that the evacuation will be conducted in accordance with Article Five of the Emergencies Act. I repeat, the evacuation will be conducted in accordance with Article Five of the Emergencies Act!'

Looking around the labyrinth of tunnels, our underground city seemed eerily normal. But I was aware of the immediate danger: of the two subterranean highways that led out of the city, one of those routes had been blocked off last year by necessary fortification work on the city's barriers. If the remaining route was also blocked, we could only escape through the vertical lift shafts that lead directly to the surface.

The carrying capacity of the lifts was very limited. It would take a long time to move all three hundred and sixty thousand residents to safety, but there was no need to scramble for a place on the lifts. The Coalition's Emergency Act had made all necessary arrangements for the evacuation.

Past generations once grappled with an ethical dilemma. A man is faced by rising floodwaters and can only save one other person. Should he save his father or his son? In this day and age, it was unbelievable that the question had ever been raised at all.

When I arrived in the plaza, I saw that people had already begun to arrange themselves in a long line according to age. At the front of the line, closest to the lifts, stood robotic nurses, each cradling an infant. Then came the kindergartners, followed by the primary school students. My place was in the middle of the line, still rather close to the front. My father was on duty in low-Earth orbit, leaving only my mother and myself in the city. Unable to see her, I began to run along the unending line of people, but did not get far before I was stopped by soldiers. I knew she stood at the very back. Our city was primarily a university town, with only a few families, so she was grouped with the city's oldest residents.

The line inched forward at an excruciating pace. After three long hours it was finally my turn, but I felt no relief as I boarded the lift. There were still twenty thousand university students standing between my mother and survival, and I could already smell the strong odor of sulfur.

Two and a half hours after I made it to the surface, five hundred meters beneath my feet, magma inundated the entire city. A knife twisted in my heart as I imagined my mother's final moments. Standing alongside eighteen thousand others who could not be evacuated in time, she would have watched magma surge into the plaza. The city's power supply would have failed, leaving only the dreadful crimson glow of the magma. The intense heat would have blackened the lofty white dome over the plaza. The victims likely never came into contact with the magma before the thousand-plus degree temperatures proved fatal.

But life went on, and even in this harsh, terrifying reality, sparks of love still flew from time to time. During the twelfth climb toward aphelion, in an attempt to ease public tension, the Coalition unexpectedly revived the Olympic Games after a two-century hiatus. I competed at the Games in the snowmobile rally. Beginning in Shanghai, athletes raced their snowmobiles across the frozen surface of the Pacific to New York.

At the sound of the starting gun, more than a hundred snowmobiles shot off across the frozen ocean, blazing across the ice at two hundred kilometers per hour. At first, there was always a competitor in my sights. Two days later, however, having fallen behind or swept ahead, they had all disappeared over the horizon.

The glow of the Earth Engines was no longer visible behind me, and I sped into the darkest part of the planet. My world was the boundless starlit sky and the ice that stretched in all directions to the ends of the universe – or perhaps this was the end of the universe. And in this universe of infinite stars and endless ice, I was alone! As an avalanche of loneliness overwhelmed me, I wanted to cry. I drove as if my life depended on it. Whether or not I placed on the podium was beside the point: I needed to get rid of this terrible loneliness before it killed me. In my mind, the opposite shore no longer existed.

At that moment, I saw a figure silhouetted against the horizon. As I grew closer, I realized it was a woman. She was standing next to her snowmobile, her long hair fluttering in the icy wind. The moment our paths crossed, it was clear that the rest of our lives had been decided. Her name was Yamasaki Kayako, and she was Japanese. The women's team had set off twelve hours before us, but her snowmobile had been caught in a crack in the ice, snapping one of the skis. As I helped her repair her sled, I shared with her the feeling that had gripped me earlier.

'I felt exactly the same way!' She exclaimed. 'It was like I was alone in the universe! You know, when I saw you appear in the distance, it was like watching the sun rise.'

'Why didn't you call a rescue plane?' I asked.

She raised her small fist. 'This race embodies the human spirit,' she declared with the tenacity so characteristic of the Japanese. 'We must remember that Earth cannot call for help as it wanders through the cosmos!'

'Well, now we have to call. Neither of us has a spare runner, so your snowmobile is beyond repair.'

'Why don't I ride on the back of yours?' she suggested. 'If you don't care about placing, that is.'

I really did not care, so Kayako and I made the rest of the long journey across the frozen Pacific together.

As we passed Hawaii, we saw a glimmer of light on the horizon. On this boundless expanse of ice, illuminated by the tiny Sun, we submitted an application for a marriage license to the Coalition Department of Civil Affairs.

By the time we reached New York City, the Olympic referees had grown tired of waiting and had packed their things and left. But an official from the municipal Bureau of Civil Affairs stood waiting for us. He congratulated us on our marriage and then began to perform his official duty. With a sweep of his hand, he summoned a hologram that was neatly lined with tens of thousands of dots. Each dot represented a couple that had registered for marriage with the Coalition in the last few days. In light of harsh environmental conditions, by law only one out of every three newly married couples was permitted to procreate. This right was awarded by lottery. Faced with thousands of dots, Kayako hesitated for a long time before picking one in the middle.

When the dot turned green, she jumped for joy. I was not sure how I felt about the prospect of starting a family. If I brought a child into this era of suffering, would it be a blessing or a calamity? The official, at least, was over the moon. He told us it was always a happy occasion when a couple got their little green dot. He pulled out a bottle of vodka, and the three of us took turns drinking from it, toasting the continuation of the human race. Behind us, the faint light of the distant Sun gilded the Statue of Liberty. Before us, the long abandoned skyscrapers of Manhattan cast long shadows over the quiet ice of New York Harbor. Feeling tipsy, tears began to stream down my cheeks.

Earth, my wandering Earth!

*

Before we parted ways, the official handed us a set of keys and said drunkenly, 'These are for your newly allotted house in Asia. Run along home, now. Run to your wonderful new home!'

'Just how wonderful is it?' I asked coldly. 'Asia's underground cities are fraught with danger – but of course you Westerners wouldn't know that.'

'We are about to face our own unique hazard,' he replied. 'Earth is about to pass through the asteroid belt, and the Western hemisphere is facing right toward it.'

'But we passed through the asteroid belt on the last few orbits. It's no big deal, is it?'

'We just swiped the edges of the asteroid belt. The Space Fleet could handle that, of course. They have lasers and nukes to clear small rocks from the Earth's path. But this time . . .' He paused. 'Haven't you seen the news? This time, Earth will pass straight through the middle of the belt! The fleet would have to deal with the large rocks, oops . . .'

On the flight back to Asia, Kayako turned to me and asked, 'Are those asteroids very big?'

My father was one of the Space Fleet officers tasked with asteroid diversion and destruction. Therefore, though the government had imposed a media blackout to prevent mass panic as usual, I still had some idea of what was about to happen. I told Kayako that some of the asteroids we faced were the size of mountains; even fifty megaton thermonuclear bombs would only pockmark their surfaces.

'They'll have to use the most powerful weapon in the human arsenal!' I added mysteriously.

'You mean antimatter bombs?' she asked.

'What else could it be?'

'What is the fleet's cruising range?'

'Currently their strength is limited. My Dad told me it extends out to about one and a half million kilometers,' I answered.

Kayako gave a little squeal. 'Then we'll be able to see it!'

'Best not to look.'

But Kayako did look, and did so without protective glasses. The first flash of an antimatter bomb arrived from space shortly after we took off. At that exact moment, Kayako had been admiring the starry sky outside the window. The flash blinded her for over an hour, and her eyes were red and watery for more than a month afterward. In the bloodcurdling moments that followed, the antimatter shells continued to bombard the asteroid. Ruinous flashes pulsed across the pitch-black sky, as if a horde of colossal paparazzi had descended upon the planet and were frenziedly snapping away.

Half an hour later, we saw the meteors, dragging streaming tails of fire across the sky, mesmerizing in their terrible beauty. More and more meteors appeared, each streaking further into the atmosphere than the last. Suddenly, a deafening roar shook the plane, immediately followed by more rumbling and shaking. Thinking that a meteor had struck the plane, Kayako screamed and threw herself into my arms. Just then, the captain's voice came on over the intercom.

'Ladies and gentlemen, please do not be alarmed. That was merely the sonic boom created by a meteor breaking the sound barrier. Please put on your headphones to avoid permanent hearing loss. Because the safety of the flight cannot be guaranteed, we will make an emergency landing in Hawaii.'

As the announcement ended, my eyes fastened on a meteor much larger than the others. I became convinced it would not burn up in the atmosphere like the ones before it. Sure enough, the fireball hurtled across the sky, shrinking as it fell, and smashed into the frozen ocean. Seen from ten thousand meters above, a small white spot appeared at the point of impact. The spot immediately spread into a white circle and rapidly expanded across the ocean's surface.

'Is that a wave?' asked Kayako, her voice trembling.

'Yes, it's a wave over a hundred meters high. But the ocean is frozen solid. The ice will soon dampen it,' I replied, mostly to comfort myself. I did not look down again.

We landed in Honolulu not long after. The local government had arranged to take us to an underground city. The drive along the coast afforded us a clear view of the meteor-filled sky. It was as if a legion of fiery-haired demons had burst all at once from a single point in space.

We watched as a meteor struck the surface not far from the coast. There was no visible plume of water, but a white mushroom cloud of water vapor bloomed high overhead. Beneath the frozen surface, roiling seawater surged toward shore. The thick layers of ice groaned as they splintered apart, rolling like waves, as if a school of giant, sinuous sea monsters was swimming beneath the surface.

'How big was that one?' I asked the official who had met us at the airport.

'Less than five kilograms, no bigger than your head. But I have just been informed that a twenty-ton meteor is splashing down eight hundred kilometers north of here.'

His wrist communicator began beeping. He glanced at it and immediately told the driver, 'We won't make it to Gate 204. Head for the nearest entrance!'

The van turned a corner and pulled to a stop in front of an entrance to the underground city. As we got out, we saw that several soldiers guarded the entrance. They stared unblinkingly into the distance, eyes filled with terror. We followed their gaze to the horizon and saw a black barrier. At first glance, it looked like a low bank of clouds, but its height was too uniform for clouds – it was more like a long wall stretching across the horizon. Closer inspection revealed the wall was edged in white.

'What is that?' Kayako timidly asked an officer. His answer made our hair stand on end.

'A wave.'

The tall steel gates to the subterranean city grated shut. Ten minutes later, we felt a deep rumble emanate from the ceiling, as if a titan was rolling about on the surface up there. We gazed at each other in speechless despair, for we knew at that moment hundred-meter waves were rolling over Hawaii and on toward the mainland. But the quakes that followed were even more terrifying. It was if a giant fist was pummeling Earth from outer space. Underground, the assault was faint, but we felt each tremor keenly in our souls. It was the barrage of meteors against the surface.

The brutal bombardment of our planet continued on and off for a week. When we finally left the underground city, Kayako cried, 'My god, what happened to the sky?'

The sky was a muddy gray. The upper atmosphere was filled with the dust that had been kicked up by the asteroid collisions. The Sun and stars were lost in this endless gray, as if the entire universe was blanketed in thick fog. On the ground, the seawater left in the wake of the monstrous waves had frozen solid. The surviving high-rises stood isolated above the ice, cascades of ice spilling down their sides. A layer of dust had settled on the ice, draining all color from the world except for that all-pervading gray.

Kayako and I soon resumed our voyage back to Asia. As the plane crossed the International Date Line, which had long since ceased to matter, we witnessed humanity's darkest night. The plane seemed to cruise silently through the inky depths of the ocean. As we gazed through the windows, searching in vain for a glimmer of light in the gloom, our moods turned equally black.

'When will it end?' Kayako murmured.

I did not know if she meant our journey or this lifetime of misery and suffering. I was beginning to think there was no end to either one. Indeed, even if Earth sailed beyond the blast radius of the helium flash, even if we escaped with our lives – then what? We stood on the bottom rung of an immeasurably tall ladder. In a hundred generations, when our descendants reached the top and glimpsed the promise of new life, our bones would have long turned to dust. I did not dare imagine the suffering and hardships yet to come, much less dare consider leading my lover and my child down that endless, muddy road. I was so tired, too tired to go on . . .

Just as sorrow and despair threatened to suffocate me, a woman's scream rang through the cabin: 'Ah! No! Darling, you can't!'

I turned and saw a woman wrest a gun from the hands of the man sitting next to her. He had just attempted to put the muzzle of the gun against his own temple. The man looked wan and emaciated, his eyes staring listlessly into the distance. The woman buried her head in his lap and broke into little chirping sobs.

'Be quiet,' the man said coldly.

The sobbing stopped, leaving only the low hum of the engines, like a steady funeral dirge. In my mind, the plane was stuck in the vast gloom, motionless. There was nothing else left in the entire universe except for the plane and the enveloping darkness. Kayako pressed herself tightly into my embrace. Her entire body felt ice cold.

Suddenly, there was a commotion at the front of the cabin and people began whispering excitedly. I looked out the window and saw a hazy light in front of the plane. The dust-filled night sky was uniformly suffused with a formless blue glow.

It was the light of the Earth Engines.

One-third of the Western hemisphere's engines had been destroyed by meteoroids, but Earth had sustained less damage than the calculations had projected before departure. The Earth Engines in the Eastern hemisphere, sheltered on the reverse side of the impact surface, had suffered no losses. In terms of power, Earth remained well equipped to make its escape.

When I laid eyes on the dim blue light ahead, I felt like a deep sea diver finally seeing the sunlit surface after a long ascent from the abyss. I began to breathe steadily again.

From a few rows away, I heard the woman's voice. 'Darling, pain, fear – we can only feel these things while we are alive. When we die, there is nothing at all. Only darkness. It is better to live, don't you think?'

The emaciated man did not reply. He was staring at the blue light up ahead, tears rolling down his face. I knew he would live through this. Just as long as that hopeful blue light still shone, we would all live through this. I remembered my father's words of hope.

When we touched down, Kayako and I did not go directly to our new underground home. Instead, we went to look for my father at the Space Fleet's base station on the surface. When we arrived at the station, however, I found only a medal of honor, posthumously awarded and ice cold. The medal was presented to me by an air vice-marshal. He told me that my father had lost his life during the operation to clear the asteroids from Earth's path. An antimatter explosion had blasted an asteroid fragment straight into his single-seater craft.

'When it happened, the rock was traveling at one hundred kilometers per second relative to his ship. The cabin was vaporized on impact. He felt no pain,' said the air marshal. 'I assure you, he felt no pain at all.'

When Earth began its fall back toward the Sun again, Kayako and I traveled to the surface to see the spring scenery. We were sorely disappointed.

The world was still a monochromatic gray. Under the overcast sky, frozen lakes of residual seawater dotted the landscape. There was not a single sprig of green to be seen. The great pall of dust in the atmosphere blocked the light of the Sun, preventing temperatures from rising again. The oceans and continents did not thaw even at perihelion. The Sun remained a faint, dim presence, like a specter lurking behind the dust.

Three years later, as the dust in the atmosphere dissipated, humanity made its last pass through perihelion. As we reached it, those living in the Eastern hemisphere were privileged to witness the fastest sunrise and sunset in Earth's history. The Sun leapt up from the sea and streaked rapidly across the sky. Shadows changed directions so quickly that they looked like second hands sweeping across the faces of countless clocks. It was the shortest day Earth had ever seen, over in less than an hour.

When the Sun plunged below the horizon and darkness fell across the planet, I felt a twinge of grief. This fleeting day seemed like a brief summary of Earth's four and a half billion-year history in the solar system. Even until the end of the universe, Earth would never return.

'It's dark,' Kayako said sadly.

'The longest night,' I replied. In the Eastern hemisphere, this night would last twenty five hundred years. One hundred generations would pass before the light of Proxima Centauri illuminated this continent again. The Western hemisphere was facing its longest day, but even so, it would last just a moment compared to the age-long night. On that side of the world, the Sun would quickly rise to its zenith, where it would remain motionless, steadily shrinking. Within half a century, it would be difficult to distinguish from any other star.

The Earth's intended trajectory called for a rendezvous with Jupiter. The Navigation Commission's plan was as follows: the Earth's fifteenth orbit around the Sun would be so elliptical that its aphelion would enter Jupiter's orbit. Earth would brush past Jupiter on a near-collision course. Harnessing the gas giant's enormous gravitational pull to assist its acceleration, Earth would finally attain escape velocity.

Two months after Earth passed perihelion, Jupiter became visible to the naked eye. At first, it appeared as a dim point of light, but it soon flattened and became disk-shaped. After another month, Jupiter had grown as large as the full Moon, reddish-brown with faintly visible banding. Then some of the Earth Engines' plasma beams, which had remained perpendicular for fifteen years, began to shift. Final adjustments were being made to Earth's orientation before the rendezvous. Jupiter sank slowly below the horizon, where it stayed for the next three months. We could not see it, but we knew the two planets were converging upon each other.

It almost came as a surprise when we heard that Jupiter was visible again in the Eastern hemisphere. Everyone thronged to the surface to take a look. When I passed through the airlock of the underground city, I saw that the Earth Engines, after running continuously for fifteen years, had been powered down. We could see the stars in the sky once again. Our final rendezvous with Jupiter was in progress.

Everyone peered nervously toward the western sky, where a dim red glow was beginning to show above the horizon. The glow swelled until it filled the entire horizon. I soon realized that the red expanse had formed a neat border against the stars; it was an arc so massive that it spanned from one end of the horizon to the other. As it slowly rose, the sky beneath it turned red, as if a velvet theater curtain was being drawn across the rest of the universe. I let out a gasp, reeling from the realization that the curtain was Jupiter. I knew that Jupiter was thirteen hundred times the size of Earth, but only when I saw its immense splendor did I truly take in its colossal size

It was difficult to describe in words the fear and oppression that accompanied the behemoth as it reared above the horizon. One reporter later wrote, 'I did not know if I was in my own nightmare, or if the whole universe was just a nightmare in the enormous, twisted mind of that deity!' As Jupiter continued its terrible ascent, it gradually came to occupy half the sky. We then had an unobscured view of the storms raging in its cloud layers, which whipped the gasses in the atmosphere into chaotic, disorienting lines. I knew that beneath those thick decks of clouds lay seething oceans of liquid hydrogen and liquid helium. The famous Great Red Spot appeared, still raging across Jupiter's surface after hundreds of thousands of years. The maelstrom was large enough to swallow the whole Earth. Jupiter now filled the entire sky. Earth was like a balloon floating on Jupiter's boiling red sea of clouds. The Great Red Spot climbed to the middle of the sky and stared down upon our world like a cyclopean eye. The entire landscape was shrouded in its ghastly light. It was impossible to believe that our tiny planet could escape the gravitational field of this colossus. From the ground, it even seemed unimaginable that Earth might become a satellite of Jupiter – no, we would certainly plummet into the hell concealed beneath that unending ocean of clouds.

But the navigational engineers' calculations were faultless, and the bewildering ruddy sky continued to drift past us. After some time, a black crescent appeared on the western horizon and swiftly widened to reveal the twinkling stars. Earth was breaking free from Jupiter's gravitational clutches. Just then, sirens began to wail, announcing that the gravitational tide Jupiter had raised was rushing back inland. We were told later that giant waves, reaching over a hundred metres high, had again swept across the continents.

As I ran toward the gates of the underground city, I stole one last glance at Jupiter, which still occupied half the sky. Distinct scoring marred the gas giant's cloud layer, which I later learned was the trail left by the gravitational pull of Earth on Jupiter's surface. Our planet, too, had left mountainous breakers of liquid helium and hydrogen in its wake. At that point, the Earth, accelerated by Jupiter's mighty gravity, was hurled into deep space.

As it departed Jupiter, Earth reached escape velocity. It no longer needed to return toward the Sun, where only death lurked. As it hurtled toward the open reaches of space, the endless Wandering Era began.

And under the dark red shadow of Jupiter, deep within the earth, my son was born.

Chapter 3
Rebellion

After we left Jupiter behind, Asia's ten thousand Earth Engines roared to life again. They would operate at full capacity for the next five hundred years, constantly accelerating the planet. During those five hundred years, the engines would consume half of the mountains on the Asian continent as fuel.

Freed at last from the fear of death after four centuries, humanity breathed a collective sigh of relief. But the expected revelry never took place, and what happened next was beyond anyone's imagining.

After our subterranean city's celebratory rally concluded, I donned my thermal suit and ascended to the surface alone. The familiar mountains of my childhood had already been leveled by mega-excavators, leaving only bare rock and hard, frozen soil. The bleak emptiness was broken by patches of stark white covering the land as far as the eye could see: the salt marshes left behind by the great ocean tide. Before me, the city in which my father and grandfather had lived out their days – a city once home to ten million – lay in ruins. In the blue light of the Earth Engine's plasma beams, the exposed steel skeletons of skyscrapers dragged long shadows behind them, like the fossilized remains of prehistoric beasts . . . The chronic floods and meteor strikes had destroyed virtually everything on the surface. All that humankind and nature had wrought over millennia lay in ruins; our planet had been rendered as barren and desolate as Mars.

Around this time, Kayako grew restless. She often left our son unsupervised while she took the car on long flights. When she returned, she would say only that she had gone to the Western hemisphere. Finally, one day she dragged me along with her.

We drove for two hours at Mach 4 before we caught a glimpse of the Sun. It had just risen above the Pacific Ocean. No bigger than a baseball, it cast a faint, cold light over the frozen surface.

At an elevation of five thousand meters, Kayako shifted the car into hover. She then pulled a long package from the backseat. After she removed its cover, I saw that it was an astronomical telescope of the sort favored by hobbyists. Kayako opened the car window, pointed the telescope at the Sun, and told me to look.

Through the tinted lens, I could see the Sun, magnified hundreds of times. I could even clearly see the light and dark sunspots slowly drifting across its surface and the faint prominences at the edges of the solar disk.

Kayako linked the telescope to the onboard computer and captured an image of the Sun. She then pulled up a different solar image and said, 'This is from four centuries ago.' The computer proceeded to compare the two images.

'Do you see that?' Kayako asked, pointing to the screen. 'Luminosity, pixel arrays, pixel probabilities, layer statistics – every parameter is exactly the same!'

'What does that prove? A toy telescope, a cheap image-processing program, and you, an uninformed amateur.' I shook my head. 'Pay no attention to those rumors.'

'You're an idiot,' she snapped, retracting the telescope and turning the car toward home. In the distance, I noticed a few other cars both above and below us. They hovered in the air just as we had, a telescope trained on the

Sun through every car window.

Over the next few months, a terrible allegation swept like wildfire across the world. More and more people made it their business to observe the Sun with the assistance of larger, more sophisticated instruments. An NGO even launched an array of probes toward the Sun, which passed through their target three months later. The data transmitted by the probes finally confirmed the fact:

The Sun had not changed at all in the past four centuries.

On every continent, the situation in the underground cities was volatile, like bubbling volcanoes building toward eruption. One day, heeding a decree from the Coalition, Kayako and I placed our son into a Foster Center. On the way home, we both sensed that the only tie that held us together was gone. As we neared the central plaza, we saw a man addressing a crowd. Others were distributing weapons to the citizens who had gathered around the speaker.

'Citizens! Earth has been betrayed! Humanity has been betrayed! Civilization has been betrayed! We are all the victims of a tremendous hoax! The sheer scale of this hoax would shock God himself! The Sun is entirely unchanged! It will not explode, not then, not now, not ever! It is the very symbol of eternity! What is explosive is the wild and insidious ambition of those in the Coalition! They fabricated all of it, just so they could establish their own tyrannical empire! They have destroyed Earth! They have destroyed human civilization! Citizens, citizens of conscience! Take up arms and rescue our planet! Rescue human civilization! We will overthrow the Coalition! We will seize control of the Earth Engines and steer our planet from the cold depths of outer space back to its original orbit! Back to the warm embrace of the Sun!'

Without a word, Kayako stepped forward to accept an assault rifle from one of the people handing out weapons, joining the column of armed citizens. She did not look back as she disappeared into the haze of the underground city alongside the ranks of her neighbors. I just stood there. In my pocket, the medal for which my father had traded his life and loyalty was clenched in my hand, so tightly that its points drew blood.

Three days later, rebellion broke out on every continent.

Wherever the rebel army went, the people rallied to its call. Few citizens still doubted that they had been deceived. Even so, I still joined the Coalition army. It was not that I had any real faith in the government, but my family had served in the military for three generations. They had sown the seeds of loyalty deep in my heart, and to betray the Coalition was simply unthinkable, no matter the circumstances.

One after another, the Americas, Africa, Oceania, and Antarctica fell to the rebels as the Coalition army drew back to defensive lines around the Earth Engines in Eastern and Central Asia, ready to defend them to the death. The rebel army quickly surrounded these lines. Their forces overwhelmingly outnumbered the Coalition forces, but because of the close proximity of the engines, the offensive made no progress for a long time. The rebel army had no desire to destroy the engines, and thus refrained from deploying heavy weapons, giving the Coalition a stay of execution. The two sides remained locked in a stalemate for three months. But after twelve field armies defected in succession, the Coalition defenses crumbled along all fronts. Two months later, with things looking bleak, the last hundred thousand government troops found themselves besieged on all sides at the Earth Engine control center on the coast.

I was a major in what remained of the army. The control center was the size of a mid-tier city, built around the Earth Navigation Bridge. A dead arm, seared by laser fire, had landed me in a cot in the combat casualty ward. It was there that I learned Kayako had been killed in action in the Battle of Australia. Like the others in the ward, all day, every day, I would drink myself blind. We lost all track of the war raging outside, and were indifferent to it. I did not know how much time had passed when I heard a voice bellow across the ward.

'You know why you have been reduced to this? You blame yourselves for standing against humanity in this war! So did I!'

As I turned my head to look, I saw that the speaker wore a general's star on his shoulder. 'No matter,' he continued. 'We have one last chance to save our souls. The Earth Navigation Bridge is only three blocks away. We will take it, and hand it over to the sane humans outside! We have done our duty to the Coalition, and now we must do our duty to humanity!'

With my good arm, I drew my pistol and followed the frenzied mass of able-bodied and wounded soldiers surging through the steel corridors toward the bridge. To my surprise, we met almost no resistance along the way. In fact, more and more people emerged from the complex maze of passageways to join us. Finally, we arrived before a metal gate so tall that I could not see the top of it. It rumbled open and we charged into the Earth Navigation Bridge.

Even though we had seen it countless times on television, everyone was still floored by the bridge's grandeur. It was difficult to judge the size of the space , as its dimensions were hidden by the huge holographic simulation of the solar system that dominated the room. The entire image was essentially black space that stretched infinitely in all directions. As soon as we came in, we were suspended in this blackness. Because the simulation was designed to reflect the true scale of the solar system, the Sun and the planets were miniscule, like fireflies in the distance, but still distinguishable. A striking red spiral expanded out from the distant point of light that represented the Sun, spreading like concentric red ripples on the surface of a vast black ocean. This was the Earth's route. At a point on the outer edge of the spiral, the route turned bright green, indicating the distance Earth had yet to travel. The green line swept over our heads. We followed it with our eyes until it vanished into the depths of a brilliant sea of stars, its end beyond our sight. Numerous specks of glittering dust floated through the black expanse. As a few of these motes drifted closer, I realized they were virtual screens, filled with scrolling streams of digits and curves.

Then my gaze fell upon the Earth Navigation Platform, known to every human on the planet. It looked like a silvery white asteroid floating in the blackness. The sight made it even harder to grasp the size of the place – the Navigation Platform itself was a plaza. It was now densely packed with over five thousand people, including the leaders of the Coalition, most of the Interstellar Immigration Committee that was responsible for implementing the voyage plan, and the last remaining loyalists. The voice of the Chief Executive rang out in the darkness.

'We could fight to the last, but we might lose control of the Earth Engines. If that were to happen, the excess fissile material could burn through the entire planet or evaporate the oceans. Instead, we have decided to surrender. We understand the people. Humanity has endured forty generations of bitter struggle, and must endure one hundred generations more. It is unrealistic to expect everyone to remain rational throughout it all. But we ask the people to remember that we, the five thousand who stand here, from the Chief Executive of the Coalition to the ordinary privates, kept our faith until the end. We know we will not see the day the truth is verified, but if humanity survives, future generations will weep over our graves! This planet called Earth will be an everlasting monument to our memory!'

The massive gate of the control center rumbled open again, and the last five thousand Takers emerged. They were then herded to the shore by rebel forces. Both sides of the road were jammed with people. The onlookers spat at the prisoners and pelted them with ice and rocks. A few of the masks on their thermal suits were shattered, exposing the faces beneath to temperatures more than a hundred degrees below freezing. But even as they were numbed by terrible cold, they trudged on, fighting for every step. I saw a little girl pick up a chunk of ice and hurl it with all her might at an old man, the wild rage in her eyes searing through her mask.

When I heard that all five thousand of the prisoners had been sentenced to death, I felt it was too lenient. One death? Could one death repair the evil they had done? Could it make amends for the crime of perpetrating an insane hoax that destroyed both the Earth and human civilization? They should die ten thousand times over! I suddenly recalled the astrophysicists who had forecast the explosion of the Sun and the engineers who had designed and built the Earth Engines. They had passed away a century ago, but I truly wanted to dig up their graves and make them die the deaths they deserved.

I felt truly thankful that the executioners had found a suitable method for carrying out the sentence. First, they confiscated the nuclear batteries that powered the thermal suits of every person sentenced to death. Then, they deposited the prisoners on the frozen ocean and let the subzero conditions sap the life from their bodies.

The most insidious, most shameful criminals in the history of human civilization stood clustered together, a dark mass atop the ice. Over one hundred thousand people had gathered on the shore to watch. Over one hundred thousand jaws clenched in anger, over one hundred thousand pairs of eyes burned with the same rage I had witnessed on the face of that little girl.

By now, all the Earth Engines had been powered down, and the stars had blinked majestically into view over the ice. I could imagine the cold piercing their skin like daggers, the blood freezing in their veins, the life draining bit by bit from their bodies. A pleasant warmth ran through my body at the thought. As they watched the prisoners slowly succumb to the agonizing cold, the mood of the crowd on the shore began to lift and they began to sing a cheerful rendition of 'My Sun.'

As I sang along, I gazed in the direction of a star that was slightly larger than the rest, its tiny disk shining with yellow light – the Sun.

Oh, my Sun, mother of life, father of all creation, my great spirit, my god above! What could be steadier than you? What could be more eternal than you? We are miniscule – carbon-based bacteria crowded on a pebble that revolves around you, no better than dust – and yet we dared to prophesy your doomsday. How could we be so foolish?

An hour passed. Out on the ice, those enemies of humanity still stood, but not one among them remained alive. Their blood had frozen in their veins.

All at once, I lost my sense of sight. Several seconds passed before my vision began to recover, and the ice, the shore, and the crowd of onlookers gradually sharpened into focus. Finally everything was clear again – even clearer than it had been before, in fact, because the world was enveloped in an intense white light. It was this abrupt glare that had blinded me a moment ago.

The stars, however, did not reappear, their radiance swallowed up, as if the cosmos had melted under the harsh light. The glare burst forth from a single point in space. That point had now become the center of the universe, and I had been staring right at it as it did so.

The helium flash had occurred.

The chorus of 'My Sun' froze mid-song. The crowd on the shore stood transfixed; like the five thousand corpses on the ice, they seemed frozen, as stiff and still as stone.

The Sun shed its light and heat upon the Earth for one last time. On the surface, the dry ice melted first, rising in plumes of white steam. Then the sea began to thaw, and the layers of ice began to creak and groan as they were heated unevenly. Gradually, the light softened and the sky took on a tinge of blue. Later, generated by the fierce solar winds, auroras appeared in the sky, great prismatic curtains of light fluttering across the heavens.

The last Takers stood firm atop the ice, five thousand statues thrown into clear relief by the sudden dazzling sunlight.

The solar explosion lasted only a short time. After two hours, the light rapidly weakened until it was extinguished altogether.

A dim red sphere had replaced the Sun. From our vantage point, it slowly swelled until it reached the size of the Sun of old, a strange memory from Earth's original orbit. It was so voluminous that its diameter exceeded the orbit of Mars. Mercury, Venus, Mars – Earth's constant companions – had been reduced to wisps of smoke by the intense thermal radiation.

But it was no longer our Sun. No longer emitting light and heat, it resembled a cold piece of red paper pasted onto the firmament, its muted glow merely a reflection of the surrounding starlight. This was the evolutionary fate common to all mid-sized stars: transformation into a red-giant.

Five billion years of majestic life were now a fleeting dream. The Sun had died.

Fortunately, we still lived.

Chapter 4
The Wandering Era

As I recall all of this now, half a century has passed. Twenty years ago, Earth sailed past Pluto's orbit and out of the solar system, continuing its lonely voyage into the vast, cold reaches of space.

My last visit to the surface was a dozen or so years ago. I was accompanied by my son and my daughter-in-law, a blonde-haired, blue-eyed girl. She was pregnant at the time.

When we arrived on the surface, the first thing I noticed was that I could no longer see the Earth Engines' massive plasma beams, even though I knew the engines were still operating at full capacity. The Earth's atmosphere had vanished, leaving nothing to scatter the plasma's light. The ground was covered with strange translucent yellow-green crystals. They were made of solid oxygen and nitrogen, the remnants of our frozen atmosphere.

Interestingly, the atmosphere had not frozen evenly across the surface. Instead, it had formed irregular mounds, like hills. The frozen surface of the sea, once flat and smooth, now rose up into a fantastic crystalline landscape. Overhead, the Milky Way stretched motionless across the sky, as if it, too, had frozen. But the stars were bright, too bright to look at for long.

The Earth Engines would operate without interruption for the next five hundred years, accelerating the planet to 0.5 percent of light speed. Earth would cruise at this incredible speed for thirteen hundred years. After it had completed two-thirds of its voyage, we would reverse the direction of the Earth Engines and Earth would enter a five hundred year deceleration period. After twenty-four hundred years of travel, Earth would finally reach Proxima Centauri. In another hundred years' time, it would lock into stabilized orbit around the star, becoming one of its satellites.

> *I know I have been forgotten*
> *This voyage wanders on and on*
> *But call me when the time comes*
> *When the East sees another dawn*
> *I know I have been forgotten*
> *Our departure is long past*
> *But call me when the time comes*
> *When men see blue skies at last*
> *I know I have been forgotten*
> *Our solar story is over now*
> *But call me when the time comes*
> *When blossoms hang from every bough*

Every time I hear that song, warmth floods this stiff, aging body of mine, and these dry old eyes fill with tears. In my mind's eye, the three golden suns of Alpha Centurai rise above the horizon one after another, bathing everything in their warm light. The solid atmosphere has melted, and the sky is clear and blue again. Seeds planted two thousand years ago sprout from the thawed soil, breathing new life into the earth. I see my great-grandchildren, one hundred generations removed, playing and laughing on green grass. Clear streams flow through the meadows, filled with small silver fish. I see Kayako, bounding toward me across the green earth. She is young and beautiful, like an angel . . .

Ah, Earth, my wandering Earth . . .

微纪元

THE MICRO-ERA

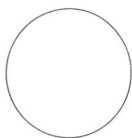

TRANSLATED BY HOLGER NAHM

霍尔格·南 译

Chapter 1
Return

The Forerunner now knew that he was the only person left in the universe. He knew that when he crossed the orbit of Pluto. From here, the Sun was but a dim star, no different from when he had left the Solar System thirty years ago.

The divergence analysis the computer had just performed, however, told him that Pluto's orbit had significantly shifted outward. Using this data, he could calculate that the Sun had lost 4.74 per cent of its mass since he had left. And that left only one conclusion, sending shivers straight through his heart, chilling his soul.

It had already happened.

In fact, humanity had known about this long before he had embarked on his journey. They had learned this after thousands upon thousands of probes had been shot into the Sun. The probes' findings had allowed astrophysicists to determine that a short-lived energy flash would erupt from the star, reducing its mass by about five per cent.

If the Sun could think and could remember, it would have almost certainly been untroubled. In the billion years of its life, it had already undergone much greater upheavals than this. When it was born from the turbulence of a spiralling stellar nebula, greater changes had been measured in milliseconds. In those brilliant and glorious moments, the Sun's gravitational collapse had ignited the fires of nuclear fusion, illuminating the grim, dark chaos of stellar dust.

It knew that its life was a process, and even though it was currently in the most stable phase of this progression, occasional minor, yet sudden, changes were inevitable. The Sun was much like the calm surface of water: perfectly still for the most part, but every so often broken by the bursting of a rising bubble. The loss of energy and mass meant very little to it. The Sun would remain the Sun, a medium-sized star with an apparent visual magnitude of -26.8.

The flash would not even have that great an effect on the rest of the Solar System. Mercury would probably dissolve, while the dense atmosphere of Venus would likely be stripped to nothing. The effect on the more distant planets would be even less severe. It could be expected that the surface of Mars would melt, likely scorching its colour from red to black. As for Earth, its surface would only be heated to four thousand degrees, probably for no longer than a hundred hours or so. The planet's oceans would certainly evaporate. On dry land, strata of continental rock would liquefy, but that would be that.

The Sun would then quickly revert to its previous state, albeit with reduced mass. This reduction would cause the orbits of all the planets to shift outward, but that would hardly be consequential. Earth, for example, would only experience a slight drop of temperature, on average falling to about -110 degrees. In fact, the cold would advance the re-solidification of the melted surface, and it would ensure that some of Earth's water and atmosphere would be preserved.

There was a joke that became popular in those days. It was a conversation with God, and it went like this:

'Oh, God, for you thousands of years are just a brief moment!'

God answered, 'Indeed, they are just a second to me.'

'Oh, God, for you hundreds of millions are just small change!'

God answered, 'Just a nickel.'

'Oh, God, please spare me a nickel!'

Upon which God then answered, 'Certainly. Just give me a second.'

Now, it was the Sun that was asking humanity for 'just a second'. It had been calculated that the energy flash would not happen for another eighteen thousand years.

For the Sun, this certainly was no more than a second, but in humanity – faced with an entire 'second' of waiting – it engendered an attitude of apathy. 'Apathism' was even elevated to a kind of philosophy. All this did not occur without repercussions; with every passing day, humanity grew more cynical.

Then again, there were at least four or five hundred generations in which humankind could find a way out.

After two centuries, humanity took the first step: a spaceship was launched into interstellar space, taxed with the mission of finding a habitable planet within one hundred light years to which humanity could migrate. This spaceship was called the *UNS Ark*, and its crew became known as the Forerunners.

The *Ark* swept past sixty stars, thus past sixty infernos. Only one was accompanied by a satellite. This satellite was a eight-thousand-mile-wide drop of incandescent, molten metal, its liquid form in constant flux as it orbited.

This was the *Ark*'s only achievement, further proof of humanity's loneliness.

The *UNS Ark* sailed for twenty-three years. However, as she travelled close to light speed, this 'Ark Time' equated to twenty-five thousand years on Earth. Had it followed its mission plan, the *UNS Ark* should have returned to Earth long ago.

Flying close to the speed of light made communication with Earth impossible. Only by reducing its velocity to less than half the speed of light could the *Ark* be contacted by Earth. This manoeuvre, however, cost significant amounts of time and energy, and therefore the *Ark* would usually only do this once a month, in order to receive a dispatch from Earth. When it slowed down, the *Ark* would pick up Earth's newest message, sent more than a hundred years after the previous one. The relative time between the *Ark* and Earth made communication much like targeting a high-powered scope; if the scope was off by even the slightest degree, its would miss the target by a vast distance.

The *UNS Ark* had received its last message from Earth thirteen 'Ark Years' after its departure. On Earth, seventeen thousand years had passed since it had left. One month after that message, the *Ark* had again slowed, but it only received silence. The predictions made many millennia ago could certainly have been off. One month on the *Ark* was more than a hundred years on Earth. That was when it must have happened.

The *UNS Ark* had truly become an actual ark – an ark with a lone Noah. Of the other seven Forerunners, four had been killed by radiation when a star had exploded in a nova four light years from the *Ark*. Two others had succumbed to illness; one man had, in the silence of that fateful slow-down, shot himself.

The last Forerunner had kept the *Ark* at communication speed for a long stretch. Finally, he had accelerated the *Ark* back to near light speed, but a tiny flame of hope burning within him had soon tempted him to again reduce the ship's speed. Again he had listened anxiously, but all he heard was silence; and so it went on. His frequent cycles of acceleration and deceleration prolonged the return journey countless times.

And through it all, the silence remained.

The *Ark* returned to the solar system twenty-five thousand years after its departure from Earth, nine thousand years later than originally planned.

Chapter 2
The Monument

Passing the orbit of Pluto, the *Ark* continued its flight deep into the solar system. For an interstellar vessel such as the *UNS Ark*, travelling in the solar system was like sailing in the calm of a harbour. Soon the Sun grew brighter. As its light began to bathe the *Ark*, the Forerunner caught his first glimpse of Jupiter. Through his telescope he could see that the huge planet had changed almost beyond recognition. Its red spot was nowhere to be seen, and its tempestuous bands appeared more chaotic than ever. He paid no heed to the other planets and continued the tranquil flight at the end of his journey, straight on to Earth.

The Forerunner's hand trembled as he pushed the button. The massive metal shield covering the porthole slowly crept open.

'Oh, my blue sphere, blue eye of the universe, my blue angel,' the Forerunner prayed, his eyelids closed firmly.

After a long while, he finally forced his eyes open.

The planet he saw was black and white.

The black was rock, melted and re-hardened, tombstone black. The white was seawater, vaporized and refrozen, corpse-shroud white.

As the *Ark* entered low-Earth orbit, slowly passing over the black land and white oceans, the Forerunner spotted no vestiges of humanity; everything had been melted to nothing. Civilization was gone, lost in a wisp of smoke.

But surely there should have been a monument, some memorial capable of withstanding the four thousand degrees that had destroyed all else.

Just as these thoughts crossed the Forerunner's mind, the monument appeared. It was a video signal, originating from the surface and being sent to his spaceship. The computer streamed the signal's contents onto his screen: a video, millennia old. Obviously shot by extremely heat-resistant cameras, it revealed the catastrophe that had befallen Earth. The moment the energy flash hit was very different from what he had imagined so many times. The Sun did not suddenly grow brighter; most of the cataclysmic radiation it blasted forth remained well outside the visible spectrum. He could see, however, the end of the blue sky. It suddenly turned inferno-red, only to change again to a nightmarish purple.

He saw the cities of that era, the so-familiar forms of skyscrapers, oozing with thick black smoke as the temperature surged by thousands of degrees. Soon they began to glow like the dim red of kindled charcoal, but they could not last, finally melting like countless sticks of wax.

Scorching red magma streamed from the mountaintops, forming cascading waterfalls of molten rock. These incandescent rapids converged to form a massive crimson river of lava that buried the earth below under its pyroclastic floods. And where there had been ocean waters, now stood only giant mushroom clouds of steam. The belly of these ferociously billowing mountains shone with the red glow of the molten world beneath. Their crests were permeated with the sky's cruel purple. The endless ranges of steam clouds expanded with relentless speed and abandon. Soon they swallowed all of the Earth…

Years passed before this haze finally dispersed, revealing that there still was a planet beneath. The burned and melted world below had begun to cool, leaving all of it covered in rippling, black rock. In some parts, magma still flowed, forming intricate webs of fire that spanned the Earth. All traces of humanity had disappeared. Civilization had vanished, forgotten like a dream from which the Earth had awoken.

A few years later, the Earth's water, having been dissociated to oxyhydrogen under the incredible heat, began to recombine. It fell as great torrents, again covering the burning world in steam. It was as if the Earth had been trapped in a titanic steamer: dark, moist and stiflingly hot. The deluge lasted for dozens of years as the Earth continued to cool. Slowly, the oceans began to fill again.

Centuries passed. The dark clouds of evaporated seawater had finally dispersed, and the sky returned to blue. In the heavens, the Sun reappeared. Earth's new, more distant orbit forced a sharp decline in temperatures, freezing the oceans. Now the sky was without clouds, and the long-dead world below froze in complete silence.

Again the picture changed, this time revealing a city: first a forest of tall, slender buildings came into view. As the camera slowly descended from some unseen place above their highest tops, a plaza came into view. Its spacious dimensions were filled with a sea of people. The camera descended further, allowing the Forerunner to discern that all of the faces in the forum were turned up, appearing to look right at him. The camera finally stopped, hovering above a platform in the middle of the plaza.

A beautiful girl, probably in her teens, stood on this platform. Through the screen, she waved right at the Forerunner, and as she waved, she shouted, 'Hey, we can see you! You came to us like a streaking star!' Her voice was delicate and fair. 'Are you the *UNS Ark One?*'

In the final years of his voyage the Forerunner had spent most of his time playing a virtual reality game. To run this game, the computer directly interfaced with the player's brain signals, using his thoughts to generate three-dimensional images. The people and objects in these images were obviously restricted in many ways, bound by the limits of the player's imagination. In his loneliness, the Forerunner had created one virtual world after another, everything from single households to entire realms.

Having spent so much time in unreal realities, he almost immediately recognized the city on his screen for what it was: just another virtual world. It was of inferior quality, at that, most likely the product of a distracted mind. Virtual images such as this one, born from the imagination, were always prone to errors. The pictures he saw now, however, seemed to have more wrong with them than right.

First and worst, when the camera passed the skyscrapers, the Forerunner had watched as numerous people exited the buildings through windows on the top floors. These people had jumped straight out, leaping hundreds of feet down to the ground below. After falling from such dizzying heights, they landed without a scratch, apparently completely unharmed. Furthermore, he saw people leap off the ground only to rise, as if being pulled by invisible wires. These strange jumps carried them several stories up a skyscraper's side. They ascended even higher, pushing off from foot-holds that ran up the side of all buildings, as though they had been put there for just that purpose. In this manner they could reach the top of any building or enter it through any of its many windows. These skyscrapers seemed to have neither elevators nor doors. At least, the Forerunner never saw them use anything except a window to enter or leave a building.

When the virtual camera moved above that plaza, the Forerunner could see another error: amongst the sea of people hung crystal balls suspended by strings. These balls were about three feet in diameter. Occasionally people would reach into these balls and pull out a part of the crystal substance with great ease. As they removed a piece, the ball would immediately recover its spherical shape. The extracted part would do the same; but even as the small piece became round, the person who had extracted it would put it into his mouth and swallow it...

In addition to these obvious mistakes, the confusion and derangement of the image's creator could best be captured by something else entirely. Bizarre objects were floating through the city's sky and air. Some were large, ranging from five to ten feet, while others were smaller, only a foot or so long. Some resembled pieces of broken sponge, while others recalled the crooked branches of some giant tree, all slowly floating through the air.

The Forerunner saw one large branch drifting toward the girl on the platform. She simply gave it a light push, sending it spiralling into the distance. The Forerunner understood then. In a world on the brink of destruction, it must have been impossible to remain of sound mind and thought.

The image was most likely being sent out by an automated installation, which had probably been buried deep beneath the surface before the catastrophe struck. Shielded from the radiation and heat, it must have lain hidden and waited, automatically rising to the surface once it was safe. This installation, then, probably kept an unending vigil, monitoring space, projecting these images to any of the scattered remnants of humanity returning to Earth. Chances were that these comical and jumbled images had been created with good will, intended to comfort the survivors.

'Did you say that other Arks were launched?' the Forerunner asked.

'Of course. There were twelve others!' the girl answered enthusiastically. The absurdity of the other parts of the image notwithstanding, this girl was not half bad at all. Her beautiful face combined the best features typical of Eastern and Western cultures. She beamed with utmost naiveté. To her, the entire cosmos was a great, big playground. Her large, round eyes seemed to sing with every flutter, while her long hair floated and unfurled in the air, appearing completely weightless. She reminded the Forerunner of a mermaid swimming in an unseen ocean.

'So, is anyone still alive?' the Forerunner asked, his final hope flaring like a wildfire.

'Aren't you?' the girl innocently returned the question.

'Of course. I'm a real human. Not like you, a computer-generated virtual person,' the Forerunner replied.

'The last *Ark* arrived seven hundred thirty years ago. You are the last *Ark* to return, but please tell us, do you have any women aboard?'the girl asked.

'It is only me,' the Forerunner replied.

'So you say that there are no women with you?' the girl asked again, her eyes widening in genuine shock.

'As I said, I am the only one. Are there no other spaceships out there that have yet to return?' the Forerunner enquired in return, desperate to keep the fire of hope alive.

The girl wrung her delicate, elfin hands before her chest. 'There are none! It's so sad, so very terribly sad! You are the last of them, if... oh...' She could barely contain her sobs. 'If not by cloning...' The girl was now crying uncontrollably. 'Oh,' she finished, her beautiful face now covered in tears. Around her, the people in the plaza were a sea of tears.

While he did not cry, the Forerunner, too, felt his breaking heart sink into new depths. Humanity's destruction had become a fact beyond denial.

'Why do you not ask me who I am?' the girl asked, raising her face again. She had reclaimed her innocent demeanour, her recent sorrow, merely seconds past, apparently forgotten.

'I couldn't care less,' the Forerunner answered flatly.

With tears in her eyes again, the girl shouted, 'But I am Earth's Leader!'

'Yes! She is the High Counsellor of Earth's Unity Government!' the people in the plaza shouted in unison, flitting from sorrow to excitement, their programming reflecting marked deficiencies.

The Forerunner felt himself growing tired of this senseless game, and he rose to turn away.

'How can you not care? All the capital has gathered here to welcome you, forefather! Do not ignore us!' the girl cried, raising a tearful wail.

Remembering his original, still unresolved question, the Forerunner turned and enquired, 'What has humanity left behind?'

'Follow our landing beacon, then you can learn for yourself!' came the happy reply.

Chapter 3
The Capital

The Forerunner climbed into his landing module. Leaving the *UNS Ark* to orbit, he began his descent to Earth, following the landing beacon's directions. He wore a pair of video specs, their lenses displaying the images being broadcast from the planet below.

'Forefather, you must immediately come to Earth's capital. Even though it is not the planet's biggest city, it is certainly the most beautiful,' the girl calling herself Earth's Leader prattled on. 'You will like it! Mind, though, that the landing coordinates we have given you will lead you to a spot a good distance from the city, as we wish to avoid possible damage...'

The Forerunner changed the image of his specs to show the area directly below his lander. Now, at only thirty thousand feet in the air, he could still see nothing but black wasteland below.

As he descended, the virtual image grew even more confusing. Perhaps its creator, thousands of years ago, had been in the grips of an unimaginable depression; or perhaps the computer projecting it, left to its own devices thousands upon thousands of years, was showing the signs of its age. In any case, for some unfathomable reason, the virtual girl had begun to sing:

Oh, you dear angel! From the macro-age you return!
Oh, glorious macro-age,
Magnificent macro-age,
Oh, beautiful macro-age,
Oh, vanished vision! In the fires the dream did burn.

As this beautiful singer began her hymn, she leapt into the air. She lifted off the platform, jumping a good thirty feet into the air. After falling back to the platform, she sprang back up, this time clearing the plaza in a single bound. She landed on top of a building, and from there she jumped again, this time across the entire width of the plaza. Landing at its other side, she looked like a charming little flea.

She leapt once more, and in mid-air she caught one of the strange objects that was floating past her. Several feet long, the object looked like the trunk of a weird tree, and it carried her spiralling through the air, above the sea of people. Even as she rose, her svelte body continued to rhythmically writhe.

The sea of people below began to agitate with raw excitement, soon boiling over into song. 'Oh, macro-age! Oh, macro-age!' As the song rose, they all began to jump. The crowd now looked like sand on a drum, rising in waves with every invisible beat.

The Forerunner simply refused to take any more of this, and he killed both the image and the sound. He was certain now that it was even worse than he had first thought. Before the catastrophe had struck, the people of Earth must have felt venomous envy toward the survivors who had slipped through time and space, thus eluding their appointed destruction. Fuelled by such emotions, they had created this gross perversion to torment those that returned.

As his descent continued, the annoyance the images had caused slowly began to ebb, but by the time he felt the shock of the landing, that annoyance had almost completely left him. For a moment he succumbed to fancy: maybe he had truly landed near a city. Perhaps it simply wasn't visible from up high?

All illusion faded to nothing as he stepped out of the lander. He was surrounded by boundless, black desolation, and despair chilled his entire body.

The Forerunner carefully slid open his visor. Immediately, he felt a surge of cold air against his face. The air was very thin, but it was enough for him to breathe. The temperature was somewhere around forty degrees below freezing. The sky was a dark blue, as it had been at dawn and dusk in the age before the catastrophe. It was neither time now, as the Sun hanging overhead clearly evidenced.

The Forerunner removed his gloves, but he could not feel the Sun's warmth. In the thin air, the sunlight was scattered and weak. He could see stars twinkle brightly in the sky above.

The ground beneath his feet had solidified about two thousand years ago. All around, he could see the ripples of hardened magma. Even though the first signs of weathering were visible, the surface remained hard and jagged. No matter how closely he looked, he could only make out the barest traces of soil. Before him the undulating land stretched to the horizon, punctuated only by small hills. Behind him lay the frozen ocean, gleaming white against the skyline.

Scanning his surroundings, the Forerunner searched for the source of the transmission. He finally spotted a transparent shield dome, embedded in the rocky ground. This hemisphere was about three feet in diameter, and it covered what appeared to be an array of highly complex structures.

The Forerunner was soon able to make out several similar domes scattered in the distance. They were spaced at distances of fifty to one hundred feet. From where he stood, they looked a little like bubbles, frozen as they burst through the Earth's surface and now glinting under the Sun.

Reactivating the left lens of his video specs, the Forerunner opened a virtual window into that strange imaginary world. That shameless impostor was still floating through the air, riding her bizarre branch, deliriously singing and writhing. As she flew, she blew kisses toward the camera. The masses below, even to the last man, cheered:

> ... *Oh, great macro-age!*
> *Oh, romantic macro-era!*
> *Oh, melancholic macro-age!*
> *Oh, frail macro-age...!*

Numbed, the Forerunner stopped cold. Standing beneath the deep blue heavens in the light of the shining Sun under the sparkling stars, he felt the entire universe revolving around him – him. The last human.

He was engulfed by an avalanche of dark loneliness. Covering his face, he sank to his knees and began to sob.

As he descended into despair, the singing ceased. Everyone in the virtual image stared straight toward him, their countless eyes filled with deep concern. The girl, still riding her branch through mid-air, beamed a sweet smile right up at him.

'Do you have so little faith in humanity?' she asked.

She continued speaking, and as she did, something that the Forerunner could not place sent a shiver through his body, setting all his senses on edge. Disturbed, he slowly began to rise back to his feet. As he stood, he suddenly saw it: a shadow was falling over the city in his left lens. It was as if a dark cloud had appeared out of the blue, blackening the entire sky from one second to the next. He took a step to the side. Light was immediately restored to the city.

He slowly approached the dome, intrigued. Standing before it, he bent forward, carefully studying it. Inside he could indistinctly make out a dense array of tiny, yet incredibly detailed, structures. He immediately noticed that something magnificently strange had completely dominated the sky in his video specs.

That something was his face.

'We can see you! Can you see us? Use a magnifier!' the girl shouted as loud as she could, as the sea of people below once more boiled over with exhilaration.

Now the Forerunner finally and truly understood it all: he recalled the people jumping out of tall buildings, which made sense because gravity could cause them no harm in their microscopic environment. This also explained their jumps. In such an environment, people would easily be able to leap up a building a thousand feet high – or should that be a thousand microns? The large crystal balls must, in fact, be drops of water. In this tiny environment, their shape would be completely at the mercy of the water's surface tension. And when these microscopic people wanted a drink, they could simply pull out a tiny droplet. Finally, the strange, elongated things that floated through the urban landscape – and that the girl was riding – these, too, made sense. They were nothing other than tiny particles of dust.

This city was not virtual at all. It was a city just as real as any city twenty-five thousand years ago had been, only it was covered by a three-foot, transparent dome.

Humanity still was. Civilization still was.

In this microscopic city floated a girl on a branch of dust – the High Counsellor of Earth's Unity Government – confidently stretching her open hand toward the man who, at the moment, filled almost her entire cosmos: The Forerunner.

'Forefather, the micro-age welcomes you!'

Chapter 4
Micro-Humanity

'In the seventeen thousand years before the catastrophe,' the girl told the Forerunner, 'humanity left no rock unturned in its search for some way out. The easiest way out would have been migrating to another star. But no *Ark*, including yours, was able to locate even a single star with a habitable planet. And it did not really matter; a mere century before the catastrophe, our spaceship technology was still not developed enough to migrate even one-thousandth of humanity.

'Another plan,' she continued, 'was to have humanity migrate deep underground, well hidden from the Sun's energy flash, ready to emerge once its effects subsided. That plan, however, would have done little other than prolong their inevitable deaths. After the catastrophe, Earth's ecosystem was completely destroyed. Humanity could not have survived.

'There was a time when humanity fell into total despair. It was in that darkest night that an idea flashed to life in the mind of a certain genetic engineer: what if humanity's size could be reduced by nine orders of magnitude?' A pensive look crossed her face.[1] 'Everything about human society could also be scaled to that size, creating a microscopic ecosystem, and such an ecosystem would only consume microscopic amounts of natural resources. It did not take long before all of humanity came to agree that this plan was the only way in which our species could be saved.'

She continued. 'The plan relied on two types of technology. The first was genetic engineering; by modifying the human genome, humans would be reduced to the height of about ten microns, no larger than a single body cell. Human anatomy, however, would remain completely unchanged. This was a completely plausible goal. In essence, there is very little difference between the genome of a bacterium and that of a human. The other piece of the puzzle was nanotechnology. This technology had been developed as far back as the twentieth century, and even in those days people were able to assemble simple generators the size of bacteria. Based on these humble beginnings, humanity soon learned to build everything from nano-rockets to nano-microwave ovens; but the nano-engineers of ages past could have never imagined where their technologies would ultimately be put to use.

'Fostering the first batch of micro-humans was very similar to cloning: the complete genome was extracted from a human cell and then cultivated to form a micro-human that resembled the original in all ways except size. They are just one billionth the size of the original ones. Later generations were born just like macro-humans. That, by the way,' she added, 'is what we call you. And, you may have already guessed that we call your era the "macro-age".

'The first group of micro-humans took to the world-stage in a rather dramatic fashion,' she told him. 'One day, about twelve thousand hundred years after the departure of your *Ark*, a classroom was shown on all of Earth's TV screens. Thirty students sat in this classroom. Everything seemed perfectly normal. The children were normal children, and the classroom was a normal

---

1 译者添加了一些补充性描述，后文不再一一标注。——编者注

classroom. There was nothing at all that would have seemed out of the ordinary. But then the camera drew back and humanity could see that this classroom in fact stood on the stage of a microscope.' The High Counsellor would have continued her account had she not been interrupted by the Forerunner's curiosity.

'I would like to ask,' he interjected, 'if micro-humans, with their microscopic brains, can achieve the intelligence levels of macro-humans?'

The girl shook her head, more bemused than angry. 'Do you take me for some kind of fool? Whales are no smarter than you are! Intelligence is not a matter of brain size. In regard to the number of atoms and quantum states in our brains, well, let us just say that our ability to process information is easily enough to match that of a macro-human brain.' She paused, then continued, curiosity ringing in her voice. 'Ah, could you please show us to your spacecraft?'

'Of course, very gladly.' It was the Forerunner's turn to pause. 'How exactly will you go?'

'Please wait just a moment!' the girl exuberantly shouted.

After saying this, the High Counsellor leapt into the air and onto a truly bizarre flying machine. The machine resembled a large, propeller-powered feather. Soon everyone on the plaza below was leaping into the air, competing for a spot on this 'feather'. It was apparent that this society obviously had neither a sense nor notion of rank or status. The people indiscriminately jumping onto this strange vehicle were certainly ordinary citizens, both young and old. Regardless of their age, they all wore the childish demeanour that seemed so out of place with the High Counsellor; the result was a noisy, excited, chaotic ruckus.

The 'feather' was almost instantly jam-packed with people, but a continuous stream of new 'feathers' was already coming into view. No sooner did one appear before it was filled with excited micro-humans. In the end, the city's sky was filled with several hundred feathers, each filled to capacity, or beyond, with people. They were all led by the High Counsellor's feather flier. The girl led this formidable flying armada to somewhere in the city.

The Forerunner again bent over the dome, carefully observing the microscopic city within. This time he was able to make out the skyscrapers. To him, they looked like a dense forest of matchsticks. He strained his eyes and was finally able to spot the feather-like vehicles. They looked like tiny white grains of powder, floating on water. If it had not been for there being hundreds of them, they would have been impossible to see with the naked eye.

The picture in the left lens of the Forerunner's video specs remained as crisp as ever. The micro-camera-person and his unimaginably small camera had obviously also boarded a feather, and from there continued to stream a live feed. Through this feed, the Forerunner was able to catch a glimpse of traffic in the micro-city.

He was in for an immediate shock; it appeared that collisions were almost constant occurrences. The fast-flying feathers were continually knocking into each other and into the dust particles floating through the air. They even regularly hit the sides of the towering skyscrapers! But the flying machines and their passengers were no worse for wear, and no one seemed to pay any heed to these collisions.

Actually, this was a phenomenon that any junior high physics student could have explained: the smaller the scale of an object, the stronger its structural integrity. There is a vast difference between two bicycles colliding and two ten thousand-ton ships ramming into each other. And if two dust particles collide, they will suffer no harm whatsoever. Because of this, the people of the micro-world seemed to have bodies of steel and could live lives free from fear of injury.

As the feathers flew, people would occasionally jump out of the skyscraper windows, trying to board one of the machines in mid-air. They were not, however, always successful, and so some would fall from what seemed like hundreds of yards. The sheer height left the watching Forerunner with a feeling of vertigo. The falling micro-humans, on the other hand, plummeted with perfect grace and composure, even taking the time to greet acquaintances through skyscraper windows as they rushed toward the ground!

'Oh, your eyes are as black as the ocean, so very, very deep,' the High Counsellor noted of the Forerunner. 'So deep with melancholy! Your melancholy shrouds our city. You should make them a museum! Oh, oh, oh...' She began to cry, clearly aggrieved.

The others, too, began to cry, and their feather fliers started bouncing between the skyscrapers, smashing into buildings left, right, front, and centre.

The Forerunner could see his own huge eyes in the image on his left video spec. Their melancholy, magnified a million times over, shocked even him. 'Why a museum?' he asked, perplexed.

'Because melancholy is only for museums. The micro-age is an age without worries!' Earth's Leader loudly acclaimed. Even though tears still clung to her tender face, there was no longer any trace of sorrow to be found behind them.

'We live in an age without worries!' the others joined in excitedly, shouting in unison.

It seemed to the Forerunner that in the micro-age moods shifted hundreds of times faster than they had ever done in the macro-age. These shifts seemed particularly pronounced when it came to negative emotions, such as sadness and melancholy. They could bounce back from such feelings in the blink of an eye.

However, there was another aspect of this discovery that was even harder for the Forerunner to truly fathom. Apparently, all negative emotions were incredibly rare in this era, so rare, in fact, that they were like fascinating artefacts to the people of the micro-age. When they encountered them, they grasped the opportunity to experience them.

'Don't be depressed like a child! You will quickly see that there is nothing to worry about in the micro-age!' the High Counsellor shouted, now full of joy.

Hearing her words, the Forerunner could not help but do a double-take. He had previously observed that the general mental state of the micro-humans seemed much like that of macro-age children, but they are even much more childish. 'Are you saying,' he asked in astonishment, 'that in this era, as people age, they grow...?' He almost couldn't believe what he was asking. 'Grow more childish?'

'We grow happier with age!' The High Counsellor giggled.

'Yes! In the micro-age we grow happier with age!' the crowd echoed loudly.

'But melancholy can be very beautiful,' the girl continued. 'Like the moon's reflection on a lake; it reflects the romanticism of the macro-age. Oh, oh, oh…' The Earth's Leader fell into plaintive cries at the imagery.

'Yes! What a beautiful age it was!' the others chimed in, their eyes brimming with tears.

The Forerunner could not help but laugh. 'You little people really don't understand melancholy. Real melancholy spills no tears.'

'You can show us!' the High Counsellor shouted, returning to her exuberant state.

'I hope not,' the Forerunner said, gently sighing.

'Look, this is our monument to the macro-age!' the High Counselor announced as the feathers flew over another square in the city.

The Forerunner saw the monument. It was a massive black pillar, vaguely reminding him of a giant broadcast tower. Its rough outside was covered with countless tiles, each about the size of a wheel. It called to mind the pattern of fish scales.

Staring at the towering structure, it took the Forerunner a long while to understand: it was a strand of macro-human hair.

Chapter 5
The Banquet

Flying upwards, the feather fliers emerged from the transparent hemisphere, passing through some unseen hole. As they left their city's cover behind, the High Counsellor turned to the Forerunner through the video screen in his specs.

'We are now a hundred miles or so from your spacecraft. If we can land on your fingers, you can carry us. It would greatly speed our journey.'

The Forerunner turned his head to his lander, which was right behind him. There was no conclusion to her reference, other than that units of measurement had also shrunk in the micro-age. He stretched out his hand, and the feather-fliers landed. They looked like a fine white powder, drifting onto his fingers.

In the video lens he could now see his fingerprints. They looked like massive, semi-translucent ranges of mountains that seemed to swallow these feathers as they floated into their great canyons. The High Counsellor was the first to leap from a feather. Immediately she fell, sprawling prone on the Forerunner's finger.

'Your oily skin is far too slippery!' she loudly complained, taking off her shoes. In frustration, she tossed them into the distance. Now barefoot, she turned, looking around curiously as the others also leapt onto his skin. A sea of people soon gathered between the semi-opaque cliffs of his fingers. By the Forerunner's best guess, there were now more than ten thousand micro-humans gathered on his hand!

The Forerunner raised himself and very, very carefully walked toward his lander, keeping his hand stretched out and steady before him.

He had not even fully entered the lander when the crowd of micro-humans began to shout. 'Wow! Just look, a metal sky! An artificial Sun!'

'Don't be so dramatic; you're being silly! This is just a small shuttle. The ship above is much larger!' the High Counsellor chastened her people. But she, too, was staring in wonder, looking in all directions, and as she did this, the crowd again began singing its strange song:

Oh, glorious macro-age,
Magnificent macro-age,
Melancholic macro-age,
Oh, vanished vision! In the fires the dream did burn.

As the lander took off, setting out on its flight to the *UNS Ark*, the High

Counsellor finally continued her account of the history of the micro-age.

'For a time, micro- and macro-society co-existed. During this period, the early micro-humans came to fully absorb the knowledge of the macro-world, and so we inherited macro-human culture,' she told the Forerunner. 'At the same time, micro-humanity began developing its own extremely technologically advanced society. It was a society based on nano-technology. This transitional era, between the macro-age and micro-age, lasted for about... hmm...' The High Counsellor's tiny mouth twisted ever so slightly as she recalled. 'About twenty generations or so.

'Then, as the catastrophe approached, the macro-humans ceased bearing children, and their numbers dwindled by the day. At the same time, the micro-human population skyrocketed, and the scope of our society expanded along with it. Soon it exceeded that of macro-human society. It was at this point that the micro-humans requested that they be handed the reins of global governance. This demand shook macro-society to its core and led to a powerful backlash. Some diehards refused to surrender political power. They claimed it would have been like a batch of bacteria ruling mankind. It ended with a global war between macro- and micro-humanity!'

'How horrible for your people!' The Forerunner gasped in sympathy.

'Horrible for the macro-humans, since they were quickly defeated,' the High Counsellor replied.

'However did that happen? A single macro-human with a sledgehammer could obliterate a micro-city of millions,' the perplexed Forerunner objected.

'But micro-humanity did not fight them in its cities, and macro-humanity's arsenal was utterly unsuitable for fighting an unseen enemy,' she told him. 'The only real weapon at their disposal was disinfectant. Throughout the history of their civilization they had used it to battle micro-organisms, yet it had never yielded a decisive victory. Now that they were seeking to vanquish micro-humans, an enemy equal to them in intelligence, their chances of victory were even slimmer. They could not track the movements of the micro-armies, and so we could corrupt their computer chips right under their noses. And what could they do without their computers? Power does not come from size,' the High Counsellor explained.

The Forerunner nodded in agreement. 'Now that I think about it...'

The High Counsellor continued, a fierce fire now burning brightly in her eyes. 'Those war criminals met their just fate. Several thousand micro-human special forces armed with laser drills parachuted onto their retinas...' She let the Forerunner's imagination do the rest before continuing more calmly, 'After the war, the micro-humans had claimed control of Earth. As the macro-age ended, the micro-age began!'

'Very interesting!' the Forerunner exclaimed.

The lander docked with the *Ark* in low-Earth orbit. The micro-humans immediately boarded their feathers-fliers again and began exploring their new surroundings. The enormous size of the spacecraft left them dumbstruck. The Forerunner at first thought their utterances reflected their admiration, but the High Counsellor soon explained her feelings about all this.

'Now we understand. Even without the Sun's energy flash, the macro-age could not have endured,' she said. 'You consume billions of times more resources than we do!'

'But consider that this spaceship is capable of travelling at near light speed. It can reach stars hundreds of light years away. This is something, small people, which could only be produced in the great macro-age,' the Forerunner countered.

'At the moment, we certainly cannot create its equal. Our space-ships at present can only reach one-tenth of the speed of light,' the High Counsellor conceded.

'You are capable of space travel?' the Forerunner stammered. The sheer surprise was enough to knock the colour out of his face.

'Certainly not as capable as you were. The spaceships of the micro-age can reach no further than Venus. In fact, we have just heard back from them, and they tell us that as things stand, it seems far more habitable than Earth,' the High Counsellor answered, paying no heed to his shock.

'How big are your ships?' the Forerunner asked, as he regained his composure.

'The big ones are the size of your age's... hmm...' She paused, searching for the right analogy. 'Soccer ball,' she finally said. 'They can carry hundreds of thousands of passengers. The small ones, on the other hand, are only the size of a golf ball, a macro-age golf-ball, of course.'

These words shattered the Forerunner's sense of superiority.

'Forefather, would you please offer us something to eat? We are starving!' the High Counsellor asked, speaking for her people as the feather fliers gathered on the *Ark*'s control console.

The Forerunner could see ten thousands of micro-humans on his command console, looking at him eagerly.

'I never thought I would be asked to invite so many to lunch,' he answered with a smile.

'We would certainly not want to ask too much of you!' the girl said, bristling with anger.

The Forerunner retrieved a tin of canned meat from storage. Opening it, he used a small knife to carefully scoop out a tiny piece. He then cautiously placed it to one side of the crowd standing on the command console. The Forerunner could make out their position with his naked eye. It was a tiny, circular area on the console, about the size of a coin. This area was less smooth than the surrounding area, like someone's breath on a cold surface

'Why did you take so much? That is very wasteful!' the Earth's Leader scolded.

Now using a large monitor, the Forerunner could see her; and behind her stood a towering mountain of meat toward which her people were swarming. As they reached the pink massif, they extracted small pieces and ate them.

Looking back to the console before him, the Forerunner could not make out even the slightest change in the size of that small piece of meat. On the screen, he could see that the crowd had quickly dispersed, some discarding half-eaten pieces of meat on the way. The High Counsellor picked a piece for herself and took a bite.

As she chewed, she began shaking her head. 'This is not very nice at all,' she commented as she finally finished.

'Of course, it was synthesized in the eco-cycler. It was impossible to make it taste any better, the machine has limited capacity for taste production,' the Forerunner acknowledged apologetically.

'Give us some alcohol to wash it down!' The Earth's Leader raised another request almost immediately. This demand caused a cheer to erupt among the gathered micro-humans. The Forerunner raised an eyebrow; after all, he knew that alcohol could kill micro-organisms!

'You drink beer?' he cautiously asked.

'No, we drink Scotch or vodka!' the Earth's Leader replied with gusto.

'Mao-tai would also do!' someone shouted.

In fact, the Forerunner still had a bottle of Mao-tai, a bottle he had kept on the *Ark* ever since its departure from Earth. He had intended it for the day they found a colonizable world. He fetched it.

Wistfully holding the white porcelain bottle, he removed its cap. He then carefully poured some of the spirits into the cap, setting it down next to the crowd.

On the screen, he could see that the micro-humans had begun to scale the unassailable cliff face that was the cap. On the micro-scale, the seemingly smooth surface of the cap offered many holds. Using the climbing skills they had honed on their home's skyscrapers, the micro-humans were quickly able to ascend to the cap's rim.

'Wow, what a beautiful lake!' the chorus of micro-humans shouted in admiration.

On the screen, the Forerunner could see the surface of that vast lake of alcohol bulge upward in a giant arc formed by the forces of its surface tension. The micro-human camera operator followed the High Counsellor as she first tried to scoop out some of the liquid with her hand. This attempt failed, however, as her tiny arms could not reach. Instead, she then sat herself down on the edge of the cap. From there, she let a slender foot brush the surface of the alcohol. Her delicate foot was immediately encased in a clear bead of liquid. Lifting her leg, she used her hands to extract a small drop of alcohol from the bead. She let the drop fall into her mouth.

'Wow!' she exclaimed, nodding in satisfaction. 'Macro-age alcohol really is a lot better than our micro-age spirits.'

'I am very glad to hear that we still have something that is better. But, using your feet to drink like that, that's very unhygienic,' the Forerunner noted.

'I don't understand,' she replied, looking up at him in puzzlement.

'You walked around on your bare feet for quite a while; they must be covered in germs,' the Forerunner explained.

'Oh, now I see!' the Earth's Leader called out. She was handed a box that one of her attendants had been carrying. She opened the box, and immediately a strange animal emerged. It was a football-sized, round being with tiny, chaotically twitching legs. The High Counsellor lifted the creature by one of its small legs and explained. 'Look, this is one of our city's gifts to you! A lacto-chicken!'

The Forerunner strained his mind trying to recall his microbiology. 'Are you saying that that is a...' He paused in disbelief. 'A lactobacillus?'

'That is what it was called in the macro-age. It is a creature that gives yogurt its taste. A very useful animal indeed!' the High Counsellor replied.

'A very useful bacterium,' the Forerunner corrected. 'But I now understand that bacteria cannot harm you at all. Our concept of hygiene has become meaningless in the micro-era.'

Earth's Leader shook her head. 'Not necessarily. Some animals, ah,' she caught herself, 'some bacteria can seriously hurt us. For example, there are the coli-wolves. Overpowering one of them is a great feat. But most animals, like the yeast pigs, are quite lovable.' As she spoke, she took another drop from her foot, placing it into her mouth. When she shook off the remains of the alcohol bead from her foot and stood up, the High Counsellor was already quite tipsy, and her speech had begun to slur.

'I never would have expected for alcohol to still be around!' The Forerunner frowned, genuinely astonished.

'We,' the Earth's Leader said, her speech faltering, 'we have inherited all that was beautiful about civilization, even though those Macros thought that we had no right to.' She stumbled a step. 'The right to become the carriers of human civilization,' she slurred. Feeling a bit dizzy, she plopped herself back down.

'We inherited all of humanity's philosophy – Western, Eastern, Greek, and Chinese!' the crowd shouted with one voice.

Sitting, the Earth's Leader stretched her hands toward heaven and intoned, 'No man ever steps in the same river twice; the Tao gave birth to One. The One gave birth to Two. The Two gave birth to Three. The Three gave birth...' Her words trailed off, but she immediately slurred on: '... Gave birth to all of creation! We appreciate the paintings of van Gogh. We listen to Beethoven's music. We perform Shakespeare's plays! To be or not to be; that is...' Again she slurred. 'That is the question.' She again rose, tipsily stumbling as she gave her best Hamlet.

'In our era, we never would have imagined a girl like you becoming the world's leader,' the Forerunner noted.

'The macro-age was a melancholic age with melancholic politics. The micro-age is a carefree age. We need happy leaders,' the High Counsellor replied, already looking a good deal more sober.

'We have not finished our discussion.' She paused, gathering herself. 'Our discussion of history. We had just talked about...' She halted again, thinking. 'Ah, yes, war. After the war between macro- and micro-humanity, a world war broke out amongst micro-humanity.'

The Forerunner interrupted in shock. 'What? Certainly not for territory?'

'Of course not,' the High Counsellor answered. 'If there is one thing that is truly inexhaustible in the micro-age, it is territory. It was because of some,' here she again paused, this time for reasons only known to her before continuing, 'some reasons that a macro-human could not understand. But know that in one of our largest campaigns, the battlefields were so large they covered...' She paused once more. 'Oh, in your units, more than three hundred feet. Imagine an area that vast!'

'You inherited much more from the macro-age than I could have ever imagined,' the Forerunner stated soberly.

'Later, the micro-age focused all of its energies on preparing for the impending catastrophe. Over five centuries, we built thousands of super-cities, deep within the Earth's crust. These cities would have looked to you like six-foot-wide, stainless-steel balls, and each one could house tens of millions. These cities were built fifty thousand miles underground...'

'Wait just a second; the Earth's radius is just under four thousand miles,' the Forerunner interjected.

'Oh, I again used our units,' the Earth's leader apologized. 'In your units, it would be about...' She did the calculation in her head. 'Yes, half a mile! When the first signs of the Sun's energy flash were observed, the entire micro-world migrated beneath the Earth's surface. Then, then the catastrophe struck.

'Four hundred years after the catastrophe, the first group of micro-humans made its way up through a massive tunnel roughly the size of a macro-era water pipe. Boring their way through the solidified magma with a laser drill, they made it to the surface,' she explained. 'It would, however, be another five centuries before micro-humanity could establish a new world for humanity on the surface. When we finally did, we built a world of tens of thousands of cities, a world of eighteen billion inhabitants.

'We were full of optimism about humanity's future then. It was an all-pervading, boundless optimism that would have been unimaginable in the macro-age. We were optimistic precisely because of our micro-society's tiny scale. It meant that humanity's ability to survive in this universe had been increased many millions of times over. For example,' she said, 'what was inside that can you just opened could feed our entire city for two years. And the can itself could supply our city with all the metal it needed for those two years.'

'As a macro-human, I now have a much better understanding of the enormous advantages of the micro-age. It's all so mythic, so very epic!' the Forerunner wholeheartedly extolled.

The High Counsellor smiled and continued. 'Evolution trends toward the small. Size does not equal greatness. Microscopic life has a much easier time coexisting with nature in harmony. When the giant dinosaurs died out, their contemporaries, the ants, persisted. Now, should another great disaster approach, a spaceship the size of your lander could evacuate all of humanity. Micro-humanity could rebuild its civilization on a smallish asteroid and live comfortably.'

A long silence followed.

Finally, the Forerunner, firmly focusing on that coin-sized sea of humanity before him, solemnly stated, 'When I saw the Earth again, when I thought myself the last human in the universe, I was heartbroken, and I felt all hope die. No one had ever faced such heartrending straits. But now, now, I am the happiest person alive; at least, I am the happiest macro-human there is. I see that humanity's civilization has persisted. In fact, civilization has achieved much more than just surviving; yours is the true apex of civilization! We are all human, hailing from the same strain. So now, I entreat micro-humanity to accept me as a citizen of your society.'

'We accepted you when we first detected the *Ark*. You can come live on Earth. It will be no problem for the micro-age to support one macro-human,' the Earth's leader replied in equally solemn tones.

'I will live on Earth, but all I need can come from the *Ark*. The ship's life eco-cycler will be able to sustain me for the rest of my natural life. There is no reason for a macro-human to ever again consume Earth's resources,' the Forerunner said, his face glowing with deep, silent joy.

'But our situation is improving. Not only has Venus's climate become far more hospitable to human life, Earth's temperature is also warming again. Maybe next year, we will even have rainfall in many parts of the world. Then plants will be able to grow again,' the Earth's Leader stated.

'Speaking of plants, have you ever seen any?' the Forerunner asked.

The High Counsellor answered. 'We grow lichen on the inside of our protective dome. They are huge plants, every filament as tall as a ten-storey building! Then there's also the chlorella in the water…'

The Forerunner interjected. 'But have you ever heard of grass? Or trees?'

'Are you talking about the macro-era plants that grew as tall as mountains?

My, they are legends of ancient times,' she replied.

The Forerunner smiled faintly and said, 'I just want to do one thing. When I return, I will show you the gifts I bring the micro-age. I think you will greatly enjoy them!'

Chapter 6
Rebirth

Alone again, the Forerunner made his way to the *Ark*'s cold storage, which was filled with neatly arranged, tall racks. Thousands upon thousands of sealed tubes filled these racks. It was a seed bank, storing the seeds of millions of Earth's plant species. The Ark had been meant to carry these seeds to the distant world that humanity would eventually adopt.

There were also a few rows that constituted the embryo storage. Here the embryonic cells of millions of Earth's animal species were banked.

When the temperatures warmed next year, the Forerunner would plant grass on the Earth below. Amongst these millions of kinds of seeds, there were strains of grass hardy enough to grow in ice and snow. They would certainly be able to grow on the present-day Earth.

If only a tenth of the planet's ecosphere could be restored to what it had been in the macro-age, the micro-age would become a heaven on earth. In fact, much more could probably be restored. The Forerunner indulged in the warm bliss of imagination: he could picture the micro-humans' wild joy when they would first see a colossal green blade of grass rising to the heavens. And what about a small meadow? What would a meadow mean to micro-humanity?

An entire grassland! What would a grassland mean? A green cosmos for micro-humanity! And a small brook in the grassland? What a majestic wonder the sight of the brook's clear waters snaking through the grassland would be in the eyes of micro-humans. Earth's Leader had said there could be rain soon. If rain fell, there could be a grassland and that brook could spring to life! Then there could certainly be trees! My God, trees!

The Forerunner envisioned a group of micro-human explorers setting out from the roots of a tree, beginning their epic and wondrous journey upward. Every leaf would be a green plain, stretching to the horizon.

There could be butterflies then. Their wings would be like bright clouds, covering the heavens. And birds, their every call angelic trumpets blaring from the heavens.

Indeed, one-trillionth of the Earth's ecological resources could easily support a micro-human population of a trillion! Now the Forerunner finally understood the point that the micro-humans had so repeatedly emphasized.

The micro-age was an age without worries.

There was nothing that could threaten this new world, nothing but...

Shivers grasped the Forerunner's mind and soul as he realized what he must do; and, it had to be done immediately. There was no time to delay. He went over to one of the racks and retrieved a hundred sealed tubes.

They contained the embryonic cells of his contemporaries, the embryonic cells of macro-humans.

The Forerunner took these tubes and dropped them into the laser waste incinerator. He then went back to cold storage, walking up and down the rows several times, carefully checking every nook and cranny. Only when he was absolutely certain that none of these tubes had been left behind did he return to the laser incinerator. He felt a sense of deep tranquillity as he pushed the button.

The laser beam burned at tens of thousands of degrees. In its blazing light, the tubes and the embryos they contained were vaporized in the wink of an eye.

全频带阻塞干扰

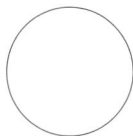

FULL-SPECTRUM BARRAGE JAMMING

TRANSLATED BY CARMEN YILING YAN

二〇一零 译

Dedicated with deep respect to the people of Russia, whose literature has influenced me all my life.

——Liu Cixin

On the subject of selecting a method of electromagnetic jamming for the battlefield, this manual recommends the use of selective frequency-targeted jamming rather than engaging in barrage jamming over a wide range of simultaneous frequencies, as the latter will interfere with friendly electromagnetic communication and electronic support as well.
—*U.S. Army Electronic Warfare Handbook*

January 5th, Smolensk front line

The fallen city had already disappeared from view. The front line had retreated forty kilometers in the span of a single night.

Under the light of the early-morning sky, the snowy plain appeared a cold, dim blue. In the distance, black columns of smoke rose from destroyed targets. There was almost no wind; the smoke ascended straight and high, like thin strands of black gauze tying heaven to earth. As Karina's gaze followed the smoke upward, she started: the brightening sky was clogged with a vast, dense bramble of white, as if a demented giant had covered the sky in agitated scrawls. They were the tangled fighter plane contrails left by the Russian and NATO air forces in their fierce night battle for control over the airspace.

The aerial and long-range precision strikes had continued throughout the night, too. To a casual observer, the bombardment wouldn't have seemed particularly concentrated. The explosions sounded seconds, even minutes apart. But Karina knew that nearly every explosion had signified some important target hit, sparking punctuation marks in the black pages of the previous night. By dawn, Karina wasn't sure how much strength was left in the defensive lines, or even whether the defensive lines had survived at all. It seemed as if she were the last one standing against the onslaught.

Major Karina's electronic-resistance platoon had been hit by six laser-guided missiles around midnight. She'd survived by pure luck. The BMP-2 armored tank carrying the radio-jamming equipment was still burning; the other electronic-warfare vehicles in the battery were now piles of blackened metal scattered around her on the snow. Residual heat was dissipating from the bomb crater Karina was in, leaving her feeling the cold. She pushed herself to a sitting position with her hands. Her right hand touched something sticky and clammy. Covered in black ash, it looked like a lump of mud. She suddenly realized it was a piece of flesh. She didn't know what body part it came from, much less whose. A first lieutenant, two second lieutenants, and eight privates had died in last night's attack. Karina vomited, though nothing came out but stomach acid. She shoved her hands in the snow, trying to wipe away the blood, but the smears of blackish red quickly congealed in the cold, as stark as before.

The suffocating stillness of the last half hour signified that a new round of ground assault was about to begin. Karina turned up the volume dial on the walkie-talkie strapped to her shoulder, but heard only static. Suddenly, a few blurry sentences emerged through the receiver, like birds flitting through thick fog.

'. . .Observation Station Six reporting! Position 1437 at twelve o'clock sees thirty-seven M1A2s averaging sixty meters apart, forty-one Bradley IFVs five hundred meters behind the M1A2s' vanguard; twenty-four M1A2s and eight Leclercs currently flanking Position 1633, already past the border of 1437. Positions 1437, 1633, and 1752, prepare to engage the enemy!'

Karina forced back shivers from cold and fear, so that the horizon line steadied in her binoculars. She saw blurry masses of snow spray, edging the horizon with fuzzy trim.

That was when Karina heard the rumble of engines behind her. A row of Russian tanks passed her position as they charged the enemy, more T-90 tanks leaving the highway behind them. Karina heard a different rumble: enemy helicopters were appearing in the sky ahead in neat array, a black lattice in the ghastly white sky of dawn. The exhaust pipes of the tanks around Karina kicked into action with low splutters, cloaking the battleground in white fog. Through its crevices she could also see Russian helicopters passing low overhead.

The tanks' 120 mm guns stormed and thundered, and the white fog became a wildly flashing pink light display. Almost simultaneously, the first enemy shells fell, the pink light replaced by the blue-white lightning of their explosion. Karina, lying on her stomach at the bottom of the bomb crater, felt the ground reverberate with the intense percussion like a drumhead. Nearby dirt and rock flew into the air and landed all over her back. Amid the explosions, she could dimly hear the whinny of anti-tank missiles. Karina felt as if her viscera were tearing apart in the cacophony, and all the universe, the pieces falling toward an endless abyss—

Just as her mind teetered on the breaking point, the tank battle ended. It had lasted only thirty seconds.

When the smoke cleared, Karina saw that the snowy ground in front of her was scattered with destroyed Russian tanks, heaps of raging flames crowned with black smoke. She looked farther; even without binoculars, she could see a similar swath of destroyed NATO tanks in the distance, appearing as black smoking specks on the snow. But more enemy tanks were rushing past the wreckage, wreathed in the snow spray churned up by their treads. Now and then the Abramses' ferocious broad wedge heads emerged from the spray like snapping turtles launching themselves out of the waves, their smooth-bore muzzles flashing sporadically like the turtles' eyes. Just above, the helicopters were still embroiled in their melee. Karina saw an Apache explode in midair not far away. A Mi-28 wobbled low overhead, trailing fuel from a leak. It hit the ground a few dozen meters away and exploded into a fireball. Short-range air-to-air missiles slashed countless parallel white lines low in the air—

Karina heard a bang behind her. She turned; not far away, a damaged and badly smoking T-90 dropped its rear hatch. No one got out, but she could see a hand hanging down from it. Karina leapt from the bomb crater and rushed to the back of the tank. She grabbed hold of the hand and pulled. An explosion rumbled inside the tank. A blast of blazing air forced Karina back several steps. Her hand held something soft and very hot: a piece of skin pulled loose from the tank crew member's hand, cooked through. Karina raised her head and saw flames burst from the hatch. Through it, she could see that the tank interior was already an inferno in miniature. Among the flames, dimly red and transparent, she could clearly see the silhouette of the unmoving crewman, rippling as if in water.

She heard two new shrills. The artillery crew to her front and left fired its last two anti-tank missiles. The wire-guided Sagger missile successfully destroyed an Abrams; the other, radio-guided missile found its signal jammed and veered upward at an angle, missing its target. Meanwhile the six missile crewmen retreated from their bunker, running toward Karina's bomb crater as a Comanche helicopter dove for them, its angular chassis resembling the profile of a savage alligator. Machine-gun bullets struck the ground in a long row, their impact abruptly standing snow and dirt up in a fence that just as quickly toppled. The fence crossed through the little squadron, felling four of them. Only a first lieutenant and a private made it over to the crater. There Karina noticed that the lieutenant was wearing an antishock tank helmet, perhaps taken from a destroyed tank. The two of them held an RPG each.

The lieutenant jumped into the crater. He took a shot at the nearest enemy tank, hitting the M1A2 head-on, triggering its reactive armor, the sound of the rocket explosion and the armor explosion mingling peculiarly. The tank charged out of the cloud of smoke, scraps of reactive armor dangling from its front like a tattered shirt. The young private was still aiming, his RPG jittering with the tank's rise and fall, too uncertain to fire. Then the tank was just fifty, forty meters away, heading into a dip in the ground, and the private could only stand on the rim of the crater to aim downward.

His RPG and the Abrams's 120 mm gun sounded simultaneously.

The tank gunner had fired a nonexplosive depleted-uranium armor-piercing round in his desperation. With an initial velocity of eight hundred meters per second, it turned the soldier's upper body into a spray of gore upon impact. Karina felt scraps of blood and meat strike her steel helmet, pitter-pattering. She opened her eyes. Just in front of her, at the edge of the crater, the private's legs were two black tree stumps, soundlessly rolling their way to the bottom of the crater next to her feet. The shattered remains of the rest of his body had spattered a radial pattern of red speckles in the snow.

The rocket had struck the Abrams, the focused jet of the explosion cutting through its armor. Thick smoke billowed from the chassis. But the steel monster was still charging toward them, trailing smoke. It was within twenty meters of them before an explosion from within stopped it in its tracks, hurling the top of its turret sky-high.

The NATO tank line went past them immediately after, the ground trembling under the heavy impact of treads, but these tanks took no interest in their bomb crater. Once the first wave of tanks was past, the lieutenant grabbed Karina's hand and leapt from the crater, pulling her after him to the side of an already bullet-scarred jeep. Two hundred meters away, the second wave of armored assault was bearing down on them.

'Lie down and play dead!'the lieutenant said. So Karina lay by the jeep's wheel and closed her eyes.'It looks more realistic with your eyes open!' the lieutenant added, and smeared a handful of somebody's blood on her face. He lay down, too, forming a right angle with Karina, his head pressing against hers. His helmet had rolled to one side, and his coarse hair pricked at Karina's temple. She opened her eyes wide, looking at the sky almost swallowed by smoke.

Two or three minutes later, a half-track Bradley infantry fighting vehicle stopped ten or so meters from them. A few American soldiers in blue-and-white snowy terrain camouflage jumped from the convoy. The bulk of them leveled their guns and advanced in a skirmish line. Only one walked toward the jeep. Karina saw two snow-speckled paratrooper boots step next to her face; she could clearly make out the insignia of the Eighty-second Airborne Division on the handle of the knife sheathed in his boot. The American crouched down to look at her. Their gazes met, and Karina tried as hard as she could to make hers blank and lifeless across from that pair of startled blue eyes.

'*Oh, god!*' Karina heard him exclaim. She didn't know if it was for the beauty of this woman with a major's star on her shoulder, or for the terrible sight of her bloody, dirty face; maybe it was both. He reached a hand to unfasten her collar. Goose bumps rose all over Karina, and she nudged her hand a few centimeters closer to the pistol in her belt, but the American only tugged the dog tag from her neck.

They had to wait longer than expected. Enemy tanks and armored convoys thundered endlessly past them. Karina could feel her body freezing almost solid on the snowy ground. It made her think of a couplet from an old army song, of all things. She'd read the words in an old book on Matrosov: 'A soldier lies on the snowy ground / like they lie on white swan down.' The day she received her Ph.D., she'd written the lines in her diary. That had been a snowy night, too. She'd stood in front of the window on the top floor of Moscow State University's Main Building; that night, the snow really did look like swan down, and through the haze of snow flickered the lights from the thousands of homes of the capital. She'd joined the army the next day.

A jeep stopped not far from them, three NATO officers smoking and conversing inside. But the area around Karina and the lieutenant was clearing. The two finally rose. They jumped in their own jeep, the lieutenant turned the ignition, and they hurtled along the route planned out earlier. Submachine guns sounded behind them; bullets flew overhead, one shattering a rearview mirror. The jeep whipped into a turn, entering a burning residential area. The enemy hadn't pursued.

'Major, you have a doctorate, right?' the lieutenant said as he drove.

'Where do you know me from?'

'I've seen you with Marshal Levchenko's son.'

After a silence, the lieutenant said, 'Right now, his son is farther from the war than anyone else in the world.'

'What are you implying? You know that—'

'Nothing, I was just saying,' the lieutenant said neutrally. Neither of them had their mind on the conversation. They were still Ling'ering on that last thread of hope.

Of the entire battlefront, this might be the only breach.

January 5th, near-sun orbit, aboard the *Vechnyy Buran*

Misha was experiencing the solitude of a lone inhabitant in an empty city.

The *Vechnyy Buran* really was the size of a small city. The modular space station had a volume equivalent to two supercarriers and could sustain five thousand residents in space at a time. When the complex was under centripetal force simulating gravity, it even contained a pool and a small flowing river. Compared to other space work environments of the day, it smacked of unparalleled extravagance. But in reality, the *Vechnyy Buran* was the product of the thrifty reasoning the Russian space program had demonstrated since Mir. The thinking behind its design went that, although combining all the functionality needed to explore the entire solar system into one structure might require a huge initial investment, it would prove absolutely economical in the long run. Western media jokingly called *Vechnyy Buran* the Swiss Army knife of space: It could serve as a space station orbiting at any height from Earth; it could relocate easily to moon orbit, or make exploratory flights to the other planets. *Vechnyy Buran* had already flown to Venus and Mars and probed the asteroid belt. With its huge capacity, it was like shipping an entire research center into space. In the field of space research, it had an advantage over the legion but dainty Western spaceships.

The war had broken out just as *Vechnyy Buran* was preparing for the three-year expedition to Jupiter. At that time, its over one hundred crew members, most of them air force officers, had left for Earth, leaving only Misha. The

Vechnyy Buran had revealed a flaw: Militarily, it presented too big a target while possessing no defensive abilities. Failing to foresee the progressive militarization of space had been a mistake on the part of the designer.

Vechnyy Buran could only take avoidance measures. It couldn't depart for farther space, with numerous unmanned NATO satellites patrolling Jupiter's orbital path. They were small, but whether armed or unarmed, any one could pose a deadly threat to the *Vechnyy Buran*.

The only option was to draw near the sun. The automatic active-cooling heat-shielding system that was the pride of the *Vechnyy Buran* allowed it to go closer to the sun than any other man-made object yet. Now the *Vechnyy Buran* had reached Mercury's orbital path, five million kilometers from the sun and one hundred million kilometers from Earth.

Most of the *Vechnyy Buran*'s hold had been closed off, but the area left to Misha was still astonishingly enormous. Through the broad, clear dome ceiling, the sun looked three times larger than it looked on Earth. He could clearly see the sunspots and the singularly beautiful solar prominences emerging from the purple corona; sometimes, he could even see the granulation formed by convection in the surface. The serenity here was an illusion. Outside, the sun pitched a raging storm of particles and electromagnetic radiation, and the *Vechnyy Buran* was just a tiny seed in a turbulent ocean.

A gossamer-thin thread of EM waves connected Misha to the Earth, and brought the troubles of that distant world to him as well. He had just been informed that the command center near Moscow had been destroyed by a cruise missile, and that the *Vechnyy Buran* 's control had passed to the secondary command center at Samara. He received the latest news of the war from Earth at five-hour intervals; at those times, each time, he would think of his father.

January 5th, Russian army General Staff headquarters

Marshal Mikhail Semyonovich Levchenko felt as if he were face-to-face with a wall, though in reality, a holographic map of the Moscow theater of war lay in front of him. Conversely, when he turned toward the big paper map hanging on the wall, he could see breadth and depth, a sense of space.

No matter what, he preferred traditional maps. He didn't know how many times he'd sought a location on the very bottom of the map, forcing him and his strategists to get on hands and knees; the thought now made him smile a little. He also remembered spending the eve of military exercises in his battlefield tent, piecing together the newly received battle maps with clear tape. He always made a mess of it, but his son had done the taping neater than he ever did, that first time he came along to watch the exercises. . .

Finding that his musings had returned to the subject of his son, the marshal vigilantly cut off his train of thought.

He and the commander of the Western Military District were the only people in the war room, the latter chain-smoking cigarettes as they watched the shifting clouds of smoke above the holographic map, their gaze as intent as if it were the grim battlefield itself.

The district commander said, 'NATO has seventy-five divisions along the Smolensk front now. The battlefront is a hundred kilometers long. They've breached the line at multiple points.'

'And the eastern front?' Marshal Levchenko asked.

'Most of our Eleventh Army defected to the Rightists too, as you know. The Rightist army is now twenty-four divisions strong, but their assaults on Yaroslavl remain exploratory in nature.'

The earth shook with the faint vibrations of some ground explosion. The lights hanging from the ceiling cast swaying shadows around the war room.

'There's talk now of retreating to Moscow and using the barricades and fortifications for a street-to-street battle, like seventy-old years ago.'

'That's absurd! If we withdraw from the western front, NATO can swing north around us to join forces with the Rightists at Tver. Moscow would fall into panic without them lifting a finger. We have three options in our playbook right now: counterattack, counterattack, and counterattack.'

The district commander sighed, looking wordlessly at the map.

Marshal Levchenko continued,'I know the western front isn't strong enough. I plan to relocate an army from the eastern front to strengthen it.'

'What? But it's already going to be a challenge to defend Yaroslavl.'

Marshal Levchenko chuckled.'Nowadays, the problem with many commanders is their tendency to only consider a problem from the military angle. They can't see beyond the grim tactical situation. Looking at the current situation, do you think the Rightists lack the strength to take Yaroslavl?'

'I don't think so. The Fourteenth Army is an elite force with a high concentration of armored vehicles and low-altitude attack power. For them to advance less than fifteen kilometers a day while not having suffered serious setbacks seems like taking things slow on purpose.'

'That's right, they're watching and waiting. They're watching the western front! And if we can take back the initiative in the western front, they'll keep on watching and waiting. They might even independently negotiate a cease-fire.'

The district commander held his newest cigarette in his hand, but had forgotten all thoughts of lighting it.

'The defection of the armies on the eastern front really was a knife in our back, but some commanders have turned this into an excuse in their minds to steer us toward passive operational policies. That has to change! Of course, it must be said that our current strength in the Moscow region isn't enough for a total turnaround. Our hope lies in the relief forces from the Caucasus and Ural districts.'

'The closer Caucasus forces will need at least a week to assemble and advance into place. If we account for possession of the airspace, it might take even longer.'

January 5th, Moscow

It was past three in the afternoon when Karina and the first lieutenant entered the city in their jeep. The air raid alarm had just sounded, and the streets were empty.

'I miss my T-90 already, Major,' sighed the lieutenant. 'I finished armored-vehicle training right around the time I broke up with my girlfriend, but the moment I arrived at my unit and saw that tank, my heart soared right back up again. I put my hand on its armor, and it was smooth and warm, like touching a lover's hand. Ha, what was that relationship worth! Now I'd found a real love! But it took a Mistral missile this morning.'He sighed again. 'It might still be burning.'

At that time they heard dense explosions from the northwest, a savage area bombing rare in modern aerial warfare.

The lieutenant was still wallowing in the morning's engagement. 'Less than thirty seconds, and the whole tank company was gone.'

'The enemy losses were heavy, too,' Karina said. 'I observed the aftermath. There were about the same number of destroyed vehicles on each side.'

'The ratio of destroyed tanks was about 1 to 1.2, I think. The helicopters were worse off, but it wouldn't have gone over 1 to 1.4.'

'In that case, the battlefield initiative should have stayed on our side. We have a sizable advantage in numbers. How did the battle end up like this?'

The lieutenant turned to eye Karina. 'You're one of the electronic-warfare people. Don't you get it? All your toys—the fifth-generation C3I, the 3-D battle displays, the dynamic situation simulators, the attack-plan optimizer, whatever—looked great in the mock battles. But on the real battlefield, all the screen in front of me ever showed was 'communication error' and 'could not log in.' Take this morning, for example. I didn't have a clue what was happening in the front and flanks. I only got one order: 'Engage the enemy.' Ah, if we'd only had half our force again in reinforcements, the enemy wouldn't have broken through our position. It was probably the same way all down the line.'

Karina knew that in the battle that had just ended, the two sides had sent perhaps over ten thousand tanks into battle along the front, and half as many armed helicopters.

At that point they arrived at Arbat Street. The popular pedestrian boulevard of yesteryear was empty now, sandbags walling off the entrances to the antiques shops and artisans' places.

'My steel darling gave as good as she got.' The lieutenant was still stuck on the morning's battle. 'I'm sure I hit a Challenger tank. But most of all, I'd wanted to take down an Abrams, you know? An Abrams . . .'

Karina pointed to the entrance of the antiques store they just passed. 'There. My grandfather died there.'

'But I don't remember any bombs getting dropped here.'

'I'm talking about twenty years ago—I was only four then. The winter that year was bitterly cold. The heating was cut off, and ice formed in the rooms. I wrapped myself around the TV for warmth, listening to the president promise the Russian people a gentle winter. I screamed and cried that I was cold, hungry.

'My grandfather looked at me silently, and finally he made up his mind. He took out his treasured military medal and took me here. This was a free market, where you could sell anything, from vodka to political views. An American wanted my grandfather's medal, but he was only willing to pay forty dollars. He said Order of the Red Star and Order of the Red Banner medals weren't worth anything, but he'd pay a hundred dollars for an Order of Bogdan Khmelnitsky, a hundred fifty for an Order of Glory, two hundred for an Order of Nakhimov, two hundred fifty for an Order of Ushakov. *Order of Victories are worth the most, but of course you wouldn't have one, those were only given to generals.* But Order of Suvorovs were worth a lot too, he'd pay four hundred fifty dollars for one. . . . My grandfather walked away then. We walked and walked along Arbat Street in the freezing cold. Then my grandfather couldn't walk anymore. The sky was almost dark. He sat heavily on the steps of that antiques store and told me to go home without him. The next day, they found him frozen to death there, his hand reaching into his jacket to clench the medal he'd earned with his own blood. His eyes were wide open, looking at the city he'd saved from Guderian's tanks fifty years ago. . . .'

January 5th, Russian army General Staff headquarters

Marshal Levchenko left the underground war room for the first time in a week. He walked in the thick snowfall, searching for the sun, half set behind the snow-draped pinewoods. In his mind's eye, he saw a small black dot slowly moving against the orange setting sun: the *Vechnyy Buran,* with his son inside, farther than any other son from a father.

It had led to many ugly rumors within his homeland, and the enemy utilized it even more fully abroad. *The New York Times* had printed its headline in black type sized for shock: no deserter has run farther. Below was a photo of Misha, captioned 'At a time when three hundred million Russians for a bloodbath defense against the 'invaders,' the son of their marshal has fled the war aboard the nation's only massive-scale spacecraft. Sixty million miles from the battlefield, he is safer than any other of his fellow citizens.'

But Marshal Levchenko didn't take it to heart. From secondary school to postgraduate studies, almost none of Misha's associates had known who his father was. The space program command center made its decision solely because Misha's field of study happened to be the mathematical modeling of stars. The *Vechnyy Buran* approaching the sun was a rare opportunity for his research, and the space complex couldn't be entirely piloted by remote control, requiring at least one person aboard. The general learned of Misha's background only later, from the Western news media.

On the other hand, whether Marshal Levchenko admitted it or not, deep down inside, he really did hope his son could stay away from the war. It wasn't solely a matter of blood ties; Marshal Levchenko had always felt that his son wasn't meant for war—perhaps he was the least meant for war of all the world's people. But he knew his notion was faulty: was anyone truly meant for war?

Besides, was Misha truly suited for the stars either? He liked stars, had devoted his life to their research, but he himself was the opposite of a star. He was more like Pluto, the silent and cold dwarf planet orbiting in its distant void, out of sight of the mortal realm. Misha was quiet and graceful. Solitude was his nourishment and air.[1]

Misha was born in East Germany, and the day he was born was the darkest day in the marshal's life. He was only a major that evening in West Berlin, standing guard with his soldiers in front of the Soviet War Memorial in the Tiergarten, keeping vigil for the fallen for the last time in forty years. In front of them were a gaggle of grinning Western officers; and a few slovenly, shiftless German police officers trailing wolfhounds on leashes to replace them; and the skinhead neo-Nazis hollering 'Red Army Go Home.' Behind him were the tear-filled eyes of the senior company commander and soldiers. He couldn't help himself; he, too, let tears blur all this away.

He returned to the emptied barracks after dark. On this last night before he left for home, he was notified that Misha had been born, but that his wife had died of complications from childbirth.

His life after he returned was difficult, too. Like the 400,000 army men and 120,000 administrators withdrawn from Europe, he had no home to go to, and lived with Misha in a temporary shack of metal sheets, freezing in winter and broiling in summer. His old colleagues would do any work for a living, some becoming gun runners for the gangs, some reduced to strip dances at nightclubs. But he stuck to his honest soldier's life, and Misha quietly grew up amid the hardship. He wasn't like the other children; he seemed to have been born with an innate ability to endure, because he had a world of his own.

As early as primary school, Misha would quietly spend the entire night alone in his small room. Levchenko had thought he was reading at first, but by chance he discovered that his son was standing in front of the window,

---

1 考虑到文化差异，译稿对原文进行了一些描述性补充，后文不再单独指出。——编者注。

unmoving, watching the stars.

'Papa, I like the stars. I want to look at them all my life.'he told his father.

On his eleventh birthday, Misha asked his father for a present for the first time: a telescope. He'd been using Levchenko's military binoculars to stargaze before then. Afterward, the telescope became Misha's only companion. He could stand on the balcony and watch the stars until the sky lightened in the east. A few times, father and son stargazed together. The marshal always turned the telescope toward the brightest-looking star, but his son would shake his head disapprovingly.'That one's not interesting, Papa. That's Venus. Venus is a planet, but I only like stars.'

Misha didn't like any of the things that the other kids liked, either. The neighbor's boy, son of the old paratrooper chief of staff, snuck out his father's pistol to play with, and ended up shooting his own leg by accident. The general of the staff's children thought no reward better than their papa taking them to the company firing range and letting them take a shot. But that affinity seemed to have completely skipped over Misha.

Levchenko found his son's apathy for weapons unsettling, almost intolerable, to the point where he reacted in a way that embarrassed him to think of to this day: Once, he'd quietly set his Makarov semiautomatic on his son's writing desk. Not long after he returned from school, Misha came out of his room with the pistol. He held it like a child, his hand closed carefully around the barrel. He set the gun gently in front of his father and said, evenly,'Papa, be careful where you put it next time.'

On the topic of Misha's future, the marshal was an understanding man. He wasn't like the other generals around him, determined that their sons and daughters would succeed them in the military. But Misha really was too distant from his father's work.

Marshal Levchenko wasn't a hot-tempered man, but as the commander in chief of the armies, he'd castigated more than one general in front of thousands of troops. He'd never lost his temper at Misha, though. Misha walked silently and steadily along his chosen path, giving his father little cause for concern. More importantly, Misha seemed to be born with an extraordinary aloofness from the world that at times elicited even Levchenko's reverence. It was as if he'd carelessly tossed a seed into a flowerpot only for a rare and exotic plant to sprout. He had watched this plant grow day by day, protecting it carefully, awaiting its flowering. His hopes had not fallen short. His son was now the most renowned astrophysicist in the world.

By this time, the sun had entirely set behind the pine forest, the white snow on the ground turning pale blue. Marshal Levchenko collected his thoughts and returned to the underground war room. All the personnel for the war meeting had arrived, including important commanders from the Western and Caucasus military districts.

Outnumbering them were the electronic-warfare commanders, all the ranks from captain to major general, most newly returned from the front. In the war room, a debate was raging between the Western Military District's ground- and electronic-warfare officers.

'We correctly determined the enemy assault's change in direction,' Major General Felitov of the Taman Infantry Division said. 'Our tanks and close air support had no problems with maneuverability. But the communications system was jammed beyond belief. The C3I system was almost paralyzed! We expanded the electronic-warfare unit from a battalion to a division, from a division to a corps, and invested more money in them these two years than we invested in all the regular equipment. And we get this?!'

One of the lieutenant generals commanding electronic warfare in the region glanced at Karina. Like all the other officers newly returned from the front line, her camo uniform was stained and scorched, and traces of blood still stuck to her face. 'Major Karina has done noteworthy work in electronic-warfare research, and was sent by the General Staff to observe the electronic battle. Perhaps her insights may better persuade you.' Young Ph.D. officers like Karina tended to be fearlessly outspoken toward superiors. They were often used as mouthpieces for tough words, and this was no exception.

Karina stood. 'General Felitov, that's hardly the case! Compared to NATO, the investment we've put into our C3I is nothing.'

'What about electronic countermeasures?' the major general asked. 'If the enemy can jam us, can't you jam them? Our C3I was useless, but NATO's worked like the wheels were greased. Just look at how quickly the enemy was able to change the direction of their attack this morning!'

Karina gave a pained smile.'Speaking of jamming the enemy, General Felitov, don't forget that in your sector, your people forced their own electronic-warfare unit to turn off their jammers at gunpoint!'

'What happened out there?'Marshal Levchenko asked. Only then did the others notice his arrival and stand to bow.

'It was like this,'the major general explained.'Their jamming was worse for our own communication and command system than NATO's! We could still maintain some wireless transmission through NATO's jamming. But once our forces turned on their own jammers, we were completely smothered!'

'But don't forget, the enemy would have been completely smothered too!' Karina said.'Given our army's available electronic countermeasures, this was the only possible strategy. At this time, NATO has already widely adopted technologies like frequency hopping, direct-sequence spread spectrum, adaptive nulling systems, burst transmission, and frequency agility.[1] Our frequency-specific aimed jamming was completely useless. Full-spectrum barrage jamming was our only option.'

A colonel from the Fifth Army spoke up.'Major, NATO exclusively uses frequency-specific aimed jamming too, with a fairly narrow range of frequencies. And our C3I system widely incorporates the technologies you mentioned as well. Why would their jamming be so effective against us?'

---

1 A simplified explanation of the electronic battle vocabulary:

Frequency hopping: The transmitter switches carrier frequencies according to a pattern possessed by the receiver.

Direct-sequence spread spectrum: The signal is distributed across a wide range of frequencies to make eavesdropping and jamming difficult.

Adaptive nulling system: An antenna array that nulls out signals coming from the direction of enemy jamming, allowing it to communicate with ally antennae in other directions.

Burst transmission: Transmitting data at a high rate over a short period of time using a wider-than-average frequency range.

Frequency agility: The signal is capable of rapidly and continuously changing frequency to avoid jamming.

'That's easy. What systems are our C3I built upon? Unix, Linux, even Windows 2010, and our CPUs are made by Intel and AMD! We're using the dogs they raised to guard our own gate! Under these circumstances, the enemy can quickly figure out, say, the frequency-hopping patterns used for our intelligence reports, while using more numerous and more effective software attacks to strengthen the effects of their jamming. The Main Command suggested the widespread adoption of a Russian-made operating system in the past, but met heavy opposition from the ranks. Your division was the most stubborn holdout of all—'

'Yes, yes, we're here today to resolve precisely that problem and conflict,' Marshal Levchenko interrupted.'I call this meeting to order!'

Once everyone was seated in front of the digital battle simulator, Marshal Levchenko called over a staff officer. The young major was tall and skinny, his eyes squinted into slits, as if they had trouble adjusting to the war room's brightness. 'Let me introduce Major Bondarenko. His most obvious trait is his severe myopia. His glasses are different from other people's—their lenses rest inside the frame, while his stick out. Ha, they're as thick as the bottom of a teacup! This morning they got smashed when the major's jeep was hit in an airstrike, which is why we don't see them now. I think he lost his contacts too?'

'Marshal, it was five days ago at Minsk. My eyes only became like this in the last half year. If it happened earlier, I wouldn't have been admitted into Frunze Military Academy.'the major said stolidly.

No one knew why the marshal had chosen to introduce the major like this, though a few chuckled in the audience.

'Since the beginning of the war,'the marshal continued,'events have shown that despite Russian losses on the battlefield, our aerial and ground weapons aren't far behind the enemy's. But in the field of electronic warfare, we've been unexpectedly left in the dust. Many events in the past contributed to this situation, but we're not here to point fingers. We're here to state this: In our situation, electronic warfare is the key to taking back the initiative in the war! We must first admit that the enemy has an advantage in this area, perhaps an overwhelming advantage. Then we must work within our army's hardware and software limitations to create an effective plan of battle. The goal of this plan is to even out our and NATO's electronic-warfare capabilities within a short period of time. Maybe you all think this is impossible—our military planning since the end of the last century has been based on the assumption of a limited-scope war. We really haven't done enough research for an invasion on all fronts by as powerful an enemy as the one we're facing right now. In our dire situation, we have to think in a completely new way. The central command's new electronic-warfare strategy, which I'm introducing next, will demonstrate the results of this mode of thinking.'

The lights went out, the computer screens and digital battle simulator dimmed, and the heavy anti-radiation doors shut tightly. The war room was plunged into total darkness.

'I had the lights turned off.' The marshal's voice came through the darkness.

A minute passed in dark and silence.

'How's everyone feeling?' Marshal Levchenko asked.

No one answered. The cloying darkness left the officers feeling as if they were at the bottom of a dark sea. It even felt hard to breathe.

'General Andreyev, tell it to us.'

'Like it felt on the battlefield these few days,' the commander of the Fifth Army said, eliciting a wave of quiet laughter from the darkness.

'Everyone else empathizes with him, I think,' said the marshal. 'Of course you do! Think of it—nothing but static in your headsets, solid white on your screens, not a clue as to your orders or the battlefield around you. That same feeling! The darkness presses down until you can't breathe!

'But not everyone feels like that. How are you, Major Bondarenko?' asked Marshal Levchenko.

Major Bondarenko's voice came from one corner of the room. 'It's not so bad for me. Everything was a blur around me anyway back when the lights were on.'

'Maybe you even feel an advantage?' asked Marshal Levchenko.

'Yes, sir. You may have heard the story of the New York blackout, where blind people led everyone out of the skyscrapers.'

'But General Andreyev's sentiments are understandable. He's eagle-eyed, a legendary marksman—when he drinks, he uses his revolver to take the caps off his bottles at ten-odd meters. Wouldn't it be interesting to picture him having a gun duel with Major Bondarenko at this moment?'

The darkened war room once again sank into silence as the officers considered this.

The lights turned on. Everyone narrowed their eyes, less because of the discomfort of the sudden brightness, and more for the shock of what the marshal had just implied.

Marshal Levchenko stood up. 'I think I've explained our army's new electronic-warfare strategy: large-scale, full-spectrum barrage jamming. With regard to EM communications, we're going to let both sides enjoy a blacked-out battlefield!'

'This will cause our own battlefield command system to completely break down!' someone said fearfully.

'NATO's will too! If we're going to be blind, let's both be blind. If we're going to be deaf, let's both be deaf. We can then reach equal footing with the enemy's electronic-warfare capabilities. This is the central tenet of our new strategy.'

'But what are we supposed to do now, send messengers on motorcycles to transmit orders?'

'If the roads are bad, they'll have to ride horses,' Marshal Levchenko said. 'Our rough prediction shows that this kind of full-spectrum barrage jamming will cover at least seventy percent of NATO's battlefield communication network, meaning that their C3I system will suffer a complete breakdown. Simultaneously, we'll be leaving fifty to sixty percent of the enemy's long-range weapons useless. The best example is with the Tomahawk satellite-guided missile. Missile guidance has changed a lot since last century. Before, it primarily navigated using onboard TERCOM with a small-scale radar altimeter, but now these methods are only used in end-stage guidance, while most of the launch process relies on a GPS system. General Dynamics and McDonnell Douglas Corporation thought this change was a big step forward, but the Americans trust their EM wave guidance from space too well. Once we disrupt the GPS transmission, the Tomahawk will be blind. The dependency on GPS exists in most of NATO's long-range weapons. Under the battlefield conditions we've planned, we'll force the enemy into a traditional battle, allowing us to fully utilize our strengths.'

'I'm still unsure about this,'the commander of the Twelfth Army which will be sent from the eastern front to the west said anxiously.'Under these battlefield communication conditions, I'm not even sure my division can smoothly reach the western front from the east.'

'Of course it will!'said Marshal Levchenko. 'The distance was nothing even for Kutuzov, in Napoleon's time. I don't believe the Russian army needs wireless to do it today! The Americans should be the ones spoiled rotten by modern equipment, not us. I know that an EM blackout over all the battlefield will put fear in your hearts. But you have to remember, the enemy will feel ten times your fear!'

Watching Karina disappear among the other camo-clad officers as they exited the war room, Marshal Levchenko felt apprehension rise in his heart. She was returning to the front, and her unit was stationed right in the middle of the enemy's most concentrated firepower. Yesterday, during his communication with his son a hundred million miles away, which had at least five minutes delay back and forth, the marshal had told him that Karina was perfectly well. But she nearly hadn't come back from this morning's battle.

Misha and Karina had met at one of the military exercises. The marshal had been eating dinner with his son one night, silently as usual, Misha's late mother looking on from her picture frame. Suddenly, Misha had said, 'Papa, I recall that tomorrow is your fifty-first birthday. I should give you a gift. I thought of it when I saw the telescope; that was a wonderful present.'

'How about you give me a few days of your time?'

Son quietly raised his head to look at father.

'You have your own work, and I'm happy for you. But surely it's not unreasonable for a father to want his son to understand his life's work! How about you come with me to observe the military exercises?'

Misha smiled and nodded. He smiled very rarely.

It had been the largest Russian war game of the century. Misha showed little interest in the torrent of steel-armored vehicles rumbling past them on the highway that night before it started; the moment he was off the helicopter, he ducked into the tent to assemble the newly arrived battle maps with clear tape in his father's stead. The next day, Misha didn't show the slightest interest through all the exercises. Marshal Levchenko had expected that. But one incident gave him all the reassurance he could ever want.

The exercise scheduled for the morning was a tank division assaulting high ground; Misha sat with some local officials on the north side of the observation station. The station was safely out of range, but in order to satisfy the curiosity of the local officials, it had been placed much closer to the action than before.

Tu-22 bombers soared in formation above, heavy aerial bombs fell like rain, and the hilltop exploded into an erupting volcano. Only then did the officials understand the difference between movies and a real battlefield. As the ground quaked and the hill shook, they pressed themselves flat against the table and covered their heads with their arms, some even crawling under the table with shrieks. But the marshal saw that Misha alone sat with his back straight, the same cool expression on his face, calmly watching the terrible volcano as the light of the explosions flashed across his sunglasses. Warmth flooded into Levchenko's heart then. In the end, son, you have a soldier's blood in your veins!

That night, father and son walked along the practice field. In the distance, the headlamps of armored vehicles densely sprinkled the valleys and plains with stars. The faint smell of gunpowder smoke still Ling'ered in the air.

'How much did it cost?'Misha asked.

'The direct cost was about three hundred million rubles.'

Misha sighed.'Our task group wanted a third-generation evolving star model to work with. We couldn't get a grant of three hundred fifty thousand for expenses.'

Marshal Levchenko at last said what he'd long wanted to tell his son. 'Our two worlds are too far apart. Your stars are all four light-years away at the least, yes? They don't have any bearing on the armies and wars on Earth. I can't claim to know much about what you do, though I'm very proud of you all the same. But as an army man, I just want my son to appreciate my own profession. What father wouldn't feel the greatest happiness telling his son about his campaigns? But you've never cared for my work, when really, it's the foundation and safeguard for your own. Without an army strong enough and big enough to keep the country safe, fundamental science research like yours would be impossible.'

'You've got it backward, Papa. If everyone were like us and spent all their life on exploring the universe, they'd understand its beauty, the beauty that lies behind its vastness and depth. And someone who truly understood the innate beauty of space and nature would never go to war.'

'That thinking's as childish as you can get. If appreciation of beauty could prevent war, we'd never be short of peace!'

'Do you think it's easy for humanity to understand this kind of beauty?' Misha pointed at the night sky, a sea of shining stars. 'Look at these stars. Everyone knows they're beautiful, but how many grasp the deepest nuances of their beauty? All these countless celestial bodies are so glorious in their metamorphosis from nebula to black hole, so vast and terrible in their explosive power. But do you know that a few elegant equations can accurately describe all of it? Mathematical models created from the equations can near perfectly predict everything a star does. Even mathematical models of our own planet's atmosphere are orders of magnitude less precise.'

Marshal Levchenko nodded. 'I can believe that. They say humanity knows more about the moon than the bottom of Earth's oceans. But the deeper beauty in space and nature you talk about still can't stop wars. No one could have understood that beauty more than Einstein, and didn't he advise the creation of the atomic bomb?'

'Einstein made little progress in his later research, largely because he became too involved in politics. I won't go down the same path as him. But, Papa, when it's necessary, I'll do my duty too.'

Misha observed the exercise for five days. The marshal didn't know when his son first met Karina; the first time he saw them together, they were already conversing on familiar terms. They were talking about stars, about which Karina knew a considerable amount. Seeing an untried youngster like Karina already wearing a major's star for her Ph.D. left the marshal feeling a little offended, but other than that, she'd made a fine first impression.

The second time Marshal Levchenko saw Misha and Karina together, he discovered there was already a deep sense of closeness between them. Their topic of conversation surprised him: electronic warfare. They were standing by a tank parked not far from the marshal's jeep. Due to their topic of conversation, they didn't seem concerned with privacy.

The marshal heard Misha say: 'Right now, your department has been focusing on only high-level pure software like the C3I, virus programs, the digital battlefield, and so on. But have you considered that this might leave you holding a wooden sword?' Seeing Karina's surprise, Misha continued, 'Have you put thought into the foundation they're built upon? The physical layer at the bottom of the seven layers of protocol defined by the Open Systems Interconnection model? Civilian networks can use fiber optics, fixed lasers, and the like for media and communication. But the terminals in a military-use C3I network are fast-moving and unpredictably located, so only EM waves can keep them in communication. And you know how EM waves are as fragile as thin ice under jamming. . . '

The marshal was quite shocked. He'd never talked about these things with Misha, and his son would never have snuck a look at his classified documents, but here Misha had neatly and clearly laid out the same considerations that he'd come up with over the years!

Misha's words had an even greater impact on Karina. She even shifted the direction of her own research to create an electromagnetic jamming unit code-named 'Flood.' It fit into an armored vehicle, and could simultaneously emit strong EM jamming waves ranging from three kilohertz to thirty gigahertz, drowning out all EM communication signals outside the millimeter radio range.

The first weapons test at one of the Siberian bases had sent a whole swarm of officials running over to protest. Flood had cut off all EM wave-based communication in the nearby city: cell phones found no reception, pagers fell silent, televisions and radios lost all signal. The impact on finance and stocks was disastrous; the local officials claimed astronomical losses.

Flood was inspired by a type of EMP bomb that utilized high explosives to create a powerful electromagnetic pulse within a one-use wire coil. As a result, Flood created shock waves like a rocket engine, shattering nearby windows in its trial. This meant that it could only be remotely operated, and its crew had to wear anti-microwave-radiation protective gear even though they were two or three kilometers away.

Flood had raised fierce debate in the armaments department and the electronic-warfare command. Many thought that it had no practical value; using it in a limited-scope battlefield would be like using a nuclear bomb in a street-to-street battle, devastating friend and foe alike. But under the marshal's insistence, two hundred Flood units had been mass-produced. Now, in the central command's new electronic-warfare strategy, it would take center stage.

That his son had fallen for a woman in the army had deeply surprised Marshal Levchenko. He assumed at the time that Misha's feelings for Karina overlooked her occupation. But Misha later brought Karina home on a few occasions. The first time, Karina wore a pretty dress; when Marshal Levchenko walked close, he overheard Misha tell her, 'You don't have to dress up for us. Wear your uniform next time, I know you feel more comfortable in it.' That disproved the marshal's original theory. Now he understood that Misha fell for Karina to some extent because she was a major in the army. He felt again what he felt that first morning of war training. The major's star on Karina's shoulder now seemed incomparably beautiful.

January 6th, Moscow theater of operations

Powerful electromagnetic waves gathered rapidly above the battlefield, at last becoming a mighty typhoon. After the war, people would reminisce: In the mountain villages far from the front line, they saw the animals fidget and stir, agitated; in the city with its enforced blackout, they saw induction trigger tiny sparks along the telephone wires.

As part of the Twelfth Army transferring from the eastern front to the west, the armored-car corps was advancing urgently. Their lieutenant general stood by his jeep parked at the roadside, watching his troops hasten through the snow and dust with satisfaction. The enemy's air raids had been far less intense than predicted, allowing his forces to travel by day.

Three Tomahawk missiles tore overhead, the low buzz of their jet engines crisp in the air. A moment later, three explosions sounded in the distance. The correspondent by the lieutenant general's side, his static-filled earpiece useless, turned to look in the direction of the explosion. He cried out in surprise. The general told him not to make a big deal out of nothing, but then a battalion commander beside him urged him to look, too. So he looked, and shook his head in confusion. Tomahawks weren't 100 percent accurate, but for three to land in an empty field, more than a kilometer from each other, really was a rare sight.

Two Su-27s flew five kilometers above the battlefield in an empty sky. They had belonged to a larger fighter squadron, but it had run into a skirmish with a NATO F-22 squadron above the sea, and the planes lost contact with the others in the turmoil of battle. Normally, regrouping would have been easy, but now the radio was down. The airspace that had seemed so small as to be cramped to a high-speed fighter plane now seemed as vast as outer space. Regrouping would be like finding a needle in a haystack. The lead pilot and his wingman were forced to fly wingtip-to-wingtip like stunt fliers to hear each other's wireless messages.

'Suspicious object to the upper left, azimuth 220, altitude 30!' the wingman reported. The lead pilot looked in that direction. The earlier snow had washed the winter sky clean and blue, and the visibility was excellent. The two planes ascended toward the target to investigate. It was flying in the same direction as them, but much slower, and it didn't take long to catch up.

Their first good look at the target was a bolt out of the blue.

That was a NATO E-4A early-warning aircraft. For a fighter-plane pilot to encounter one was like seeing the back of their own head. An E-4A could monitor up to one million square kilometers, completing a full sweep in just five seconds. It could locate targets two thousand kilometers from the defensive area, providing more than forty minutes of advance notice. It could separate out up to a thousand EM signals within one thousand to two thousand kilometers, and each scan could query and identify two thousand targets of any kind, land, sky, or sea. An early-warning aircraft didn't need the protection of escorts when its all-seeing eyes allowed it to easily avoid any threats.

That was why the lead pilot naturally assumed it was a trap. He and the wingman searched the surrounding sky carefully, but there was nothing in the cold, clear sky. The lead pilot decided to take a risk.

'Ball lightning, ball lightning, I'm going to attack. Guard azimuth 317, but be careful not to leave range of sight!'

Once his wingman flew in the direction he thought most likely for an ambush, he activated the afterburner and yanked at the controllers. Trailing black exhaust, the Su-27 lunged toward the early-warning aircraft above like a striking cobra. Now the E-4A discovered the approaching threat and turned to rush southeast in an escape maneuver. Magnesium heat pellets popped from its tail one after another to disrupt heat-seeking missiles, the trail of little fireballs looking like bits of its soul startled out of its mortal shell. An early-warning aircraft before a fighter plane was as helpless as a bicycle trying to outrun a motorbike. In that moment, the lead pilot decided that the order he'd given the wingman had turned out to be terribly selfish.

He followed the E-4A from above at a distance, admiring the prey he'd caught. The pale blue radar dome atop the E-4A was lovely in its curves, charming as a Christmas ornament; its broad white chassis was like a fat roast duck on its platter: so tempting, yet too lovely to violate with knife and fork. But instinct warned him not to drag this on any longer. He first fired a burst with the 20 mm cannon, shattering the radome, and watched scraps of the Westinghouse-made AN/ZPY-3 radar antenna scatter across the sky like silver Christmas confetti. He next severed a wing with the cannon, then at last lashed down the fatal blow with the 6,000 rpm double-barreled cannon, cutting the already tumbling and falling E-4A in two.

The Su-27 wheeled downward to follow the halves in their plunging descent. The pilot watched crew and equipment fall from the hold like chocolates from a box, a few parachutes blooming against the sky. He remembered the battle earlier, the sight of his comrade escaping from his hit plane: an F-22 had purposely flown low over the parachute, swooping past, three times, to knock it over. He'd watched as his comrade dropped like a stone, disappearing against the white backdrop of the ground.

He forced back the impulse to do something similar. Once he regrouped with his wingman, the pair abandoned the area at top speed.

They still suspected a trap.

The two weren't the only aircraft separated from their unit. A Comanche armed attack helicopter from the US Army First Cavalry Division flew with no target in sight, but its pilot, Lieutenant Walker, felt a rush of adrenaline all the same. He'd transferred from an Apache to the Comanche recently, and had yet to adjust to this sort of attack helicopter with troop-carrying capabilities, an innovation from the end of the previous century. He was unaccustomed to the Comanche's lack of foot pedals, and he thought the headset with its binocular helmet-mounted display wasn't as comfortable to use as the Apache's single sight. But most of all, he wasn't used to Captain Haney, the forward director sitting in front of him.

'You need to know your place, Lieutenant,'Haney had told him the first time they met. 'I'm the brain controlling this helicopter. You're a cogwheel in its machinery, and you're going to act like one!' And Walker hated nothing more than that.

He remembered the retired navy pilot who'd toured their base, a WWII vet pushing a hundred years old. He had shaken his head when he saw the Comanche's cockpit. 'Oh, you kids. My P-51 Mustang back in the day had a simpler control panel than a microwave today, and that was the finest control panel I ever used!' He patted Walker's ass. 'The difference between our generations of pilots is the difference between knights of the sky and computer operators.'

Walker had wanted to be a knight of the sky. Here was his opportunity. Under the Russians' berserk jamming, the helicopter's combat mission integration system, the target analysis system, the auxiliary target examination and classification system, the RealSight situation imager, the resource burst system, whatever, they were all fried! All that was left was the two 1,000-horsepower T800 engines, still loyally churning away. Haney normally earned his spot with his electronic gewgaws, but now his incessant orders had gone silent with them.

Haney's voice came through the internal mic system. 'Attention, I've found a target. It seems to be to the left and front, maybe by that little hill. There's an armored-car unit that seems to be the enemy's. You . . . do what you can.'

Walker nearly laughed aloud. Ha, that bastard. What he would have said in the past was, 'I've found a target at azimuth 133. Seventeen 90-series tanks, twenty-one 89-series soldier convoys, moving toward azimuth 391 at an average speed of 43.5 klicks per hour and an average separation of 31.4 meters. Execute the AJ041 optimized attack plan and approach from azimuth 179 at a vertical angle of 37 degrees.' And now? 'It 'seems' to be an armored-car unit, 'maybe by' that little hill.' *Who the hell needed you to say that? I saw it ages ago! Leave it to me, because you're useless now, Haney. This is my battle, and I'm going to use my ass for an accelerometer and be a knight! This Comanche's gonna fight like its namesake in my hands.*

The Comanche charged toward its open target and launched all sixty-two 27.5-inch Hornet missiles. Walker watched rapt as his swarm of fire-stingered little bees buzzed happily toward their target, swamping the enemy in a sea of fire. But when he turned to fly over the results of the encounter, he realized that something was wrong. The soldiers on the ground hadn't tried to conceal themselves. Instead, they stood in the snow, pointing at him. They seemed to be cussing him out.

Walker flew closer and clearly saw the destroyed armored car's insignia for himself: three concentric circles, blue at the center, white in the middle, red on the outside. Walker felt as if he'd dropped into hell. He started cussing, too.

'You son of a bitch, are you blind?!'

But he still had the wisdom to fly away in case the enraged French returned fire. 'You son of a bitch, you're probably thinking of how to pin the blame on me in military court right this moment. I'm telling you here, you won't get away with this. You were the one in charge of identifying targets, are you clear?'

'Maybe . . . maybe we'll still have the chance to make up for our mistake,' Haney said timidly. 'I found another unit, right across—'

'Fuck you!' Walker said.

'They're definitely the enemy's this time! They're exchanging fire with the French!'

Walker perked up at that. He steered toward the new target and saw that the enemy force was primarily infantry without much armored-vehicle strength. This did support Haney's assessment. Walker launched his last four Hellfire missiles, then set his double-barreled Gatling gun to 1,500 rpm and started shooting. He felt the comfortable vibration of the machine gun through the chassis, watching as it scattered snow and powder like ground white pepper over the enemy skirmish line on the ground. But the intuition of a veteran armed helicopter pilot warned him of danger. He turned, only to see a soldier standing on a jeep fire a shoulder-mounted rocket launcher to his left. Walker frantically shot off magnesium heat pellets as lures and swung backward for evasive maneuvers, but too late. The missile, trailing cobwebs of white smoke, had punched into the Comanche right under the nose.

When Walker woke from his brief explosion-induced concussion, he found that the helicopter had crashed in the snow. Walker scrambled desperately from the smoke-filled interior, bracing himself against a tree that had been severed neatly at waist height by the propeller. When he looked back, he could see the remains of Captain Haney in the front seat, blasted into a pulp by the explosion. When he looked forward, he saw a band of soldiers running toward him with submachine guns raised, their Slavic features clear.

Shaking, Walker dug out his handgun and set it on the snow in front of him. He dug out his Russian phrase book and began to clumsily read out his surrender.

'Y-ya postavil svoye oruzhiye. Ya voyennoplennym. V Zhenevskoy konventsii—'

Walker took a gun butt to the back of his head, then a boot to his belly. But as he collapsed into the snow, he was laughing. They might beat him half to death, but only half. He'd seen the eagle insignia of the Polish army on the soldiers' collars.

January 7th, Minsk, NATO combat operations center

'Get that goddamn doctor over here!' General Tony Baker roared.

The gangly military doctor ran over.

'What the hell went wrong?' Baker demanded. 'You've messed with my dentures twice and they're still buzzing!'

'I've never seen anything like it, General. Maybe it's your nervous system. How about I give you a shot of local anesthetic?'

'Give me the dentures, sir,' said a major on the staff, walking over. 'I know how to fix them.' Baker took out his dentures and set them on the major's proffered paper towel.

According to the media, the general lost his two front teeth when his tank was hit during the Gulf War. Only Baker himself knew that this wasn't true.

That time he'd broken his lower jaw; he'd lost the teeth earlier.

It had been at Clark Air Base in the Philippines, during the Mount Pinatubo eruption, when the world around seemed to be volcanic ash and nothing else. The sky was ash, the ground was ash, the air was ash, too. Even the C-130 Hercules that he and the last of the base personnel were about to board was coated with a thick layer of white. The dim red of magma glimmered intermittently in the gray distance.

Elena, the Filipina office worker he had been sleeping with, tracked him down after all this. The base was gone, she said, and she'd lost her job. Her house was buried under ash. How were she and the child in her belly supposed to live? She pulled at his hand and begged him to take her to America. He told her it was impossible. So she took off a high-heeled shoe and whacked him in the face, knocking out two of his teeth.

Where are you now, my child? Baker wondered, gazing at the gray ocean. *Are you living out your days with your mother in the slums of Manila? In a way, your father is fighting for your sake. Once the democratic government takes over in Russia after the war, NATO's vanguard will be at China's borders, and Subic Bay and Clark will once again become America's Pacific naval and air bases, even more prosperous than they were last century. You'll find work there!* The major returned, cutting short the general's woolgathering. Baker accepted the dentures on the paper towel, put them in, and after a few seconds, looked at the major in astonishment. 'How did you do that?'

'Sir, your dentures were buzzing because of electromagnetic resonance.'

Baker stared at the major in clear disbelief.

'Sir, it's true! Maybe you've been exposed to strong EM waves before, for example near radar equipment, but the frequency of those waves must have been different from your dentures' resonant frequency. But now, the air is filled with powerful EM waves at all frequencies, which caused this condition. I've modified the dentures to make their resonant frequency much higher. They're still vibrating, but you can't feel it anymore.'

After the major left, General Baker's gaze fell onto the clock standing beside the digital battle map. Its base was a sculpture of Hannibal riding an elephant, engraved with the caption ever victorious. The clock had originally inhabited the Blue Room of the White House; when the president saw his gaze straying again and again in its direction, he'd personally picked up the clock from its century-old resting place and gifted it to him.

'God save America, General. You're God to us now!'

Baker pondered for a long time, then slowly said, 'Tell all forces to halt the offensive. Use all our available airpower to find and destroy the source of the Russian jamming.'

January 8th, Russian army General Staff headquarters

'The enemy has disengaged, but you don't seem happy,' Marshal Levchenko said to the commander of the Western Military District, newly returned from the front line.

'I don't have reason to be happy. NATO has concentrated all their airpower on destroying our jamming units. It's really proving an effective countertactic.'

'It's no more than we expected,' Marshal Levchenko said evenly. 'Our strategy would catch the enemy unprepared at first, but they'd come up with a way to counter eventually. Barrage-type jammers emitting strong EM waves at all frequencies wouldn't be hard to find and destroy. But fortunately, we've managed to stall for a considerable length of time. All our hopes now rest on the reinforcement armies' swift arrival.'

'The situation might be worse than we predicted,' said the district commander. 'We might not be able to give the Caucasus Army enough time to move into position before we lose the upper hand in the electronic battle.'

After the district commander had left, Marshal Levchenko turned to the digital map display of the frontline terrain and thought of Karina, right now under the enemy's massed fire, and as a result thought again of Misha.

That one day, Misha had returned home with his face bruised blue and purple. Marshal Levchenko had heard the gossip already: his son, the only anti-war factionist at the college, had been beaten up by students.

'I only said that we shouldn't speak of war lightly,'Misha explained to his father.'Is it really impossible to reach a reasonable peace with the West?'

The marshal replied, his tone harsher than it had ever been toward his son, 'You know your position. You can choose to stay silent, but you will not say things like that in the future.'

Misha nodded.

Once they were through the door that night, Levchenko told Misha,'The Russian Communist Party has taken office.'

Misha looked at his father.'Let's eat,' he said, without inflection.

Later, the West declared the new Russian government unlawful. Tupolev assembled an extreme rightist alliance and instigated civil war. Marshal Levchenko didn't need to tell any of it to Misha. Every night, father and son silently ate dinner together as usual. Then one day, Misha received his order from the spaceflight base, packed his things, and left. Two days later, he boarded a spaceplane for the *Vechnyy Buran,* waiting in near-Earth orbit.

All-out war broke out a week later, an invasion by an unprecedentedly powerful enemy, from an unexpected direction, aiming to dismember Russia piece by piece.

January 9th, near-sun orbit, the *Vechnyy Buran* passes Mercury

Due to the *Vechnyy Buran*'s high velocity, it couldn't settle into orbit around Mercury, only sweep past the sunward side. This was the first time humanity observed Mercury's surface at close range with the naked eye.

Misha saw cliffs two kilometers tall, winding hundreds of kilometers through plains covered with huge craters. He saw the Caloris Basin, too, thirteen hundred kilometers across, termed 'Weird Terrain' by planetary geologists. The weird part came from the similar-sized basin exactly opposite it on the other side of Mercury. It was hypothesized that a huge meteor had struck Mercury, and that the powerful shock waves had passed right through the planet, simultaneously creating nearly identical basins in both hemispheres. Misha found new, thrilling things, too. The surface of Mercury was covered in shiny speckles, he saw. When he used the screen to zoom in, the realization took his breath away.

Those were lakes of mercury on Mercury, each with a surface area of thousands of square kilometers.

Misha imagined standing by the lake banks in the long Mercury days, in the 1,800-degree-Celsius heat: what a sight it would be. Even in a tempest, the mercury would lie calm and still. And Mercury didn't have an atmosphere, or wind. The surface of the lakes would be like mirrored plains, faithfully reflecting the light of the sun and Milky Way.

Once the *Vechnyy Buran* passed by Mercury, it was to continue approaching the sun until its insulation reached the absolute limit of what the fusion-powered active-cooling system could sustain. The sun's heat was its best protection; none of NATO's spacecraft could enter the inferno.

Gazing at the vastness of space, thinking of the war on his mother planet a hundred million kilometers away, Misha once again sighed at the shortsightedness of humanity.

January 10th, Smolensk front line

As she watched the gradual encroachment of the enemy's skirmish line, Karina understood why her location alone had survived where the surrounding sources of jamming had been destroyed one by one. The enemy wanted to capture a Flood unit intact.

The helicopter squadron, three Comanches and four Blackhawks, had easily located this control unit. Due to Flood's massive EM radiation emissions, it could only be remotely operated via fiber-optic cable. The enemy had followed the cable to Karina's control station three kilometers from the Flood unit, a lone abandoned storehouse.

The four Blackhawks, carrying more than forty enemy infantry, had landed less than two hundred meters from the storehouse. At the time they arrived, there had still been a captain and a staff sergeant in the station with Karina. Hearing the sound of an engine, the sergeant had gone to open the door; a sniper aboard the helicopter immediately shot off the top of his skull. Enemy fire was careful and restrained after that, fearful of damaging the precious equipment inside the storehouse, allowing Karina and the captain to hold their ground for a while.

Now, to Karina's left, the captain's submachine gun that had sounded her only comfort went silent. She saw the captain's unmoving body behind the tree stump he'd used for cover, a circle of bright red blood blooming in the snow around him.

Karina was in front of the storehouse, behind the crude cover of a few piled sandbags. Eight submachine-gun cartridge clips lay at her feet, and the hot gun barrel hissed in the snow atop the sandbags. Every time Karina opened fire, the enemy opposite her would crouch down, the bullets splattering snow in front of them, while the enemy on the other side of the semicircular encirclement would spring up and push a little closer. Now Karina only had three cartridge clips left. She began to fire single shots, but this inexperienced tactic only announced to the enemy that she was running out of ammunition. They began to push forward more boldly and quickly. The next time Karina reloaded, she heard a sharp squeaking sound from the thick snow on top of the sandbags. Something flew out and struck her on the right, hard. There wasn't any pain, just a rapidly spreading numbness, and the heat of blood running down her right flank. She endured, firing the remnants of this clip wildly. When she reached for the last clip on the sandbags, a bullet cut through her forearm. The clip fell to the ground. Her forearm, connected by a last strip of skin, dangled in the air. Karina got up and went for the storehouse door, a thin trail of blood following her steps. When she pulled open the door, another bullet pierced her left shoulder.

Captain Rhett Donaldson's SEAL team approached the storehouse cautiously. Donaldson and two marines stepped over the Russian sergeant's body, kicked open the door, and rushed in. They found a single young officer inside.

She was sitting beside their target, Flood's remote control equipment. One broken forearm hung uselessly from the control desk, the other hand was clenched in her hair. Her blood dripped down steadily, forming little puddles at her feet. She smiled at the American intruders and the row of gun barrels pointing at her, a greeting of sorts.

Donaldson exhaled, but wouldn't get the chance to inhale: he saw her turn her good hand from her hair to a dark green ovoid object resting on the remote control equipment. She picked it up, dangling it in midair. Donaldson instantly recognized it as a gas bomb, sized small for use on armed helicopters. It was triggered by a laser proximity signal and would explode twice at half a meter aboveground, first to disperse a gaseous explosive, second to trigger the vapor. He couldn't escape its range now if he were an arrow in flight.

He extended a placating hand. 'Calm down, Major, calm down. Let's not get too hasty here.' He gestured around him, and the marines lowered their guns. 'Listen, things aren't as serious as you might think. You'll get the finest medical care. You'll be sent to the best hospitals in Germany and return in the first POW exchange.'

The major smiled at him again, which encouraged him somewhat. 'You don't have to do something so barbaric. This is a civilized war, you know. It would go like clockwork, I could tell already when we crossed the Russian border twenty days ago. Most of your firepower had been destroyed by then. That remaining little scatter of gunfire was just the perfect confetti to greet this glorious expedition. Everything will go like clockwork, you see? There's no need—'

'I know of an even more beautiful beginning,'the major said in unaccented English. Her soft voice could have come from heaven, could have made flames extinguish and iron yield. 'On a lovely beach, with palm trees, and welcome banners hanging overhead. There were beautiful girls with long, waist-length hair and silk trousers that rustled as they moved among the

112

young soldiers and adorned them with red-and-pink leis, smiling shyly at the gawking boys. . . . Do you know of this landing?'

Donaldson shook his head, confused.

'March eighth, 1965, at nine a.m. It was the scene awaiting the first American marine forces landing at China Beach, the start of the Vietnam War.'

Donaldson felt as if he'd been plunged into ice. His momentary calm vanished; his breathing sped and his voice started to shake. 'No, Major, don't do this to us! We've hardly killed anyone, they're the ones who do all the killing,' he said, pointing out the window to the helicopters hovering in midair. 'Those pilots there, and the computer missile guidance gentlemen in the mother ships out in space. But they're all good people too. All their targets are just colored icons on their screen. They press a button or click a mouse, wait a bit, and the icon goes away. They're all civilized folks. They don't enjoy hurting people or anything, honest, they're not *evil*—are you listening?'

The major nodded, smiling. Who ever said that the god of death would be ugly and terrible?

'I have a girlfriend. She's working on her Ph.D. at the University of Maryland. She's beautiful like you, honest, and she attended the anti-war rally . . .' *I should have listened to her,* Donaldson thought. 'Are you listening to me? Say something! Please, say something.'

The major gave her foe one last radiant smile. 'Captain, I do my duty.'

A unit from the reinforcing Russian 104th Motorized Infantry Division was half a kilometer from the Flood operation station. They first heard a low explosion and saw the little storehouse in the broad, empty fields disappear in a cloud of white mist. Immediately after, a terrible cacophony a hundred times louder shook the ground. An enormous fireball emerged where the storehouse had been, the flames embroiled in black smoke rising high, transforming into a towering mushroom cloud, like a flower of lifeblood blooming in the expanse between heaven and earth.

January 11th, Russian army General Staff headquarters

'I know what you want. Don't waste words, spit it out!'Marshal Levchenko said to the commander of the Caucasus Army.

'I want the electromagnetic conditions on the battlefield for the last two days to last another four days.'

'Surely you're aware that seventy percent of our battlefield jamming teams have been destroyed? I can't even give you another four hours!'

'In that case, our army won't be able to arrive in position on time. NATO airstrikes have greatly slowed the rate at which our forces can assemble.'

'In that case, you might as well put a bullet in your head. The enemy is approaching Moscow. They've reached the position Guderian held seventy years ago.'

As he exited the war room, the commander of the Caucasus Army said in his heart, *Moscow, endure!*

January 12th, Moscow defensive line

Major General Felitov of the Taman Division was fully aware that his line could endure at most one more assault.

The enemy's airstrikes and long-range strikes were slowly growing in intensity, while the Russian air cover was diminishing. The division had few tanks and armed helicopters left; this last stand would be borne on blood and flesh and little else.

The major general, dragging a leg broken by shrapnel, came out of the shelter using a rifle as a crutch. He saw that the new trenches were still shallow, unsurprising given that the majority of the soldiers here had been wounded in some way. But to his astonishment, neat breastworks about a half meter tall stood in front of the trenches.

What material could they have used to build a breastwork so quickly? He saw that a few branch-like shapes stuck out from the snow-covered breastwork. He came closer. They were pale, frozen human arms.

Rage boiled through him. He seized a colonel by the collar. 'You bastard! Who told you to use the soldiers' corpses as building materials?'

'I did,' the divisional chief of staff said evenly behind him. 'We entered this new zone too quickly last night, and this is a crop field. We truly had nothing else to build with.'

They looked at each other silently. The chief of staff's face was covered in rivulets of frozen blood, leaked from the bandage on his forehead.

A time passed. The two of them began to walk slowly along the trenches, along the breastworks made from youth, vitality, life. The general's left hand held the rifle he used as a crutch; his right hand straightened his helmet, then saluted the breastworks. They were inspecting their troops for the last time.

They passed by a private with both legs blown off. The blood from his leg stumps had mixed with the snow and dirt into a reddish black mud, and the mud was now crusted over with ice. He lay with an anti-tank grenade in his arms. Raising his bloodless face, he grinned at the general. 'I'm gonna stuff this into an Abrams's treads.'

The cold winds stirred up gusts of snow mist, howling like an ancient battle paean.

'If I die first, please use me in this wall too. There's no better place for me to end, truly,' the general said.

'We won't be too long apart,' said the chief of staff, with his characteristic calm.

January 12th, Russian army General Staff headquarters

A staff officer came to inform Marshal Levchenko that the general director of the Russian Space Agency wanted to see him—the matter was urgent, involving Misha and the electronic battle.

Marshal Levchenko started at the sound of his son's name. He'd already heard that Karina had been killed in action, but aside from that, he couldn't imagine what Misha had to do with the electronic battle a hundred million miles away. He couldn't imagine what Misha had to do with any part of Earth now.

The general director came in with his people behind him. Without preamble, he gave a three-inch laser disc to Marshal Levchenko. 'Marshal, this is the reply we received from the *Vechnyy Buran* an hour ago. He added afterward that this isn't a private message, and that he hopes you'll play it in front of all relevant personnel.'

Everyone in the war room heard the voice from a hundred million kilometers distant. 'I've learned from the war news updates that if the electromagnetic jamming fails to last for another three to four days, we may lose the war. If this is true, Papa, I can give you that time.

'Before, you always thought that the stars I studied had nothing to do with the ways of the world, and I thought so too. But it looks like we were both wrong.

'I remember telling you that, although a star generates enormous power, it's fundamentally a relatively elegant and simple system. Take our sun, for example. It's composed of just the two simplest elements: hydrogen and helium; its behavior is the balance of just the two mechanisms of nuclear fission and gravity. As a result, it's easier to model its activity mathematically than our Earth. Research on the sun has given us an extremely accurate mathematical model by this time, work to which I've contributed. Using this model, we can accurately predict the sun's behavior. This would allow us to take advantage of a tiny disturbance to rapidly disrupt the equilibrium conditions inside the sun. The method is simple: use the *Vechnyy Buran* to make a precision strike on the surface of the sun.

'Perhaps you think it no more than tossing a pebble into the sea. But that's not the case, Papa. This is dropping a grain of sand into an eye.

'From the mathematical model, we know that the sun is in an extremely fine-tuned and sensitive state of energy equilibrium. If correctly placed, a small disturbance will create a chain reaction from the surface to a considerable distance down, spreading to disrupt the local equilibrium. There are recorded precedents: the latest incident was in early August of 1972, when a powerful but highly localized eruption created a massive EMP that heavily affected Earth. Compasses in planes and boats jumped wildly, long-distance wireless communications failed, the sky shone with dazzling red lights in high northern latitudes, electric lights flickered in villages as if they were in the center of a thunderstorm. The reactions continued for more than a week. A well-accepted theory nowadays is that a celestial body even smaller than the *Vechnyy Buran* collided with the surface of the sun at that time.

'These disruptions on the sun's surface certainly occurred many times, but most would have happened before humanity invented wireless equipment, and therefore went undetected. In addition, since these collisions were placed by random chance, the disturbances in equilibrium wouldn't have been optimal in strength and area.

'But the *Vechnyy Buran*'s impact location has been meticulously calculated, and the disturbance it will create will be orders of magnitude larger than the natural examples mentioned. This time, the sun will blast powerful electromagnetic radiation into space in every frequency, from the highest to the lowest. In addition, the powerful X-ray radiation generated by the sun will collide violently with Earth's ionosphere, blocking off short-wave radio communications, which are reliant on the layer.

'During the disturbance, the majority of wireless communications outside of the millimeter radio range will fail. The effect will weaken somewhat at night, but during the day, it will even exceed your jamming of the previous two days. Based on calculations, the disturbances will last a week.

'Papa, the two of us always did live in worlds far away from each other's. We could never interact much with each other. But now our worlds have come together. We're fighting for the same goal, for which I'm proud. Papa, like all your soldiers, I await your order.'

'Everything Dr. Levchenko said is true,' said the general director. 'Last year, we sent a probe to enact a small-scale collision with the sun according to calculations based on the mathematical model. The experiment confirmed the model's predictions of the disturbance. Dr. Levchenko and his research group even hypothesized that this method could be used to alter Earth's climate in the future.'

Marshal Levchenko walked into a side room and picked up the red telephone that was a direct line to the president. A little later, he walked back out.

The historical records give different accounts of this moment: some claim that he spoke immediately, while others recount that for a minute he was silent. But they concur on the words he said.

'Tell Misha to carry out his plan.'

January 12th, near-sun orbit, aboard the *Vechnyy Buran*

The *Vechnyy Buran* fired all ten fission engines, jets of plasma hundreds of kilometers long erupting from every engine nozzle as it made final corrections to trajectory and orientation.

In front of the *Vechnyy Buran* was an enormous and lovely solar prominence, a current of superheated hydrogen wheeling upward from the sun's surface. Like long ribbons of gauze drifting high above the fiery sea of the sun, they shifted and changed like a dreamscape. Their ends anchored to the surface of the sun, forming a gigantic gateway.

The *Vechnyy Buran* passed slow and stately through the four-hundred-thousand-kilometer-tall triumphal arch. More solar prominences appeared in front, one end attached to the sun, but the other extending into the depths of space. The *Vechnyy Buran* with its blinking blue engine lights threaded through them like a firefly amid burning trees. Then the blue lights slowly dimmed. The engines stopped. The *Vechnyy Buran*'s trajectory had been meticulously established; the rest depended on the law of gravity.

As the spaceship entered the corona, the outermost layer of the sun's atmosphere, the black backdrop of space above turned a magenta all-pervading in its radiance. Below was a clear view of the sun's chromosphere, twinkling with countless needle-shaped structures, discovered in the

118

nineteenth century, they were jets of incandescent gas emanating from the surface of the sun. They made the atmosphere of the sun look like a burning grassland, where each stalk of grass was thousands of kilometers tall. Underneath the burning plain was the sun's photosphere, a sea of endless fire.

From the last images relayed from the *Vechnyy Buran*, people saw Misha rise to his feet in front of the giant monitoring screen. He pressed a button to retract the protective cover outside the transparent dome, revealing the magnificent sea of fire before him. He wanted to see the world of his childhood dreams with his own eyes. The view was distorting and rippling; that was the half-meter-thick insulation glass melting. Soon the glass barrier fell in a sheet of transparent liquid. Like someone who had never seen the sea facing the ocean wind in rapture, Misha spread his arms to greet the six-thousand-degree hurricane that roared toward him. In the last seconds of video before the camera and transmission equipment melted, one could see Misha's body catching alight, a slender torch melding into the sun's sea of fire. . . .

What sight would have followed could only be conjecture. The *Vechnyy Buran*'s solar panels and protruding structures would have melted first, surface tension making silver beads of fluid of them on the spaceship's surface. As the *Vechnyy Buran* traversed the boundary between the corona and chromosphere, its main body would begin to melt, fully liquefying at a depth of two thousand kilometers into the chromosphere. The beads of liquid metal would cohere into a huge silvery droplet, diving unerringly toward the target its now-melted computers had calculated. The effect of the sun's atmosphere would become apparent: a pale blue flame would emanate from the droplet, trailing hundreds of meters behind it, its color gradating from the pale blue, to yellow, to a gorgeous orange at the tail.

At last, this lovely phoenix would disappear into the endless sea of flames.

January 13th, Earth

Humanity returned to the world as it had been before Marconi.

As night fell, undulating auroras flooded the sky, even into the equatorial zones.

Facing television screens filled with white noise, most people could only guess and imagine at the situation in that vast land where war raged.

January 13th, Moscow front line

General Baker pushed aside the division commander of the Eighty-second Airborne and the assorted NATO frontline commanders attempting to drag him onto a helicopter. He raised his binoculars to continue surveilling the horizon, where the Russian front was rumbling in advance.

'Calibrate to four thousand meters! Load number-nine ammunition, delayed fuse, fire!'

From the sounds of artillery behind him, Baker could tell that no more than thirty of their 105 mm grenade launchers, last of the defensive heavy artillery, could still fire.

An hour ago, the German tank battalion that had been the last remaining armored-vehicle force in the position had launched an admirably courageous counterattack. They'd achieved outstanding results: eight kilometers away, they'd destroyed half again their number of Russian tanks. But under the crushing disadvantage in numbers, they had disappeared under the Russian army's roaring torrent of steel like dew under the noon sun.

'Calibrate to thirty-five hundred meters, fire!'

The explosive missiles hissed as they flew, and flung up a barrier of earth and fire in front of the Russian tank lines. But they were like a landslide before a flood, the earth a short-lived impediment against the implacable waters.

Once the earth blasted up by the explosions fell back to the ground, the

Russian armored cars reappeared in view through the dense smoke. Baker saw that they were arranged as densely as if they were receiving inspection. Attacking in this formation would have been suicide a few days ago, but now, with almost all of NATO's aerial and long-distance firepower jammed, it was a perfectly feasible way to concentrate armored-vehicle strength as much as possible, ensuring a break in the enemy line.

Baker had expected that the defensive line would be poorly arranged. Under the electromagnetic conditions on the battlefield, it had been effectively impossible to quickly and accurately determine the direction the main enemy assault would take. As to how the defense would proceed, he didn't know. With the C3I system completely down, quickly adjusting the defensive dispositions would be enormously difficult.

'Calibrate to three thousand meters, fire!'

'General, you were looking for me?' The French commander Lieutenant General Rousselle came over. Beside him were only a French lieutenant colonel and a helicopter pilot. He wasn't wearing camouflage, and the medals on his chest and general's stars on his shoulders shone brightly polished, making the steel helmet he wore and the rifle he held seem incongruous.

'I hear that the French Foreign Legion is withdrawing from the fortifications on our left wing.'

'Yes, General.'

'General Rousselle, seven hundred thousand NATO troops are in the process of retreat behind us. Their successful breakthrough of the enemy encirclement depends on our steadfast defense!'

'Depends on your steadfast defense.'

'Care to explain that comment?'

'You have plenty to explain yourself! You hid the real battle situation from us. You knew from the beginning that the Rightist allies would independently negotiate a cease-fire in the east!'

'As the commander in chief of the NATO forces, I had the right to do so. General, I think you're also clear on the duty placed on you and your troops to follow the orders given.'

A silence.

'Calibrate to twenty-five hundred meters, fire!'

'I only obey the orders of the president of the French Republic.'

'I do not believe you could have received orders to that effect right now.'

'I received them months ago, at the National Day reception at Élysée Palace. The president personally informed me of how the French army should conduct itself under the present conditions.'

Baker finally lost his temper. 'You bastards haven't changed a bit since de Gaulle's time!' [1]

'Don't make it sound so unpleasant. If you won't leave, I will stay here without my retinue as well. We will fight and die honorably together on the snowy plain. Napoleon lost here too. It's nothing to be ashamed of,' Rousselle said, gesturing with his French-made FAMAS rifle.

A silence.

'Calibrate to two thousand meters, fire!'

Baker turned slowly to face the frontline commanders in front of him. 'Relay these words to the American soldiers defending these lines: We didn't start out as an army dependent on computers to fight our battles. We come from an army of farming men. Decades ago, on Okinawa, we fought the Japanese foxhole by foxhole through the jungle. At Khe Sanh, we deflected the North Vietnamese soldiers' grenades with shovels. Even longer ago, on that cold winter night, our great Washington himself led his barefoot soldiers across the icy Delaware to make history—'

'Calibrate to fifteen hundred meters, fire!'

'I order you, destroy all documents and excess supplies—'

'Calibrate to twelve hundred meters, fire!'

General Baker put on his helmet, strapped on his Kevlar vest, and clipped his 9 mm pistol to his left side. The grenade launchers went silent; the gunners were shoving the grenades into the barrels. Next sounded a mess of

---

1. In 1966, General de Gaulle withdrew all French armed forces from the NATO integrated military command, a serious blow to NATO's Cold War efforts at the time.

explosions.

'Troops,' Baker said, looking at the Russian tanks spread in front of them like the veil of death. 'Bayonets up!'

The sun faded in and out of the thick smoke of the battlefield, throwing shifting light and shadow onto the snowy plain as the battle raged.

地球大炮

CANNONBALL

TRANSLATED BY ADAM LANPHIER

亚当·兰菲尔 — 译

Prologue

Since mankind depleted the Earth's natural resources, the world turned its gaze towards the last pristine continent – Antarctica. This shifted the Earth's political center of gravity, and the Antarctic Treaty was discarded. Due to their proximity to Antarctica, two South American countries suddenly emerged as global powers, attaining a geopolitical status that rivaled their status on the soccer field. Mankind had also entered into the final phase of the complete eradication of nuclear weapons. This victory of enlighted reason over barbarism made humanity's struggle for Antarctica devoid of the fearful shadow of a thermonuclear apocalypse.

Chapter I
New Solid State

In the immense cavern, Shen Huabei felt as if he were walking on a dark plain under a starless sky. Beneath his feet, rock that had melted in the heat of a nuclear blast had already cooled and solidified, though a powerful warmth still penetrated the thermal insulation of his boots, causing the soles of his feet to sweat. Far away, a section of cavern wall had not yet cooled. It glowed faintly red in the darkness, like a murky dawn sky.

Shen Huabei's wife, Zhao Wenjia, walked to his left, and their eight-year-old son, Shen Yuan, was in front of them. Shen Yuan skipped ahead, heedless of his heavy radiation suit. They were joined by members of the UN Nuclear Inspection Team, their headlamps sending long beams of light into the darkness.

Two methods were employed to destroy nuclear weapons: disassembly and underground detonation. This was one of China's subterranean detonation sites.

Professor Kavinsky, leader of the inspection team, caught up to Shen Huabei. His headlamp shined on the three people ahead of him and threw their long, swaying shadows across the cavern floor.

'Doctor Shen, why did you bring your family? This is no place for a picnic.'

Shen Huabei halted to allow the Russian physicist to catch up. 'My wife is a geological engineer working for the central command of the Eradication Operation. As for my son, I think he likes it here.'

'Our son has always been fascinated by the strange and the extreme,' Wenjia agreed, more to her husband than the head of the team. Even though her face was partially concealed by the radiation suit's visor, Huabei could still clearly see the unease in his wife's eyes.

The boy was practically dancing in front of them. 'When they started, this hole was only as big as our basement. After just two blasts, it got gigantic! Think of the fireballs those blasts made – it was probably like there was a huge BABY under the ground, having tantrums, kicking and screaming. It must have been amazing!'

Shen Huabei and Zhao Wenjia exchanged glances. He was grinning slightly, but the worry in her expression had only deepened.

'My boy, there were eight babies!' Professor Kavinsky said to Shen Yuan with a laugh. He turned to face Shen Huabei. 'Doctor Shen, this is what I meant to discuss with you. In the last blast, you detonated the warheads of eight Giant Wave submarine-launched ballistic missiles, each with a yield of 100 kilotons. The warheads were on a rack, stacked in a cube—'

'What is the issue?'

'Before the detonation, I clearly saw on the monitor that there was a white sphere in the center of the cube.'

Shen Huabei again stopped walking. Looking squarely at Kavinsky, he said, 'Doctor, the provisions of the Destruction Treaty prohibit us from detonating less than our mandated quota, but I do not believe they restrict us from detonating more. There were five independent observations that verified the size of the blast. Anything else is immaterial.'

Kavinsky nodded. 'That is why I waited until after the detonation to raise this issue with you. I am simply curious.'

'I imagine you have heard of "sugar coating."'

Shen Huabei's words fell like a curse over the site. The cavern went silent as everyone stopped walking, and the beams of light from their headlamps became still, shining off in every direction. They conducted their conversation over a wireless intercom system in their radiation suits, so even the people far ahead heard his words. The silence ended as the members of the inspection team walked over and gathered around Shen Huabei. Everyone in this select group, no matter what part of the world they hailed from, was a luminary in the field of nuclear weapons research, and they had all clearly heard.

'It really exists?' an American asked, gawping at Shen Huabei.

The latter just nodded his head.

The key to designing fission weapons is the ability to apply compression. When a nuclear bomb goes off, a package of conventional explosives detonates around a mass of fissile material, compressing it into a dense sphere. When that sphere reaches critical density, a violent chain reaction begins, which results in a nuclear explosion. All of this takes place within a millionth of a second, so the pressure on the fissile core must be calibrated with extreme precision, as even a minuscule imbalance can easily result in the core failing to reach critical density. If that happens, the weapon will only produce a normal chemical blast. Since the inception of nuclear weapons, researchers have used complex mathematical models to design a variety of compression charge arrays. New technologies developed in recent years had enabled researchers to design compression mechanisms with groundbreaking accuracy, and 'sugar coating' was one of the techniques that allowed them to achieve this.

A 'sugar coat' was a kind of nanomaterial that was used to encase the core of a nuclear weapon. Once applied, it was in turn covered in a layer of conventional explosive charges. 'Sugar coating' had the function of automatically balancing compressive stress, so even if the outer layer of explosives did not produce uniform pressure, the 'sugar coat' would balance its distribution, resulting in the precise compression necessary to bring fissile material to critical density.

'The white sphere you saw between the warheads was an alloyed material wrapped in a "sugar coat,"' Shen Huabei said. 'It ought to have undergone extreme compressive stress in the explosion. This is part of a research project we plan to continue throughout the process of weapon destruction. Once all the nuclear weapons on Earth have been destroyed, it will be difficult to produce momentary compressive stress of this magnitude, for a while at least. It will be interesting to see what happens to the test material under such pressure – what it will turn into. We hope this research can help us find some promising uses for "sugar coating" in civilian hands.'

Considering the possibilities, one UN official said, 'You should encase graphite in sugarcoating, so we could produce a large diamond with every explosion. Maybe this costly project of nuclear weapon destruction could turn a profit.'

Laughter erupted in their headphones. Officials without technical backgrounds were often the butt of jokes in situations like this. 'Let's see, 800 kilotons... How many orders of magnitude greater is that than the pressure needed to turn graphite into a diamond!' someone said.

'Of course it didn't make a diamond!' Shen Yuan's bright voice crackled in their earphones. 'I bet it made a black hole! A tiny black hole! It's going to suck us in, suck the whole world in, and we'll wind up in a prettier universe on the other side!'

'Haha, the explosion wasn't quite that large, my boy. Doctor Shen, your son has a fascinating mind!' said Kavinsky. 'So, what were the test results? What did the alloy turn into? I assume you probably could not find it.'

'I don't know yet. Let's go see,' said Shen Huabei, pointing ahead. The explosion had blasted an enormous, spherical cavity into the Earth, whose curved bottom formed a small basin. In the basin's center, the lights of a few headlamps flitted around. 'Those are people from the "sugar coating" research team.'

They walked down the gentle slope towards the center of the basin. Suddenly, Kavinsky stopped, then laid his hands flat against the ground. 'There's a tremor!'

The others felt it, too. 'It couldn't have been induced by the explosion, could it?'

Zhao Wenjia shook her head. 'We have carried out repeated surveys of the geological structure of the area around the destruction site. There is no way for an explosion to cause an earthquake here. The tremor began after the explosion and has continued uninterrupted since. Doctor Deng Yiwen said it has something to do with the "sugar coating" experiment, though I don't know the details.'

As they approached the center of the basin, the tremor became stronger, eminating from deep below the ground. Soon, it was strong enough to send a tingling sensation up their legs, as if a giant, uneven wheel was rumbling wildly in the Earth beneath them. Reaching the center, one suited researcher at the bottom of the basin rose to greet them. It was Deng Yiwen, the scientist responsible for the experiments involving the compression of materials with nuclear explosions..

'What's that you're holding?' Shen Huabei asked, pointing at a large, white ball in Deng Yiwen's hand.

'Fishing line,' said Doctor Deng. Around him, a ring of people crouched on the ground, peering into a small hole in the surface of the rock, which had melted and recondensed in the explosion. The hole's rim was a near-perfect circle, around 10 centimeters in diameter, and its edge was quite smooth, as if it had been bored with a drill. One end of the fishing line in Deng Yiwen's hand was in the hole, and he unravelled more line in a continuous stream.

'We've already fed more than 10,000 meters of line into the hole and we're nowhere near the bottom. Our radars say it's more than 30,000 meters deep and getting deeper.'

'How did it form?' someone asked.

'The compressed test alloy sank into the Earth like a stone in the sea. That's what made this hole. The alloy is passing through dense layers of rock as we speak, which is what's causing the tremor.'

'My God, that is astonishing!' Kavinsky exclaimed. 'I assumed the alloy would be vaporized in the heat of the blast.'

'If it had not been "sugar coated," that would have been the result.' Professor Deng agreed. 'As it was, it didn't have time to evaporate – the "sugar coat" redistributed the force of the blast, compressing the alloy into a new state of matter, which ought to be called a super-solid state. That name was taken, so we are calling it "new solid-state".'

'Are you saying that this thing's density, compared to the density of the earth below, is analogous to the density of a stone dropped into water?' Professor Kamensky asked, still somewhat incredulous.

'It's much denser than that. The main reason stones sink in water is unrelated to either material's density. It's that water is a liquid – when water freezes, its density doesn't change considerably, but if you place a stone on ice, it won't sink through it. New solid-state matter, however, actually *sinks through* rocks, so we can only imagine how dense it must be.'

'You mean it turned into something like neutron-star material?'

Deng Yiwen shook his head. 'We haven't determined its precise density yet, but just by looking at the speed of its descent, we can be sure it's not as dense as the degenerate matter of a neutron star. If it were, it would be falling as fast as a meteorite through the atmosphere, and it would cause volcanic eruptions and large earthquakes. It's a state of matter somewhere between ordinary solid-state and degenerate matter.'

'Will it sink to the center of the Earth?' asked Shen Yuan.

'It is possible. Below a certain depth, the rock strata of the Earth's crust and mantle give way to the liquid core, where it will be even easier for the thing to sink!'

'Awesome!'

While everyone's attention was on the hole, Shen Huabei and his family quietly parted from the group and walked off into the darkness. Except for the hum of the tremor, it was silent away from the hole. The beams of their headlamps dissolved into the immense darkness around them, and their presence was subsumed into the vast, featureless void. They turned their intercoms to a private channel. Here, Shen Yuan was to make a choice that would decide the course of his life – would he follow his father or his mother?

Shen Yuan's parents faced a problem worse than divorce – his father had terminal leukemia. Shen Huabei did not know whether his work in nuclear research had caused the disease, but he knew he had no more than six months to live. Fortunately, the technology existed to induce artificial hibernation. Shen Huabei would enter a state of suspended animation until there was a cure for leukemia. Shen Yuan could either enter hibernation with his father or continue his life with his mother. The second choice seemed more prudent, but it was hard for a child to resist the idea of following his father into the future. Shen Huabei and Zhao Wenjia tried once again to win him over.

'Mom, I'm going to stay with you. I won't go to sleep with daddy!' said Shen Yuan.

'You changed your mind?!' asked Zhao Wenjia, overjoyed.

'Yes! I don't need to go to the future to have fun. There is plenty of fun stuff around now, like that thing, the one that's sinking into the ground. I want be around to see that!'

'That's your decision?' asked Shen Huabei. Zhao Wenjia glared at him, worried her son might change his mind again.

'Yeah,' said Shen Yuan. 'I'm gonna go try to see what's down that hole.' He took off running towards the basin, where the others' headlamps flickered.

Zhao Wenjia watched her son run off. 'I worry I won't be able to give him what he needs. He's just like you – lost in his dreams. Maybe the future will suit him better.'

Shen Huabei put his hands on his wife's shoulders. 'No one knows what the future will be like. And what's wrong with him being like me? The present needs dreamers, too.'

'There's nothing wrong with being a dreamer. That's why I fell in love with you. But you must know he has another side to him – he was chosen as class head of two of his classes!'

'Yes, I heard. I don't know how he managed that.'

'He has a thirst for power, and he knows what it takes to achieve it. In that way, he's nothing like you at all.'

'Yes. How can he reconcile that with his fantasies?'

'I'm more worried about what will happen when he does.'

Shen Yuan had arrived at the basin, his headlamp indistinguishable from the others. His parents stopped watching him, turned off their headlamps, and sank into darkness.

'No matter what, life will continue. They may develop a cure next year, or it might be a century, or... they may never develop one. Without question, you'll live at least another forty years. I need you to promise me something. In forty years, if there is still no cure, I need you to wake me up. I want to see you and our son again. This can't be our final goodbye.'

'Do you want to see an old woman and a grown man ten years your senior in the future? But it is as you said, life goes on.' In the dark, Wenjia managed a miserable smile.

In that giant cavern, hollowed out by nuclear blasts, they spent a final, silent moment together. The next day, Shen Huabei was to enter into a dreamless sleep. Zhao Wenjia would be left to live with Shen Yuan, whose life was consumed by his dreams. Together, they would continue down the treacherous road of life, toward an unknown future.

Chapter 2
Awakening

It took a day for him to wake up fully. When he first opened his eyes, he saw only a white mist, from which blurred figures gradually emerged over the next ten hours. The figures were white, and after another ten hours, he was able to recognize them as doctors and nurses. People in suspended animation are unaware of the passage of time, and Shen Huabei thought that his weak consciousness was part of the process of entering hibernation, that perhaps the hibernation systems had suffered a malfunction as he was going under. As his vision continued to improve, he examined the hospital ward around him, which was softly lit by sconces on its white walls. This place was familiar, which confirmed to him the idea that he had not yet entered hibernation.

In the next moment, it became clear that he was mistaken. The white ceiling of the ward began to glow blue, and against this backdrop, sharp, white characters emerged.

> *Greetings! Living Earth Cryonics, your suspended animation provider, filed for bankruptcy in 2089. Responsibility for your care was transferred to Jade Cloud Corporation. Your hibernation serial number is WS368200402-118. You retain all rights and privileges granted to you in your contract with Living Earth Cryogenics. You underwent medical treatment before being awoken, and you are successfully cured of all disease. Please accept Green Cloud Corporation's congratulations on your new life.*
>
> *You have been in hibernation for 74 years, 5 months, 7 days, and 13 hours. Your account is paid in full.*
>
> *The current date is April 16th, 2125. Welcome to the future.*

His hearing began gradually to return, and three hours later, he was able to speak. After 74 years of deep sleep, his first words were, 'Where are my wife and son?'

A tall, thin doctor stood next to his bed. She handed him a folded piece of paper. 'Mr Shen, this is a letter from your wife.'

Shen Huabei cast a strange glance at the doctor. Even before I went under, people hardly ever wrote paper letters, he thought to himself. He managed to unfold the letter, though his hands were still half-numb. Here was more proof that he had travelled through time: the paper, blank at first, began to emit an azure light that formed letters as it travelled down the page. Soon, the page was full of writing.

Before entering cryo-sleep, he had on countless occasions imagined the first words his wife might say to him as he woke up, but what was written on the paper exceeded his wildest fantasies:

Huabei, my love, you are in great danger!
By the time you read this letter, I will no longer be alive. The person who gave you this letter is Dr. Guo. You can trust her; in fact, she may be the only person left on Earth you can trust. Follow whatever directions she gives you.
Forgive me for breaking my promise. I did not wake you in forty years. You cannot imagine the person Yuan has become, the things he has done. As his mother, I felt unable to look you in the eye. My heart is broken. My life has been wasted. Please take care of yourself.

'My son – where is Shen Yuan?' shouted Huabei, rising with great effort onto his elbows.

'He died five years ago.' The doctor's answer was icy, utterly indifferent to the heartache this message inflicted. As if realizing this, she softened and added, 'Your son was 78 years old.'

Doctor Guo took a card from her coat pocket and handed it to Huabei. 'This is your new identity card. The information it contains is explained in your wife's letter.'

Huabei examined the paper, checking it back and front. There was nothing on it except for Wenjia's brief note. As he turned it over, the creases in the paper seemed to ripple, like the LCD screens of his day did when touched. Doctor Guo reached over and pressed on the letter's lower right corner, and the paper's display switched over to a spreadsheet.

'Sorry about that. Paper as you know it no longer exists.'

Huabei looked at her quizzically.

'There are no forests anymore,' she explained, shrugging. She then returned to the spreadsheet. 'Your new name is Wang Ruo. You were born in

2097. Your parents are deceased, and you have no close family. You were born in Hohhot, Inner Mongolia, but you now reside here,' she said, indicating a cell on the spreadsheet. 'It is a remote village in the mountains of Ningxia. It was the best place we could find, considering. You won't attract attention there. Before you depart, you will need to undergo plastic surgery. Under no circumstances should you talk about your son. Do not even express an interest in him if someone else mentions him.'

'But I am Shen Yuan's father! I was born in Beijing!'

Doctor Guo stiffened and became cold again. 'If you say that publicly, your hibernation and treatment will have been for nothing. You'll be dead in an hour.'

'Whatever happened?' Huabei finally needed to know – *now*.

The doctor smiled coldly as she began. 'Perhaps you're the only one who didn't know what happened.' She ever so slightly shook her head. 'Well, we should hurry. You should first get out of bed and learn to walk again. We then need to get you out of here as quickly as possible.'

Just as Huabei opened his mouth to ask another question, a loud banging erupted from the door. It crashed open, and six or seven people rushed in and surrounded Huabei's bed. They were of all different ages and they had different clothes, except for a strange sort of hat that some of them wore and some carried. The hats had brims wide enough to cover their wearers' shoulders, like the straw hats farmers used to wear. Each of them also had a transparent oxygen mask, which some of them had removed when they entered the room. They all stared at Huabei menacingly.

'This is Shen Yuan's father?' one of them asked. He appeared to be the oldest member of the group, at least 80 years old, and he had a long, white beard. Without waiting for the doctor to answer, he turned to the rest of his group and nodded his head.

'He looks just like his son. Doctor, you've done your duty. He's ours now.'

'How did you know he was here?' asked Dr. Guo coolly.

Before the doctor could answer, a nurse spoke up from the corner of the room. 'I told them.'

136

Dr. Guo turned and glared angrily at the nurse. 'You betrayed a patient's confidence?'

'Happily,' said the nurse, her lovely face marred by a grimace.

A young man grabbed Huabei's gown and dragged him off the bed. He lay paralyzed on the ground, still too weak to move. A girl kicked him in the gut so hard that the sharp toe of her boot almost pierced his stomach; the pain was excruciating, and he writhed on the floor like a fish. The old man took hold of Huabei's collar and hauled him to his feet with an unexpected strength. He held Huabei upright in a futile effort to make him stand. He released his grip and Huabei fell backwards, smacking his head on the floor. His eyes blurred with pain. Someone said, 'Great, that'll cover a small bit of this bastard's debt to society.'

'Who are you people?' asked Huabei weakly. From his vantage on the floor between their feet, he felt as if his captors were a menacing group of giants.

'You should know who I am, at least,' said the old man, sneering vindictively. Seen from below, his face appeared twisted and grotesque. Huabei shuddered. 'I am Deng Yang, Deng Yiwen's son.'

The name made Huabei's stomach lurch. He turned and grabbed the hem of the old man's trousers. 'Your father was my coworker and close friend! You were my son's classmate! Don't you remember? My goodness, you're Yiwen's son? I can't believe it! Back then, you were—'

'Get your filthy hands off me!' shouted Deng Yang.

The young man who had pulled Huabei off the bed crouched down and leaned close to his face, his eyes full of malice. 'Listen, kid. You aren't any older than you were when you went to sleep. This man is your elder, and you need to show him some respect.'

'If Shen Yuan were still alive, he'd be old enough to be your father,' said Deng Yang loudly, eliciting a round of laughter. He pointed at one of the people he came with. 'When this young man was four years old, both his parents died in the Central Breach Disaster,' he said to Huabei. 'And this young lady lost her parents in the Lost Bolt Disaster. She wasn't even two years old.' Deng Yang gestured towards two more members of his group. 'These people invested their life savings in the Project. When this man learned it had failed, he attempted suicide. And this man simply lost his mind.' He paused, then added, 'And as for me, I was tricked by your bastard son. I threw my youth and my talent into that goddamn hole, and the whole world hates me for it.'

Huabei still lay on the floor, shaking his head in confusion.

'Shen Huabei, this is a court, and we, the victims of the Antarctic Entry Project, are your judge and jury! Everyone in this country is a victim, but we have the special privilege of administering your justice. We could have sent you to a real court, but our justice system is even more convoluted now than it was in your day. Lawyers would have spent a year spewing bullshit about your case, and then you'd probably have been acquitted, like your son was. We won't take more than an hour to deliver our righteous judgment, and believe me: once we have, you'll wish the leukemia had taken you 70 years ago.'

They began jeering at Huabei. Two people lifted him by his arms and hauled him towards the door. He was too weak to struggle, and his legs dragged on the floor.

'Mr. Shen, I did what I could,' said Doctor Guo as Huabei neared the door. He wanted to look back at her, the only person he could trust in these vicious times, according to his wife's letter, but the position he was held in made it impossible. She spoke again from behind him.

'Don't despair too much. Living in these times isn't easy, either.'

As he was dragged out the door, Huabei heard Doctor Guo call out, 'Close the door and turn up the air purifiers! Do you want to choke to death?!' Her tone was urgent, and it was clear that she was already indifferent to his fate.

Once they got out of the hospital ward, Huabei understood Doctor Guo's last words: the air was acrid and hard to breathe. He was dragged out through the hospital's main corridor. They exited the building, and the two people dragging him put his arms over their shoulders and began to carry him. He took a deep breath, relieved to be outside of the hospital, but what he inhaled

138

was not the fresh, outdoor air he expected but a gas even more noxious than the air in the hospital. His lungs erupted in pain, and he was racked by a sudden, violent cough that did not stop. As he began to suffocate, he heard someone say, 'Give him a respirator. We don't want him to die before we can administer justice.' Someone fitted a device over his nose and mouth. The air it provided had a strange taste, but at least he could breathe. Someone else said, 'You don't need to give him a screen hat. He won't be alive long enough for the UV to give him leukemia again.' This drew a burst of cruel laughter from the group. Huabei's breathing became somewhat more regular, and the tears caused by his cough began to dry, restoring his vision. He raised his head and took his first look at the future.

The first thing he noticed was that the people on the street; all of them were wearing the transparent respirator masks and every head was covered by one of those large straw hats his kidnappers had just called a 'screen hat.' He also noticed that despite the warm weather, everyone was swaddled in clothes, without an inch of skin showing. The street was lined with enormous skyscrapers on both sides, so tall that he felt like he was in a deep valley. 'Skyscraper' was an apt term for these buildings – they literally stretched into the grey clouds overhead. In the narrow strip of sky between the buildings, the sun shone indistinctly behind the clouds. Streaks of smoke passed in front of the sunlight, and he soon realized that the clouds themselves were in fact plumes of pollution.

'A great time to be alive, isn't it?' asked Deng Yang. His friends laughed heartily, as if they hadn't laughed for ages.

They carried him towards a nearby car – different from the cars of Huabei's day, but he was able to recognize it as a car. It was similar in size to a sedan, able to fit four or five people. As they approached it, two people passed by them, walking with purpose in another direction. They wore helmets, and though their uniforms were unfamiliar to Huabei, he could guess at their profession. He called out to them.

'Help! I'm being kidnapped! Help me!'

The two police officers abruptly turned around and ran over to Huabei.

They looked him up and down, taking special notice of his hospital gown and bare feet. One of them asked, 'You're just out of cryo, aren't you?'

Huabei nodded weakly. 'They're kidnapping me...'

The other police officer nodded at this. 'Sir, this sort of thing is common. Many people have been waking from cryosleep recently, and getting them established in society takes a lot of resources. People are resentful and angry, and they often lash out.'

'That's not what's happening here...' began Huabei, but the officer cut him off with a wave of his hand.

'Sir, you're safe now.' The police officer turned toward Deng Yang and his gang. 'This man obviously still requires medical attention. Two of you have to take him back to the hospital. We will investigate this matter thoroughly, but for now, all seven of you are under arrest on suspicion of kidnapping.' He lifted the radio on his wrist to his mouth and called for reinforcements.

Deng Yang rushed over and interrupted him. 'Officer, wait a moment. We aren't anti-cryo thugs. Look closely at this man. Doesn't he look familiar?'

The police officers peered at Huabei's face for a long time. One of them pulled down his respirator for a moment to see him better.

'It's Mi Xixi!'

'He's not Mi Xixi, he's Shen Yuan's father!'

Mouths agape, the two policemen looked back and forth between Shen Huabei and Deng Yang. The young man whose parents had died in the Central Breach disaster pulled the policemen over to him and whispered to them. As he spoke, the policemen glanced occasionally over at Huabei, and with each glance their eyes grew colder. The last time they looked at him, his heart sank. Deng Yang had two more accomplices.

The policemen walked over, avoiding Huabei's eye. One of them stood sentry and the other approached Deng Yang. In an urgent whisper, he said, 'We saw nothing. Whatever you do, don't let anyone figure out who he is – there'd be a riot.'

It wasn't just the policeman's words that terrified Huabei, but the way he said them. He spoke without regard to whether Huabei heard, as if Huabei were part of the landscape. The members of Deng Yang's gang quickly pushed Huabei into the car and boarded it behind him. As soon as the car's engine revved up, its windows grew darker, preventing the Sun from shining in and him from looking out. The car was self-driving and completely devoid of any visible means of manual control. No one spoke as they took to the road.

At last, Huabei ventured a question, if only to break the ominous silence.

'Who is Mi Xixi?'

'A movie star,' the Lost Bolt orphan sitting next to him advised. 'He is famous for playing your son. Shen Yuan and alien monsters are the media's villains of the day.'

Huabei squirmed in his seat, trying to move away from the girl. As he did, he inadvertently brushed his arm against a button beneath the window. The window's glass immediately turned clear again. Through it, Huabei saw they were driving on an enormous, complex highway overpass. The structure was packed with vehicles with no more than two meters between them. Alarmingly, the cars were not stopped in traffic, as their proximity suggested they should be – they were all moving at full speed, at least 100 kilometers per hour! The whole overpass looked like an unsafe amusement park ride.

Their car sped ahead towards a junction in the road. As they approached the junction, their car turned to change lanes, and just as it seemed they would crash into another car, a gap opened in the lane beside them, allowing them to merge. In fact, a gap opened for every merging vehicle, with an action so quick and so regular that the two lanes seemed to meld into one. Huabei had already realized that the car was self-driving; now, he realized that the AI operating the car enabled an extremely efficient use of the highway.

A person in the back seat reached over and hit the button to darken the window again.

'I don't know anything that's going on, and you still want to kill me?' asked Huabei.

From his seat in front, Deng Yang turned to face Huabei. After a pause, he unenthusiastically said, 'Well, then I guess I'll just have to tell you.'

Chapter 3
The Antarctic Doorstep

'People rich in imagination are usually weak in reality, and most strong people – the people who make history – lack imagination. Your son was a remarkable exception: a man with imagination and the strength of will to bring his visions into being. To him, reality was just a small, remote island in a vast ocean of fantasies; but when he wanted to, he could reverse the two, making his fantasies into an island and reality into the ocean. He navigated both oceans with incredible skill—'

Huabei interrupted him. 'I know my own son. Stop wasting my time.'

'No matter how well you knew him, you could never have imagined the status that Shen Yuan attained, the power he held. He was in a position to bring his darkest visions to life. Unfortunately, the world did not recognize how dangerous this was until it was too late. Perhaps there have been others like him in history, but they were like asteroids that flew by the Earth. They never made impact – they just flew off into the vastness of space. History gave Shen Yuan the means to realize his twisted vision. His asteroid made impact, to our great misfortune.'

'In your fifth year of cryonic hibernation, the world took a preliminary step towards resolving the problem of who should control Antarctica. The continent was declared a shared region of global economic development. Strong nations circumvented this declaration and carved out large areas of the continent for their own, exclusive benefit. Each of those nations wanted to exploit the resources of its own region as quickly as possible. Doing so was their only hope to escape the economic depression that resource depletion and pollution had brought about. There was a saying back then – The future lies at the bottom of the world. It was then that your son proposed his insane idea. He claimed that implementing it would turn Antarctica into China's backyard, that he could make it simpler to get from Beijing to Antarctica than to Tianjin. This was not a metaphor – it actually was faster to get to Antarctica than to Tianjin, and the trip used fewer resources and created less pollution. When he began announcing his plan in a televised press conference, the whole country laughed, as if they were watching a ludicrous comedy. But before the conference was over, we had all stopped laughing. We realized it really was possible! Thus began the disastrous Antarctic Doorstep Project.

Deng Yang abruptly stopped talking.

'Well, what is the Antarctic Doorstep Project?' asked Huabei, urging Deng Yang to continue.

'You'll know soon enough,' said Deng Yang icily.

'Can you at least tell me what I have to do with any of this?'

'You are Shen Yuan's father. What else is there to say?'

'So we've regressed to genetic determinism now?'

'Of course not, but by your son's own admission, bloodline is relevant in this case. After he became famous around the world, he said in countless interviews that his way of thinking and his personality were already largely formed by the time he was eight years old and that it was his father who had formed them. He said that all his work over the years was meant only to supplement the knowledge his father gave him. He even declared outright that his father was the original innovator of the Antarctic Doorstep Project.'

'What? Me? Antarctica? That is simply—'

'Let me finish. You also provided the technological foundation for the project.'

'What are you talking about?'

'New solid-state matter. Without it, the Antarctic Doorstep Project would have been a pipe dream. It made it possible to turn this twisted fantasy into a reality.'

Shen Huabei shook his head in confusion. He was completely unable to imagine how super-dense new solid-state matter could enable such fast travel to Antarctica.

Just then, the car came to a stop.

Chapter 4
The Gate of Hell

They got out of the car, and Huabei saw a strange, small hill in front of them. The color of rust and completely barren, there wasn't even a single blade of grass on its surface.

Deng Yang nodded towards the slope, 'That's an iron hill,' and seeing the surprise on Huabei's face, he added, 'It's a single, huge piece of metal.' Huabei looked around and saw there were several more 'iron hills' nearby, jutting out from the ground at odd intervals, their color strange against the large plain on which they stood. It looked like an alien landscape.

By now, Huabei was able to walk again, though shakily. He staggered along behind the people who had brought him here, towards a large structure in the distance. The structure was a perfect cylindar, more than 300 feet tall, and its surface was completely smooth, with no visible entrance. As they approached, a heavy iron panel slid open in the side of the structure, allowing them to enter. It closed tightly behind them.

Shen Huabei saw that he was in a dimly-lit room that resembled an airlock chamber. On the smooth, white wall hung a long row of what looked like spacesuits. Each person took one off the wall and put it on, and two people helped Huabei into one. He looked around the room and saw another sliding door on the far wall. Above the door glowed a red light, and next to the light was a digital display that showed the current atmospheric pressure in the room. When his heavy helmet was tightened into place, a transparent liquid crystal display appeared in the upper right corner of his visor, showing a string of numbers and figures in quick succession. He recognized that it was the suit's internal diagnostic system. Then, he heard the deep drone of machinery start up. The number on the atmospheric pressure display above the door was falling fast. In less than three minutes, it hit zero. The red light turned green and the door slid open, revealing the dark interior of the airtight structure.

Huabei's guess had been correct: the room they were in was an airlock chamber that enabled passage between an area with atmosphere into a vacuum. The interior of the huge cylinder was a vacuum.

The group walked through the door, which shut behind them, leaving them in pitch darkness. The lights on a few people's helmets turned on, sending feeble shafts of light into the void. A feeling of deja-vu came over Huabei, and he shivered with dread.

'Walk forward,' crackled Deng Yang's voice in Huabei's headphones. His helmet light illuminated a small bridge ahead of them, no more than three feet wide. Its far end was obscured by darkness, so he couldn't see how long it was. Beneath the bridge was blackness. With trembling steps, Huabei walked on. The heavy boots of his airtight suit produced a hollow clang against the metal surface of the bridge. He walked a few yards out onto the bridge and turned his head to see if anyone had followed him. As he did, everyone's helmet lamps suddenly turned off, and all was engulfed in darkness. A few seconds later, a blue light suddenly began to glow beneath the narrow bridge. Huabei looked behind him and saw that he was the only one on the bridge – everyone else had gathered at its foot, and they were all looking at him. Lit from below by the blue light, they looked like ghosts. Tightly grasping the bridge's railing, Huabei looked down, and what he saw made his blood run cold.

He was standing above a deep well.

The well was around 30 feet in diameter. Rings of light were evenly spaced along its interior wall; it was only by their glow that was he able to discern the well's presence. The bridge spanned the mouth of the well, and he stood in its exact center. He couldn't see the well's bottom. He saw only countless rings of light on the wall of the well, shrinking with perspective into the distance and finally coming to a point. It was like looking down at a glowing blue target.

'Your judgment is at hand – you will pay your son's debt!' shouted Deng Yang. He grabbed hold of a wheel at the foot of the bridge and began to turn it, muttering, 'This is for my stolen youth, my wasted talent...' The bridge tilted to one side, and Huabei tightly gripped the higher railing, trying with all his might to keep his footing.

Deng Yang gave control of the wheel to the Central Breach orphan, who turned it forcefully. 'This is for my mother and father, for their melted bodies...' The incline of the bridge increased.

The girl whose parents died in the Lost Bolt Disaster stepped up. She turned the wheel, her wrathful gaze on Huabei. 'This is for vaporizing my parents...'

The man who had attempted suicide after losing his fortune took the girl's place at the wheel. 'This is for my money – my Rolls Royce, my Lincoln, my villa on the beach, my swimming pool. This is for my ruining my life, for making my wife and son stand in that long, cold welfare line...'

The bridge was now tilted on its side, leaving Huabei hanging on to the top railing as he desperately caught a foothold on the railing now below him.

The man who had lost his mind joined the man who had attempted suicide at the wheel, and they turned it together. He was clearly still ill, and he said nothing – he just looked down into the well and laughed. The bridge flipped over completely. Huabei clutched the railing with both hands and dangled over the pit.

His fear had actually subsided somewhat. As he gazed through the gate of hell into the bottomless pit beneath him, Huabei's life flashed before his eyes. His childhood and youth had been a drab and joyless time for him. He had found success as a student and a researcher, yet even after inventing 'sugar coating' technology, he still felt ill at ease in the world. Personal relationships had always felt to him like a spider's web whose strands bound him more tightly the more he struggled. He had never known true love; he had married out of obligation. As soon as he decided never to have children, a child came to him and his wife. He was a man who lived in a world of dreams and fantasies, the sort of man most people despise. He had never found his place among other people. His life was one of isolation, of going against the current. He used to put all his hope in the future. Now, the future had arrived: he was a widower whose son was the enemy of humanity, in a polluted city, surrounded by hateful, twisted people... He was nearly overcome with disappointment in the era in which he found himself and in his own life. He had once resolved to know the reason why people treated him like this before he died; now, that no longer mattered to him. He was simply a weary traveller whose only desire was to rest.

Cheers rose as Huabei's grip finally failed and he plummeted towards his fate, towards the glowing blue rings beneath him.

He shut his eyes and gave himself over to weightlessness. It felt like his body was dissolving away, and with it, the crushing burden of existence. In these, the last few seconds of his life, a song suddenly popped into his mind. His father had taught it to him – an old Soviet tune, already forgotten by the time he had entered cryonic hibernation. He had once gone to Moscow as a visiting scholar, and while there, he tried to find someone who knew the song. No one had heard of it, so it became his own, private song. He would only have time to hum a note or two in his head before he hit the bottom of the well, but he was sure that after his soul left his body, it would enter the next world humming.

Before he knew it, Huabei had already hummed half of the song's slow melody to himself. He suddenly became aware of how much time must have passed. Opening his eyes, he saw himself flying past ring after ring of blue light.

He was still falling.

'Ha ha ha ha!' Deng Yang's maniacal laugh came through his headphones. 'You're about to die – what a feeling that must be!'

Huabei looked down at the row of concentric rings glowing blue beneath him. They whizzed by him, one after the other, and each time passed through the largest circle, a new one emerged at its center, tiny at first but growing rapidly. He looked up at the concentric rings of light above him, whose expansion off into the distance mirrored the sight below.

'How deep is this well?' he asked.

'Don't worry, you'll hit the bottom soon enough. There's a hard steel plate down there, and you're going to splat against it like a bug on a windshield! Ha ha ha ha!'

As Deng Yang spoke, Huabei noticed that the small display in the upper right corner of his visor had flickered back to life. In glowing red letters, it read:

You have reached a depth of 50 miles.
Your speed is 0.86 miles per second.
You have passed the Mohorovičić discontinuity
Having passed the crust, you are now entering the Earth's mantle.

Huabei shut his eyes again. This time, there was no music. His mind was like a computer, dispassionate and fast, and after 30 seconds of thought he opened his eyes. Now he understood everything. This was the Antarctic Doorstep Project. There was no steel plate at the end. This well was bottomless.

This was a tunnel straight through the Earth.

Chapter 5
The Tunnel

'Is its path tangential or does it go straight through the Earth's core?' wondered Huabei aloud.

'Clever! You figured it out!' exclaimed Deng Yang.

'As clever as his son,' someone added – the Central Breach orphan, by the sound of his voice.

'It goes through the Earth's core, from Mohe to the easternmost part of the Antarctic Peninsula,' said Deng Yang, responding to Huabei's question.

'The city we were just in was Mohe?'

'Yes, it experienced a boom once the tunnel was constructed.'

'As far as I know, a tunnel from there straight through the Earth would reach the southern part of Argentina.'

'That's correct, but this tunnel curves slightly.'

'If that's the case, won't I hit the wall?'

'No – in fact, you would hit the wall if the tunnel went to Argentina. A perfectly straight tunnel would only be workable between the Earth's poles, along its axis. To make a tunnel at an angle to the axis, you must consider the rotation of the Earth. This tunnel's curvature is necessary for smooth passage.'

'This tunnel is a remarkable achievement!' exclaimed Huabei, sincerely.

You have reached a depth of 185 miles.
Your speed is 1.5 miles per second.
You have entered the Earth's asthenosphere.

Huabei saw that he was passing through the rings of light at an increasing rate. The concentric circles of light above and below him now appeared considerably denser.

Deng Yang spoke. 'Digging a tunnel through the Earth isn't exactly a new idea. As early as the 18th century, at least two people had already considered it. One was the mathematician Pierre Louis Maupertuis. The second was none other than Voltaire. After them, the French astronomer Flammarion raised the idea again, and he was the first to take into account the rotation of the Earth.'

Huabei interrupted him. 'So how can you say the idea came from me?'

'Because those people were just doing thought experiments, while your idea influenced someone – someone talented, with vision, who went on to make this outlandish idea a reality.'

'I don't remember mentioning anything like that to Shen Yuan.'

'Then you have a bad memory. You had a vision that changed the course of human history, and you forgot it!'

'I honestly can't recall.'

'Surely you remember a man called Delgado, from Argentina, and the birthday present he gave your son.'

You have reached a depth of 930 miles.

Your speed is 3.2 miles per second.
You have entered the Earth's mesosphere.

Huabei finally remembered. It was Shen Yuan's sixth birthday, and Huabei had invited the Argentine physicist Dr. Delgado, who happened to be in Beijing, to his home. Argentina was one of the two South American nations that emerged from the struggle for Antartica as a superpower. It had vast territorial claims on the continent, and large numbers of Argentine citizens had gone to live there.

In the subsequent process of global nuclear disarmament, it was natural that Argentina should join the UN's Nuclear Eradication Committee. Shen Huabei and Delgado were both serving as technical experts within that committee.

Delgado had given Shen Yuan a globe. It was made of a novel kind of glass, one of the products of Argentina's rapid technological development. The refractive index of this glass was equal to that of air, so it was entirely invisible. On the globe, the continents appeared as if they were floating in space between the Earth's poles. Shen Yuan loved his gift.

As they chatted after dinner, Delgado took out a prominent Chinese newspaper and showed Huabei a political cartoon. It was a drawing of a famous Argentine soccer player kicking the Earth like a soccer ball.

'I don't like this cartoon,' said Delgado. 'China knows nothing about Argentina except that we play soccer well, and this limited understanding affects international politics.'

'Well, Doctor, Argentina is the furthest nation from China on Earth. You are on the opposite end of the globe,' said Zhao Wenjia, smiling. She took the transparent globe from Shen Yuan and held it up. China and Argentina overlapped through the perfectly clear glass.

'I know a way to improve communication between our countries,' said Huabei, taking the globe. 'We'd just need to dig a tunnel through the center of the Earth.'

'That tunnel would be more than 7,500 miles long. That's not much shorter than a direct flight path,' said Delgado.

'But the travel time would be much shorter than flying. Think about it – you'd pack your bags, hop into one end of the tunnel, and...'

Huabei had only raised this idea to turn the conversation away from politics. It worked. Delgado's interest was piqued, and he said, 'Shen, your way of thinking is truly original. Let's see – after I jumped into the hole, the speed of my fall would continuously accelerate. The deeper I fell, the slower my acceleration would be, but I would continue to accelerate all the way to the center of the Earth. At the center, I will have achieved my maximum velocity, and my acceleration would be zero. Then, as I began to ascend the far side of the hole, I would decelerate, and my rate of deceleration would increase the further I ascended. When I arrived at the surface of the Earth in Argentina, my speed would be exactly zero. If I wanted to return to China, I could simply jump back into the hole. I could continue this sort of travel forever, if I wished, moving in simple harmonic vibration between the northen and southern hemispheres. Yes, it's a wonderful idea, but the travel time...'

'Let's calculate it,' said Huabei. He turned on his computer.

Completing the calculation took only a moment. Based on the planet's average density, if you jumped into the tunnel in China, travelled 7,917 miles through the Earth, and emerged from the tunnel in Argentina, your travel time would be forty two minutes and twelve seconds.

'Now that's what I call fast travel!' said Delgado, clearly pleased.

You have reached a depth of 1740 miles.
Your speed is 4 miles per second.
You are passing the Gutenberg discontinuity and entering the Earth's core.

As Huabei continued to fall, Deng Yang spoke. 'You certainly didn't notice it at the time, but clever little Shen Yuan hung onto your every word that evening. You also wouldn't know that he didn't sleep a wink that night.

He just stared at the transparent globe next to his bed. Your influence on his thinking was enormous. Over the years, you planted countless seeds in his imagination. This one happened to bear fruit.'

The wall of the tunnel was around fifteen feet from Huabei, and he watched it fly upwards. The rings of light now sped by so rapidly that they appeared as a blur on the wall.

'Is this wall made of new solid-state material?' he asked.

'What else could it be? Is there another material strong enough to construct a tunnel like this?'

'How did you produce such an enormous quantity? How can you transport and machine a material so dense that it sinks through the Earth?'

'The short answer is this: new solid-state material is produced in a continuous series of small nuclear explosions, using your 'sugar coating' technology, of course. Producing it is a long and complex process. We can produce new solid-state material in a range of densities. Lower-density material does not sink into the ground, so it is used to build large foundations that can bear the weight of high-density material without sinking, by dispersing its pressure. The same principle can be applied in transporting the material. The technology used to machine the material is more complex; you don't have the background knowledge to understand it. Suffice it to say that new solid-state material is an enormous industry, larger in scale than steel production. The Antarctic Doorstep Project is not the material's only application.'

'How was this tunnel built?'

'I'll tell you first that the basic component of the tunnel's structure is a wellbore casing. Each section of casing is around 320 feet long, and the tunnel is made of around 240,000 sections linked together. As to the specific construction process, you're a smart man – you figure it out.'

You have reached a depth of 2550 miles.
Your speed is 4.6 miles per second.
You are at the center of the Earth's liquid core.

'A caisson?'

'Yes, we used a caisson. First we sank the wellbore casing from sites in China and Antarctica. Linked together, the sections of casing formed an unbroken line through the Earth. The second step was to excavate the material from inside the casing, forming the tunnel. The metal hills you saw outside the entrance to the tunnel are made of excavated material, iron and nickel alloys from the core of the Earth. The actual work of linking the casing was carried out by 'subterranean ships,' machines made of new solid-state material that are capable of travel among and between the strata of Earth. Some models are able to operate at core depth. We used these machines to maneuver the sinking sections of casing into place.

'By my calculation, the process you describe would only require 120,000 sections of casing.'

'Super dense solids are able to withstand the high pressures and temperatures found in the interior of the Earth, but the movement of liquid matter within the Earth is more problematic. There is magma at relatively shallow depths, but the real danger is in the core, where the flow of liquid iron and nickel produces enormous shearing force against the tunnel. New solid-state matter is strong enough to withstand these forces, but the joints in the casing aren't. Therefore, the tunnel is constructed out of two layers of casing, one wrapped tightly around the other. By staggering the joints of the two layers, we were able to achieve sufficient resistance to the shearing forces.'

You have reached a depth of 3350 miles.
Your speed is 4.8 miles per second.
You are approaching the Earth's solid core.

'I suppose you'll tell me next about the disasters that this project caused.'

153

Chapter 6

Disaster

'Twenty-five years ago, the Antarctic Doorstep suffered its first disaster, just as the project entered the final phase of survey and design,' Deng Yang resumed. 'This stage required substantial underground navigation. On one exploratory voyage, a ship called Sunset 6 experienced a malfunction while in the Earth's mantle and sank down to the core. Two members of the three-person crew were killed. Only the young, female pilot survived. She is still down there, sealed off in the core of the Earth, doomed to live out her remaining days encased in that subterranean ship. The neutrino communication device on the ship is no longer able to transmit messages, though it might still receive ours. Oh, that's right – her name is Shen Jing. She is your granddaughter.'

Huabei's heart skipped a beat.

At this speed, the rings of light on the wall of the tunnel were completely indistinct, making the wall itself appear to glow with a harsh, blue light. Huabei felt as if he were falling into a tunnel through time, into the recent past, the past he had not known.

You have reached a depth of 3600 miles.
Your speed is 4.8 miles per second.
You have entered the solid core and are approaching the center of the Earth!

'In the sixth year of construction, the tragic Central Breach Disaster struck. As I mentioned before, the tunnel's wall is composed of two staggered layers of casing. Before installing a section of the inner layer, it was necessary to join the adjacent outer sections and extract all material from inside them, as any debris could have compromised the seal between the layers. This was time-sensitive work, especially in the liquid core. After two sections of the outer ring were coupled and before the inner section was inserted, the outer layer had to hold on its own against the force of the nickel-iron flow. The riveting used to join the rings was exceptionally strong. Its design was projected to be able to withstand the force of the flow almost indefinitely during a considerable period of time. 300 miles into the core, two sections of outer ring that had just been coupled were struck by an aberrant surge in the nickel-iron flow, five times more forceful than anything observed in prior surveys. The force of the surge dislocated the sections and in an instant, high-temperature, high-pressure core material rushed through the breach, into the caisson, and up the tunnel rapidly. As soon as the breach was detected, Shen Yuan, as general director of the project, immediately ordered the closure of the Gutenberg Gate, a safety valve located at the Gutenberg Discontinuity. More than 2500 engineers were working in the 310 miles of tunnel beneath the valve at the time. These workers boarded high-speed freight elevators to evacuate the tunnel as soon as they became aware of the breach. There were 130 elevators in total. The final one departed around 20 miles ahead of the crest of the nickel-iron flow. In the end, only sixty-one elevators made it through the Gutenberg Gate before it closed; everyone else was trapped on the wrong side, swallowed by torrents of the core flow, burning at over seven thousand degrees. One thousand five hundred and twenty-seven people lost their lives.

'News of the disaster shook the world. There was a consensus that Shen Yuan was to blame, but people disagreed about how he should have responded. One group asserted he had had time to wait for all the elevators to pass through the Gutenberg Gate before closing it. The last elevator was 20 miles ahead of the flow – it would have been a close call, but possible. Even if the flow had overtaken the Gutenberg Gate before it could be closed, there was still the Moho Gate, another safety valve at the Mohorovičić discontinuity. Outraged members of the victims' families accused Shen Yuan of murder. His public response was a single sentence: I should avoid any possibilities of larger disasters. He wasn't wrong – hesitating might have caused a cataclysm. There was a whole subgenre of disaster films about the Antarctic Doorstep. The most famous, *Metal Fountain*, was a nightmarish depiction of what would have happened if the core material had breached the surface. In it, a column of liquid nickel and iron shot out of the tunnel into the stratosphere, where it blossomed outwards like a flower of death. It glowed with a blinding white light that illuminated the whole Northern Hemisphere, and a rain of molten metal began to fall over the Earth, turning all of Asia into a furnace. Humanity met the same fate as the dinosaurs.

'This wasn't artistic license; it was a probable outcome, and because of this, Shen Yuan faced another line of accusation that contradicted the first: he should have closed the Gutenberg Gate immediately, without waiting for 61 elevators to ascend. This was the more popular view, and its adherents labelled Shen Yuan's crime as 'criminal negligence against humanity.' There was no proper legal basis for either accusation, but Shen Yuan resigned from his leadership position on the Project. He refused to be reappointed elsewhere, and he continued his work on the tunnel as an ordinary engineer.'

The light on the wall of the tunnel suddenly turned from blue to red.

You have reached a depth of 3900 miles.
Your speed is 5 miles per second.
You are passing through the center of the Earth!

Deng Yang's voice came again through Huabei's earphones. 'Your current speed would be fast enough to carry you into orbit, but your location at the center of the planet means that the world is revolving around you. The continents and oceans of Earth, its cities and people, are all orbiting you.'

Bathed in the solemn red light, another piece of music came to Huabei, this time a magnificent symphony. He was travelling at first cosmic velocity in a tunnel through the center of the Earth, whose glowing, red walls gave Huabei the impression that the Earth itself was alive and he was floating through one of its veins. His own blood ran hot at the thought.

Deng Yang continued. 'New solid-state material is an excellent insulator, but the air around you is still above 2700 degrees. Your suit's cooling system is running at full power.'

After about ten seconds, the red light on the wall suddenly turned back to a tranquil blue.

You have passed through the center of the Earth and begun your ascent and deceleration.
You have ascended 300 miles.
Your speed is 4.8 miles per second.
You are in the Earth's solid core.

The blue light soothed Huabei. He had already gotten used to weightlessness, and he slowly turned his body so that he was moving head-first. In this position, he felt he was rising rather than falling. 'Wasn't there a third disaster?' he asked.

'The Lost Bolt Disaster happened five years ago, after the Antarctic Doorstep Project had been completed and officially opened for use. Core trains travelled through the tunnel nonstop. The cars of the trains were cylindrical, 27 feet in diameter and 165 feet long; a single train was made up of as many as 200 cars that could carry 22,000 tons of freight or nearly 10,000 passengers. A one-way trip through the center of the Earth took only 42 minutes and required no resources besides gravity.

'At the Mohe Station, a repair technician carelessly dropped a bolt into the tunnel. It was no thicker than five inches in diameter, but it was made of a new material that is able to absorb electromagnetic waves, so the radar safety system was unable to detect it. The bolt fell down the tunnel, through the Earth, and arrived at the Antarctic Station, where it began to fall again. Near the center of the Earth, it struck a core train ascending to Antarctica. The speed of the bolt relative to the train was close to ten miles a second; its kinetic energy made it like a missile. It penetrated the first two cars of the train, vaporizing everything in its path, and the explosion sent the rest of the train off course. It crashed into the wall of the tunnel at five miles per second, tearing it to shreds in an instant.

'Debris from the crash oscillated back and forth in the tunnel. Some pieces rose as high as the surface, but most of the debris had lost momentum in the crash and simply swung around near the core. It took a month to clean the shards out the tunnel. We were unable to recover the bodies of the 3,000 passengers on board – they had been incinerated in the heat of the core.'

You have ascended 1360 miles from the center of the Earth.
Your speed is 4.6 miles per second.
You have reentered the Earth's liquid core.

'The biggest disaster of all was the project itself. The Antarctic Doorstep Project may have been an unprecedented feat of engineering, but from an economic standpoint, it was incredibly stupid. People still can't figure out how such a patently foolish project could ever have made it off the drawing board. Shen Yuan's reckless ambition certainly played a role, but the true reason it succeeded was people's frenzied desire for new lands to claim and their blind worship of technology. The economic benefits of the project dried up on the day it was completed. It was true that the tunnel enabled extremely fast travel through the Earth and consumed almost no resources – people used to say "just toss it in the tunnel" or "just hop in the tunnel." But it had been a huge investment, and the transport fees on core trains were astronomical. Despite its speed, the high cost of using the tunnel eliminated its competitive advantage over traditional modes of transport. '

You have ascended 2170 miles from the center of the Earth.
Your speed is 4 miles per second.
You are passing Gutenberg discontinuity and are reentering the Earth's mantle.

'Humanity's Antarctic dream was soon shattered. The last pristine land on Earth was over-exploited and destroyed in a swarm of industry, and Antarctica became like everywhere else: used up, covered in refuse – a landfill. The ozone layer over Antarctica was completely destroyed, which affected the whole world. Even in the northern hemisphere, strong ultraviolet rays made it necessary for people to cover their skin outdoors. The melting of the Antarctic ice sheet accelerated sharply, causing a dramatic rise in sea levels across the globe. In the midst of these crises, human reason once again prevailed. Member States of the United Nations unanimously signed a new Antarctic Treaty that mandated an immediate, complete withdrawal from the continent. It is once again a wilderness, and we expect its environment to recover gradually. The treaty caused a sudden, sharp drop in demand for shipping to Antarctica, and after the Lost Bolt Disaster, all core train operations ceased. The tunnel has now been closed for eight years, but its effects on the economy still Ling'er. Thousands of people who had bought stock in the Antarctic Doorstep Company lost everything, which caused serious social unrest. The tunnel was a black hole for investors, and it brought the country's economy to the brink of collapse. Even today, we are still mired in the troubles and pain it caused.

'That is the story of the Antarctic Doorstep Project.'

As Huabei's speed decreased, the blur of blue light on the wall of the tunnel began to flicker, and soon he was again able to distinguish each ring as it passed. In each direction, the lights appeared once again as the dense, concentric rings of a target.

> *You have reached a height of 2980 miles above the Earth's core.*
> *Your speed is 3.1 miles per second.*
> *You are passing through the Earth's mesosphere.*

Chapter 7
The Death of Shen Yuan

'What became of my son?' asked Huabei.

'After the tunnel was closed, Shen Yuan stayed on as part of a skeleton crew at the Mohe Station. I called him on the phone one day; he said he was "with his daughter" and hung up. I didn't learn the truth behind those cryptic words until several years later. It nearly defies description. He spent all his time in an airtight suit, falling back and forth through the tunnel. He slept in the tunnel. He only returned to the station to eat and recharge his suit. He passed through the Earth roughly 32 times each day. Day after day, year after year, he travelled from Mohe to the Antarctic Peninsula and back again, in a simple harmonic wave with a cycle of 84 minutes and an amplitude of 7830 miles.'

You have ascended 3730 miles from the center of the Earth.
Your speed is 1.5 miles per second.
You are passing through the Earth's asthenosphere.

'No one knows exactly what Shen Yuan did during his endless fall. According to his colleagues, each time he passed through the center of the Earth, he used a neutrino communicator to hail his daughter. He often had long conversations with her as he fell – one-sided, of course. But Shen Jing, trapped in the Sunset 6 as it drifted in the nickel-iron flow of the Earth's core, was probably able to hear him.

'He subjected his body to long periods of weightlessness, interrupted by two or three exposures each day to the normal force of Earth's gravity, when he returned to the station to eat and recharge his suit. He was an old man, and the constant change in gravity weakened his heart. His heart gave out as he fell. No one noticed. His body continued to travel through the tunnel for two days until his sealed suit exhausted its charge. The tunnel was his crematorium. His final pass through the center of the Earth burned his body to ashes. I believe your son would have been satisfied with this fate.'

You have reached a height of 3,850 miles above the Earth's core
Your speed is 0.9 miles/sec
You have passed through the Mohorovicic Discontinuity, and are entering the Earth's crust

'That will be my fate as well, won't it?' asked Huabei, calmly.

'It should satisfy you, too. You saw everything you wanted to see before your death. We had originally planned to throw you into the tunnel without a suit, but in the end, we decided that you should get a thorough look at the thing your son made.'

'Yes, I am satisfied. This life has been enough. I am sincerely grateful to each of you.'

There was no answer. The hum of Huabei's headphones abruptly disappeared as his executioners, standing on the other side of the world, cut off communications.

Huabei looked up. The concentric rings of light above him were quite sparse now. It took two or three seconds to pass each one, and the interval was getting longer. A beeping sound came through his headphones, and words appeared on his visor:

Attention!
You are approaching the Antarctic Terminal

At the center of the rings above him was emptiness, which grew as he approached the final ring of blue light. He passed it and rose slowly towards a bridge spanning the mouth of the tunnel, identical to the bridge on the other end. On the bridge stood several people in airtight suits. As he ascended through the mouth of the tunnel, they reached out to grab him and pulled him up onto the bridge.

The interior of the Antarctic station was also dark, lit only from below by the glow of the blue rings. Huabei looked up and saw a huge cylindrical object suspended above him. Its diameter was slightly smaller than that of the tunnel. He walked along the bridge to the rim of the tunnel and looked up again. There was a whole row of cylinders hanging above the mouth of the tunnel. He counted four of them and guessed that there were more in the darkness above those. This, he knew, had to be the decommissioned core train.

Chapter 8
Antarctica

Half an hour later, Huabei walked out of the tunnel's Antarctic terminal station, accompanied by the police officers who had saved his life. He stood on a snowless expanse of Antarctic plain. There was an abandoned city in the distance. The sun hung low over the horizon, casting its weak rays over the vast and uninhabited continent. The air here was better than on the other side of the Earth, and no respirator was necessary.

A policemen told Huabei that they were members of a small police force left to guard the empty city. They had rushed to the station after receiving an alert from Doctor Guo. The tunnel's mouth was sealed when they arrived, so they immediately contacted the tunnel's management department and lodged an urgent request to remove the cover. Huabei was approaching the mouth of the tunnel just as it opened, and they saw him rise towards them in the blue light, like something floating up from the depths of the ocean. If it had opened a few seconds later, Huabei would have certainly perished. The tunnel's seal would have blocked his ascent, and he would have begun falling again towards the northern hemisphere. His suit would have run out of power before he reached the core, and he would have been burned to ashes, just as his son was.

'Deng Yang and his gang have been arrested and will be charged with attempted murder. However...' The police officer paused and glared at Huabei. 'I understand what drove them.'

Huabei was still dizzy from the weightlessness of his fall. He looked off towards the sun at the edge of the sky and sighed. 'This life has been enough,' he said.

'If that's how you feel, you'll find it easier to accept your fate,' said another officer.

'My fate?' Huabei's senses came back to him and he turned his head to face the second officer.

'You can't live in these times or this sort of thing will happen again.

Fortunately for you, the government has a "temporal emigration program" aimed at reducing population pressures on the environment. Under this program, a portion of the population is obliged to enter cryonic hibernation, to be awoken at some future date. We have already received our orders – you will be a temporal emigrant. I don't know how long it will be until you are awoken.'

It took Huabei a long time to fully comprehend what he had been told. Once he did, he gave the police officer a deep bow. 'Thank you. How am I always so lucky?'

'Lucky?' asked the officer, clearly confused. 'Temporal emigrants from this era will have a hard enough time adapting to the society of the future. There is no hope for someone from the past like you!'

A faint smile crossed Huabei's face. 'That doesn't matter. What matters is that I will have the chance to see the Earth Tunnel restored to glory!'

The policemen scoffed. 'I wouldn't bet on it. The project was a catastrophe! It will stand forever as nothing more than a monument to you and your son's failure.'

'Ha ha ha ha!' Huabei burst into laughter. He was still weak from weightlessness and could barely stand straight, but his spirit soared. 'The Great Wall and the Pyramids were utter failures, too. The Mongols invaded China from the north, and the pharaoh's mummy never came back to life. But is that how we think of these colossal projects now? No, we think of them as glorious monuments to the human spirit!' He pointed behind him, at the towering cylinder of the tunnel station. 'This tunnel is a Great Wall through the center of the Earth itself, and here you are at its edge, weeping like Meng Jiang! How pitiful! Ha ha ha ha!'

Huabei opened his arms to embrace the cold Antarctic wind. 'Yuan, our lives were enough,' he said happily.

Epilogue

The next time Huabei woke up half a century had passed. His experience was almost identical to the last time: he was taken by a group of people to a car, which drove to the tunnel's Mohe terminal station. He was put into an airtight suit – for some reason, much heavier than the one he had worn 50 years before – and was thrown, once again, into the tunnel. After 50 years, the tunnel looked much the same as it did before – a bottomless hole, lit by an endless series of blue, ring-shaped lights on its walls.

This time, however, someone had jumped in with him. She was young and beautiful, and she introduced herself as his tour guide.

'A tour guide? So my prediction was right – the tunnel has become a wonder of the world, like the Great Wall or the Pyramids!' Huabei said excitedly as he fell.

'No, not like those places. The tunnel has become...' She was holding Huabei's hand, to ensure that they fell at the same speed, and her speech trailed off as she carefully adjusted her grip in the weightless environment.

'What has it become?'

'The World Cannon!'

'What?' Huabei looked again at the walls of the tunnel as they flew by, trying to understand.

The tour guide explained, 'After you entered hibernation, the environment became even worse. Pollution and the destruction of the ozone layer killed what little vegetation on Earth. Breathable air became a commodity. At the time, we were left with one option if we wanted to save the Earth: shut down all heavy energy industries'

'That may help the environment, but it would also mean the end of civilization,' Huabei interrupted.

'Many people were willing to accept that as a side effect, given the size of the problem. However, other people continued looking for another way out. The most feasible alternative was to move all the planet's industrial operations to the moon and outer space.'

'You built a space elevator?'

'No, though we tried. It turned out to be even harder than digging the Earth Tunnel.'

'Did you invent anti-gravity spacecraft?'

'No. In fact, that has been proven to be theoretically impossible.'

'Nuclear-powered rockets?'

'Those we have, but they're not much cheaper to operate than traditional rockets. Using them to move all industry to space would have been an economic disaster of the same scale that this tunnel was.'

'So you weren't able to move anything to space in the end.' Huabei smiled grimly. 'Has the world entered . . . a post-human age?'

The guide did not respond. Together, they fell in silence into the abyss as the rings of light flying past them grew denser and blended together into a single, luminescent surface on the wall of the tunnel. Ten minutes later, the light turned red, and they wordlessly passed through the center of the Earth at five miles per second. The walls soon turned blue again, and Huabei's guide deftly turned her body 180 degrees, so that she ascended head-first. Huabei followed her motion clumsily.

'Oh!' Huabei shouted in surprise. The display in the upper right corner of his visor said their current speed was 5.3 miles per second.

They had passed the center of the Earth, but they were still accelerating!

Something else alarmed Huabei: he felt the force of gravity. The process of falling through the Earth was supposed to take place entirely in weightlessness, but he distinctly felt his own weight! His scientist's intuition told him that what he felt was not in fact gravity – it was thrust. Some force was thrusting them forward and causing them to continue to accelerate, even as gravity should have been slowing them down.

'I take it you've read From the Earth to the Moon, by Jules Verne?' asked the guide suddenly.

'When I was young. It was the dumbest book I'd ever read,' Huabei answered, absent-mindedly. His attention was on his surroundings as he tried to figure out what strange force was acting on them.

'It's not dumb at all. To implement large-scale, fast transportation into space, a cannon is ideal.'

'Unless the speed of the launch squashes you flat.'

'The reason you'd get squashed would be if you accelerated too quickly, and you'd only accelerate too quickly if the barrel of the cannon was too short. With a long enough barrel, the payload could accelerate gently, just as we are right now.'

'So we're in Verne's cannon?'

'As I said, it's called the World Cannon.'

Huabei looked up at the blue tunnel and tried to imagine it as the barrel of a cannon. At this speed, the wall appeared as a single, uninterrupted object, so he had no sense of movement. He felt as if they were motionless, hovering in a glowing, blue tube.

'In your fourth year of hibernation, we developed a novel type of new solid-state material. It possesses all the properties of the previous material, but it is also an excellent conductor. A thick wire made of this material is wrapped around the exterior of the Antarctic half of the tunnel, making it function as a 4,000 mile-long electromagnetic coil.

'What powers the coil?'

'There is a strong electric current in the core of the Earth. It's what produces the Earth's magnetic field. We used core ships to assemble more than one hundred 1000-mile-long loops of conductive solid-state wire in the core. These loops collect the current in the core and transfer it to the coil around the tunnel, filling the tunnel with a powerful electromagnetic field. In the shoulder and waist of our suits are two superconducting coils that produce the opposite magnetic field. That's how we achieve thrust.'

Continuing to accelerate, they quickly approached the end of the tunnel. As they did, the walls again began to glow red.

'Our speed is 9.3 miles per second, well above escape velocity. We're about to be fired from the Earth cannon!'

The towering Core Train station above had long been dismantled, replaced with nothing but a sealed gate, covering a simple opening right up into the sky.

A recorded message played over their headphones: Attention passengers: the World Cannon is about to commence today's 43rd launch. Please put on your protective eyewear and insert your earplugs. Failure to do so will cause permanent damage to your eyesight and hearing.

Ten seconds later, the sealed mouth of the tunnel slid open loudly, revealing its 30-foot-wide mouth. Air roared into the vacuum of the tunnel's interior. With a noise like thunder, a long tongue of flame leapt out of the mouth of the tunnel, so bright that it outshone the weak, low-hanging Antarctic sun. Instantly, the sealed gate slid closed again, the tunnel's air pumps roaring to life. Soon they had removed all the air that had rushed into the tunnel during the three seconds that the gate had been open; then the cannon was ready for the next launch.

People looked up to see two shooting stars, trailing tails of fire as they streaked upwards and disappeared into the deep blue Antarctic sky.

Huabei didn't see the mouth of the tunnel came to him as he had imagined. He travelled too fast to see that. Only he could see is the endless tunnel glowing red light disappeared in an instant. Simultaneously the blue sky came to his vision. It was just like two frames on the screen without any transition. He looked back to see the ground receding beneath his feet. He recognized the city next to the tunnel's terminal, which soon appeared only as big as a long, rectangular basketball court. He saw the color of the sky quickly transitioning from blue to black, as if a screen were being dimmed. Turning his gaze below, he saw the long arc of the Antarctic peninsula surrounded by ocean. A long tail of flame trailed behind him, emanating from the red-hot surface of his suit. He was enveloped in a thin cloak of fire.

He looked over at his guide, some thirty feet away. She was also wrapped in flames, like some fantastic creature of living fire. The air resistance felt like a giant hand pressing relentlessly down on his head and shoulders. As the sky grew darker, this giant hand was conquered by another more powerful force and the pressure subsided. Looking down, he saw all of Antarctica, noticing with joy that it was white once again. In the distance, the curvature of the Earth became clear. The sun appeared to move upwards from the arc of the horizon, scattering its resplendent light throughout the planet's thin atmosphere. Once more, Huabei looked up and saw the constellations spread out above him. He had never seen the stars shine so brightly.

The fire on his body subsided as they shot out of the atmosphere. They were now floating in the vast silence of space.

Huabei felt as light as a feather. His sealed suit, or spacesuit, was much thinner than before, as its top layer of heat-dispersing material had burned off in the friction of the atmosphere. Their communications had been interrupted by atmospheric disturbance, but now they were back online. Huabei's guide spoke. 'Atmospheric resistance slowed us down a bit, but we are still travelling at escape velocity. We're leaving the Earth. Look over there.'

She pointed beneath them at the Antarctic peninsula, which was now tiny. Huabei saw a flash of light from the spot where the tunnel emerged, and a shooting star shot upwards into the sky, trailing fire behind it. As it exited the atmosphere, the fire dimmed and went out.

'That was a spaceship leaving the World Cannon. It's going to pick us up. At every moment, five or six "payloads" are travelling through the barrel of the cannon, firing off at eight to ten minute intervals, so getting into space is as fast and easy as taking the subway. It fired even more rapidly when the great industrial migration began twenty years ago. There were often more than twenty ships accelerating through the barrel at a time, with two or three-minute intervals between shots. Back then, the spaceships shot into the sky like a never-ending shower of meteors. The job was enormous, but humanity's fate hung in the balance. It was truly magnificent!'

Huabei spotted numerous fast moving stars, easy to see against the stillness of the stars in the background, and Huabei realized that they were in fact objects in orbit around the Earth. Squinting, he was able to make out some of their shapes: some were ring-shaped, others were circular, and some appeared to be irregular assemblies of many different shapes. They looked like jewels against the deep blackness of space.

'That one is Baoshan Iron & Steel Company,' said Huabei's guide, pointing towards a glowing, ring-shaped object. She pointed out several other bright objects. 'Those are Sinopec which, of course, no longer handles oil. Those cylindrical ones are the European Metallurgy Association. Over there are solar power stations – they collect solar energy and send it to the surface using microwaves. The shining parts are just their control centers; their panels and transmission arrays are invisible from here.

Huabei was enraptured by the sight. He looked down at the lush, blue orb of Earth, and tears flowed from his eyes. His heart went out to everyone, living or dead, who had participated in the Antarctic Doorstep Project. He wished that all of them could see this. And one of them especially – a certain young woman, who would remain forever young in his heart.

'Did they find my granddaughter?' he asked.

'No. We don't have the technology to conduct long-range scans in the core. The search area is vast, and no one knows where the iron-nickel flow has carried her.'

'Can we send this image to the core as a neutrino transmission?'

'We already are. I believe she can see it all.'

乡村教师

THE VILLAGE TEACHER

TRANSLATED BY ADAM LANPHIER

亚当·兰菲尔 — 译

He knew he'd have to teach his final lesson early.

He felt another shot of pain in his liver, so strong he almost fainted. He didn't have the strength to get out of bed, and, with great difficulty, he pulled himself closer to the bedside window, whose paper panes glowed in the moonlight. The little window looked like a doorway leading into another world, one where everything shone with silver light, a diorama of silver and frostless snow. He shakily lifted his head and looked out through a hole in the paper window, and his fantasy of a silver world receded. He found himself looking into the distance, at the village where he had spent his life.

The village lay serenely in the moonlight, and it looked as if it had been abandoned for a hundred years. The small flat-roofed houses were almost indistinguishable from the mounds of soil surrounding them. In the muted colors of moonlight, it was as if the entire place had dissolved back into the hills. Only the old locust tree could be seen clearly, a few black crows' nests scattered among its withered branches, like stark drops of black ink on a silver page.

The village had its good times, like the harvest. When young men and women, who had left the village in droves to find work, came back, and the place was bustling and full of laughter. Ears of corn glistened on the rooftops, and children did somersaults in the piles of stalks on the floor of the threshing ground. The Spring Festival was another cheerful time, when the threshing ground was lit with gas lamps and decorated with red lanterns. The villagers gathered there to parade lucky paper boats and do lion dances. Now, only the clattering wooden frames of the lions' heads were left, stripped of paint. The village had no money to buy new trains for the heads, so they had been using bedsheets as the lions' bodies, which worked in a pinch. But as soon as the Spring Festival ended, all the youths of the village left again to look for work, and the place fell back into torpor.

At dusk every day, as thin wisps of smoke rose from the chimneys of the houses, one or two elderly villagers, their faces grooved like walnuts, would stand and gaze down the road that led beyond the mountains, until the last ray of gloaming light got caught in the locust tree and disappeared. People turned their lamps off and went to bed early in the village. Electricity was expensive, at ¥1.8 per kilowatt hour.

He could hear a dog softly whimpering somewhere in the village, whining in its sleep, perhaps. He looked out at the moonlit yellow soil surrounding the village, which suddenly seemed to him like a placid sheet of water. If only it *were* water—this year was the fifth consecutive year of drought, and they had had to carry water to the fields to irrigate them.

His gaze drifted into the distance, landing on the fields on the mountain, which looked in the moonlight like the footprints of a giant. Small, scattered plots were the only way to farm that rocky mountain, covered as it was with vines and brush. The terrain was too rough for agricultural equipment—even oxen would have had no good footing—so people were obliged to do all the labor by hand.

Last year, a manufacturer of agricultural machines had visited to sell a kind of miniature walking tractor, small enough to work those meager fields. It wasn't a bad little machine, but the villagers weren't having it. How much grain could those tiny plots produce? Planting them was detailed work, more like sewing than sowing, and a crop that could feed a man for a year was considered a success. In a year of drought, as it was, those fields might not even produce enough to recoup the cost of planting. A five-thousand-yuan tractor, and on top of that, diesel fuel at more than two yuan a liter—outsiders just didn't understand the difficulties of life in these mountains.

A few small silhouettes walked past the window. They formed a circle on a ridge between two fields and squatted down, inscrutable. He knew these were his students—as long as they were nearby, he could detect their presence even without seeing them. This intuition had developed in him over a lifetime, and it was particularly keen now that his life was drawing to a close.

He could even recognize the children in the moonlight. Liu Baozhu and Guo Cuihua were there. Those two were originally from the village and didn't have to live at school; nevertheless, he had taken them in.

Liu Baozhu's father had bought a woman from Sichuan as his wife ten years before, and she had given birth to Baozhu. Five years after that, when Baozhu had grown a bit, his father loosened his grip on his wife. And eventually she left him and returned to Sichuan with all his money[1].

After that, Baozhu's father lost his way. He began gambling, just like the old bachelors of the village, and before long he had lost everything but four walls and a bed. Then he began drinking. Every night, he spent 0.8 yuan to buy a pound of spirits which were made from sweet potatoes and drank himself useless. Useless and angry: he hit his son every day, and twice a week he hit him hard. One night the month before, he'd nearly beaten his son to death with the stick which was used to add the firewood into the hearth .

Guo Cuihua's home life was even worse. Her father had found a bride for himself through decent channels, a rare thing here, and he was proud. But good things seldom last, and right after the wedding, it became apparent that Cuihua's mother was unwell. No one could tell at the wedding—she'd likely been given a drug to calm her. Why would a respectable woman come to a village like this in the first place, so poor that even the birds wouldn't shit as they flew over? Nevertheless, Cuihua was born and grew up, and her mother got sicker and sicker. She attacked people with cooking knives in the daytime, and at night she would try to burn the house down. She spent most of her time laughing to herself like a ghoul, with a sound that would set your hair on end.

The rest of the children were from other villages, the closest of which was

---

1　本段原版翻译为：Liu Baozhu's father had paid the dowry for a bride from Sichuan ten years before, and she had come and given birth to Baozhu. Five years after that, when Baozhu had grown a bit, his father began to neglect his wife, the small bit of closeness they'd had slipping away, and eventually she left him and returned to her family in Sichuan. 根据中文原义，编者有修改。

at least ten miles away on mountain roads, so they had to live at school. In a crude village school like this, they would spend the whole term there. The students brought their own bedding, and each hauled a sack of wheat or rice from home, which they cooked themselves on the school's big stove. As night fell in the winter, the children would gather around the stove and watch the cooking grain bubble and purl in the pot, their faces lit by straw-orange flames. It was the most tender sight he'd ever seen. He would take it with him into the next world.

On the ridge outside the window, within the ring of children, little stars of fire began to shine, bright in the moonlit night. They were burning incense and paper, and their faces were lit red in the firelight against the silver-gray night. He was reminded of the sight of the children by the stove. Another scene emerged from the pool of his memory. The electricity had gone out at school (due perhaps to a faulty circuit, or, as happened more often, a lack of funds) while he was teaching an evening class. He held a candle in his hand to illuminate the blackboard. 'Can you see it?' he'd asked, and the children answered, as they always did, 'Not yet!' It really was hard to read the blackboard with so little light, but they had a lot of material to cover, so night class was the only option. He lit a second candle and held them both up. 'It's still too dark!' yelled the children, so he lit a third candle. It was still too dark to read the board, but the children stopped yelling. They knew their teacher wouldn't light another candle no matter how much they yelled. He couldn't afford to. He looked down at their faces flickering in the candlelight, those kids, who had fought off darkness with every fiber of their beings.

The children and firelight, the children and firelight. It was always the children and firelight, always the children at night, in the firelight. The image was forever embedded in his mind, though he never understood what it meant.

He knew the children were burning incense and paper for him, as they had done so many times before, but this time he didn't have the strength to criticize them for being superstitious. He had spent his whole life trying to ignite the flame of science and culture in the children's hearts, but he knew that, compared to the fog of ignorance and superstition that enshrouded this remote mountain village, it was a feeble flame indeed, like the flame of his candles in the classroom that night. Six months earlier, a few villagers had come to the school to scavenge rafters from the roof of the already-dilapidated dorm, with which they meant to renovate the temple at the entrance to the village. He asked where the children would sleep if the dorm had no roof, and they said they could sleep in the classroom.

'In the classroom? The wind blows right through the walls. How can the children sleep there in the winter?'

'Who cares? They're not from here.'

He picked up a pole and fought them fiercely, and he wound up with two broken ribs. A kind villager propped him up and walked with him all the way to the nearest town hospital, fifteen miles or more on mountain roads.

While assessing his injuries, the doctor had discovered that he had esophageal cancer. There was a high incidence of this sort of cancer in the region, so it wasn't a rare diagnosis. The doctor congratulated him on his good fortune—he had come while the cancer was still in an early stage, before it had started to metastasize. It was curable with surgery; in fact, esophageal cancer was one of the types of cancer against which surgery was most effective. His broken ribs might well have saved his life.

After, he had gone to the province's main city, which had an oncology hospital, and asked a doctor there how much such a surgery would cost. The doctor told him that, considering his situation, he could stay in the hospital's welfare ward, and that his other expenses could also be reduced commensurately. The final amount wouldn't be too much—around twenty thousand yuan. Recalling that his patient came from such a remote place, the doctor proceeded to explain the details of hospitalization and surgery.

He listened silently and suddenly asked: 'If I don't get the surgery, how long do I have?'

The doctor regarded him blankly for a long moment and said, 'Maybe six months.'

The teacher heaved a long sigh, as if greatly relieved, and the doctor was nonplussed. At least he could see this graduating class off.

He really had no way to pay twenty thousand yuan. Over his life, he could have saved up some money. Community teachers may not make much, but he had worked for so many years, and he had never married, nor did he have other financial obligations. But he had spent it all on the children. He couldn't remember how many children's tuition he had paid, how many of their incidental expenses he had covered. Recently, there were Liu Baozhu and Guo Cuihua, but more often, he would see that the school's big cooking pot had no oil in it, so he would buy meat and lard for the children. All the money he had left would cover perhaps a tenth of the surgery.

After the appointment with the doctor, he had walked along the city's wide avenue toward the train station. It was already dark out, and neon lights had come on in a dazzling blur of stripes and dots, bewildering him. At night, the tall buildings of the city were like rows of enormous lamps extending into the clouds, and snippets of music, alternately frenetic and gentle, filled the air along his way.

In that strange world of the city, he reflected on his own short life. He was feeling philosophical, calmly considering that each person has their own path in life, and that he had chosen his own path twenty years prior, when he had graduated from middle school and decided to return to the village. In fact, his destiny had been given to him by another village teacher.

He had spent his own childhood at the school where he now taught. His father and mother had died early, and the school had been his home. His teacher had raised him as a son, and while his childhood might have been poor, it was not lacking in love. When school had gone on winter break one year, his teacher decided to take him home for the season.

His teacher's home was far away, and snow had lain deep on the mountain road. It was the middle of the night by the time they laid eyes on the lights of his teacher's village. Not far behind them, they saw four glints of green, the eyes of two wolves. There were many wolves in the mountains back then, and you could find piles of wolf shit all around the school. Once, as a prank, he had taken a gray-white pile of the stuff, lit it on fire, and thrown it into the classroom, which filled with acrid smoke, choking his classmates. His teacher was furious.

The two wolves in the forest had slowly approached them. While his teacher had snapped a thick branch off a tree and brandished it in the wolves' path, yelling loudly, he had run off toward the village, scared out of his wits, running with all his might. He worried the wolves would go around his teacher and come after him; he worried he would run into another wolf on his way. He ran heaving into the village. Several men assembled with hunting rifles, and he went back with them to look for his teacher. They found him lying in a pool of blood and slush, half of his leg and most of his arm bitten off. His teacher took his final breath on the way to the town hospital, and he saw his teacher's eyes in a ray of torchlight. A large chunk of his cheek had been bitten off and he was unable to speak, but his eyes expressed an urgent plea, one that he'd understood and remembered.

After he graduated from middle school, he had turned down a promising opportunity to work in the town's municipal government. Instead, despite having no family or friends there, he returned directly to the mountain village, to the village primary school that his teacher had pleaded with him to save. By the time he returned, the school was abandoned, having had no teacher for several years.

Not long before that, the Board of Education had begun enforcing a policy that replaced community teachers with state-supported teachers. Some community teachers were able to obtain state support by taking a test. He passed that test and got his teaching certificate, and when he found out he was a licensed, state-supported teacher, he was happy, but that was the extent of his reaction. Other members of his cohort had been elated. But he didn't care whether he was a community teacher or a state-supported teacher; he only cared about the classes of children who would graduate from his primary school and go out into the world. Regardless of whether they left the mountains or stayed, their lives would be different in some way from the lives of children who had never gone to school.

Those mountains were one of the most impoverished areas in the country.

But worse than the poverty was the apathy of the people there toward their condition. He remembered how, many years ago, when agricultural output quotas were set for each household, the village had divided and distributed its fields, and then its possessions. The village had one tractor, and the villagers couldn't come to a consensus on how to pay for its fuel or allot time to use it. The only solution everyone could accept was to divide the tractor itself. They literally disassembled it—you get a wheel, he gets an axle. And two months ago, a factory had sent poverty relief in the form of a submersible pump, and, electricity being expensive, they also sent a diesel generator along with plenty of fuel to operate it. They had barely left the village before the villagers sold the machines, the pump and the generator together, for just fifteen hundred yuan. Everyone ate two good meals and spent a good Spring festival, that's all.

Another time, a leather manufacturer had bought some land in the village on which to build a tannery—who knew how it got sold to them in the first place. Once the tannery was up, lye and niter flowed into the river and seeped into the well water. The people who drank it broke out in red boils all over their bodies—but no one cared! They were just happy the land sold for a good price. It was a village of old, hopeless bachelors who spent all day gambling and drinking, never planting. They had it figured out—as long as they stayed poor, the county would receive small amounts of poverty relief every year, more than they could make plowing their tiny fields of rocks and dust. They had come to accept this sort of life because they knew nothing else. The village's fruitless ground and poison water were dispiriting, but what could truly make you lose hope was the dull eyes of the villagers.

This walking had tired him, so he sat down next to the sidewalk. In front of him was a large, glamorous restaurant. Its façade was a single, transparent window, through which the restaurant's luxurious chandeliers cast their light onto the street. The restaurant looked like a huge aquarium, and the customers inside, in their fancy clothes, looked like a school of colorful fish. A heavyset man sat at a table by the window. His hair and face were slicked with oil, making him look like a painted wax sculpture. Two tall young women sat next to him, one on each side. The man turned and said something to one of the women, which made her burst out in laughter, and he started laughing, too. Who knew women could get so tall, he thought. Xiuxiu would have only come up to their waists. He sighed—he was thinking about Xiuxiu again.

Xiuxiu had been the only girl in the village who hadn't married out of the mountains. Maybe she was afraid of the outside world because she, like most of the villagers, had never left. Maybe she had a different reason. Either way, the two of them had spent more than two years together, and it had seemed things might work out—her family had asked for a reasonable birth-pain price,[1] only fifteen hundred yuan. But soon, some villagers who had left to find work came back with a bit of money. One of them, about the same age as him, was a clever guy, though illiterate. He had left for the city, where he'd gone door-to-door, cleaning people's kitchen exhaust hoods, and in a year he had made a bundle.

This cleaner had spent a month in the village two years ago, and Xiuxiu had somehow wound up with him. Her family were all illiterate. The rough walls of her family's home were covered in melon seeds and scratched tallies. That was how her father kept accounts over the years. Xiuxiu hadn't gone to school, but she had an affinity for people who could read. He knew that was the main reason she had initially been attracted to him. But the village boy gave her one chip bottle of perfume, one gold-plated necklace, and eventually won her over.

'Being able to read won't put food on the table,' she told him. He knew it could, but with his job, it wasn't *good* food, especially compared to what the cleaner could give her. So, he'd had no response. Xiuxiu had walked out the door and left only the smell of her perfume, which made him scrunch up his nose.

A year after marrying the village boy, Xiuxiu died in childbirth. He

---

1 A form of dowry payment in some rural areas of northwestern China, meant to compensate the bride's mother for the pain of having borne her.

still remembered the midwife holding her rusty forceps over a flame for a second before poking them inside her. Xiuxiu's blood filled the copper basin beneath her. She died on the way to the town hospital. The village boy had spent thirty thousand yuan on the wedding, and it had been a spectacle like nothing the village had seen. Why wasn't he willing to part with a little more money so Xiuxiu could give birth in the hospital? He had asked around about the cost of delivering a child in the hospital. It was only two or three hundred yuan. But the village had its ways, and no villager had ever gone to the hospital to give birth. No one blamed the boy. They threw up their hands and said it was her fate. He heard later that compared to the cleaner's mother, Xiuxiu had been lucky. His mother had gone into obstructed labor. When the cleaner's father heard from the midwife that the child was a boy, he'd chosen to save the child. His mother was placed on the back of a donkey and driven around in circles, in order to spin the baby out. People who were there said that there was a ring of her blood in the dust.

The teacher took a deep breath and felt the ignorance and despair of the village sitting heavily on his chest. It was an ever-present sensation, and even here in the city he felt it just as strongly.

There was still hope for the children, he told himself, even as they sat in the freezing classroom in the winter and looked at the blackboard by candlelight. He was the candle. For as long he could, with as much brightness as he could muster, he would burn, body and soul, for those children.

Eventually, he had risen from the city sidewalk and continued walking for a while, before stepping into a bookstore. The city was a good place—it even had bookstores that were open at night. There he spent all the money he had brought on books for the school's tiny library, saving for himself only enough to cover the fare home. In the middle of the night, clutching two heavy bundles of books, he had boarded the train.

In the center of the Milky Way, fifty thousand light-years from Earth, an interstellar war that had lasted for twenty thousand years was nearing its resolution.

A square-shaped, starless region was visible there, as distinctly as if it had been cut from the background of shining stars with a pair of scissors. Its sides were six thousand miles long, and its interior was blacker even than the blackness of space—a void within a void. Several objects began to emerge from within the square. They were of various shapes, but each was as large as Earth's moon, and their color was a dazzling silver. As more appeared, they took on a regular, cube-shaped formation. The cube of objects continued to emerge from the square, a mosaic set into the eternal wall of the universe itself, whose base was the complete, velvet blackness of the square and whose tiles were the luminescent silver objects. They were like a cosmic symphony given physical form. Slowly, the black square dissolved back into the stars, leaving only the cube-shaped array of silver objects floating ominously.

The interstellar fleet of the Galactic Federation of Carbon-Based Life had completed the first space-time warp of its journey.

The High Archon of the Carbon Federation looked out from the fleet's flagship onto a metallic, silver landscape. An intricate network of paths snaked across the land like circuits etched into an infinitely wide, silver circuit board. Teardrop-shaped craft appeared occasionally on the surface of the land; they shot at blinding speed along the paths, and after a few seconds, noiselessly disappeared into ports that suddenly opened in the surface to receive them. Cosmic dust had clung to the fleet during its warp travel; it formed clouds over the landscape that glowed faintly red as they ionized.

The High Archon was known for his cool demeanor. The endlessly tranquil, azure smart field that usually surrounded him was like a symbol of his personality. At this moment, however, traces of yellow light emerged from his smart field, as they did from the fields of the people around him.

'It's finally over.' The High Archon's smart field vibrated, transmitting his message to the senator and the fleet commander, who stood on either side of him.

'Yes, it's over. This war went on too long—so long that we have forgotten its beginning,' the senator replied.

The fleet began to cruise at sub-light speed. The ships' sub-light engines engaged simultaneously, and thousands of blue suns suddenly appeared around the flagship. The silver land below them reflected the engines' lights like an edgeless, infinite mirror, and each blue sun was doubled in the reflection.

The beginning of the war was a distant, ancient memory, and though it seemed to have been burned away in the fighting, no one had truly forgotten it. It was a memory that had passed through hundreds of generations, but to the trillion citizens of the Carbon Federation, it was still vivid, engraved into their hearts and minds.

Twenty thousand years earlier, the Silicon-Based Empire had launched a full-scale attack against the Carbon Federation from the periphery of the galaxy. The Empire's five million warships leapt from star to star along the ten-thousand-light-year-long battlefront. Each ship first drew power from its star to open a wormhole through space-time, then traveled through the wormhole to another star, which it likewise harnessed to create another wormhole and continue its travel.

Opening a wormhole depleted a large amount of a star's energy and shifted its light toward the red end of the spectrum. After the ship had jumped, the star's light would gradually return to its original state. The collective effect of millions of ships traveling in this way was terrifying. A band of red light ten thousand light-years long appeared at the edge of the galaxy and began moving toward its center, invisible to light-speed observations but clearly visible on hyperspace monitors. The band, created by the red-shifted light of stars, rushed toward the borders of Carbon Federation space, a tide of blood ten thousand light-years across.

The first Carbon Federation planet to be hit by the vanguard of the Silicon Empire forces was Greensea. It was a beautiful planet that orbited a pair of binary stars. Its surface was covered completely by ocean, on which floated great forests of soft, long, vine-like plants. These forests were home to the temperate, beautiful inhabitants of Greensea, who, swimming lithely among the plants with their crystal-clear bodies, had created an Edenic civilization. Tens of thousands of harsh beams of light suddenly pierced the sky of the planet—the lasers of the Silicon Empire fleet—and began evaporating the ocean. In a short time, Greensea's surface became a boiling cauldron, and all life on the planet, including its five billion inhabitants, died in agony in the boiling water. The ocean was completely evaporated in the end, and Greensea, which had once been so beautiful, was left a hellish, gray planet, shrouded in thick steam.

There was virtually nowhere in the galaxy untouched by the war. It was a ruinous fight for survival between carbon-based and silicon-based civilization. Yet neither side had expected the war to last twenty thousand galactic years!

Except for historians, no one remembers how many battles were waged between forces of a million or more ships. The largest-scale battle was the Battle of the Second Arm, which took place in the second spiral arm of the Milky Way Galaxy. In total, more than ten million warships from both fleets participated as combatants. Historical records tell that more than two thousand stars went supernova in the huge battle zone, like fireworks in the black void. They turned the whole spiral arm into an ocean of super-strong radiation, with groups of black holes floating like ghosts in its midst.

By the end of the battle, both sides had lost nearly their entire fleets. Fifteen thousand years had elapsed, and the story of the battle sounded like an ancient myth, except for the fact that the battle zone itself still existed. Ships rarely entered the zone. It was the most terrifying region of the galaxy, and not just because of the radiation and black holes.

During the battle, squadrons of ships from both unthinkably huge fleets made short-distance space-time jumps as a tactical maneuver. It was thought that in dogfights, some interstellar fighters made almost incredible jumps of a few miles at most! These jumps left space-time in the battle zone riddled with holes, more like rags than fabric. Any ship unfortunate enough to stray into the region risked hitting a patch of distorted space. A patch like that could twist a ship into a long, thin, metal pole, or press it into a sheet hundreds of millions of square miles in area and a few atoms thick, which the gale of radiation would immediately shred to pieces. More often, a ship that hit a patch of distorted space-time would regress into the pieces of steel it was made of, or immediately age into a broken husk, everything inside the ship decaying into ancient dust. Anyone aboard would revert in an instant to an embryonic state, or collapse into a pile of bones. . . .

The war's decisive battle was not a myth. It took place a year ago. The Silicon Empire assembled its remaining forces, a fleet of 1.5 million warships, in the desolate space between the galaxy's first and second spiral arms. They set up an antimatter cloud barrier around their location, with a radius of one thousand light-years.

The first Carbon Federation squadron to attack jumped directly to the edge of the cloud and entered it. The cloud was very thin, but it was lethal against warships, and it turned those ships into brilliant fireballs. Dragging long tails of flame from their hulls, the ships bravely continued to advance on their target, streaks of fluorescence in their wakes. An array of thirty thousand or more shooting stars, rushing bravely forward—it was the most magnificent, tragic image from the Carbon-Silicon War.

But these shooting stars thinned out as they passed through the antimatter cloud, and at a location very close to the battle array of the Silicon Empire fleet, they disappeared. They had sacrificed themselves to open a tunnel through the cloud for the rest of the attack fleet. In the battle, the last fleet of the Silicon Empire was driven back to the most desolate region in the Milky Way: the tip of the first spiral arm.

Now, the Carbon Federation fleet was about to complete its final mission: constructing a five-hundred-light-year-wide isolation belt in the middle of the spiral arm. They would destroy most of the stars in the belt to prevent the Silicon Empire from making interstellar jumps. Interstellar jumps were the only way in the Milky Way system for large battleships to carry out fast, long-range attacks, and the greatest distance a ship could jump was two hundred light-years. Once the belt was built, the heavy warships of the Silicon Empire would have to cross five hundred light-years of space at sub-light speeds to get to the central region of the galaxy. In effect, the Silicon Empire would be imprisoned at the tip of the first spiral arm, unable to pose any serious threat to carbon-based civilization in the center of the galaxy.

The senator used his vibrating smart field to speak to the High Archon. 'The will of the Senate is as follows: We maintain our strong recommendation to conduct a life-level protective screening in the belt before commencing stellar destruction.'

'I understand the Senate's caution,' said the High Archon. 'In this long war, the blood of all forms of life has flowed, enough to fill the oceans of thousands of planets. Now that the war has ended, the most pressing concern for the galaxy is to reestablish respect for life—all forms of life, not only carbon-based life, but silicon-based life, as well. The Federation stopped completely annihilating silicon-based civilization on the basis of this ideal. Yet the Silicon Empire has no such qualms. They have an instinctual love for warfare and conquest. It has always been so, even before the Carbon-Silicon War. Now, these inclinations are embedded in each of their genes and in each line of their code. They are the ultimate goals of the Empire. Silicon-based life is far superior to us at storing and processing information. Even here, at the tip of the first spiral arm, their civilization will recover and develop quickly. It is therefore imperative that we construct a sufficiently wide isolation belt between the Federation and the Empire. Given the circumstances, a life scan on each of the hundred million stars in the belt is unrealistic. The first spiral arm may be the most barren region of the galaxy, but there are likely enough stars with inhabited planets to achieve leap density. Medium warships could use them to cross the belt, and just one Silicon Empire medium warship could cause immense damage if it managed to enter Federation space. We cannot conduct a life-level protective screening for each planet, only civilization-level. We must sacrifice the primitive life-forms in the belt, in order to save the advanced *and* primitive life-forms in the rest of the galaxy. I have explained this to the Senate.'

'The Senate recognizes this imperative, sir. You have explained it, as has the Federal Defense Committee. The Senate's statement is a recommendation, not a piece of legislation. However, stars in the belt with life-forms that have reached 3C-civilization status and above must be protected.'

'Rest assured,' said the High Archon, his smart field flashing a determined red. 'We will be extremely thorough in conducting civilization tests for each planetary system in the isolation belt!'

For the first time, the fleet commander's smart field emitted a message. 'I think you are worried over nothing. The first spiral arm is the most barren wasteland in the galaxy. There won't be any 3Cs or above.'

'I hope you are right,' said the High Archon and the senator simultaneously. Their smart fields vibrated in resonance and sent a solitary ripple of plasma into the sky above the metallic land below.

The fleet began its second space-time leap, traveling at near-infinite speed toward the first spiral arm of the galaxy.

It was late at night. The children had gathered by candlelight at the foot of their teacher's sickbed.

'Teacher, you should rest. You can teach us the lesson tomorrow,' said a boy.

The teacher managed a pained smile. 'Tomorrow we have tomorrow's lesson.'

If he could make it to tomorrow, then he would teach tomorrow's lesson. But his gut told him he wouldn't last the night.

He made a gesture, and one of the children placed a small blackboard on the sheet covering his chest. This was how he had been teaching them for a month. The children passed him a half-worn piece of chalk; he grabbed it weakly and put its tip to the blackboard with great effort. A sharp, strong pain shot through him. His hand trembled, knocking the chalk against the blackboard and leaving white dots.

He had not gone to the hospital since he returned from the city. His liver had begun to ache two months later—the cancer had spread.

The pain got worse with time until it overwhelmed everything. He groped under his pillow for a pain pill, the common, over-the-counter kind, packaged in plastic. They were completely ineffective at relieving the agony of late-stage cancer, but they had a bit of value as a placebo. Demerol wasn't expensive, but patients weren't allowed to take it out of the hospital, and even if they were, there was no one to administer the shot. As usual, he pushed two pills out of the plastic strip. He thought for a moment, then pushed out the remaining twelve pills and swallowed them all. He knew he would have no use for them later.

Again, he turned his attention to the blackboard and struggled to write out the lesson, but a cough overcame him. He turned his head to the side, where a child had rushed to hold up a bowl next to his mouth. He spit out a mouthful of red and black blood, then reclined on his pillow to catch his breath.

Several of the children stifled sobs.

He abandoned his effort to write on the blackboard. He waved his hand, and a child came over to remove it from his chest. In a small voice, almost a whisper, he began to speak.

'Like our lessons yesterday and the day before, today's lesson is meant for middle schoolers. It is not on your syllabus. Most of you will never have a chance to attend middle school, so I thought I would give you a taste of what it's like to study a subject in greater depth. Yesterday, we read Lu Xun's *Diary of a Madman*. You probably didn't understand much of it, but I want you to read it a few more times, or, better yet, learn to recite it from memory. You'll understand it when you're older. Lu Xun was a remarkable man. Every Chinese person should read his books. I hope all of you would in the future.'

He stopped speaking to rest for a moment and catch his breath. He looked at the flickering candle flame. Another passage of Lu Xun came to him. It wasn't from *Diary of a Madman*, and it hadn't been in his textbook. He had encountered it many years before, in his own incomplete, thumbed-through set of Lu Xun's collected works. Since the first time he read it, he hadn't forgotten a single word.

'Imagine a windowless, iron room. Many people lie asleep inside. They will soon suffocate and die in their sleep. However, from sleep to death, people won't feel the agony. You shout, and a few hopeless sleepers awaken to a wretched fate that you are powerless to prevent. Have you done them a favor?'

'But if there are several people awaken, there will be hope to destroy the iron room.'

With the last of his strength, he continued his lecture.

'Today's class is middle school physics. You may not have heard of physics before. It is the study of the principles of the physical world. It's an extremely rich, deep field of knowledge.

'We will learn about Newton's three laws. Newton was an important English scientist who lived a long time ago. He came up with three remarkable rules. These rules apply to everything in heaven and on Earth, from the sun and moon in the sky down to the water and air of our own planet. Nothing can escape Newton's three truths. With them, we can calculate to the second when solar eclipses—when the 'sun dog eats the sun,' as our village elders say—will happen. Humans can fly to the moon using Newton's three laws.

'The first law is as follows: A body at rest or moving in a straight line at a constant speed will maintain its velocity unless an outside force acts upon it.'

The children watched him silently in the candlelight. No one stirred.

'This means that if you took the grindstone from the mill and gave it a good push, it should keep rolling, all the way to the horizon. What are you laughing at, Baozhu? You're right, that wouldn't actually happen. That's because a force called friction will bring the stone to a halt. There is nowhere in the world without friction.'

That's right, nowhere in the world without friction—his life, especially. He didn't have the village surname,[1] so his words carried no weight. And he was so stubborn! Over the years he had offended practically everyone in the village in one way or another. He had gone door-to-door persuading each family to put their kids in school, and he had gotten some kids to stop following their parents to work by swearing he'd cover their tuition himself. None of this endeared him to the villagers. The plain truth was that his ideas about how to live were just too different from theirs. He talked all day about

---

1   In many Chinese villages, residents share a common, ancestral surname.

things that were meaningless to them, and it annoyed them.

Before he'd learned of his cancer, he had gone once to town and brought back some funds from the Education Bureau to repair the school. The villagers took a bit of the money to hire an opera troupe to perform for two days in an upcoming festival. This bothered the teacher deeply. He went to town again, and this time he brought back a vice county head, who made the villagers return the money. They had already built a stage for the singers. The school was repaired, but that was the end of what little goodwill there was for him in the village, and his life was even more difficult from then on.

First, the village electrician, the village head's nephew, cut off the school's electricity. Then they stopped giving the school cornstalks for heating and cooking, forcing him to abandon planting and spend his time in the hills instead, looking for kindling. Then there was the incident with the rafters in the dorm. Friction was omnipresent, exhausting his body and soul, making him unable to move in a straight line at a constant speed. He had to come to a stop.

Maybe the place he was heading was a frictionless world where everything was smooth and lovely. But what was there for him in a place like that? His heart would still be in this world of dust and friction, in the primary school he had devoted his whole life to. After he left, the two remaining teachers would leave, too, and the school would grind to a halt, like the village millstone. He fell into a deep sorrow—in this world or the next, he had no hope of changing the world.

'Newton's second law is a little tricky, so we'll leave it for last. His third law is as follows: When a body exerts force on a second body, the second body will exert an equal force on the first body in the opposite direction.'

The children were silent for a long time.

'Do you understand? Who can explain it back to me?'

Zhao Labao, his best student, stood and spoke. 'I get the idea, but it doesn't make sense. This morning I got into a fight with Li Quangui and he hit me right in the face. It really hurt, and I've got a lump, right here. Those aren't equal forces!'

The teacher took a while to catch his breath, then explained, 'The reason you hurt is that your cheek is softer than Quangui's fist. They exerted equal forces against each other.'

He wanted to make a gesture to illustrate his point, but he couldn't lift his hand anymore. His limbs felt as heavy as iron, and soon his whole body felt heavy enough to collapse the bed and sink into the ground.

There wasn't much time.

Target Number: 1033715
Absolute Magnitude: 3.5
Evolutionary Stage: Upper Main Sequence
Two planets found, average orbital radii 1.3 and 4.7 Distance Units
Life discovered on Planet One
This is Vessel Red 69012 reporting

The hundred thousand warships of the Carbon Federation's interstellar fleet had spread out across a ten-thousand-light-year-long band of space to begin construction of the isolation belt. The first stage of the project was the trial destruction of five thousand stars. Only 137 of those star systems had planets; this was the first planet they had found with life.

'The first spiral arm is truly a barren place,' said the High Archon, sighing. His smart field vibrated, initiating a holographic projection that concealed the floor of the flagship and the stars overhead. The High Archon, the fleet commander, and the senator all appeared to be floating in a limitless void. Then, the High Archon switched the hologram feed to display the information sent back by the probe, and a glowing, blue fireball appeared in the middle of the void. The High Archon's smart field produced a white, square box; it adjusted its shape and moved to enclose the image of the star, plunging the space into near-darkness again. This time, however, a small point of yellow light remained. The focal length of the image adjusted rapidly, and in an instant, the yellow dot zoomed into the foreground, fully occupying half of the void. The three of them were bathed in its reflected, orange radiance.

It was a planet covered in a thick, tempestuous atmosphere, like an orange ocean. The motion of the gas produced an extremely complex, ever-changing lattice of lines. The image of the planet continued to grow until it seemed to occupy the whole universe, and they were swallowed by its orange, gaseous ocean. The probe took them through the thick clouds to a place where the fog was slightly thinner, enabling them to see the planet's life-forms.

In the upper part of the thick atmosphere floated a school of balloon-shaped animals. Their bodies were covered in kaleidoscopic patterns that changed from stripes to spots to all sorts of wonderful designs—perhaps a sort of visual language. Each balloon had a long tail whose tip occasionally produced a flash of light that traveled up the tail and into the balloon's body, where it became a diffuse fluorescence.

'Commence the four-dimensional scan!' said the pilot in command of Vessel Red 69012.

An extremely thin beam swept quickly across the balloons from top to bottom. Though the beam was only a few atoms thick, the interior of the beam had one more spatial dimension than normal space. It transmitted data from the scan back to the ship, and in the storage of the ship's main computer, the balloon creatures were cut into hundreds of billions of thin slices. Each slice was an atom-thick cross section that recorded everything with near-perfect accuracy, down to the state of each quark.

'Commence data mirror assembly!'

The ship's computer rearranged the hundreds of billions of cross-sectional images in its storage in their original order, superimposing them. Soon, a hollow balloon took shape—a perfect replica of the life-form they had found on the planet, re-created in the computer's vast digital universe.

'Commence 3C Civilization Test!'

The computer quickly identified the being's thinking organ, an elliptical structure that hung at the center of an intricate plexus of nerves. The computer analyzed the structure of the brain in an instant and established a direct, high-speed information interface with it, bypassing all of the creature's lower sensory organs.

The civilization test consisted of a set of questions selected at random from an enormous database. Three correct answers were considered a pass. If a life-form failed to answer the first three questions correctly, the tester had two options: He could end the test and declare a failure, or he could provide more questions. Three correct answers were considered a pass, regardless of how many questions the tester asked.

'3C Civilization Test, Question One: Please describe the smallest unit of matter you have discovered.'

'Dee-dee, doo-doo-doo, dee-dee-dee-dee,' answered the balloon.

'Incorrect. 3C Civilization Test, Question Two: According to your observations, in what direction does thermal energy flow through matter? Can its flow be reversed?'

'Doo-doo-doo, dee-dee, dee-dee-doo-doo,' answered the balloon.

'Incorrect. 3C Civilization Test, Question Three: What is the ratio of a circle's circumference to its diameter?'

'Dee-dee-dee-dee-doo-doo-doo-doo-doo,' answered the balloon.

'Incorrect. 3C Civilization Test, Question Four . . .'

'That's enough,' said the High Archon, after the tenth question. 'We don't have much time.' He turned and signaled to the fleet commander.

'Fire the singularity bomb!' ordered the commander.

Strictly speaking, a singularity bomb was a sizeless object, a point in space, infinitely smaller than an atom. It had mass, though: the largest singularity bombs were billions of tons, and the smallest were more than ten million tons. When the bomb slid out of the arsenal of Vessel Red 69012, it appeared as a sphere, several thousand feet in diameter, that glowed with a faint fluorescence—radiation generated as the miniature black hole consumed the space dust in its path.

Unlike black holes formed by the collapse of stars, these miniature black holes were formed at the beginning of the universe, tiny models of the universal singularity that preceded the big bang. Both the Carbon Federation and the Silicon Empire maintained fleets of ships that cruised the empty space beyond the galactic equator collecting these primordial black holes. Inhabitants of some marine planets called these fleets 'deep-sea trawlers.' The 'catches' that these fleets brought back were one of the most potent weapons in the galaxy, and the only weapon that could annihilate a star.

The singularity bomb left its guide rail and accelerated along a force-field beam from the ship toward its target star. It arrived in short order, a dusty black hole that quickly plunged into the star's fiery exterior. Stellar matter rushed from all directions in a turbulent arc toward the center of the black hole, where it disappeared. Copious radiation poured from the black hole, which appeared now as a blinding ball of light on the surface of the star, a diamond on the ring of the star's circumference.

As the black hole sank into the star's interior, the radiant orb grew dimmer, revealing the enormous, hundred-million-mile-wide vortex that encircled the orb. The rotating vortex scattered the orb's light in a kaleidoscopic display that looked, from the vantage of the ship, like a hideous, prismatic face. A moment later, the orb disappeared, as did the vortex, though more slowly; the star appeared to have returned to its original color and luminosity. This was the eye of the storm, the final moment of silence before annihilation.

The voracious black hole sank toward the dense center of the star, devouring everything in its path. In less than a second, it swallowed a mass of stellar material greater than the mass of a hundred medium-sized planets. Super-strong radiation spread out from the black hole toward the surface of the star. Some of it escaped, but most of it was blocked by stellar material, adding enough energy to the star to disrupt its convection and knock it out of equilibrium. The star's color began to shift, first from red to bright yellow, then to bright green, then to a deep, sapphire blue, and then to a forbidding violet. The radiation from the black hole by now was orders of magnitude more intense than the radiation from the star itself, and as more energy flowed out of the star in the form of nonvisible light, its violet color intensified—a spirit in agony, floating in the vastness of space. Within an hour, the star's billion-year journey had come to a close.

There was a flash of light that seemed to swallow the whole universe, then faded slowly away. Where the star had been, there was now a thin, spherical layer of material expanding rapidly, like a balloon being blown up. This was the surface of the star, swept outward in the explosion. As it expanded, it became transparent, and a second hollow sphere grew in its center, followed by a third. These waves of material were like exquisitely painted glass orbs, one inside another, and even the smallest of them had a surface area tens of thousands times larger than the original surface area of the star. The first wave vaporized the orange planet in an instant, though it was impossible to see its destruction against such a magnificent background. Compared to the size of the expanding stellar layer, the planet was a speck of dust, not even a dot on the surface of the orb.

The smart fields of the High Archon and the senator darkened. 'Do you find this work distressing?' asked the fleet commander.

'Another species gone, like dew in the sun.'

'Think of the Battle of the Second Arm, Your Excellency—more than two thousand supernovas detonated, one hundred and twenty thousand planets with life vaporized. We do not have the luxury to be sentimental.'

The senator ignored the fleet commander. He addressed the High Archon directly. 'Random planetary spot checks are unreliable. There may be signs of civilization elsewhere on a planet's surface. We should implement area scans, as well.'

The High Archon said, 'I have discussed that possibility with the Senate. We must destroy hundreds of millions of stars in the isolation belt. We estimate the belt contains ten million planetary systems and fifty million planets. Our time is limited; we will not be able to conduct a full area scan on each planet. All we can feasibly do is widen the detection beam to scan larger random samples . . . and pray the civilizations that might exist here have spread uniformly across their planets' surfaces.'

'Next, we'll learn Newton's second law.'

He spoke as quickly as he could, to teach the children as much as possible in the short time he had left.

'An object's acceleration is directly proportional to the force acting on it, and inversely proportional to its mass. To understand that, you need to know what acceleration is. Acceleration is the rate at which an object's speed changes over time. It's different from speed—an object that's moving fast isn't necessarily *accelerating* rapidly, and a quickly accelerating object may not be moving fast. For example, say there's an object moving at 110 meters per second. Two seconds later, it is moving at 120 meters per second. Its acceleration is 120 minus 110, divided by two . . . that's five meters per second—no, five meters per second squared. Another object is moving at ten meters per second, but two seconds later, it's moving at thirty meters per second. Its acceleration is thirty minus ten, divided by two—ten meters per second squared. The second object may not be as fast as the first, but its acceleration is greater! I mentioned squares—a square is just a number multiplied by itself . . .'

He was surprised that his thinking was suddenly so clear. He knew what this meant: If life is a candle, his had burned to its base, and its wick had fallen and ignited the last bit of wax there, with a flame ten times brighter than before. His pain was gone and his body no longer felt heavy; in fact, he was barely aware of his body at all. The life he had left seemed to be in his brain, which worked furiously to convey all its knowledge to the children gathered around him. Language was a bottleneck—he knew he didn't have enough time. He fantasized that the knowledge he had spent his life accumulating—not much, but dear to him—was lodged in his brain like small pearls, and that as he spoke, a crystal ax chopped the pearls out of his brain onto the floor, where the children scrambled to gather them like sweets at New Year's. It was a happy fantasy.

'Do you understand?' he asked restlessly. He could no longer see the children around him, but he could still hear them.

'We understand! Now please rest, teacher!'

He felt his flame begin to sputter. 'I know you don't understand, but memorize it anyway. Someday, it will make sense to you. *The acceleration of an object is directly proportional to the force acting on it, and inversely proportional to the object's mass.'*

'We really do understand, teacher! Please, please rest!'

With his last ounce of strength, he gave the children a command. 'Recite it!'

Through tears, the children began to chant. 'The acceleration of an object is directly proportional to the force acting on it, and inversely proportional to the object's mass. The acceleration of an object is directly proportional to the force acting on it, and inversely proportional to the object's mass. . . .'

Hundreds of years ago, one of the world's great minds emerged in Europe, wrote down these words. Now, in the twentieth century, they filled the air of China's most remote mountain village, recited by a chorus of children in a thick, rural accent. In the sound of that sweet hymn, his candle burned out.

The children gathered around his body and wept.

> *Target Number: 500921473*
> *Absolute Magnitude: 4.71*
> *Evolutionary Stage: Middle Main Sequence*
> *Nine planets found*
> *This is Vessel Blue 84210 reporting*

'What an exquisite planetary system,' the fleet commander exclaimed.

The High Archon agreed. 'Indeed. Its small, rocky planets and gas giants are spaced with wonderful harmony, and its asteroid belt is in a beautiful location, like a necklace. And its farthest planet, a little dwarf covered in methane ice, suggesting the end of one thing and the beginning of another, like the final note of a musical cadence . . .'

'This is Vessel Blue 84210. We are commencing a life scan on Planet One. This planet has no atmosphere, a slow rotation, and a huge temperature differential. Scan beam is firing. First random site: white. Second random site: white. . . . Tenth random site: white. Vessel Blue 84210 reports that this planet has no life.'

'You could smelt iron on the surface of that planet. We shouldn't waste time,' said the fleet commander.

'We are commencing a life scan on Planet Two. This planet has a thick atmosphere; a high, uniform temperature; and substantial acidic cloud cover. Scan beam is firing. First random site: white. Second random site: white. . . . Tenth random site: white. Vessel Blue 84210 reporting—this planet has no life.'

'I have a strong feeling that Planet Three harbors life. Scan thirty random sites,' said the High Archon, his message traveling instantly over the four-dimensional communicator to the duty officer of Vessel Blue 84210, over one thousand light-years away.

'Excellency, our schedule is very tight,' said the fleet commander.

'You have your orders,' said the High Archon resolutely.

'Yes, Your Excellency.'

'We are commencing a life scan on Planet Three. This planet has a medium-density atmosphere, and most of its surface is covered by ocean . . .'

The first shot of the life-scan beam struck a circle of land in Asia around three miles across. In the light of day, the effect of the beam would have been visible to the naked eye—it turned every nonliving object in its field transparent. The scan hit the mountains of northwest China; in daylight, an observer would have seen a spectacular sight as sunlight refracted through the mountain range and the ground under her feet seemed to disappear, revealing an abyss into the depths of the planet. Living things—people, trees, grass—remained opaque, and their forms would have stood out clearly against the crystal background. However, this effect only lasted for the half a second it took the beam to initialize, and onlookers would likely assume they had imagined it. Besides, it was nighttime.

In the direct center of the beam's field was the village school.

'First random site . . . we've got green! Vessel Blue 84210 reporting—we have discovered life on target number 500921473, Planet Three!'

The beam began automatically to sort the many life-forms it had hit, entering them into its database in order of complexity and according to an initial intelligence estimate. At the top of the list was a group of life-forms inside a square shelter. The beam narrowed and focused on the shelter.

The High Archon's smart field received an image transmission from Vessel Blue 84210. He projected it onto the black background, and in an instant, he was standing within a projection of the village school. The image-processing system had removed the shelter from view, but the life-forms inside were still hard to make out, as their bodies were so similar to the silicon-based planetary surface around them. The computer eliminated all nonliving objects in the image, including the larger, lifeless body the other beings encircled, and the beings now appeared suspended in a void. Even so, they were still dull and colorless, like a bunch of plants. This was clearly not a species with any remarkable phenotypic features.

Vessel Blue 84210 was an interstellar warship as large as Earth's moon, and in its position outside Jupiter's orbit, it was like an extra planet in the solar system. It fired a four-dimensional beam that moved through three-dimensional space nearly instantaneously. In a moment, the beam had arrived at Earth and pierced the roof of the village school's dorm. It scanned the eighteen children inside down to their elementary particles and transmitted the enormous amount of data back into space at an unimaginable rate. The main computer of Vessel Blue 84210 had a storage capacity larger than the universe itself; in an instant, digital copies of the children were constructed and stored there.

The eighteen children floated in an endless void whose color was indescribable. In fact, it didn't strictly have a color. It was a limitless field of perfect transparency. The children instinctively tried to grab hold of nearby classmates, but their hands passed through their bodies without resistance. They were terrified. The computer detected their fear and judged that they required some familiar objects for comfort, so it altered the color of the simulation's background to match their home planet's sky. Immediately, the children saw a cloudless, sunless, deep blue sky. There was no ground beneath them, just endless blue, the same as above, and they were the only things in it.

The computer reassessed the digital children and found they were still panicking. In a hundred-millionth of a second, it understood why: Whereas most life in the galaxy had no fear of floating, these creatures were different in that they lived on land. The computer added Earth-like gravity and a ground to the simulation. The children were astonished to find under their feet a pure white plain, extending into infinity in all directions and crossed by a neat, regular black grid, like a huge piece of writing paper. A few children crouched down to touch the ground, and it was the smoothest surface they had ever touched; they tried taking a few steps, but the ground was completely frictionless and didn't move beneath them. They wondered why they didn't fall down. One child took off a shoe and threw it level with the ground. It slid along at a regular speed, and the children watched it glide off into the distance, never decelerating.

They had seen Newton's first law.

A melodious, ethereal voice permeated the digital universe.

'Commencing 3C Civilization Test. Question One: Please describe the basic principles of biological evolution on your planet. Is it driven by natural selection or spontaneous mutations?'

The children had no idea. They stayed silent.

'3C Civilization Test, Question Two: Please briefly describe the source of a star's power.'

Silence.

. . .

'3C Civilization Test, Question Ten: Please describe the chemical composition of the liquid in your planet's oceans.'

The children still did not speak.

The shoe had slid off into the horizon, where it became a black point and disappeared.

'That's enough!' said the fleet commander to the High Archon, one thousand light-years distant. 'We won't be able to complete the first phase of the project on time if we keep on like this.'

The High Archon's smart field vibrated slightly, signaling his consent.

'Fire the singularity bomb!'

The beam containing the command shot through four-dimensional space and arrived immediately at Vessel Blue 84210, which was holding its position in the solar system. A faintly glowing ball left the long track at the front of the ship and accelerated along an invisible force field toward the sun.

The High Archon, the senator, and the fleet commander turned their attention to another region of the isolation belt, where several planetary systems with life had been discovered, the most advanced of which was a brainless, mud-dwelling worm. Exploding stars filled the region, like galactic fireworks. They all thought of the Battle of the Second Arm.

A while later, a small portion of the High Archon's smart field split off from the rest and turned its attention back to the solar system. He heard the captain of Vessel Blue 84210.

'Prepare to exit the blast radius. T minus thirty to warp. Commence countdown!'

'A moment, please. How long until the singularity bomb reaches its target?' asked the High Archon, attracting the attention of the fleet commander and the senator.

'It's passing the orbit of the system's first planet. Approximately ten minutes to impact.'

'We will take five minutes to continue the test.'

'Yes, Your Excellency.'

The duty officer of Vessel Blue 84210 continued administering the test. '3C Civilization Test, Question Eleven: What is the relationship between the three sides of a right triangle on a flat plane in three-dimensional space?'

Silence.

'3C Civilization Test, Question Twelve: Where is your planet's position relative to the other planets in your star system?'

Silence.

'This is pointless, Your Excellency,' said the fleet commander.

'3C Civilization Test, Question Thirteen: How does an object move when it is not subjected to any external forces?'

Beneath the endless blue sky of the simulated universe, the children recited, 'A body at rest or moving in a straight line at a constant speed will maintain its velocity unless an outside force acts upon it.'

'Correct! 3C Civilization Test, Question Fourteen . . .'

'Wait!' called out the senator, interrupting the duty officer administering the test. 'The next question is also about heuristics in low-speed mechanics. Doesn't that violate the test guidelines?' he asked the High Archon.

'Of course not, as long as the question is in the database,' interjected the fleet commander. He was shocked that these unassuming life-forms had answered a question correctly, and all his attention was now on them.

'3C Civilization Test, Question Fourteen: Please describe how two objects exerting force on each other interact.'

'When a body exerts force on a second body, the second body will exert an equal force on the first body in the opposite direction!' said the children.

'Correct! 3C Civilization Test, Question Fifteen: Please describe the relationship between an object's mass and acceleration when an external force acts upon it.'

In unison, the children said, 'The acceleration of an object is directly proportional to the force acting on it, and inversely proportional to the object's mass!'

'Correct! You have passed the Civilization Test! Confirming that there is a 3C-level civilization on Planet Three of Target Star 500921473.'

'Reverse the singularity bomb! Disengage!!' The High Archon's smart field flashed and vibrated frantically as he sent his order through hyperspace to Vessel Blue 84210.

The force-field beam began to bend. Its hundred-million-mile path through the solar system curved away from the sun, like a tree branch that had been weighed down. As the force-field engine on board Vessel Blue 84210 worked at maximum power, its enormous heat sink glowed, first dark red, then with a bright white incandescence. The beam's new thrust vector began to affect the trajectory of the singularity bomb, which curved away from its target. However, it was already inside the orbit of Mercury, very close to the sun, and no one was confident that the force-field engine could bend its course enough to prevent impact.

The whole galaxy watched over hyperspace as the fuzzy, dark ball veered and grew substantially brighter, a worrisome sign that it had already entered the particle-rich space around the sun. The captain's hand rested on the red hyperspace button, ready to leap away from the solar system the moment before impact.

In the end, the bomb shot by the very edge of the sun, only a few dozen miles from its surface, sucking in huge amounts of material from the sun's atmosphere as it brushed past. It glowed intensely with a blue-white light, and for a moment, the sun appeared to have a brighter twin star locked in close, binary orbit, a phenomenon that was to become an enduring mystery to the inhabitants of Earth. The sun's fiery surface darkened beneath the bomb, like the wake of a speedboat in calm water, and as the black hole swept past the solar surface, its gravity consumed the sun's light, scratching a dark, crescent scar into the sun's surface which grew to eclipse the whole solar hemisphere. As the bomb left the sun, it dragged an enormous solar prominence behind it, a beautiful string of flame one million miles long. The tip of the prominence flared violently outward, blossoming into a mass of whirling plasma vortices.

After the singularity bomb brushed past the sun, it grew dark again. Soon, it disappeared into the infinite night of space.

'We almost destroyed a carbon-based civilization,' said the senator, heaving a sigh of relief.

'A 3C-level civilization here, in this desert—unbelievable!' exclaimed the fleet commander.

'Yes. Neither the Carbon Federation nor the Silicon Empire has included this region in its plans for expansion and cultivation. If this civilization were to have evolved entirely on its own, that would be a rare thing indeed,' said the High Archon.

'Vessel Blue 84210, you are to hold your position in that star system and commence a full-surface civilization test on Planet Three. Another ship will take over your prior mission,' ordered the fleet commander.

The children in the village didn't notice anything amiss, unlike their digital replicas outside of Jupiter's orbit. They were still crying over their teacher's body in their candlelit dormitory. After a long time, they quieted down.

'We should go tell a grown-up,' said Guo Cuihua, stifling a sob.

'What for?' asked Liu Baozhu, his eyes on the floor. 'No one in this village cared about him when he was alive. I bet they won't even pay for a coffin!'

In the end, the children decided to bury their teacher themselves. With pickaxes and shovels, they dug a grave in a hill next to the school, and the brilliant stars above silently watched them work.

The senator watched Vessel Blue 84210's test results as they streamed instantly across a thousand light-years of space. 'The civilization on this planet isn't 3C—it's 5B!' he exclaimed, astonished.

The skyscrapers of human cities appeared as holograms aboard the flagship.

'They have already begun using nuclear energy, and they can fly into space using chemical propellants. They've even landed on their moon.'

'What are their basic features?' asked the fleet commander.

'You'll have to be more specific,' said the duty officer of Vessel Blue 84210.

'Well, how advanced is their heritable memory?'

'They don't inherit memories. They acquire all their memories during their lives.'

'What method do they use to communicate information to each other?'

'It's very primitive, and very rare. There is a thin organ in their bodies that vibrates, producing waves in their planet's atmosphere, which is primarily composed of nitrogen and oxygen. By modulating the vibrations, they encode information into the waves. They have separate organs—thin membranes—that receive the waves.'

'What's the transmission rate of that method?'

'Approximately one to ten bits per second.'

'What?!' Everyone on the flagship laughed out loud.

'It's true. We were incredulous at first, but it's been verified repeatedly.'

'Captain, this is lunacy!' yelled the fleet commander. 'You are telling us that an organism without *any* hereditary memory that transmits information using sound waves at *one to ten bits per second* can form a 5B-level civilization?! And that they developed this civilization entirely on their own, without any external assistance from an advanced civilization?!'

'Sir, that is the case.'

'If that's so, they have no way to pass knowledge between generations. Accumulated knowledge across generations is necessary for civilization to evolve!'

'There is a class of individuals, a certain proportion of the population spread evenly among their civilization. They act as mediums for the transmission of knowledge between generations.'

'That sounds like a myth.'

'It's not,' said the senator. 'Such a concept existed in the galaxy in prehistoric times, but even then, it was extremely rare. No one would know about it except historians of the evolution of civilization like me in the star systems where the idea had currency.'

'By 'concept,' you mean individuals that transmit knowledge between generations of a species?'

'Yes. They're called 'teachers.''

'Tea—cher?'

'An ancient word that was once in currency among a few long-lost civilizations. It's rare enough that it does not appear in most ancient vocabulary databases.'

The holographic feed from the solar system zoomed out to display the blue orb of Earth rotating slowly in space.

The High Archon said, 'A civilization evolving independently is rare enough, but I know of no other civilization in the Milky Way that has attained 5B level on its own, at least in the era of the Carbon Federation. We should let this civilization continue its evolution without interference, observing it as it does, not only to further our understanding of ancient civilizations, but also, perhaps, to gain insight into our broader galactic civilization.'

'I'll have Vessel Blue 84210 leave the star system immediately and designate a hundred-light-year no-fly zone around it,' said the fleet commander.

Insomniacs in the northern hemisphere might have seen a small group of stars begin to flutter slightly, then the stars around those, and so on across the whole sky, as if a finger had been dipped into the still water of the night sky.

The space-time shock wave caused by Vessel Blue 84210's hyperspace leap was considerably attenuated by the time it hit Earth. Every clock jumped three seconds ahead. Humans, confined as we are to three-dimensional space, were unaware of the disturbance.

'It's a pity,' said the High Archon. 'They'll be confined to sub-light speeds and three-dimensional space for another two thousand years without the intervention of a more advanced civilization. It will be at least a thousand years before they can harness the energy of matter-antimatter annihilation. Two thousand more years before they can transmit and receive multidimensional communications . . . and as for hyperspace galactic travel, that will take them at least five thousand years. It will be at least ten thousand years before they attain the minimum conditions for entry into the galactic family of carbon-based life-forms.'

The senator said, 'Independent evolution of this sort happened only in the prehistoric era of the galaxy. If our records of those times are correct, my distant ancestors lived in the deep ocean of a marine planet. They lived and died there in darkness, their governments rose and fell, and then, at some point, they felt adventurous. They launched a craft toward space—a buoyant, transparent ball that rose slowly to the surface of the ocean. It was the dead of night when they reached the surface. The people inside the craft were the first of my ancestors to see the stars. Can you imagine how they felt? Can you imagine how glorious and mysterious that sight was to them?'

The High Archon said, 'It was an era full of passion and yearning. A terrestrial planet was a complete, limitless world to our ancestors. From their home in a planet's green waters or on its purple grasslands, they looked up at the stars with awe. We have not known such a feeling for tens of millions of years.'

'I feel it now!' said the senator, pointing at the holographic image of Earth. It was a lustrous, blue ball, with white clouds floating above its surface, streaking and billowing. The senator felt as if he had found a pearl in the depths of his ancestors' ocean home. 'Such a small planet, populated by organisms living their lives, dreaming their dreams, completely oblivious to us and to the strife and destruction in their galaxy. To them, the universe must seem like a bottomless well of hopes and dreams. It's like an ancient song.'

And he began to sing. The smart fields of the three became as one, rippling with rose-colored waves. The song he sang was old, passed down from the forgotten beginnings of civilization itself. It sounded distant, mysterious, forlorn, and as it propagated through hyperspace to the hundreds of billions of stars in the galaxy, countless beings heard its sound and felt a long-forgotten kind of comfort and peace.

'The most incomprehensible thing about the universe is that it is comprehensible,'[1] said the High Archon.

'The most comprehensible thing about the universe is that it is incomprehensible,' said the senator.

There was light in the east by the time the children had finished digging the grave. They tore the door off the classroom and put their teacher's body on it, and they buried him with two boxes of chalk and a used textbook. They stood a stone slab on top of the mound, and wrote on it in chalk: *Mister Li's Grave.*

The faint letters would wash off in the first rainfall, and not long after that, the grave and the person it contained would be forgotten completely.

The tip of the sun rose above the hills, casting a golden ray into the

---

1   Albert Einstein, *Physics and Reality.*

sleeping village. The grass of the valley was still in shadow, but its dew glowed with the light of dawn. A bird or two began timidly to sing.

The children walked along the narrow road back into the village. Their little shadows soon disappeared into the pale blue morning mist of the valley.

They were going to live their lives on that ancient, barren land, and though their harvests would be meager, they would always have hope.

中国太阳

SUN OF CHINA

TRANSLATED BY ELIZABETH HANLON

韩恩立 译

Prologue

Shui Wah took the small parcel from his mother's trembling hands. It contained one pair of thick-soled shoes she had sewn herself, three steamed buns, two heavily patched coats, and twenty yuan. His father squatted by the roadside, sullenly smoking a long-stemmed pipe.

'Our son is leaving home. Would it kill you to put on a good face?' Ma scolded Pa. When she met with stony silence, she added, 'Fine, don't let him go. Can you afford to build him a house and find him a wife?'

'Go then! East, west, they all leave in the end! I'd have been better off raising a litter of puppies!' Pa bawled, without looking up.

Shui[1] lifted his eyes to the village in which he had been born and raised. Condemned to perpetual drought, the villagers scraped by on what little rainwater they could collect in cisterns. Shui's family had no money to build a cistern out of cement, and had to make do with an earthen one instead. On hot days, the water stank. In years past, the foul water had been safe to drink after boiling, just a little bitter, a bit astringent. This summer, however, even the boiled water gave them diarrhea. They had heard from a local military doctor that some toxic mineral had leached into the water from the ground.

With one last glance at his father, Shui turned and walked away. He did not look back. He did not expect Pa to watch him go. When Pa felt miserable, he would crouch over his pipe for hours, unmoving, as if he had become a clod of dirt on the yellow earth. But he still clearly saw Pa's face, or perhaps it was better to say he walked upon it. Northwestern China stretched

---

1　虽然水娃并不姓水，但考虑到文化习惯，此处保留了"水"的简称。——编者注

around him, a vast expanse of parched ochre, lined with cracks and gullies carved by erosion. Was the face of an old farmer any different? The trees, the soil, the houses, the people — everything was blackened, yellowed, wrinkled. He could not see the eyes of this face that stretched toward the horizon, but he could feel their presence, staring toward the sky. In youth, that gaze had been filled with longing for rain; in old age, it had grown glassy.

In fact, this giant visage had always been dull and impassive. He did not believe this land had ever been young.

There was a sudden gust of wind, and the path out of the village was swallowed in yellow dust. Shui followed this road, taking his first step toward his new life. It was a road that would lead him to places beyond his wildest dreams.

Life Goal #1:
Drink some water that is not bitter, make some money.

'Oh, there are so many lights!'

Night had fallen by the time Shui reached the cluster of many small, unauthorized coal pits and kilns that constituted the mining district.

'Those? Hardly. Now in the city, that's a lot of lights,' said Guo Qiang, who had come to meet him. Guo was from the same village as Shui, but he had left many years ago.

Shui followed Guo to the workers' bunkhouse for the night. At dinnertime, he was delighted to discover that the water tasted pleasantly sweet. Guo told him a deep well had been drilled in the district, so naturally the water was good. 'But go to the city,' he added, '*that's* sweet water!'

Before bed, Guo handed Shui a hard, wrapped bundle to used as a pillow. He opened it and saw round sticks covered in black plastic. Peeling back the plastic, he saw that the sticks were yellowish, like soap.

'Dynamite,' Guo mumbled before he rolled over and started snoring. Shui noticed that his head rested on the same sort of 'pillow'. There was a stack of dynamite beneath the bed, and a cluster of blast caps dangled above his head. Later, Shui learned that there were enough explosives in the bunkhouse to blow his whole village sky high. Guo was the mine's blast technician.

Work at the mine was hard and tiring. Shui ran back and forth, digging coal, pushing carts, erecting props, and doing other odd jobs. He was dead tired at the end of each day. But Shui had grown up with hardship, and he did not fear it. What did frighten him were the conditions in the pit. The descent felt like burrowing into a dark anthill. At first, it felt like a waking nightmare, but later he grew accustomed to this, too. He was paid a piece rate, and he could make 150 yuan every month. He could even earn 200 when the work was good. He was quite content with this.

But what satisfied Shui most of all was the water. After his first day of work, his entire body was blackened with soot, so he followed his fellow miners to the showers. When he entered, he watched as they used washbasins to ladle water from a large pool. They then rinsed themselves, letting the water stream down from head to toe, black rivulets running across the earth. He was utterly astounded. *Ma, how can they waste such sweet water like this?* In Shui's eyes, it was that sweet, fresh water that made this dusty, blackened world beautiful beyond comparison.

Guo, however, urged Shui to move to the city. He had previously worked as a laborer there, but because he had stolen from a construction site, he had been labeled a vagrant and sent back to his registered home. He assured Shui that he could earn more money in the city. Moreover, he could do so without having to work himself to death, as in the mine.

Shui hesitated, but as he struggled to make up his mind, Guo met with an accident in the pit. He was removing a dud stick of dynamite when it exploded. He had to be carried from the pit, his body riddled with shards of rock. Before he died, he turned to Shui and rasped, 'Go to the city... there are more lights there . . .'

Life Goal #2:
Go to a city with more lights and sweeter water, make more money.

'Night here is as bright as day!' exclaimed Shui. Guo had not been mistaken. There really were many more lights in the city. At that moment, he was following Junior, carrying a shoeshiner's trunk on his back. They were walking along the main thoroughfare of the provincial capital toward the train station. Junior was from a village that neighbored Shui's home, and he had once worked together with Guo in the provincial capital. Despite Guo's directions, it had taken Shui a while to track him down. Junior, it turned out, no longer worked in construction, he had switched to shining shoes. But luck was on Shui's side: not only did he find the shoeshiner but one of Junior's flatmates, who plied the same trade, had just returned home to attend to a personal matter. Junior quickly walked Shui through the polishing process, and then told him to pick up the other guy's trunk and follow behind.

As he walked, Shui decided he had very little confidence in his new trade. He could see the use in repairing shoes. But shining shoes? Anyone who spent one yuan on a shine – three yuan for the good polish – surely had a screw loose. In front of the station, however, their first customer arrived before they had even finished setting up their stall. To his surprise, by eleven o'clock that night, Shui had earned fourteen yuan!

Junior, on the other hand, wore a surly expression on his face as they returned home. He griped that business had been bad that day, and Shui did not miss the implication that he had stolen Junior's business.

'What are those big metal boxes under the windows?' Shui asked, pointing at a building up ahead.

'Air-conditioning units. It feels like early spring in there.'

'The city is incredible!' Shui exclaimed, wiping the sweat from his face.

'If you're not afraid of hard life, it will be easy to earn enough money for a bowl of rice, but if you want to marry and settle down, forget about it,' Junior said, gesturing with his chin toward the building. 'An apartment in there costs two, three thousand per square meter!'

'What's a square meter?' Shui asked innocently.

Shaking his head in disdain, Junior did not reply.

*

Shui split the rent on a small makeshift apartment with a dozen other men. Most of them were migrant laborers or farmers peddling their produce in the city. But the man who occupied the mattress right next to Shui was a proper city-dweller, although he did not come from this city. He was really no different from the other men. He ate no better than anyone else, and at night he, too, would strip to the waist to enjoy the cool evening air. Every morning, however, he would don a sharp suit and leather shoes. As he walked out the door, he seemed to become a different person. It was like watching a golden phoenix soar out of a chicken coop.

The man's name was Zhuang Yu. The others did not resent him, mainly because of something he had brought with him. It looked liked a large umbrella to Shui, only it was made from mirrors. The inside was very bright and reflective. Zhuang first placed the upturned umbrella on the ground beneath the sun. Then, he set a pot of water on a bracket where the handle should be. The reflected glare heated the bottom of the pot and the water quickly came to a boil. Later, Shui learned it was called a solar cooker. The men used it to boil water and cook food, which saved them quite a bit of money. On overcast days, however, it was useless.

The so-called 'solar cooker' umbrella had no ribs; it was just a very thin sheet. Shui looked on with fascination when Zhuang collapsed the umbrella. A long thin electrical wire ran from the top of the cooker into the apartment. To close it, Zhuang simply pulled the plug from the socket. The umbrella drooped to the ground with a small puff of air, suddenly transformed into a length of silver cloth. Shui picked up the cloth and inspected it carefully. It was soft and smooth and so light that it hardly seemed to weigh anything all. His own distorted likeness was reflected on its surface, glinting with the iridescent sheen of a soap bubble. As soon as he relaxed his grip, the silver cloth slipped through his fingers and fell to the ground without a sound, like an airy handful of quicksilver. When Zhuang reinserted the plug into the power socket, the cloth lazily unfurled like a lotus in full blossom. After a short time, it reverted to its round, upside-down umbrella shape. When he touched the its surface again, it was thin and firm. Giving it a light tap, he was rewarded with a pleasant, metallic ping. In this state, it was extremely strong, able to support a full pot or kettle once fixed to the ground.

'It's a type of nanomaterial,' Zhuang told Shui. 'The surface finish possesses excellent reflective properties, and it is also very strong. Most importantly, it is soft and flexible under normal conditions, but becomes rigid when a weak electric current is applied.'

Shui later learned that this 'nano mirror film' was one of Zhuang's own research achievements. After applying for a patent, he had invested everything he had into bringing products made from the new material to market. But no one had showed any interest in his products, even his portable solar cooker, and he lost all of his capital. Now he was so poor that he had to borrow money from Shui to make rent. But even though he had fallen so low, he remained relentlessly upbeat. Day in and day out, he scoured the city in pursuit of outlets for his new material. He told Shui that this was the thirteenth city he had visited in search of opportunities.

Besides the solar cooker, Zhuang also owned a smaller sheet of the mirror film. Normally, it rested on his bedside table, looking like a small silver handkerchief.

Every morning before he went out, Zhuang would hit a tiny power switch, and the silver handkerchief would immediately stiffen into a thin panel. Using it as a small mirror, he would groom and dress himself in front of it. One morning, as he brushed his hair in the mirror, he cast a sidelong glance at Shui, who had just rolled out of bed.

'You really ought to pay attention to your appearance,' he remarked. 'Wash your face regularly, tame your hair a bit. Not to mention your clothes. Can't you spare a little money for new ones?'

Shui reached for the mirror and held it to his face. Finally he laughed and shook his head. It was too much hassle for a shoeshiner.

'Modern society is full of opportunities,' Zhuang said, leaning toward Shui. 'The skies are thick with golden birds. Perhaps one day you will reach out and seize one, but only if you learn to take yourself seriously.'

Shui looked around, but he did not see a single golden bird. He shook his head and said, 'I never got an education.'

'That is certainly regrettable, but who knows? Maybe it will turn out to your advantage in the end. The greatness of this era lies in its unpredictability. Miracles can happen to anyone.'

'You,' Shui asked haltingly, 'went to university, right?'

'I have a doctorate in solid-state physics. Before I resigned, I was a professor.'

For a long time after Zhuang left, Shui sat with his mouth agape. Finally, he shook his head. If someone like Zhuang Yu could not catch a bird in thirteen different cities, he stood no chance. He felt like Zhuang was making fun of him, but in any case, the guy was pitiable and ridiculous himself.

That night, while some of the men slept and others played a game of poker, Shui and Zhuang went to watch television in the small restaurant just a few doors down.

It was already midnight, and a news broadcast was on. The screen showed only the anchor, and there were no other graphics.

'In a press conference held this afternoon, a spokesperson revealed that the remarkable China Sun Project has formally launched. As a large-scale ecological engineering project, its construction is expected to fundamentally transform our nation's soil . . .'

Shui had heard of the project before, and he knew it involved constructing another sun in the sky. The second sun would bring more rain to the arid Northwest.

It all sounded very farfetched to Shui. He wanted to ask Zhuang about it, as he usually did when he encountered such matters. When he turned his head, however, his friend was staring with wide eyes at the television, slack-jawed, as if the screen had snatched the soul from his body.

Shui waved his hand in front of the other man's face, but received no response. Zhuang did not recover his senses until long after the broadcast had ended. 'Really,' he mumbled to himself, 'how did I not think of the China Sun?'

Shui looked at him blankly. If even he knew about it, there was no way Zhuang was not aware of the China Sun. Who in China had not heard of it? Of course he knew about it – he just hadn't thought about it until now. But what new possibility had captured his attention? What could this project possibly have to do with Zhuang Yu, a down-and-out tramp living in a stuffy, slapdash apartment?

'Do you remember what I said this morning?' Zhuang asked. 'Right now, a golden bird has swooped in front of me, and it is *huge*. It has been right overhead all this time, but I never noticed!'

Shui continued to stare at him in total confusion.

'I am going to Beijing,' Zhuang announced, rising. 'I'll catch the 2:30 train. Come with me, brother!'

'To Beijing? To do what?'

'Beijing is so big, what can't be done?' he replied. 'Even if you just shine shoes, you'll still make much more money there than you do here!'

And so, that very night, Shui and Zhuang boarded a train so crowded that there was not a single seat available. All through the night, the train rolled across the vast open spaces of the West, racing toward the rising sun.

Life Goal #3:
Go to a bigger city, see more of the world, make even more money.

When Shui saw the capital for the first time, one thing became clear: some things had to be seen to be understood. The power of his imagination alone was inadequate. For instance, he had imagined nighttime in Beijing countless times. At first, he had simply doubled or trebled the lights in his village or at the mining district; after he moved to the provincial capital, he repeated the trick with the lights there. But when the bus he and Zhuang had boarded at Beijing West Railway Station turned onto Chang'an Avenue, he knew he could multiply the lights of the provincial capital a thousand times and never match the spectacle of Beijing at night. Of course, the lights of Beijing were not really a thousand times brighter than those of the provincial capital, but there was something about Beijing that the cities out west could never hope to capture.

Shui and Zhuang stayed the night in a cheap basement motel, and then went their separate ways in the morning. Before he took his leave, Zhuang wished Shui good luck, and said that if he ran into any trouble, he could always come find him. But when Shui asked him for a telephone number or address, he admitted he had neither.

'Then how will I find you?' asked Shui.

'Just wait a while. Soon, you'll know where I am by glancing at the television or the newspaper.'

As he watched Zhuang's receding figure, Shui shook his head in bewilderment. What a puzzling response! The man did not have a cent to his name. Today, he had not been able to afford the room at the motel, and Shui had bought their breakfast. Before they left for Beijing, he had even given his solar cooker to the landlord in place of rent. Now, he was no better than a beggar with a dream.

After he parted from Zhuang, Shui immediately went out in search of work, but the city shocked him so deeply he soon forgot his original objective. He spent the entire day strolling aimlessly through the city streets. It was as though he had walked into a fairyland, and he did not feel tired in the slightest. As dusk fell, he stood before one of the new symbols of the capital. Completed just last year, the Unity Tower stood five hundred meters tall. Shui craned his neck to look up at the glass precipice that rose above the clouds. On its surface, the fading glow of the sunset and the swiftly brightening sea of lights below staged a breathtaking performance of light and shadow. Shui watched until his neck grew sore. Just as he turned to leave, the lights of the tower itself came on. The potent spectacle took possession of

Shui, and he stood transfixed, his gaze turned skyward.

'You've been staring for a long time. Are you interested in this sort of work?'

Shui turned to see who had addressed him. It was a young man. He was dressed like any other resident of the city, but he held a yellow hardhat in his hand.

'What work?' Shui asked, confused.

'What were you looking at just then?' the man asked in return, pointing upward with the hand that still held the helmet.

Shui lifted his head and looked in the direction the man was pointing. To his surprise, he spotted several people high up on the glass precipice. From the ground, they looked like little black dots.

'What are they doing so high up there?' Shui asked as he strained for a closer look. 'Cleaning the glass?'

The man nodded. 'I'm the human resources manager of Blue Skies Window Cleaning Company. Our company primarily provides high-rise cleaning services. Are you willing to do that kind of job?'

Shui raised his head again. Looking at the antlike black dots high above him, he felt dizzy. 'It seems . . . scary.'

'If you are concerned about safety, you can rest assured. The job looks dangerous, and that does make recruitment quite difficult. We're short of hands right now. But I guarantee you that our safety precautions are very thorough. As long as you follow the operating procedures to the letter, there is absolutely no danger. And we pay higher wages than companies in similar industries. You could make fifteen hundred per month plus free lunch on work days, and the company would buy you personal insurance.'

Shui was taken aback by the sum. Astonished, he just stared at the manager. The other man misunderstood his silence. 'Fine, I'll cancel your probation period and throw in another three hundred. That's eighteen hundred per month. I can't go any higher than that. The base pay for this kind of work used to be four or five hundred yuan, plus additional piece work. Now we pay a fixed monthly salary, which is not bad in comparison.'

So Shui became a high-rise window cleaner, otherwise known as a 'spiderman.'

Life Goal #4:
Become a Beijinger.

Together with four other window cleaners, Shui cautiously descended from the top floor of the Aerospace Tower. It took them forty minutes to reach the eighty-third floor, where they had left off the previous day. One of the spidermen's biggest headaches was cleaning canted facades, those that formed angles smaller than ninety degrees with the ground. The architect of the Aerospace Tower, in a display of his own pathological creativity, had designed the entire building on a slant. The top of the tower was supported by a slender column driven into the ground. According to the celebrity architect, the slanted design was supposed to impart the sensation of rising upward. His statement seemed reasonable, and the skyscraper became famous throughout the world as a landmark of Beijing. But the architect and eight generations of his ancestors were routinely and inventively cursed by Beijing's spidermen. For them, cleaning the Aerospace Tower was a nightmare. The entirety of one side was at an incline, which stood four hundred meters tall and met the ground at a sixty-five degree angle.

After he reached his workstation, Shui looked up. Above him, the huge glass face looked like it was toppling down on him. With one hand, he removed the cap from his detergent container. With his other hand, he clutched the handle of his suction cup. This kind of suction was specially made for cleaning surfaces beyond the vertical, but even so, it was difficult to use and often came unsealed. When this happened, the spiderman would swing away from the wall, dangling from his safety line. Such accidents were frequent while cleaning the Aerospace Tower, and each time, it would near frighten the soul out of the cleaner's body. Just yesterday, Shui's workmate lost suction and swung far out from the building. As he swung back in, he was caught by gust of wind and sent crashing into the building, shattering a large sheet of glass. His forehead and arms were cut to ribbons, and the cost of replacing the expensive coated architectural glass set him back an entire year's wages.

Shui had joined the ranks of the spidermen more than two years ago, but the work had not grown easier with time. Category two winds on the Beaufort scale on the ground strengthened to category five winds at one hundred meters. On buildings that exceeded four or five hundred meters, the winds were stronger still. That the job was hazardous went without saying. Since the beginning of the twenty-first century, plummeting to death in the streets below hasn't been an unusual fate for spidermen. In winter, strong winds felt as sharp as knives, and the hydrofluoric acid solution commonly used to clean glass windows was so corrosive that it would cause their fingernails to turn black and fall off. To protect themselves from the detergent, the spidermen had to wear watertight jackets, pants, and boots, even in summer. When cleaning coated glass, the blazing sun would beat down on their backs, and the reflected glare in front of them was so blinding it was difficult to keep their eyes open. It made Shui feel like he had been placed into Zhuang's solar cooker.

But Shui loved his job. The past two years had been the happiest time of his life. It undoubtedly helped that the spidermen were highly paid relative to the other uncultured migrant laborers who flocked to Beijing. More importantly, however, he derived a wonderful sense of fulfillment from his work. He relished the jobs his fellow spidermen were unwilling to do: cleaning newly constructed super-skyscrapers. All of these buildings stood at least two hundred meters tall, and the tallest topped five hundred meters. Hanging off the sides of these skyscrapers, he commanded a magnificent view of Beijing, stretched out below him. The so-called 'high-rises' built during the previous century looked squat from up there. A little farther away, they became small bunches of twigs stuck in the ground. In the heart of the city, the Forbidden City looked like it had been built with golden toy blocks. From this height, he could not hear the clamor of Beijing, and he could survey the city with a single glance. It breathed quietly below him, a super-organism surrounded by a spider web of arterial roads. Sometimes, a skyscraper he was cleaning would push through the clouds. Half of the skyscraper could be enveloped in a dark and dreary rainstorm even as the other half was bathed in bright sunshine. Looking at the endless sea of clouds billowing beneath his feet, Shui always felt as though the howling winds above blew right through him.

The experience taught Shui a philosophical truth: some things only became clear when seen from above. Swallowed up in the capital, everything around him seemed hopelessly complicated. On the ground, the city was like an unending labyrinth. Up here, it was nothing more than an anthill with ten million inhabitants, and the world around it was so vast!

The first time he received his paycheck, Shui had gone for a stroll through a large shopping mall. Riding the elevator to the third floor, he was met by a peculiar scene. Unlike the bustling floors below, this hall was empty except for a few staggeringly large, low tables. The broad tabletops were covered with clusters of tiny buildings, each one no taller than a book. The space between the buildings was filled with bright green grass, dotted with white pavilions and winding corridors. The little structures were lovely, like they were carved from ivory or cheese. Together with the green lawn, they formed an exquisite miniature world. In Shui's eyes, it looked like a model of paradise. At first he guessed that these were some sort of toys, but he did not see any children in the hall. All of the adults at the tables wore attentive, serious expressions. Bewitched, he stood next to one of the tiny paradises and studied it for a long time. It was not until an attractive young woman came over to greet him that he realized this was a real estate office. He pointed to a building at random and asked how much the apartment on the top floor cost. The saleslady told him it was a three-bedroom, one-den apartment and that it cost thirty-five hundred yuan per square meter, which worked out to three hundred and eighty thousand yuan in total. Shui drew a sharp gasp when he heard the number, but the woman's next statement softened the brutal figure considerably: 'You can pay by monthly installments of fifteen hundred to two thousand yuan.'

'I-I'm not from Beijing. Could I still buy it?' he asked carefully.

The saleslady flashed him a winning smile. 'You are too funny. The household registration system was dismantled years ago. Is there such a thing as a 'real' Beijinger anymore? If you settle down here, doesn't that make you a Beijinger?'

After Shui left the mall, he had wandered aimlessly through the streets for a long time. All around him, Beijing's brilliant mosaic of lights glittered in the night. In his hand he held the colorful fliers the saleslady had given him, and every so often he stopped to look at them. Just two years ago, in that rundown room in that distant western city, even owning an apartment in the provincial capital had seemed like a fairytale. Now, he was still a long way away from buying an apartment in Beijing, but it was a fairytale no longer. It was a dream, and like those delicate little models, it was right before his eyes. He could reach out and touch it.

Just then, someone rapped on the window Shui was cleaning, interrupting his daydream. This was a common nuisance. For white collar workers, the appearance of high-rise window cleaners on their office windows was a source of indescribable irritation. It was like the cleaners really were large, aberrant spiders, as their nickname suggested, and far more than a single pane of glass separated the workers without from those within.

While the spidermen worked, the people inside would complain that they were too noisy, or that they were blocking the sunlight, or about any of the million other ways in which the cleaners had ruined their day. The glass of the Aerospace Tower was semi-reflective, and Shui had to strain to see through it. When he finally made out the man inside, he was astonished to see Zhuang Yu.

After they parted ways, Shui had often worried about Zhuang. In his mind, the man had remained a dapper tramp, making his way through the big city step by arduous step. Then, one night in late autumn, as Shui sat in his dormitory silently fretting about Zhuang's winter wardrobe, he saw him on television. The China Sun Project had begun the selection process for the critical technology at the heart of the project: the material that would be used to build its reflector. In the end, Zhuang's nano mirror film was chosen from among a dozen other materials. Overnight, the scientifically inclined vagrant was transformed into one of the chief scientists of the China Sun Project, recognized the world over. Afterward, even though Zhuang made frequent media appearances, Shui gradually forgot about him. He believed they no longer had anything to do with each other.

When Shui arrived in that spacious office, he saw that Zhuang had not changed one bit over the past two years. He even wore the same suit. Shui now saw that the attire he had once considered so luxurious was, in truth, very shabby. He told Zhuang all about his life in Beijing. 'It looks like we've both done well here,' he concluded, grinning.

'Yes, yes, very well!' Zhuang agreed, nodding excitedly. 'To tell the truth, that morning when I told you about the opportunities of these times, I had lost faith in just about everything. I was mostly saying those things for my own benefit, but these days the world truly is brimming with opportunities!'

Shui nodded too. 'There are golden birds everywhere.'

Shui took stock of large, modern-looking office around him. A few unusual decorations stood out from the rest of the room. A holographic image of the night sky was projected across the entire ceiling of the office; anyone who stood in the center of the room would feel as though they had been transported to a courtyard beneath the brilliant stars. A curved silver plate hung suspended against the background of stars. It was a mirror that looked very similar to Zhuang's solar cooker, but Shui knew that the real thing was likely twenty or thirty times larger than Beijing.

In one corner of the ceiling, there was a spherical lamp. Like the mirror, it floated in the air without any means of support, shining with a bright yellow light. The mirror reflected its rays onto a globe next to Zhuang's desk, creating a circle of light on its surface. As the lamp slowly floated across the ceiling, the mirror rotated to track it, throwing its light upon the globe without interruption. The starlit sky, the mirror, the lamp, its light, the globe and the illuminated spot composed an abstract and mysterious mural.

'This is the China Sun?' Shui asked in awe, pointing to the mirror.

Zhuang nodded. 'It is a thirty thousand square kilometer reflector. From geosynchronous orbit – at an altitude of thirty-six thousand kilometers – it will reflect sunlight onto Earth. Viewed from the surface, it will look like there is another sun in the sky.'

'There's something I don't understand. How does an extra sun in the sky bring more rain?'

'This artificial sun can employ many different methods to influence the weather. For instance, by disturbing the thermodynamic equilibrium of the atmosphere, it can influence atmospheric circulation, increase ocean evaporation, or shift weather fronts,' Zhang answered. 'But that doesn't really explain it. In fact, the orbital reflector is just one part of the China Sun Project. The other part is a complex model of atmospheric motion, which will run on multiple supercomputers. It will be able to accurately simulate motion in any given region of the atmosphere and then identify a critical point. If heat from the artificial sun is brought to bear upon this point, the effect would be dramatic enough to completely transform the climate of a targeted area for a period of time.' He paused. 'The process is extremely complicated, and it is outside my area of expertise. I don't quite understand it myself.'

Shui decided to ask another question which Zhuang could certainly answer. He knew his question was foolish, but he steeled his nerve and asked anyway. 'How can something so big hang in the sky without falling down?'

Zhuang gazed silently at Shui for several long seconds. Finally, he glanced down at his watch and then clapped Shui on the shoulder. 'Let's go. I'm treating you to dinner. I'll explain why the China Sun will not fall while we eat.'

The explanation did not turn out to be as easy as Zhuang expected. He was forced to set aside his original topic and start with the basics. While Shui knew he lived on round planet, the traditional Chinese model of a heavenly dome over a square earth was still rooted deep in his mind. It required a great deal of effort from Zhuang to make Shui really understand that the world in which he lived was a small spherical rock floating through an endless void.

Although Shui came no closer to understanding why the China Sun would not fall, the universe was greatly changed in his mind's eye that evening. He entered his own Ptolemaic Era. The second evening, Zhuang ate dinner with Shui at a roadside food stall and successfully dragged him into the Copernican Era. Over the next two evenings, Shui slogged through the Newtonian Era, acquiring an elementary understanding of universal gravitation. The evening after that, with the help of the globe in his office, Zhuang ushered Shui into the Space Age. On the next public holiday, in front of that globe, Shui finally grasped the meaning of a geosynchronous orbit. At last, he understood why the China Sun would not fall down.

That day, Zhuang took Shui on a tour of the China Sun Command Center. At the center, a massive monitor displayed a panoramic view of the ongoing construction of the China Sun in geosynchronous orbit. Several thin silver sheets floated in the blackness of space, so large that the space shuttles hovering next to them seemed like tiny mosquitoes.

But what shook Shui the most was an image on another monitor. It showed Earth from an altitude of thirty-six thousand kilometers. The continents floated on the oceans like large scraps of brown packing paper. Mountain ranges became creases in the paper, and clouds looked like residual smudges of powdered sugar on its surface.

Zhuang showed Shui the location of his home village and Beijing. He gawked at the monitor for a long minute before he blurted, 'People must think differently up there.'

The main construction of the China Sun was finished three months later. As night fell on National Day, the reflector was turned towards the night-shrouded Earth, training its immense spotlight on Beijing and Tianjin. That night, standing amid a crowd of several hundred thousand people gathered in Tiananmen Square, Shui witnessed a magnificent sunrise. In the western sky, a star began to brighten dramatically, creating a little ring of blue around itself. As the China Sun approached peak luminosity, the halo expanded, filling half the sky. Around its edges, the clear blue bled into yellow and then orange-red and dark purple, forming a circular rainbow that became known as the 'Wreath of Dawn'.

By the time Shui returned to his dormitory, it was already four o'clock in the morning. As he lay on his narrow upper bunk, the light of the China Sun streamed through his window, illuminating the real estate fliers pasted to the wall above his pillow. He ripped the glossy pages down.

Under the divine radiance of the China Sun, the ideal that had once thrilled him now seemed dull and insignificant.

*

Two months later, the manager of the cleaning company came to find Shui. He told him that Director Zhuang of the China Sun Command Center wished to see him. Shui had not seen Zhuang since he had finished his work on the Aerospace Tower.

'Your sun is really something!' Shui exclaimed in heartfelt admiration when he met Zhuang in his office at the Aerospace Tower.

'It is our sun, and yours especially!' answered Zhuang. 'Right now you cannot see it from Beijing because it is bringing snow to your village!'

'My parents mentioned in their letter that they were getting more snow than usual this winter!'

'However, the China Sun has a big problem,' said Zhuang, pointing to a large monitor behind him. Two images of a single circular spot of light were displayed on the screen. 'These images of the China Sun were taken from the same location, two months apart. Can you see the difference?'

'The one on the left is brighter.'

'You see, the decrease in reflectivity can be seen with the naked eye after just two months.'

'How can that be? Has the mirror grown dusty?'

'There is no dust in space, but there is the solar wind, or the stream of particles ejected by the sun. With time, the wind will transform the China Sun's mirrored surface. As the reflector accumulates a fine film of particles, its reflectivity will decrease. One year from now, it will look like it is covered with water vapor. Then, the China Sun will have become the China Moon, and it will be useless,' explained Zhuang.

'You didn't think of this earlier?'

'Of course we thought of it!' Zhuang paused. 'Let's talk about you. How do you feel about switching jobs?'

'Switching jobs? What else could I do?'

'You would still be working as a high-altitude cleaner, but you would be working for us.'

Shui glanced around in confusion. 'Wasn't your tower just cleaned? Why would you need to specially employ a high-rise window cleaner?'

'No, we don't want you to clean buildings. We want you to clean the China Sun.'

Life Goal #5:
Fly to space, clean the China Sun.

It was a meeting of the senior directors of the China Sun Project Operations Division to discuss the establishment of a reflector cleaning unit. Zhuang introduced Shui to the assembled parties and explained his profession to them. When someone inquired about his educational background, Shui honestly replied that he had only finished three years of primary school.

'But I can recognize characters and can read without problems,' he told the attendees.

The conference room dissolved in a gale of laughter.

'Director Zhuang, is this a joke?' someone shouted indignantly.

'I'm not joking,' Zhuang replied evenly. 'If we assembled a crew of thirty cleaners, it would take them six months to clean the entire China Sun if they worked around the clock. In reality, we would need at least sixty to ninety people working in shifts. If the new aerospace labor protection law goes into effect as scheduled, we may need even more, perhaps one hundred and twenty to one hundred and fifty cleaners. Can we really send one hundred and fifty astronauts with doctorates and three thousand flight hours in high-performance fighter jets up into space to do the job?'

'Surely we can find more qualified candidates? Higher education is practically universal in the cities these days. How can we send an illiterate hick into space?'

'I am not illiterate!' Shui objected.

The man ignored him and continued speaking to Zhuang. 'You would debase this great project!'

The other participants nodded in agreement.

Zhuang nodded, too. 'I thought you might react like this. Ladies and gentlemen, except for this cleaner, you all hold doctorates. Well then, let us see the quality of your cleaning work! Please come with me.'

A dozen bewildered participants followed Zhuang out of the conference room and into the elevator. Three types of lifts had been installed in the tower: standard, fast, and express. They boarded the fastest elevator and shot up at breakneck speed to the top floor of the building.

'This is my first time in this elevator,' someone remarked. 'I feel like I am blasting off in a rocket!'

'After we enter geosynchronous orbit, everyone will experience what it is like to clean the China Sun,' said Zhuang, drawing strange glances from the people around him.

After they stepped out of the elevator, Zhuang led the group up a narrow flight of stairs. Finally, they emerged from a low metal door onto the open roof of the tower. They were immediately thrust into bright sunlight and powerful winds. The blue sky overhead seemed even clearer than usual, and the directors looked all around, admiring the panoramic view of Beijing. Another small group of people stood waiting for them. Shui was startled to see his company's manager and his fellow spidermen!

'Now, everyone will try their hand at Shui's profession!' Zhuang announced in a loud voice.

The spidermen stepped forward and strapped each director into a safety harness. They then led them to the edge of the roof and carefully helped them onto narrow suspended platforms that normally served as a workstation for a dozen or more spidermen. The boards were slowly lowered until they were suspended five or six meters beneath the edge of the rooftop, where they halted. Unadulterated screams of terror rose from where the directors dangled against the glass face of the tower.

'Ladies and gentlemen, let us continue the meeting where we left off!' Zhuang called down to his colleagues below, leaning over the edge of the roof.

'You bastard! Quick, pull us up!'

'Every one of you has to clean a pane of glass before I let you up!'

It was an impossible demand. The people below could only cling to their safety harnesses or the ropes supporting the platforms for dear life, not daring to move. They were utterly incapable of loosening one hand to pick up a squeegee or remove the lid from the detergent bucket. Every day, these aerospace officials dealt with altitudes as high as tens of thousands of kilometers in the form of blueprints and documents; but now, as they gained a first-hand feel for four hundred meters, they were scared witless.

Zhuang rose and walked to the spot above an air force colonel. Of the dozen people hanging off the side of the building, he was the only one who remained calm and collected. The colonel began to clean the glass, keeping his motions steady and controlled. What astonished Shui most, however, was that the man was working with both hands, and he had relinquished his grip on anything he might use to steady himself. Even so, his board remained motionless against the wall in the strong wind, a feat that only veteran spidermen could accomplish. When Shui recognized the man, the scene in front of him no longer seemed as strange; he was an astronaut who had flown on the Shenzhou 8 spacecraft more than a decade earlier.

'Colonel Zhang, in your candid opinion, is the task before you really easier than a spacewalk in orbit?' asked Zhuang.

'With respect to the physical ability and skill required, the difference is not great,' the former astronaut replied.

'Well said. According to studies conducted at the Aerospace Training

Center, from an ergonomic standpoint, there are many similarities between cleaning skyscrapers and cleaning the reflector in space. Both tasks require workers to constantly maintain their balance in the face of danger, while performing repetitive, monotonous, physically demanding labor. Both tasks require constant vigilance, as the slightest carelessness can lead to an accident. For an astronaut, that might mean deviation from orbit, lost tools or materials, or a malfunction in his life support system. For a spiderman, that might mean shattered glass, dropped tools or detergent, or breakage or slippage of his safety harness. In terms of physical strength, technical skill, and especially psychological fortitude, the spidermen are fully qualified to work as reflector cleaners.'

The former astronaut lifted his head and nodded at Zhuang. 'I am reminded of that old parable about the oil peddler who could pour oil into a bottle through the square hole in a copper coin. He was every bit as skilled as a general who never missed a bulls-eye. The only difference between them was their social status.'

'Columbus discovered America and Cook discovered Australia, but these New Worlds were settled by ordinary people, pioneers who came from the lowest rungs of European society,' added Zhuang. 'The development of space is no different. In the next Five Year Plan, we have designated near-Earth space as a second western frontier. The era of exploration has ended, and the aerospace industry will never again be the exclusive domain of an elite minority. Sending ordinary people into orbit is the first step toward the industrialization of space!'

'Okay! Fine! You have made your point! Now quickly, let us up!' his colleagues shouted hoarsely below.

In the elevator on the way down, the manager of the cleaning company leaned toward Zhuang and whispered in his ear. 'Director Zhuang, that was a moving and impassioned speech back there, but wasn't it a little much? But of course, it is difficult to discuss the key issue at hand in front of Shui and my boys.'

'Eh?' Zhuang shot him an inquiring look.

'Everyone knows that the China Sun Project is a quasi-commercial operation. Halfway to completion, a funding shortfall nearly led to the project's cancellation, and now you have next to no operations budget. In the commercial aerospace sector, the annual salary of a qualified astronaut is over one million yuan. My guys will save you tens of millions every year.'

Zhuang smiled enigmatically. 'You think such a paltry sum would be worth the risk? Today, I deliberately slashed the educational standards required of reflector cleaners to set a precedent. After this, I will be able to hire ordinary university graduates to fill the jobs in orbit needed to operate the China Sun. This way, we will save a lot more money than just a few tens of millions. As you said, it is the only course of action available. We really don't have any money left.'

'Growing up, going to space was such a romantic endeavor. I can clearly remember when Deng Xiaoping visited the Johnson Space Center, he called an American astronaut a god. Now,' said the manager with a bitter smile, shaking his head and slapping Zhuang on the back, 'I am no better or worse than you.'

Zhuang turned to look at the young spidermen and then told the manager in a raised voice, 'But, sir, the salary I am offering is eight to ten times better than what you pay them!'

The next day, Shui and sixty of his fellow spidermen arrived at the National Aerospace Training Center in Shijingshan. Each and every one of them was a farm boy who had come from some remote corner of China's vast countryside to Beijing, looking for work.

Mirror Farmers

At the Xichang Space Center, the nose cone of the space shuttle *Horizon* emerged from the billowing white clouds of exhaust produced by its engines. With a thunderous roar, it rose straight into the clear blue sky. Shui and fourteen other reflector cleaners sat strapped into their seats in the cabin.

After three months of training on the ground, they had been chosen from the sixty candidates to be part of the first crew assigned to actual operations in space.

To Shui, the lift-off g-forces were not nearly terrible as the tales said they would be. He even found a familiar comfort in them. It was the feeling of being held tightly in his mother's arms as a child. Outside the porthole to his upper right, the blue sky began to deepen. There was a faint pop of bolts blasting apart outside the cabin, and the booster rockets separated. As they left the rockets behind, the earsplitting roar of the engines became a mosquito-like drone. The sky faded to dark purple and then full black. The stars appeared, unblinking and intensely luminous.

The drone ceased abruptly, and silence fell over the cabin. The vibration of Shui's seat disappeared along with the pressure pinning his torso to the seatback. They had entered microgravity. Shui and the other spidermen had trained in a colossal swimming pool to prepare for weightlessness. It really did feel like he was floating in water.

But it was not yet safe to unfasten his seatbelt. The hum of the engine returned, and the shuttle's acceleration pressed the men back into their seats. The long maneuver into orbit had begun. The starry sky and the ocean appeared by turns in the tiny porthole. One moment the cabin flooded with the blue glow reflected by Earth, the next with the white light of the Sun. Each time Earth appeared in the porthole, the curvature of the horizon grew more conspicuous, and more of the planet's surface came into view. From start to finish, it took six hours to maneuver into geosynchronous orbit. The continuous alternation of sky and earth outside the porthole had a hypnotic effect on Shui, lulling him into an unexpected sleep. He was jarred awake by the commander's voice over the intercom. He informed them that the orbit insertion maneuver was complete.

One after another, his companions floated from their seats, pressing their faces to the viewing ports to peer outside. Shui unfastened his own seatbelt and, using swimming motions, floated clumsily through the air to the nearest porthole. For the first time, he saw Earth in its entirety with his own eyes.

Most of the other men, however, had gathered in front of the viewing ports on the other side of the cabin. He pushed off against the bulkhead with his foot and shot across to join them. Unable to control his speed, he bumped his head on the opposite wall. As he gazed through a porthole, he realized the *Horizon* was already directly beneath the China Sun. The reflector took up most of the starry sky. Their space shuttle seemed like a small mosquito trapped under a silver dome. As the *Horizon* continued its approach, Shui gradually came to appreciate the sheer immensity of the reflector. Its mirrored surface occupied the entire view from the porthole, and its curvature was imperceptible, as if they were flying above a boundless silver plain. A reflection of the *Horizon* appeared on its surface as the distance continued to shrink. Shui could see long seams on the silver ground, which formed a grid like the latitude and longitude lines on a map. The grid was his sole reference point for judging the shuttle's relative velocity. After a time, the longitude lines no longer ran parallel. They began to converge in one direction, gradually at first and then more sharply, as if the *Horizon* was bound for a pole on this great map. Soon, the pole came into view. All of the longitudinal seams met at a small black dot. As the shuttle began its descent toward the dot, Shui realized with a start that it was actually a gigantic tower rising above the silver plain. He knew that this hermetically-sealed cylinder was the China Sun Control Station. For the next three months, it would be their only home in the desolation of space.

*

And so the spidermen began their new lives in space. Every day – the China Sun orbited Earth once every twenty-four hours – they piloted small tractor-like machines onto the mirrored surface to polish it. They drove their tractors to and fro across the wide expanse of the reflector, as if they were tilling the silver earth. As a result, the Western media coined a more poetic name for the spidermen. They were now 'mirror farmers'.

The world in which these farmers lived was quite peculiar. A silver plain lay beneath their feet. Though the reflector's curved form caused the plain to rise slowly in the distance in every direction, it was so vast that it looked as flat and calm as still water. Overhead, both Earth and the Sun were visible. The latter appeared much smaller than Earth, as if it was the planet's radiant satellite. On the surface of the Earth, which occupied most of the sky, they could see a slowly moving circle of light. It was a particularly striking sight when it drifted onto the nighttime hemisphere. This was the region illuminated by the China Sun. The reflector could change the size of the light spot by adjusting its own shape. When the silver plain rose steeply in the distance, the spot grew smaller and brighter. When the slope was gentler, the spot grew larger and dimmer.

The work of the reflector cleaners was extremely difficult. They soon realized that buffing the reflector was far more monotonous and draining than scrubbing skyscrapers on Earth. When they returned to the control station at the end of each day, they were often too exhausted to even take off their spacesuits. As more personnel arrived from Earth, the control station began to feel cramped, and they lived like crewmen aboard a submarine. Nonetheless, they considered themselves fortunate if they could return to the station at all. The most remote point on the reflector was nearly one hundred kilometers from the station. Cleaners working on the reflector's outer rim often could not make it back after a day on the job, and had to spend the 'night' in the 'wilderness'. After suctioning a liquid dinner from their suit, they would then fall asleep suspended in space.

The work was incredibly dangerous to boot. Never before in the history of human spaceflight had so many people performed space walks. In the 'wilderness', the slightest malfunction in one's space suit could mean death. There were also micrometeorites, bits of space debris, and solar storms to worry about. The control station engineers carped bitterly about these living and working conditions, but the mirror farmers, who had been born into hardship, adapted to their new circumstances without complaint.

On his fifth day in space, Shui received a call from his family. He was working more than fifty kilometers away from the control station, and the

China Sun had its beam trained on his home village.

He heard Pa's voice. 'Wah, are you on that sun? It's shining above our heads right now. The night is as bright as day!'

Shui replied, 'Yeah, Pa, I'm right above you.'

Then Ma spoke. 'Wah, is it hot up there?'

'You could say it's both hot and cold. Right now, everything outside of my shadow is hotter than ten summers in our village, but inside my shadow is colder than ten winters.'

'I can see our Wah,' Ma told Pa, 'That little black dot on the sun right there!'

Shui knew this was impossible, but as tears rolled down his cheeks, he said, 'Pa, Ma, I can see you, too. There are two little black dots on the Asian continent where you are! Dress warmly tomorrow. I can see a cold front moving in from the north!'

*

Three months later, the second cleaning crew arrived to relieve the first of its duties, and Shui and his coworkers returned to Earth for three months leave. After they landed, the first thing that every one of them did was buy a high-powered monocular telescope. When they returned to the China Sun three months later, they used their new purchases to observe the planet below during the breaks between work. They most often turned their lenses toward home, but at an altitude of nearly forty thousand kilometers, it was impossible to see their villages. One of the men scrawled a simple, inelegant poem on the reflector with a felt-tip pen:

> *From this silver earth, I watch my distant home*
> *On the edge of the village, my mother looks up at the China Sun*
> *Its disc is the image of her son's eye*
> *The yellow earth is clad in green under his gaze*

The mirror farmers did an outstanding job. Over time, they began to take on responsibilities beyond the scope of their cleaning work. At first, they simply repaired damage done to the reflector by meteor strikes, but later they were tasked with more demanding work: monitoring and reinforcing sections at risk for overstress failure.

As the China Sun moved in orbit, it was constantly reorienting itself. These adjustments were accomplished by three thousand engines distributed across the back face of the reflector. The actual mirrored surface of the reflector was very thin, and it was joined to the whole structure with a great number of slender beams on its back. When the engines fired, parts of the reflector surface could become overstressed. If the engine outputs were not corrected in time, or the location was not reinforced, the unchecked overstress could tear the mirrored surface. Discovering and reinforcing stress points required both great technical skill and ample experience.

Apart from reorientation or reshaping periods, overstress was most likely to occur during an 'orbital haircut', or a 'Radiation Pressure and Solar Wind-Induced Drag Correction', as the operation was formally known. Together, solar wind and radiation exerted a significant force on the enormous surface of the reflector. Approximately two kilograms of pressure pushed against every square kilometer of the reflector, causing an outward drift in its orbit. The earthbound control centre constantly monitored these changes, comparing the altered track to the intended orbit on a large screen. On screen, it looked as if long, wavy hairs were sprouting from the intended orbit, hence the curious name for the operation.

The reflector's acceleration was much greater during an orbital haircut than during reshaping or reorientation and the work of the mirror farmers was critical during this period. Flying above the silver plain, they would scrutinize every anomaly on its surface and perform emergency reinforcements when necessary. They acquitted themselves splendidly and their salaries were raised accordingly. But the greatest beneficiary was Zhuang Yu, who rose to the highest office of the China Sun project – without having to hire a single university graduate.

Nevertheless, it was clear to the mirror farmers that they would be the first and last group of workers in space to receive only a primary school education. Those who followed them would be university graduates at the very least. Still, they served the purpose envisioned by Zhuang. They had proven that skill, experience, and the ability to adapt to adverse circumstances were more important than knowledge and creativity in the blue-collar jobs created by space development. Ordinary people were fully up to the task.

However, space did alter the way the mirror farmers thought. No one else had the privilege of gazing down upon Earth from thirty-six thousand kilometers every day. With a glance, they could take in the whole planet. To them, the global village was no longer just a metaphor, but a reality before their very eyes.

As the first laborers in space, the mirror farmers had been a global sensation but the industrial development of near-Earth orbit was now in full swing. Mega projects were commissioned, including vast solar power stations that beamed microwave energy down to the planet below, micro-gravity processing plants, and many others. Construction even began on an orbital city that could accommodate one hundred thousand residents. Industrial workers arrived in space in droves. They, too, were ordinary people, and so the world gradually forgot about the mirror farmers.

*

Several years passed. Shui bought a house in Beijing, married, and had a child. He spent half of every year at home, and the other half in space. He loved his job. His long patrols on that silver land more than thirty thousand kilometers above Earth filled his heart with detached peacefulness. He felt as though he had found his ideal life, and the future stretched before him as level and smooth as the silver plain underfoot. But then something happened that shattered his tranquility and thoroughly changed the course of his mental journey. Shui encountered Stephen Hawking.

No one had expected that Hawking would live to be one hundred. It was a medical miracle, but it was also a testament to his force of will. After the first low-gravity assisted living facility was constructed in near-Earth orbit, he became its first resident. However, the hypergravity of launch nearly claimed his life. Because he would have to endure the same forces during reentry, returning to Earth was out of the question, at least until the invention of a space elevator, antigravity cabin module, or similar delivery vehicle. In fact, his doctors advised him to permanently settle in space, as the weightless environment perfectly suited his body.

At first, Hawking expressed little interest in the China Sun. Only a survey of anisotropy in the cosmic background radiation was sufficient to persuade him to subject himself to the g-forces generated by the trip from near-Earth orbit to geosynchronous orbit (though, of course, these forces were smaller than those he had experienced during launch). The observation station had been installed on the back face of the China Sun, as the reflector would block all interference from the Sun and Earth. But when the survey was complete, the observation station dismantled and the survey team withdrawn, Hawking did not want to leave. He said he liked it there and wished to stay a while longer. Something had drawn his attention to the China Sun. The press had a field day with speculations of all kinds, but only Shui knew the whole truth.

What Hawking enjoyed most about his life on the China Sun, were his daily excursions across the surface of the reflector. To the consternation of many, he would simply drift along the underside of the reflector for several hours every day. Shui, who by now was the China Sun's most experienced spacewalker, was assigned to accompany the professor on his outings. At that time, Hawking's fame rivaled Einstein's – even Shui had heard of him. Nevertheless, Shui was shocked when they met for the first time in the control center. He had never imagined that someone with such a severe disability could achieve so much – not that he understood the great scientist's achievements in the slightest. On their excursions, however, Hawking betrayed no hint of his paralysis. Perhaps it was his experience controlling an electric wheelchair that allowed him to operate the micro-engines in his spacesuit as nimbly as any able-bodied person.

Hawking found it difficult to communicate with Shui. He did have an implant that allowed him to control a speech synthesizer with his brain waves, which made speaking less of a chore than it had been in the previous century. However, his words still had to be run through a device that provided real-time translation into Chinese so that Shui could understand him. Shui's superiors instructed him that he was never to initiate conversation with the professor in case he disturbed his thoughts. Hawking, however, was more than willing to talk to him.

He first asked Shui for an account of his life, and then began to reminisce about his own early years. Hawking told Shui about his cold, sprawling childhood home in St Albans; in winter, the frigid, lofty parlor would ring with the music of Wagner. He told him about the Gypsy caravan his parents placed in a field at Osmington Mills, and how he and his younger sister Mary would ride it to the seashore. He talked about the times he and his father visited the Ivinghoe Beacon in the Chiltern Hills. Shui marveled at the centenarian's memory, but he was even more amazed that they shared a common vocabulary. The professor greatly enjoyed Shui's accounts of life in his home village. Floating on the outer rim of the reflector, he asked Shui to point out its location.

After a while, their conversations inevitably turned to science. Shui feared this would bring their discussions to an end, but it was not the case. For the professor, it was relaxing to discuss deep topics in physics and cosmology using language that even ordinary people could follow. He told Shui about the Big Bang, black holes, and quantum gravity. When Shui returned to the station, he began to wrestle with the thin little book Hawking had written in the previous century, consulting the station's engineers and scientists when he encountered something he did not understand. He grasped far more of its contents than anyone thought he would.

One day, the two men travelled to the outskirts of the reflector. 'Do you know why I like this place?' the professor asked Shui, facing a sliver of Earth visible beyond the rim of the reflector. 'This huge mirror separates us from

Earth below. It lets me forget about the world and devote my entire focus to the cosmos.'

'The world below is complicated,' agreed Shui, 'but seen from so far away, the universe seems so simple, just stars scattered in space.'

'Yes, my boy, it does indeed,' said the professor.

Just like the reflector's front face, its back face was also mirrored. The only real difference was that it was dotted with the engines that adjusted the reflector's orientation and shape, which resembled small black towers. On their daily strolls, Shui and the doctor would leisurely float along, staying just above the ground. They often drifted all the way from the control station to the outer rim. When the Moon was not visible, the back face of the reflector was extremely dark, and its surface reflected the starlit sky. Compared to the front face, the horizon was closer here, and visibly curved. By the light of the stars, the black latitude and longitude lines formed by the support beams passed beneath their feet, as if they were skimming above the surface of a tiny, tranquil planet. Whenever the reflector was reoriented or reshaped, the engines on the back face would ignite. Illuminated by countless jets of flame, the surface of this tiny planet seemed even more beautiful and mysterious. And shining above, always, the Milky Way, bright and unwavering.

It was here that Shui first encountered the deepest secrets of the cosmos. He learned that the starry sky that filled his vision was but a speck of dust in the unimaginable vastness of the universe, and that this entire creation was nothing but the embers of a ten-billion-year-old explosion.

Many years ago, when he had taken his first step as a spiderman onto the roof of a skyscraper, Shui had seen all of Beijing. When he arrived on the China Sun, he had seen all of Earth. Now, Shui faced the third such glorious moment of his life. Standing on the roof of the cosmos, he could see things beyond his wildest dreams. Although he possessed only a superficial understanding of those distant worlds, they still held an irresistible attraction for him.

Once Shui expressed his confusion to an engineer in the station. 'Humanity landed on the Moon in the sixties. And what next? Even now, we have not set foot on Mars. We don't even visit the Moon anymore.'

'Humans are practical creatures,' replied the engineer. 'What was driven by idealism and faith in the middle of the last century was not viable in the long term.'

'What's wrong with idealism and faith?'

'There's nothing wrong with them per se, but economic interests are better. If in the sixties humanity had spared no expense in the pursuit of spaceflight and racked up enormous losses, Earth might still be mired in poverty. Ordinary people like you and I would never have made it to space at all, even if we are no further than near-Earth orbit. Pal, don't let Hawking poison you. Normal folk shouldn't toy with the things he does.'

The conversation changed Shui. On the surface he appeared calm, working as hard as ever, but deep down he was contemplating new horizons.

*

Twenty years flew by. From an altitude of thirty-six thousand kilometers, Shui and his compatriots commanded a clear view of two decades of changes creeping across the globe. They watched as the Three-North Shelter Belt formed a verdant ribbon that traversed north-western China, slowly turning the yellow desert green. Their home villages would never lack for rain or snow again, the dry riverbeds on the outskirts of the villages flowed once more with clear, clean waters.

The China Sun deserved the credit for all of this. It had played a major role in the great campaign to transform the climate of northwestern China. Not only that, it also performed a number of innovative extracurricular activities: once it melted the snows of Mount Kilimanjaro to ease a drought in Africa; on another occasion it turned an Olympic host city into a city that truly never slept.

But with the advent of newer technologies, the China Sun's methods of manipulating the weather began to seem clumsy and encumbered with too many side effects. The China Sun had accomplished its mission.

The Ministry of Space Industry held a grand ceremony to decorate the first group of industrial workers in orbit. They were honored not only for their twenty years of exceptional hard work, but more importantly, these sixty men were recognized for the singular accomplishment of entering space as youths with nothing but an elementary or middle school education. In doing so, they had thrown the doors of space development wide open to everyone. Economists unanimously agreed that this had been the true beginning of the industrialization of space.

The ceremony attracted widespread attention from the press. In addition to the aforementioned reasons, the mirror farmers' story had acquired a legendary quality in the hearts of the public. It was also an excellent opportunity to indulge in nostalgia in an age where things were rapidly acquired and then forgotten.

Those simple and honest lads were already well into middle age, but they did not appear greatly changed. Audiences could still recognize them on their holographic television sets. Over the years most of the men had attained some form of higher education, and a few had even earned the title of space engineer. In their own eyes and the eyes of the public, however, they remained that same group of migrant laborers from the countryside.

Shui gave a speech on behalf of his companions. 'With the completion of the electromagnetic conveyor system, the cost of entering near-Earth orbit is only half the cost of a flight across the Pacific Ocean,' he said. 'Space travel has become an ordinary, unglamorous affair. New generations are hard-pressed to imagine what traveling to space meant to an ordinary person twenty years ago, how the opportunity would excite him, how it would make his blood boil. We were the lucky ones.

'We are ordinary men, and there is little to be said about us. Our extraordinary experience was entirely thanks to the China Sun. Over the past twenty years, it has become our second home. In our hearts, it is like a miniature Earth. At first, we used the seams on the reflector's mirrored surface to represent the latitude and longitude lines of the northern hemisphere. When we marked our positions, we would specify our coordinates in degrees north and degrees east or west. Later, as we grew familiar with the reflector, we gradually blocked out the continents and oceans on it. We would say were in Beijing or Moscow. Each of our home villages had a corresponding position on the reflector's surface, and we cleaned those areas the hardest.'

Shui became momentarily lost in thought. 'We worked hard on that small, silver Earth, and we did our duty. All in all, five reflector cleaners gave their lives for the China Sun. Some had no time to take cover from solar magnetic storms, and others were hit by meteors or space debris. Soon, our silver world, where we lived and worked for two decades, will vanish. It is difficult to express our feelings in words.'

Shui fell silent. Zhuang, who had risen to the office of Minister for Space Industry, picked up the thread. 'I completely understand how you must feel, but I am pleased to be able to tell everyone that the China Sun will not disappear! As I expect you all know, such a massive object cannot be allowed to burn up in the atmosphere, as was common practice in the last century. But there is another, rather elegant, way to find the China Sun a final resting place. If we simply discontinue the orbital haircuts and make the appropriate adjustments to its orientation, solar wind and radiation pressure will accelerate it until it reaches the second cosmic velocity. In the end, it will escape Earth orbit and become a satellite of the Sun. Perhaps, many years in the future, interplanetary spaceships will rediscover it. We could turn it into a museum, and return to that silver plain and reminisce about these unforgettable years.'

Shui lit up with sudden excitement. 'Minister, do you really think that day will come?' he asked Zhuang in a loud voice. 'Do you really think there will be interplanetary spaceships?'

Zhuang stared at him, at a loss for words.

'In the middle of the last century,' Shui continued, 'when Armstrong left the very first footprint on the Moon, almost everyone believed that humanity would land on Mars with in the next ten to twenty years. Now, eighty-six years have passed. No one has returned to the Moon, let alone Mars. The reason is simple: it is a losing proposition.

'Since the end of the Cold War, economics has come to rule our day-by-day lives and under its rule, humanity has made great strides. Today, we have eliminated war and poverty and restored the environment. Truly, Earth is becoming a paradise. This has reinforced our belief in the efficiency of the economic principle. It has grown paramount, permeating our very DNA. There is no doubt, human society has become an economic society. Never again will we undertake any endeavor that yields less than the investment it requires. The development of the Moon makes no economic sense, the large-scale manned exploration of the planets would qualify as an economic crime, and as for interstellar flight, that is downright lunacy! Now humanity knows only input, output, and consumption.'

Zhuang nodded. 'In this century, human development of space has been confined to near-Earth space. That is a fact,' he said. 'There are many underlying reasons for it, but they are beyond the scope of today's topic.'

'No, they are well within it! We have been given an opportunity. If we just spend a little money, we can leave near-Earth space behind and embark on a great voyage into the cosmos. Just as solar radiation pressure can push the China Sun out of orbit around Earth, it can also push it to more distant places.'

Zhuang chuckled and shook his head. 'Oh, you mean to use the China Sun as a solar sail? That might work in the abstract. The body of the reflector is thin and light, and its surface area is large. After a long period of acceleration by radiation pressure, it would become the fastest spacecraft ever launched by humanity. However, I am only speaking in a theoretical sense. In reality, a ship with only a sail cannot travel far. It needs a crew. An unmanned sailboat will only drift in circles on the ocean without ever sailing out of the harbor – I recall Stevenson's *Treasure Island* contained a particularly vivid description of such a ship. Returning from a long voyage by means of radiation pressure requires precise, complex control over the reflector's orientation. But the China Sun was designed to operate in orbit around Earth. Without human control, it will follow an aimless path as it drifts blindly through space, and it will not make it far.'

'Yes, but it will have a crew aboard. I will pilot it,' Shui replied calmly.

At that moment, the audience measurement system indicated that the channel's ratings had risen sharply. The eyes of the entire world were focused upon them.

'But you cannot control the China Sun by yourself. Its orientation controls require at least—'

'At least twelve people,' Shui interrupted. 'Taking other factors of interstellar travel into account, at least fifteen to twenty people. I believe we will have that many volunteers.'

Zhuang gave a helpless laugh. 'I truly did not expect that today's conversation would take this turn.'

'Minister Zhuang, over twenty years ago, you changed the course of my life on more than one occasion.'

'But I never, ever imagined you would travel so far, much further than I have.' Zhuang sighed deeply. 'Well, this is very interesting. Let us continue our discussion! Ah,' he said, frowning, 'I'm afraid your idea is not feasible. The most sensible target for the China Sun is Mars, but you have not considered that the China Sun cannot land. If you want to land, it will require a huge expenditure, and the plan will lose its economic viability. If you do not want to land, the whole endeavor is tantamount to launching an unmanned probe. What would be the point?'

'The China Sun is not bound for Mars.'

Zhuang looked at Shui, baffled. 'Then where? Jupiter?'

'Not Jupiter, either. Even farther afield.'

'Farther? To Neptune? Pluto?' Zhuang abruptly stopped. For a long while, he gazed at Shui in disbelief. 'My god, you don't mean to say – '

Shui nodded firmly. 'Yes, the China Sun will fly beyond the solar system and become the first interstellar spaceship!'

All around the world, people stared at their televisions with the same open-mouthed incredulity as Zhuang.

Zhuang stared straight ahead and nodded mechanically. 'Well, if you are not joking, let me make a quick estimate . . .' he said, his eyes half-closed as he began to do mental calculations.

'I have it figured out. Using solar radiation pressure, the China Sun would accelerate to one-tenth of the speed of light. Taking into account the time needed to accelerate, it would reach Proxima Centauri in forty-five years.

'The China Sun would then use the radiation pressure of Proxima Centauri to decelerate. After you complete a survey of the Alpha Centauri system, you would accelerate in the opposite direction, returning to the solar system after another few decades. It sounds like a marvelous plan, but in fact, it is a dream that cannot be realized.'

'Wrong again,' Shui replied. 'When we reach Proxima Centauri, the China Sun will not decelerate. We will skim by it at a speed of thirty-thousand kilometers per second, using its radiation pressure to accelerate even faster as we fly toward Sirius. If possible, we will continue to leapfrog through space, to a third star, a fourth . . .'

'What the hell is your game plan here?' Zhuang shouted, losing patience.

'All we ask of Earth is a highly reliable but small-scale ecological life support system—'

'And you would use this system to sustain the lives of twenty people for over a century?'

'Let me finish,' Shui replied. 'And a cryogenic hibernation system. We will spend most of the voyage in a dormant state, only powering up the life support system when we approach Proxima Centauri. At the current level of technology, this should be enough to let us travel through the cosmos for over a thousand years. Of course, these two systems do not come cheap, but it will require just one-thousandth of the capital required to build a manned interstellar probe from scratch.'

'Even if you did not want a cent, the world cannot permit twenty people to commit suicide.'

'This is not suicide, it is exploration,' Shui countered. 'Maybe we will not even make it past the asteroid belt right in front of us, but maybe we will reach Sirius or beyond. If we do not try, how will we know?'

'But there is something that sets this expedition apart from exploration,' said Zhuang. 'There is no possibility of return.'

Shui nodded. 'Yes, we will not return. Some people are satisfied with a wife, children, and a warm bed, never so much as glancing at the parts of the world that do not concern them. But some people will spend their whole lives trying to glimpse something humanity has never seen before. I have been both of these people, and I have the right to choose the life I want to lead,' he concluded. 'That includes living out my days on a mirror, drifting through space ten light-years away.'

'One final question,' Zhuang said. 'In one thousand years' time, as you race past stars at speeds of tens or hundreds of thousands of kilometers per second, it will take decades or even centuries for humanity to receive the weak radio signals you send out. Is it worth the sacrifice?'

With a smile, Shui announced to the whole world, 'As the China Sun flies beyond the solar system, humans will look away from all our creature comforts and up toward the starry sky again. We will recall our dream of space travel and rekindle our desire for interstellar exploration.'

Life Goal #6:
Fly to the stars, draw humanity's gaze back to the depths of the cosmos.

Zhuang stood on the roof of the Aerospace Tower and gazed at the China Sun as it moved swiftly through the sky. Its light caught the capital's high-rises and threw countless fast-moving shadows, as if Beijing was an upturned face following the China Sun.

This was the China Sun's last revolution around Earth. It had already reached escape velocity and would soon fly beyond the planet's gravitational field, entering into orbit around the Sun. There were twenty people aboard humanity's first manned interstellar spaceship. Besides Shui, the others had been selected from among more than one million volunteers. They included three other mirror farmers who had worked with Shui for many years. The China Sun had accomplished its goal before it ever began its journey.

Humanity's enthusiasm for exploring beyond the solar system was reborn.

Zhuang's thoughts returned to that sultry summer night in that northwestern city twenty-three years ago, when he and a farm boy from the arid countryside had boarded the night train to Beijing.

In parting, the China Sun trained its spot of light on each major city in turn, giving humanity one last look at its radiance. Finally, the spot of light came to rest on northwestern China. At its center lay the little village in which Shui had been born.

By the side of the road on the outskirts of town, Shui's parents stood together with their neighbors, watching the China Sun fly east.

Pa shouted into the phone, 'Wah, you are going somewhere far away?'

'Yeah, Pa,' Shui replied from space. 'I am afraid I will not come home.'

'Is it very far away?' Ma asked.

'Very far, Ma,' Shui answered.

'Farther than the Moon?' Pa asked.

Shui fell silent for a few seconds. Then, in a voice much lower than before, he said, 'Yeah, Pa, a little farther than the Moon.'

Shui's parents were not especially distraught. Their son was going to do great things at that place beyond the Moon! Besides, these were extraordinary times. Even from the remotest corners of the earth, they could talk to him at any time, they could even see him on their little television. It was no different from speaking to him face-to-face. It did not occur to them that there would be an ever longer delay; that Shui's answers to their concerned questions would come slower and slower. At first, it would only be a few seconds, but the pauses would grow. In a year's time, every question would require hours for a response.

Finally, their son would vanish. They would be told that Shui had gone to sleep and that he would not wake for forty years.

After that, Shui's parents would continue to tend that plot of once-barren but now fertile land and live out the remainder of their once-backbreaking but now satisfying lives. Their last wish would be that, some day in the distant future, their son return to see an even more beautiful homeland.

As the China Sun left Earth orbit, it steadily dimmed in the eastern sky, its blue halo shrinking to a star-like point as it dissolved into the night. Then dawn arrived, and its light was completely swallowed by the glow of the morning Sun.

The morning Sun also shone down on the path that led out of the village. Now white poplars lined the path, and a short distance away a small river ran parallel to it. On that day twenty-four years ago, in the small hours of the morning, under the same light of dawn, the son of north-western peasants gradually disappeared into the distance on this very road, nursing vague hopes.

It was now broad daylight in Beijing, but Zhuang remained standing on the roof of the Aerospace Tower, gazing at the point where the China Sun had vanished. It had embarked on its endless voyage of no return. The China Sun would first pass Venus' orbit, getting as close as possible to the Sun to boost radiation pressure and maximize the distance it had in which to accelerate. This would be realized through a complex series of orbital transfer maneuvers, much like the way ocean-going vessels of the Age of Navigation would tack and jibe upwind. After seventy days, it would pass Mars' orbit. After one hundred and sixty days, it would sweep by Jupiter. After two years, it would fly beyond Pluto's orbit and become an interstellar spaceship, and its crew would enter hibernation. After forty-five years, it would fly past Alpha Centauri, and its crew would briefly reawaken. One century after the China Sun began its journey, Earth would receive information obtained during their exploration of Alpha Centauri. By then, the China Sun would already be soaring toward Sirius. Thanks to the speed boost from Alpha Centauri's three suns, it would have reached fifteen percent of the speed of light. Another sixty years later, one hundred and sixty years after setting out from Earth, it would reach Sirius. After it passed the binary star system formed by Sirius A and Sirius B, its speed would increase to twenty percent of the speed of light, and it would hurtle even deeper into the night sky. Given the limits of the onboard cryogenic hibernation system's lifespan, the China Sun might reach ε Eridani or – though the probability was quite small – even 79 Ceti. Both star systems were thought to harbour planets.

No one knew how far the China Sun would fly, or what strange worlds Shui and the others would behold. Perhaps one day they would send a message to Earth, but it would be over a thousand years before they received a reply.

No matter what happened, Shui would always remember a country called China on his mother planet. He would always remember a little village in that country's arid northwest. He would always remember the path that led out of that village, the path on which his journey began.